SHE TOOK A DEEP BREATH AND HALF SWUNG AROUND TO FACE HIM.

Oh, God, she thought helplessly as she stared at him. I'm in big trouble. He looked so right lounging against the pillows of her bed, his hands behind his head and that mocking smile on his lips, the half-shuttered eyes full of sensual promise.

"We have to talk," she said levelly, holding on to her churning emotions by a thread.

"No, we don't," Sloan said. Before she realized it, she was caught and dragged across the bed. "Talking," he muttered against her mouth, "always seems to get us into trouble. But never this. Never this."

His lips took hers in a kiss that sent her senses spinning. . . .

"A satisfying read."
—*Publishers Weekly* on *Swear by the Moon*

Please turn to the back of this book for a preview of Shirlee Busbee's new novel, *Coming Home*.

Also by Shirlee Busbee

Lovers Forever

A Heart for the Taking

Love Be Mine

For Love Alone

At Long Last

Swear by the Moon

Return to Oak Valley

SHIRLEE BUSBEE

WARNER BOOKS

An AOL Time Warner Company

WARNER BOOKS EDITION

Cover design by Diane Luger
Cover illustration by Ben Perini

Warner Books, Inc.
1271 Avenue of the Americas
New York, NY 10020

Visit our Web site at
www.twbookmark.com.

An AOL Time Warner Company

Printed in the United States of America

First Printing: December 2002

10 9 8 7 6 5 4 3 2 1

This is long overdue, but I've been saving it for a special occasion. To JAY ACTON, my longtime, long-suffering agent—one of the best around. The concept was yours and without your insight and persistence the book would never have happened. Thank you. Thank you. *Thank you!*

And, per usual, HOWARD, the man who makes my life fun and full of adventure—even some adventures I could do without!

Acknowledgments

I'd like to thank the following individuals, in no particular order, for graciously taking the time out of their busy days to patiently answer my questions. Any mistakes are, of course, my own.

Leonard LaCasse, Attorney at Law; Norm Vroman, Mendocino County District Attorney; Dr. Lovejoy, Mendocino Medical Group; Dr. Lee, Kaiser Permanente; Bill Baker, Covelo Volunteer Fire Department; "Linda", Willits sub-station Mendocino Sheriff's Department; Maja Reid, Bank of America and last, but not least, my dear friend and fellow horse lover, Sandy Reimer. If I forgot anybody—forgive me. Please.

Return to Oak Valley

Chapter One

❦

When she reached the turnout at Inspiration Point overlooking Oak Valley, Shelly pulled to the side of the road and turned off the ignition. Utter silence fell. Having lived most of her adult life in New Orleans, with all its constant bustle and city noise, it was the sort of silence she had not heard in years . . . seventeen years to be exact.

She sat there in her new dark gray Bronco and let the silence seep into her consciousness, feeling her tense muscles ease and her jangled nerves calm. The Bronco was shrouded in silence and darkness, the gleam of stars overhead and the beckoning glitter of the few lights on the valley floor the only break in the blackness of the night.

She had chosen to return at night, even knowing that the narrow two-lane road to St. Galen's, the only town in Oak Valley, was nearly thirty miles of twisting, twining curves that required careful concentration even in daylight, but even more so after dark. At night the curves leaped out at one; deer, skunks, raccoons, and the occasional bear or bobcat could appear suddenly in the headlights, and in some places, a small scattering, and not so small scattering, of rocks could litter the blacktop, making the drive interesting, if not downright hazardous.

Smiling to herself, she reached for the cherry-colored sweater that lay on the seat next to her. The road to St.

Galen's was probably one of the main reasons Oak Valley had not grown much in the 150 years or so since the first white man had stumbled across it. Once she had taken pleasure in the very perversity of the road, calling it, as did others, their long driveway home, but during her years away, she had forgotten just how curving and narrow it could be. *A mistake*, she thought wryly, *I'd not make again. From now on, kiddo, daylight will be the best time to travel in and out of the valley.*

Stepping out from the warmth of the Bronco, she caught her breath at the sharp chill of the night. She'd also forgotten just how cold it could be in the mountains of northern California—even in mid March.

Arms wrapped around her slender body, she walked to the edge of the turnout and stared down at the valley. She had chosen to return at night, as much because she had not wanted to see the changes over a decade and a half had wrought, as she had not wanted to face the stares and curiosity of the inhabitants. Looking at the occasional twinkle of light below her, she sighed. The next few weeks were going to be difficult. With her brother's death so recent and tragic, once her presence in the valley became common knowledge, there would be many kindhearted souls coming to call to express their sympathy. She grimaced. Her return, after so many years away, was also bound to bring to her doorstep quite a few not-so-kindhearted callers.

Counting the residents of St. Galen's and a surrounding radius of thirty or forty miles, there were probably only about five thousand people who inhabited that vast space of mountains and forest. Which, she admitted, could be a good thing—just about everybody knew everyone else, and in many cases, were related, even if distantly, to each other. The valley was quick to rally around neighbors and friends in need or trouble and, considering Oak Valley's isolation, that meant just about everyone helped everyone else. Her lips twisted. Except in a few notable exceptions, such as her family, the Grangers, and their longtime opponents, or enemies if you really wanted the unvarnished truth, the Ballingers. Which brought her to one of the worst things about such a small, tight-knit community—everyone knew your business, bad or good, and the valley could be, upon occasion, rife with gossip and speculation. If there was animosity between certain factions, it was a sure bet everyone knew about it and would be quick to share news of the latest clash between the principals with their nearest crony, embroidering the tale just a tad for a little added interest. Which was a good way in such a small community to keep controversy smoldering and ensuring that some feuds, as in the case of her family and the Ballingers, lasted for generations. And as for keeping anything private. . . . Shelly snorted. You didn't dare sneeze at the north end of the valley before someone at the south end immediately sang out, "God bless you!"

It was going to take some getting used to, she thought ruefully. Not that she had been without relatives, friends, and acquaintances while she had lived in New Orleans, but that had been different. New Orleans was so huge and sprawling, so full of a constant ebb and flow of tourists, and strangers just passing through, that keeping your privacy was easy. In Oak Valley, where practically everyone had known you since birth . . . and your mother . . . and your father, and all of *their* relatives back to when Christ had the croup, well, it made things sticky. Worse, if at the tender age of seven, you had gone skinny-dipping with the present fire chief, one of the current resident deputy sheriffs, and the owner of the biggest grocery store in town, it would be kind of tricky to remain aloof. She grinned. Yeah, it would be hard to pretend that they all hadn't seen you bare-ass naked—and knowing her three compatriots in youthful mischief, unless they had changed a great deal, they weren't about to let her forget it.

Shelly started as the stillness of the night was broken by a cacophony of shrill yips and howls. It came from the foothills across the valley from her, and she recognized the sound immediately. A delighted smile crossed her face. Coyotes! So they hadn't been able to wipe them all out, she thought with satisfaction, in spite of all the poison, traps, and dynamiting of dens that had been done over the years. She supposed that if she were a sheep rancher and/or had a flock of chickens, she wouldn't be quite so pleased to hear their call, but for someone used to the muted roar of city life, it was a thrill to hear that chorus peal forth through the quiet night. To her amusement, every dog in the valley immediately answered the coyotes' song. Listening to the yelping canine choir, she grinned. There were going to be a lot of irate owners in the morning, complaining about the damned coyotes last night setting off Ole Blue or Jesse or Traveler.

She had thought that after her years away from the valley and its ways it would be impossible to return to the place of her birth. She had feared that everything would seem foreign and strange, boring and dull—especially after nearly two decades of living in one of the most glamorous cities in the world. Yet as she stood looking down at the occasional blinking light, the clean, cool night air brushing against her cheeks, she was amazed at how right it felt to be here. She was astonished at how eager she was suddenly to see the valley, to rediscover familiar haunts and meet old friends again and discover the changes that had occurred in their lives during her absence. But if there was eagerness within her, there was also anguish, for it was death that had caused her to leave behind New Orleans and return to Oak Valley.

Grief swept through her as she thought about the real reason that had brought her home after all these years. Standing here on this cool March night overlooking the valley, she could feel the same sensation of disbelief and pain that had knifed through her when she had gotten the telephone call from the family attorney, Michael Sawyer, two and a half weeks ago, telling her of Josh's death. A suicide.

She and Josh had been close—as close as siblings could be with a fifteen-year gap in their ages. A child born late in the life of her parents, Shelly had lost both of them at an early age and had few clear memories of them. It had been Josh who had stepped into their father's shoes when Stanley Granger, at fifty-five, had overturned his jeep while searching for some cattle and had been killed instantly. She had been seven at the time, and it was Josh who became the dominant male in her life. Her mother, Catherine, had died just as she had been entering her teens, and it had been Josh who had been left to deal with all the mood swings and gyrating hormones of that age. Shelly smiled wistfully. He had done very well, even if half the time he had been bewildered by the demands of the girl-woman growing up before his very eyes.

A raw sense of loss swept through her again. *I should have come home*, she berated herself, feeling the sting of tears. *I should have visited him, instead of allowing telephone calls and his vacations with me to suffice. I should have*—She let out a shaky breath, knowing that beating herself up over the past wouldn't change a thing.

At least, she reminded herself, she didn't have a funeral to face and all the attention, some of it kind, some of it not, that a formal service would have entailed. Josh had made arrangements for his cremation years ago, with the request that his ashes be spread over the valley from Pomo Ridge— the highest of the long, curving arm of foothills that surrounded the valley on the west. He had not wanted any sort of public service to mark his passing—much like her father, who had often vented his loathing of funerals and funeral homes. While a part of her had rebelled against Josh's wishes, she had heard his pungent comments on funerals enough times to know that it would be unfair of her to go against his express desires when he was no longer around to enforce them. Following the instructions he had left with the family lawyer seemed to be the last favor she could do for him.

She sighed, suddenly feeling lonely and overwhelmed. She had left behind the familiar and was facing not only her brother's death but the need to oversee the Granger holdings—no small task, since the family holdings were sizable. Via the telephone, Mike Sawyer had already been giving her a crash course on what was facing her. Fortunately, the bulk of the Granger holdings were in a living trust, so she would not have to deal with the dispersal of the entire estate. Josh had left a will, but it covered only his personal possessions, and Sawyer had already told her that most of it was just a few bequests to friends and family.

There were still Grangers in the valley, second and third cousins, maybe a great-uncle or great-aunt, but with Josh's death, she became the sole living member of her branch of the Granger family. That thought depressed her and made her feel even more isolated. She was conscious of a deep longing for the warm, comforting arms of her Louisiana relatives. They were even more distantly related than the Grangers living in the valley were but at least she *knew* them and it hadn't been almost seventeen years since she'd last seen them. For a moment she regretted that she had declined her cousin Roman's escort and that of his younger sister, Angelique. They had both offered to come with her, but she had refused, feeling her return would be enough for Oak Valley to gossip about without adding in her handsome cousin and his dark-eyed Southern belle sister. There was also Uncle Fritzie and Aunt Lulu and Roman's and Angelique's other siblings—they were a large family and had taken her to their collective bosoms or chests, depending.

Thinking about Roman and Angelique and the others made her feel better, not quite so alone; but aware that she was letting her thoughts stray, she focused on the valley below and what it might hold for her. Seventeen years, she thought moodily, was a long time to have been away. At eighteen, her heart wounded, her pride battered when she had fled the valley all those years before, she had severed most ties. Her friends must have thought she was crazy, but a few had understood the situation. They'd been very kind, she realized, not to press for answers to explain her abrupt withdrawal and had endeared themselves to her even more by not mentioning Sloan Ballinger—especially not the details of his engagement to Nancy Blackstone and their subsequent marriage ten months later. She grimaced. What a little coward she had been.

The sound of an approaching vehicle broke up her thoughts, and deciding that she had lingered long enough, she walked back to the Bronco. She was just ready to nose the Bronco out onto the road when the other vehicle swept around the curve, its headlights pinning her where she sat, almost blinding her. She blinked, framed for a brief second in the bright light. The new arrival slowed, dimmed its lights, and she stepped on the gas, pulling away from the turnout. A moment later the Bronco was sweeping slowly down the twisting blacktop toward the valley floor. Suddenly the vista opened up, and after the previous thirty miles of narrow, snake-backed road it was a pleasure to step on the gas and almost fly along the straight, flat road before her, broad open fields flanking either side of the pavement.

Forty-five minutes and two locked gates later, having left

the valley floor again for the three-mile climb to the old home site, Shelly pulled up in front of the house where Josh had lived. It wasn't the home that she had grown up in—that one, originally built by her great-grandfather, had burned to the ground ten years ago. The house had been a valley landmark, a grand Victorian rising up nearly four stories of pristine whiteness against the green of the trees. Everyone knew the Granger house, and it was pointed out with pride by those on the valley floor. Josh had phoned the day after the tragedy and had said that there had been a chimney fire that had gotten out of hand. Since the old redwood framed house was situated in the foothills, by the time the fire trucks had reached it, there was nothing to be done. Before the fire had gotten too bad, fearing the worst, Josh and some of the early arrivals had frantically thrown several items, mostly heirlooms, out the windows, but most everything else had been lost when the house had burned. The heat from the roaring fire had been so intense and furious by then that Josh, half the valley, and the fire crew had been forced to stand at a distance and watch helplessly as over a hundred years of family and valley history went up in flames.

When Josh had rebuilt, against the advice of nearly everyone, it had been on the exact same spot, and it had been a log house—a handsome, metal-roofed affair, multileveled and surrounded by wide, covered decks. To show that he hadn't forgotten the reason he was rebuilding in the first place, there was a sprinkler system throughout the house and smoke alarms everywhere. He had installed all the safety features, but he hadn't been able to give up the idea of a cozy fire on a cold evening. In several of the rooms there were elegant brass-and-enameled fireplace inserts, fitted into the river rock facings so that they looked like nothing more than glass-fronted fireplaces.

Josh's Mexican-American housekeeper, and Shelly's

childhood nursemaid, Maria, lived in a small house a quarter of a mile down the gravel road, and she had left a light on on the deck and one inside the house. Shelly was glad of it as she turned off the ignition. The house looked welcoming, the lights beckoning her forward, inviting her to enter—she could almost envision Josh bounding down the steps to greet her.

Ignoring the stab of pain, she grabbed her purse and the smaller of several suitcases she had brought with her. Locking the Bronco, she slowly walked up the wide, stone-lined gravel walkway that led to the front of the house.

Now that she was actually here, exhaustion claimed her. During the time since she had learned of Josh's death, and knew she would be returning to Oak Valley indefinitely, she had been run ragged. There had been a multitude of tasks to perform; notification of her apartment manager, the utility company, and then packing and selling her furniture and larger belongings. Saying good-bye to all her relatives and the friends she had made in New Orleans had been the hardest part—especially their sympathy as she coped with the horror of Josh's suicide. Being an artist of some repute, there had been no employer to worry about—although several of her friends had wondered about her decision to sell her furniture and give up her apartment. Surely, Roman had asked, concern in his emerald eyes, you will come back to New Orleans after you have seen to Josh's affairs? She had hunched a shoulder, unable to answer him. Seated in the first-class section of the plane for the flight to San Francisco, her gaze fixed on the disappearing runway below her, Shelly finally admitted that she had known the answer to his question, had known the answer from the moment she had learned of Josh's death. No, she wasn't coming back to New Orleans—no matter what she found in Oak Valley, no matter how painful her return might be. She took a deep breath. She was returning to Oak Valley for good. Returning home to stay after seventeen years away. She could not have explained it—it was simply something she felt she needed to do—even if everyone thought she was peculiar for doing so. She could live with peculiar, she thought, as she pushed open the door to Josh's house and stepped inside—right now, all she wanted was a bed.

Shutting the heavy oak door with its stained-glass window behind her, she headed for the wide staircase that dominated the large entry hall. Josh had sent her the architect's plans and had told her a lot about the house so, despite never having stepped foot in the place, she knew exactly where everything was situated.

A mixture of guilt and longing swept though her again as she pushed open the door to the main guest room on the second floor. Josh had told her all about it, his pleasure in the then-new house almost palpable. We should have been doing this together, she admitted with a lump in her throat, tears welling up in her eyes. She bit her lip, assailed by remorse, not even seeing the room in front of her.

What a selfish little bitch she had been, she thought, not to have come home even once during all these years. It didn't matter that she and her brother had talked almost weekly on the phone, or that Josh had flown to New Orleans to share most holidays and vacations with her . . . and to gamble, she thought wryly, remembering his passion for the turn of a card. He would have made a great Regency buck, with his love for every kind of game of chance.

She was lost in thought for several moments, remembering Josh laughing when he had had a particularly good night and his cheerful insouciance when he lost. "Next time," he'd murmur, his green eyes twinkling. "You wait and see—next time the story will be different."

Josh had been such an optimist and had had such a joy for

life that it was hard to believe that he was gone. Dead. Bleakly, she wondered if Josh would still be alive had she faced her own demons and come back. If she had been here, would she have seen the signs of depression? Would she have realized that he was suicidal? Could she have prevented him from taking his own life? She had been asking herself those bitter questions ever since the news of his death had been relayed to her. There had been no real reason for her not to have come home before now—even if only briefly from time to time. Other than that she had been a coward, whispered a sly voice.

She dashed away a tear. Enough. She was home now, and even if Josh was not at her side, she could still appreciate the pleasure he had taken in his home.

The room in which she stood was gorgeous—huge and airy, one whole end a wall of glass that extended from the open wooden beams of the ceiling to the floor; in the middle, a pair of sliding doors led to a small, partially covered balcony beyond. Through the glass she could see an iron table and chairs sitting outside on the balcony.

The oatmeal-colored carpet muffled her steps as she walked farther into the room, her gaze touching the furniture Josh had chosen—she remembered his excitement at its arrival and his delight in how the room had all come together. "Wait till you see it, kiddo, you're gonna love it," he'd said during one of their marathon phone conversations. "I even picked out a four-poster for it." He laughed. "Hell, honey, I'm turning into a damned interior decorator! If I start walking with a mince, punch me."

His words playing in her memory, she glanced at the cherrywood four-poster bed with a canopy of soft peach netting that sat against the far wall; a pair of matching night tables with brass lamps had been placed on either side of it. She remembered him talking about those, too—and the

small sofa near the glass sliding door done up in a wild print
of orange poppies and blue lupine.

Setting her suitcase down near the door, she noticed for
the first time the two sets of doors at the opposite end of the
room. One, she discovered, was a walk-in closet with recessed cupboard and drawers and enough room to hold a
wedding reception. The other door opened into a bathroom
that was large enough for a family of twelve. Or thereabouts,
she thought with a smile.

Too tired to unpack, she picked up her suitcase and
walked to the closet. After pulling out the few things she
would need, she left the suitcase on the floor and wandered
into the bathroom. A few minutes later, her teeth brushed,
her face washed, and wearing a pair of yellow shorty paja-
mas, she climbed into bed.

Shelly had thought she would fall immediately to sleep,
but she discovered that she was too restless, too wired after
the long drive and the anxious anticipation of finally returning to the valley. Her lips curved. She had wanted to return
alone, and by heaven, she had! Now she wished that she
hadn't been so adamant about it. Having someone to talk to
wouldn't have been such a bad thing.

After tossing and turning for several minutes, she gave
up and slipped out of bed. Hoping that Maria had had the
forethought to stock the refrigerator, she padded down the
stairs, flipping on lights as she went.

Pushing open the swinging door that led to the kitchen,
she turned on the light and stared around her. The kitchen
was charming, large and spacious; the gold-flecked toffee-
colored tiled countertops were a pleasing contrast to the pale
oak cabinets that lined two walls. The floor was wild—a
Mexican tile that, oddly enough, went very well with the
rest of the kitchen, the copper-bottomed pans hanging over
the island in the center of the room adding another splash of

color. She smiled wistfully when she spied the fireplace insert at the far end of the kitchen. Josh had so loved his fireplaces—the kitchen in the old house had had a fireplace in which she and Josh had popped corn over the leaping flames at Christmastime.

She blinked back tears at the memory and walked over to the huge built-in oak-fronted refrigerator. Someone, probably Maria, had been thoughtful enough to stock it with necessities. Taking a carton of milk from the refrigerator's cavernous interior, she found a glass in one of the cupboards. A few minutes later, having fumbled her way through the various choices of the gleaming black microwave on the counter, she was wandering through the house, sipping her glass of warm milk.

Eventually she made her way into Josh's den/office. It was a masculine room, the walls covered in knotty pine, the floor in a hunter green carpet. Heavy, comfortable chairs in russet leather were arranged in front of the black-marble-fronted fireplace insert; a long plaid couch was set under one of the windows, and at the far end of the room was a large rolltop desk made of oak. Bookshelves and windows were interspersed along the remaining walls of the room; a pair of glass doors, she knew, led to a private patio.

The chairs she recognized. They had been in the family for as long as she could remember—family gossip said that they had come with Jeb Granger when he had left New Orleans after the end of the Civil War. She had been thrilled when Josh had told her they had been among the few things saved from the fire that had destroyed the old house.

Her hand caressed the soft leather, obviously reupholstered, and as she looked closely at the wooden legs, she could make out the faint signs of charring the refinishers had not been able to obliterate. Sinking down into one of the chairs, she stared blankly into space.

It seemed impossible that Josh was dead. Her brain knew that he was dead, but her heart was still having trouble accepting that he was actually gone. He would have turned fifty in April, she had teased him about the big five-oh, but as far as she knew he had been in excellent health, which made his death all the more senseless. Why, she wondered for the hundredth time since Michael Sawyer had called with the devastating news of Josh's death, had he killed himself? She was positive that there had been no hint, nothing that would have alerted her to the fact that he was depressed, that he planned to kill himself when she had last spoken to him. She hesitated. Except, now that she considered it, for those few odd comments at the beginning of their conversation . . . She shook her head. She was just being fanciful—trying to read something into nothing. He had sounded, she decided firmly, his usual cheerful self, and mostly they had talked about what a great time they'd had together in February during Mardi Gras when he'd flown out to visit. The phone call had ended with his promise to call her the following week. And three days later, he had ridden to Pomo Ridge on his favorite horse and shot himself in the old family hunting shack.

Her breath caught, pain knifing through her. Thinking of her laughing, pleasure-loving brother, it seemed inconceivable that Josh had killed himself. But if he hadn't killed himself . . . She frowned. Did she really think that he *hadn't* killed himself? The coroner's report had stated clearly that his death had not been accidental—one didn't accidentally shoot oneself in the temple. So that left what? Murder? Had someone else placed the pistol at his temple and pulled the trigger? A shudder went through her. The notion of Josh being murdered was just as hard to accept as the idea that he had killed himself. *Everyone* loved Josh! Her mouth twisted. Except, of course, the Ballingers.

The warm milk was having the effect she had hoped for, and, yawning, she finally made it upstairs to bed. Snuggled in bed, she let her thoughts drift, forcing her mind away from Josh. It was weird to be lying here with no screaming sirens, no honking horns or the sound of swishing, screeching tires on pavement to disturb the silence. And the darkness! It was complete, only the stars winking in the sky overhead splintering the blackness. There were no street-lights, no flashing neon signs, and no headlights spearing through the darkness to disrupt the black velvet cloak of night. She'd forgotten that. The utter lack of light was al-most unnerving, but she stilled the impulse to turn on a lamp. The lack of sound, too, was strange and, at first, it bothered her, the only noises she heard just the natural creak and squeak of the house. As the minutes passed, the night and the silence began its magic, just as it had when she was a child—she'd forgotten that, too. Oh, how she had missed the soft quiet, the soothing dark, and she suddenly wondered how she had stood all the blaring noise, the con-stant bustle and glaring light that was New Orleans. *This*, she thought drowsily, *is where I belong. This is my home. My roots.*

It wasn't something she could explain. She had been away from home for a long, long time and though she had told herself there was nothing in Oak Valley for her, there had always been a faint persistent longing to see the valley again. To see if it was as lovely as she remembered—the sky as blue, the creeks and streams as crystal clear and the trees as green. She'd been aware of a growing need to see if the people were as friendly and dear as her memories of them. And to learn if others were as treacherous as she remem-bered. Even before Josh's death, she'd touched once or twice on the idea of coming back to Oak Valley. A frown marred her forehead. Now that she thought of it, Josh had not seemed thrilled at the notion. He had not precisely discouraged her, but he hadn't *en*couraged her either.

So why was she back? Especially now when there was no real reason to return? She had a good life in New Orleans. She was successful, and she had friends and a family, albeit distant, who lived there. Her closest, dearest relative was dead. Mike Sawyer would see to it that the Granger holdings in Oak Valley were properly handled. Looking at it logically, except to spread Josh's ashes, she could not think of one reason why she was here. Except that I want to be, she finally admitted. I have wanted to come back home ever since I left. And she realized something else rather disturbing: It was Josh's death that had finally allowed her to return. All these years away, while she had been telling herself how much she loved New Orleans, how happy she was with her career and friends, she had been merely marking time, waiting for the moment she could return. There had been, she admitted, a part of her that had lain dormant like a daffodil waiting for spring to arrive. Had she been waiting for the sweet warmth of the sun, the return to Oak Valley, before bursting out of the cold ground and into life again? Her lips twisted. Well, since she seemed to think she was a damned flower, was spring really just around the corner? Or was winter still lurking in the wings? She shook her head. One thing was sure: She'd soon find out.

Chapter Two

Long after Shelly Granger's Bronco had disappeared from view, the driver of the vehicle that had disturbed her sat there staring at the darkness, his hands clenching the steering wheel as if it were the only thing between him and annihilation. He was a handsome man even though his features were not conventionally handsome. His nose was too big, his mouth too wide, the chin stubborn and the amber-gold eyes beneath a pair of winged black brows had been known to stop a man in his tracks at ten yards. There was nothing open and friendly about his face, the features hard and controlled, and yet it was a face that most people trusted and had, to date, never found their trust misplaced—twisted perhaps, but never misplaced. At the moment that face wore an expression that would not have engendered trust in anyone; in fact, anyone seeing that expression would have crossed the street and given him a wide berth. His size and build alone would have given most people pause; he stood six-foot-four in his bare feet, and his wide shoulders and muscled forearms made one instantly think of a steel worker and not the business executive he was. He fit the word *brawny* to perfection—muscular, strong, powerful.

Several more minutes passed as he stared in the direction of Shelly's disappearing taillights, then he took a deep breath and guided the big silver-and-black Suburban into the turnout so recently vacated by Shelly and turned off the ignition. He sat there frozen, his gaze blank. Then he shook his head. Shelly Granger. Christ on a mule! Shelly was the last person he ever expected to see—or wanted to see.

Levering his long body out of the vehicle, Sloan Ballinger walked to the edge of the overlook and stared down at the vast darkness of the valley floor. The twinkling lights that signaled habitation were sparse and widespread, except for the cluster of lights that marked the town of St. Galen's near the north end of the valley. From the location of the lights strung out along the lone road that cut through the middle of the valley, he could recite the names of all who lived there, for how many generations, the acreage and what was raised; sheep, cattle, horses, pears, hay, or alfalfa . . . and who was a newcomer or weekender and who wasn't. It was one of the blessings, or curses, of having been born and raised in the valley—as well as having ancestors that were among the first white people to settle the area.

His lips thinned. The Grangers had arrived first, followed within a year or two by the Ballingers—and they'd been at each other's throats ever since, he thought grimly. He reached for the pack of cigarettes that used to rest in his left-hand pocket and made a face when his fingers found nothing but empty space. He'd quit smoking ten years ago and generally didn't miss it, but sometimes he still automatically reached for a cigarette. Mostly from habit, he admitted, and mostly in times of stress. He shook his head. Who'd have thought that seeing Shelly Granger's face after seventeen years, he'd recognize her in an instant and would feel as if he'd been sucker-punched in the gut. Jesus! He'd damn near kill for a cigarette about now.

She had changed in seventeen years—they all had, he conceded, thinking of the sprinkling of silver throughout his own thick thatch of black hair and the faint sun creases that radiated from the corners of his eyes—but she hadn't changed much. Her hair was still a wild, curly, tawny mane that framed those high cheekbones and stubborn chin, her skin looked just as honey-hued and smooth as he remembered. His mouth tightened—and probably felt just as silky as it had been when she'd been eighteen. He hadn't been able to see the color of her eyes, but he remembered them. Oh, yeah, he remembered them all right; the way they could gleam like emeralds or freeze over, making them look like frosty green glass. *Very* frosty green glass. Yeah, he remembered. There wasn't much about Shelly that he didn't remember—or that bastard, Josh. His attitude toward Josh was that the world was a better place without him in it. A lot better.

He snorted. You'd think that after 150 or so years of living side by side that the Ballingers and Grangers would have come to some sort of meeting of the ways. A bitter laugh came from him. Might happen, but he wouldn't put money on it.

The two families had been feuding since York Ballinger and his younger brother, Sebastian, had arrived in Oak Valley in 1867, after the Civil War. Almost immediately they had begun to carve out an empire—which had inevitably led to the locking of horns with Jeb Granger, who had settled with the surviving members of his family in the valley the previous year. York had been a major in the Union Army and Jeb Granger had held the same rank . . . in the Confederate Army. The scars and bitterness instilled in each man during the War Between the States had been too recent, too deep for either man to put aside, and predictably it had led to trouble. Right from the git-go they'd tangled over right-of-ways and water rights, and in the ensuing years, the families had squabbled over timber grants, cattle vs. sheep . . . You name it, they'd argued over it. It wasn't long before the pattern was set, and everyone in Oak Valley and for fifty miles around knew that if a Granger was for it, a Ballinger would be against it . . . or vice versa. Sloan's expression grew bleaker as he thought of Shelly and their aborted affair. And, of course, they'd fought over women now and then.

He took a deep breath. So forget about it. So you shared a tumble or two when you were both young and consumed by hormones. That's all it had been, a lustful mating of two young healthy animals, remember? To his everlasting disgust, he did remember—too goddamn well, for his own liking. And, Jesus, he wished he had a cigarette.

The past wasn't something that he dwelled on. Irritated with himself and most especially with his reaction to the mere glimpse of Shelly Granger, Sloan spun on his heels and climbed back into the big Suburban.

The weight of a small warm body landing in his lap immediately softened his bleak expression. A pair of paws hit his chest, and a damp tongue caressed his cheek. His mood lightened, and he grinned down into the luxuriously bewhiskered face of a tiny silver-and-black miniature schnauzer female. Two expressive black eyes regarded him fixedly from beneath a pair of overhanging silver eyebrows.

"OK. OK. I know you're there and anxious for us to reach the cabin," he muttered, as he ran a hand over her haunches, wondering not for the first time how he had ended up with a bearded and mustached dog no bigger than a cat. Fastidious as a cat, too, and as arrogant and demanding— and downright prissy in the bargain, Sloan admitted with a grin. Pandora was certainly not the sort of dog he had ever thought to own . . . or the sort of dog he had thought to be owned by!

Away from the boardrooms and offices of Ballinger Development, headquartered in Santa Rosa, Sloan was an avid rider and outdoorsman, his heart firmly lodged in Oak

Valley and the sprawling ranch that his many-times-great-grandfather, York, had first torn from the wilderness. In York's day and for some generations after that, the Ballingers had raised cattle and logged the forests, but in the last fifteen or so, under Sloan's guidance, they had begun to raise horses. Very, *very* expensive horses—American paint horses of impeccable lineage and breathtaking performance abilities—as anyone who had seen them cut cattle could attest. Being a big, athletic man, used to hard, physical work when it was called for and with his rock-carved features, he wouldn't have hesitated to say that his taste in dogs ran to the larger and more robust. If it had been a rottweiler or pit bull sharing the vehicle with him, no one would have thought it strange—least of all Sloan.

It was all Samantha's fault, he thought as he avoided another swipe of the pink tongue, and it had come about a couple of years ago when he had driven up to his youngest sister's house on the outskirts of Novato to wish her a happy trip to Mexico. She was flying down the next day to visit the Mexican branch of the family for an extended stay—her marriage had ended two months previously, and Sloan had thought that it would be a good idea for her to get away for a while. Not only had he stopped by to wish her a good trip, but he'd wanted to be easy in his own mind that she was definitely going to be on the plane tomorrow and hadn't slid back into the blue funk she'd been in since the divorce. She'd looked fine, happier than he had seen her in several months. He was just congratulating himself on his clever engineering of getting her away for a while when he had found himself gingerly holding a tiny black ball of fur.

As a hobby Sam showed and raised miniature schnauzers, specializing in the uncommon black and silvers. Sloan knew that the puppy was out of Sam's favorite bitch, Gemini, a finished champion—he'd been by to admire the litter several times during the past weeks, using the puppies as an excuse to check on Sam's well-being. Not a stupid man, he had felt alarm flags fly all over the place when he looked down at the little creature leaning confidingly against his chest and then across at his sister's expectant features.

"Uh, is there a reason I'm standing here holding this fur-ball? I thought you'd sold all of them."

"Well, not exactly," Sam had hedged. "There's a lady in the LA area who thinks she might want this one. She just hasn't made up her mind yet."

One of Sloan's eyebrows cocked. "And this affects me how?"

"Um. I thought maybe you could keep her for me, until either the lady makes up her mind, or I get back."

"Correct me if I'm wrong, but aren't you going to be gone for six weeks or so?"

"Oh, I'm sure you won't have to keep her that long," Sam said airily. "Midge is bound to make up her mind within a week or two."

Sloan smiled sweetly and thrust the puppy at Sam. "Then I suggest that you tell Midge in which kennel you have placed the animal, and if she decides to buy it, that she can make arrangements for its delivery through them."

Sam jumped nimbly away, her eyes laughing at him as she put her hands behind her back. "Sloan, she's only three months old! She's too young to be put in a kennel for six weeks while I'm gone."

"Aha! I knew there was no Midge involved. Sorry, kiddo, but it won't work. The furball's all yours."

Sam made a face. "I knew I shouldn't have tried to trick you. But what am I going to do with her? I've already tried to get Ross or Roxanne to keep her for me, but they both said absolutely not! And Ilka is out of town—she went with Mom and Dad on that trip to Greece. The puppy is just too young to be placed in a kennel for that long." She sighed. "Of course, if you won't take her, I suppose I'll just have to cancel my trip." A hint of tears suddenly appeared in her eyes. "It's been such a long time since I've gone anywhere and I've been so looking forward to seeing Tio Ward and Tia Madalena and all the others. . . ." A quiver entered her voice, and she turned her head away, a curtain of dark hair hiding her features. Nobly she said, "It was my decision to breed Gemini, and so it's my responsibility to take care of her offspring. If you won't watch her for me, I'll just forget about my trip."

Sloan knew when he was being manipulated, and while he had a reputation as a cold, hard negotiator in business, his family saw an entirely different side of him. He glanced down at the puppy, which had begun to chew happily on one of his fingers, then across at his sister—his sister who he suspected was grinning to herself. He sighed. "All right. I'll *watch* her for you. But I'm warning you, Sam, I want you to pick her up within twenty-four hours of your arrival back in the States. And dammit, I mean it!"

Tears magically gone, Sam had giggled and bounced over to kiss his cheek. "Of course, that goes without saying."

Sloan smiled at the memory, and Pandora gave him another lick on the chin, then jumped back into her carrying case on the other seat of the vehicle. When Sam had returned, there had never been any question of giving Pandora back—as his wily sister had known.

His sour mood vanquished, he put the key in the ignition, and the engine turned over. Gliding back onto the road, he kept his foot steady on the gas. Since he planned to stay at his cabin in the mountains at the northern end of the valley, he'd better get a move on. He hadn't planned on arriving this late, but that last meeting over dinner at Ross's town house before he began an extended vacation, one he hoped would become permanent, had taken much longer than he or his younger brother had estimated. By the time they'd hashed out all the final details of Ross taking over the reins as CEO of Ballinger Development, it had been near midnight. At almost thirty-two, Ross was well qualified to run their various development deals—he'd grown up in the business and had been Sloan's right-hand man for the past three years. Sloan grinned. If it worked out as expected, both of them were getting what they wanted; Ross got to run Ballinger Development, and Sloan got to devote his full attention to his passion; raising horses. A yawn overtook him. He was looking forward to arriving at his destination—after he'd traveled the final ten, eleven miles of road—the last six of it, winding and graveled.

⋙⋘

Shelly woke the next morning, disoriented and confused. She lay in bed, blinking up at the netting, trying to get her bearings. Then she remembered. She was home. In Oak Valley. And Josh was dead.

She buried her head in the pillows, wondering how long it would be before she stopped waking up and facing each day with that painful knowledge. From the moment she'd received Mike Sawyer's phone call, it seemed that a black pall had settled over her. *Maybe*, she thought, *once Josh's ashes are scattered.* And today, she reminded herself, was the day she would do that one last thing for Josh. Mike Sawyer was driving up from Ukiah this morning, bringing the urn with Josh's ashes in it. Together they planned to carry out Josh's final wish. She sighed. Not exactly a task she was looking forward to, and yet once it was done . . .

She sighed again. Once it was done, she could begin to heal. She hoped.

Shelly glanced at the clock on the nightstand and groaned. Ten o'clock, but her body felt as if she had never gone to sleep. Not getting to bed until three-thirty in the morning would have been bad enough on her system, but jet lag added its very own problems. She made a face. By the time her plane had landed and she'd picked up the new Bronco from the dealership where it had been waiting for her, it had been well into evening. She should have stayed overnight in San Francisco—as her more seasoned traveling friends had advised. Oh, well, she had never been very good at taking advice—"but you'd think I'd learn," she muttered, as she dragged herself from the bed and staggered toward the bathroom.

Half an hour later, freshly showered, her wet hair hanging around her shoulders and wearing a worn pair of blue jeans, she wandered down the stairs. The scent of coffee teased her nostrils the same moment her bare feet hit the bottom step. Maria?

A flutter in her stomach, tension knotting across her shoulders, Shelly pushed open the door to the kitchen. A sturdy, dark-haired woman, her salt-and-pepper hair neatly caught in a bun at the back of her neck, was in the act of pouring a cup of coffee. At Shelly's entrance she glanced in her direction.

An uncertain smile curved the woman's lips. There was just the faintest hint of a Mexican accent as she said, "Good morning, Miss Shelly. I hope you slept well after the long drive in last night. Did you find everything you needed?"

Maria Rios had not changed overmuch in seventeen years. She was not quite the same dark-eyed, smiling young woman Shelly remembered so well from her youth, but she recognized her instantly. As well she should! Maria had come to work for the family when Maria had been a shy twenty-year-old and Shelly had been a two-year-old toddler. Some of her earliest memories were of Maria's lilting voice and soft, warm, comforting body. There were a lot more strands of gray these days in the gleaming black hair and more lines and creases on the smooth olive skin of her face than there had been when Maria had been thirty-six and Shelly had seen her last. But she was still Maria.

Seeing Maria, the kindness and sympathy, the pain reflected in her brown eyes, Shelly's tension fled. "Oh, Maria," she cried, the missing years vanishing as if they had never been as they met in the center of the kitchen and embraced, "it is *so* good to see you—even under these circumstances."

There were more hugs, tearful exchanges, half-started sentences, smiles that crumpled, but above all Shelly was aware of the warm welcome and the shared grief.

"Well, well," drawled a half-remembered voice, "what you don't see when you haven't got a gun."

Shelley spun around, noticing for the first time the sun-worn face of the old cowboy seated at the oak table in the sunroom attached to the kitchen. She stared at him for several seconds, trying to place that dark, creased face, the white hair of his head, and the truly magnificent handlebar mustache that draped the lower half of his face. It was the mustache that gave him away.

"Acey!" she cried happily. "I didn't expect you to be here."

He rose to his feet, revealing a small, wiry frame, the worn blue jeans fitting his narrow hips in a way that younger men envied. "No reason you should, girl," he said as he swept her into a hard embrace. "It's damn fine to see you again—even under these circumstances."

Acey Babbitt had to be over seventy, and yet there was

nothing but his lined features and heavily veined hands to reveal it. Certainly his age was not apparent in the bear hug he gave her. When she caught her breath again, Shelly grinned at him, and said, "How have you been? Still teaching hardheaded little know-it-alls, like I was, to ride?"

He nodded, a twinkle in his dark eyes. "Yep. And chasing wimmen, too." His eyebrows wriggled suggestively. "Got my eye on a comfy widow lady this time." He smacked his lips. "By golly, but she's an armful. Demanding, too. Why, she's likely to plumb love me into my grave." His mustache twitched. "You know that old saying, girl—there may be snow on the mountain, but there's still a fire in the furnace."

"A roaring fire where you're concerned," Maria said tartly. She shook a finger at him. "I heard about you and that woman up at Shawnee Dick. You better take care, old man. Jim Madden has been keeping company with her for the past six months. And you know that Jim doesn't have red hair for nothing. Get him mad enough, and he's likely to take a scrawny old rooster like you apart—and in about ten seconds flat!"

Acey waved a dismissing hand. "Don't you worry none. I ain't *serious* about the widow."

Maria snorted and rolled her eyes at Shelly. "He'll be seventy-three in June, and you'd think that at his age, he'd have learned some sense."

"Well at least I've got more sense than to spout gossip to the girl here on her first morning back," he commented as he picked up his hat from the table and put it on his head with a flourish. "I got stock to see to. Don't have time to sit around and yammer." He flashed Shelly a glance. "You grew up just fine, honey. Good to see you." And strolled out the door with the rolling gait of a man who had spent most of his life in the saddle.

Maria looked stricken, but Shelly laughed and put her

arms around the older woman. "Nothing could make me feel more at home than listening to you two still squabbling—and about the same thing! Don't let him get you all ruffled—you know he does it on purpose." For as long as Shelly could remember, Maria had always scolded Acey about his women, and she had suspected even then that he made up half the stories of his amatory exploits just to get a rise out of Maria. It still seemed to work.

Maria smiled. "I know, but I can't help worrying about the old devil. He acts as if he's not a day over forty—he continues to train horses and work cattle—by himself most of the time, although a lot of the other ranchers try to keep an eye on him. He can still work rings around most men half his age, but I worry about him riding out in the hills by himself—he just doesn't seem to realize that he is not a young man anymore. Accidents happen, and they are harder and more dangerous on someone his age. Nick volunteered to go with him last fall to gather cattle, and he came home exhausted—said Acey might be old and he might move slower these days, but he *keeps* moving. It took Nick a week to recover from the pace Acey set, and he's only thirty!"

The conversation became more general, but it was several minutes later when both women were seated at the oak table that Acey had vacated before Shelly was finally able to ask the question that had been uppermost in her mind.

"Why, Maria? Why did Josh do it?"

Her dark eyes full of sadness, Maria shook her head. "I do not know, *chica*. I have asked myself that same question a dozen times, but I cannot come up with an answer."

"Did he seem different? Did he say anything to you that day that seemed odd, something that seemed out of place, anything that might have been a clue to what he planned to do?"

"No. The afternoon it happened . . ." Her voice faltered,

then picked up. "He pinched my cheek before he left for the barn to saddle his horse—you remember how he used to do. He said that he wanted to get away for a while—and that he wanted a heart attack on a plate for dinner—steak, French fries, and apple pie with ice cream for dessert." Her eyes filled. "I cannot believe that he is gone."

They were silent for several minutes as they sipped their coffee and brooded over Josh's suicide. Eventually, though, they began to talk of other things, Maria asking about Shelly's life in New Orleans; Shelly catching up on some of the major events that had happened in the valley since she had left—there weren't many—change came slowly to Oak Valley—one of its charms. Maria relayed news of the marriages, births, and deaths of the various residents and mentioned the few new businesses in town before the conversation drifted to Maria's two children.

Shelly remembered them; the boy, Nick, as an adventurous holy terror, the younger girl, Raquel, as a wide-eyed little shadow silently following Maria around as she did her work in the house.

"I can't imagine them all grown-up," Shelly exclaimed. "My God—they were just kids when I last saw them. And now you tell me that Raquel is working in Santa Rosa as a dental assistant and Nick has started his own business. Wow! I can hardly believe it! It doesn't seem possible that so many years have passed."

Maria smiled and rose to her feet, picking up the two mugs. "It does to me—especially every morning when my knees pop and creak when I get out of bed."

The sound of an approaching vehicle cut off Shelly's reply. "Oh, jeez! That's Mike Sawyer, and I'm not ready." Jumping up from her chair, she said, "Would you let him in and serve him some coffee? I need to change my clothes." She looked down at her faded blue jeans. "Josh wouldn't care what I wore, but I'd feel better if I were dressed better than this."

A shadow crossed Maria's face. "Are you going to spread his ashes today?"

Shelly nodded, the primary reason why she was here crushing down on her. "Yes. Mike thought I would want to get it behind me as soon as possible. He said he didn't want me to think about it too long. He offered to come with me— he feels that I should have someone else with me." She made a face. "I think, as the family lawyer, he wants to see for himself that I actually do scatter Josh's ashes and don't just set the urn on the top shelf of my closet."

"Would you mind if I came with you when you do it . . . your brother was very good to me and my children. He was very dear to me—and to Nick and Raquel."

"Of course not! And if I hadn't been so busy with my own feelings, I would have suggested it myself." Guilt washed over her. During her years away, she and Josh had had an exclusive relationship, just the two of them, and she had forgotten that he had another life away from her, that there were other people who had cared about him, who had loved him. He had specified that his ashes were to be spread privately, but surely he wouldn't object to Maria's presence? And as for Nick and Raquel . . . Maria's husband, Juan, had been a mostly absent one—at least as far she knew— and for as long as she could remember, Josh had shouldered the responsibility for their well-being. Just as he had with her. Her brother, she thought with a wistful smile, had had strong patriarchal tendencies and should have had his own brood of a half dozen children or so to oversee. Instead, there had been only her. And upon occasion, Nick and Raquel. They had loved him, too.

Impulsively, Shelly asked, "Do you think Nick and

Raquel would like to be there? I have no set time to do it. Do you want to get in touch with them and ask them?"

Maria did and consequently, it was a somber group of five who stood on Pomo Ridge overlooking the valley that afternoon. Thirty-six hundred feet below them lay the valley, still not having escaped the grip of winter, as the patchwork of colors revealed. The planted fields were a soft green, though the fallow ground still sported patches of yellow and brown—last year's dead grass and weeds, the new growth not yet tall enough to hide them. While many trees were already covered in green, the oaks that dotted the valley floor had not yet leafed out, the only sign of life on their naked branches the faint rosy tips that bespoke a spring yet to come. Gazing across to Mount Sebastian, towering over the ascending foothills to the east, Shelly wasn't surprised to see that the mountaintop was cloaked in white, the firs and pines standing tall and dark above the snow.

From here Shelly could make out most of the landmarks of the valley. She easily picked out the state highway that ran through the valley and the short string of businesses that straggled along it for five or six blocks. Below and almost directly in front of where she stood was the self-serve tiny Oak Valley Airport and a half mile or so to the left and beyond the airport lay the high school and grammar school. She noticed the high school still didn't have outside lights for night games—a sore point with everyone who had ever sat on the metal bleachers on a hot September afternoon to watch a football game. She had endured a few herself, although she had not attended the local high school. Josh had been adamant about that, too—when they reached high school age, all of the Grangers had been packed off to private schools, and whether she liked it or not, she would go to the very pricey private school in San Francisco that he had picked out. Shelly frowned. She'd forgotten how determined to get his own way Josh could be—or that he'd been a bit of a snob.

Feeling disloyal and uncomfortable with her thoughts, she stared down at the heavy bronze urn she held in her hands. It seemed strange that an object that she could hold in her hands contained all the physical remains of Josh Granger. The finality of what she was about to do suddenly overwhelmed her. Her head bent as anguish tore through her, and tears burned her eyes. *Oh, Josh! How could you have done this to yourself—and to the rest of us?*

She glanced back at the others where they stood in a half circle behind her. It was an odd little group, the housekeeper, her two grown children, and the family lawyer. Mike Sawyer looked the part; his dark blue suit creased and pressed, his white shirt and tie neat and tidy, the only unlawyerly note a pair of discreet black cowboy boots. Shelly liked that—it made him seem more approachable, less stiff and professional. Like her, Maria was simply dressed—pressed slacks and shirt, and a light jacket for protection against the faint chill in the air, despite the pale sunshine. Beside their mother stood Nick and Raquel, Nick towering over the two women, his eyes shuttered, his mouth held in a tight line. Raquel reminded Shelly of Maria, small, square-shouldered, and sweet-faced, her features hidden behind a handful of tissues as she tried to contain her tears.

Shelly looked away, feeling her own tears clogging her throat. Clearing her throat, she asked, "Does anyone want to say anything?"

Maria hesitated, then nodded and stepped forward. Laying her hand on the urn, she said in a trembling voice, "You were a good man, Josh Granger—I shall miss you. Rest in peace."

Maria's children shook their heads, Nick's eyes dropping to the ground between his boots, Raquel burying her head deeper into damp tissues. Mike Sawyer spoke up. "I brought a small Bible with me—I could read the Twenty-third Psalm, if you like. I think it's the twenty-third they always read at funerals."

Shelly shook her head. "That's not necessary—Since he never set foot in a church unless he had to, I don't think Josh would care."

She turned and looked down at the valley. Taking a deep breath, she undid the lid and began to shake out the ashes. A slight breeze had sprung up and the gray ash, all that remained of the physical Josh Granger, drifted away. *Good-bye, Bro*, Shelly said softly to herself, tears stinging the corners of her eyes, her spirits low. *Find peace.*

It was a silent and awkward group that rode the three miles back to Josh's house in Shelly's Bronco. Only when they were once more inside, all five of them seated in the kitchen sipping the hot coffee Maria had prepared before they had left to spread the ashes, did they start to speak.

At first the conversation was slow and uncertain and was mostly of a "getting-to-know" type. Shelly knew of Mike Sawyer, had talked to him quite a bit recently but had never met him. Beyond the most basic facts and a few blurry memories, Nick and Raquel were almost strangers to her. And it had been seventeen years since she had last seen Maria. With Josh's death lurking just over their shoulders, it wasn't what one could call a comfortable time, but as the conversation ebbed and flowed around her, Shelly began to relax.

Meeting Mike's eye, she said, "I really appreciate you taking the time to drive up here." Smiling faintly she added, "I doubt that delivering ashes to the bereaved family is why you became a lawyer."

Mike appeared to be in his mid-to-late thirties, and leaning back in the kitchen chair, his coat discarded and his tie half-undone, he appeared even less the proper family lawyer and far more attractive than Shelly had first thought. Standing about six feet tall, with a slender build and light brown hair and blue eyes, she found herself warming to him, liking the intelligence in his gaze and the sensitive curve of his mouth.

Mike waved a dismissing hand. "I wanted to do it. Your brother was more than a client—he was a friend as well. I hope that you will consider me in the same light."

Shelly nodded and, looking warmly around the table at the others, lifted her mug, and said, "Here's to friendship."

Maria beamed at her, Raquel nodded, and Mike grinned. Sprawled across from her, his long legs stretched in front of him, Nick regarded her for a moment, then shrugged and raised his mug. "Why not."

It was a less-than-enthusiastic response, but Shelly was willing to take it. The toast was drunk and the conversation ambled on a few more minutes before Raquel asked abruptly, "How long do you intend to stay?"

Shelly's gaze dropped to her brown ironstone mug. "I, um, don't have any set date." She swallowed, saying in a firmer voice, "Actually, I may not be returning." She looked up. "I'm thinking of staying . . . permanently."

"Oh, *chica*! I am so happy to hear you say that," Maria exclaimed. "I know it is what Josh hoped would happen one day." A cloud crossed her face. "It's not for me to criticize, and I do not mean it to sound as if I am, but how sad that you make this decision now—and not when Josh was alive. He spoke so often of how much he wanted you to come back to Oak Valley. He longed for you to return and was always saying how much he missed you. He was very lonely for your company."

Shelly frowned. That wasn't how she remembered it. The few times she brought up the subject of returning, Josh had brushed it aside, rushing on to talk about other things. In fact, if she'd had to hazard a guess, she would have said that Josh had *not* wanted her to come back. He had seemed content and more than willing for her to remain in New Orleans, yet Maria was telling her the exact opposite. If he'd wanted her to come home, why hadn't he said something?

Confused, she shrugged, and muttered, "Well, I'm here now, even if a bit late."

Breaking into the uncomfortable mood that seemed ready to settle over them, Mike said briskly, "Speaking of the time, I had better think of leaving. I've an hour and half drive in front of me. But before I leave, I thought perhaps we could get the reading of Josh's will out of the way. I brought it with me just on the off chance the opportunity presented itself— I didn't see the need for all of you to drive to my office for that particular formality. If you'll excuse me long enough to get it out of my briefcase in the car?"

"Of course," Shelly replied, her initial favorable impression of the lawyer increasing.

An awkward silence fell with the departure of Sawyer, Shelly once again realizing that she was in the midst of strangers, and she wished that Roman and Angelique were with her. Her eyes on her mug in front of her, she waited for Mike's return, tension coiling in her stomach as the minutes ticked by.

A strained smile on her face, she glanced around at Maria and her children. "It was kind of you to come with me to spread his ashes."

"Kindness had nothing to do with it," Nick growled, his expression resentful and determined at the same time.

"Oh, Nick, don't! Not now," cried Raquel, reaching out a hand to clasp his arm. "Please! We've just said good-bye to him. I know how you felt about him, but don't start now."

"Your sister is right," said Maria firmly. "Now is the time to grieve. There will be time later for, for . . . other things."

Bewildered, Shelly looked from one shuttered face to the other. "Would someone mind telling me what's going on?"

A bitter smile curved Nick's mouth as he stared at her. "You don't get it, do you?" He shook his head. "Figures. Ole Josh wouldn't want anything to distress his innocent little princess or to disturb the pedestal you obviously put him on." He laughed, but there was no amusement in the sound. "Allow me to strike the first blow at that golden image he presented to you." He bowed mockingly. "Meet your nephew, auntie. Of course, I'm not legitimate. Oh, no. Josh could sleep with the hired help and get her pregnant, but God forbid that a great and powerful Granger would ever marry his Mexican housekeeper or publicly acknowledge his own child." At Shelly's stunned expression, he added, "Yeah, that's right, auntie. I'm your brother's bastard. Welcome to the family secret."

Chapter Three

❦

Shelly blinked. A couple of things occurred to her at once. The contradiction of Josh's statements to her and those expressed by Maria were the most immediate. Not having ever mentioned or even hinted at the existence of a child, Josh sure as hell wouldn't have wanted her to come back to Oak Valley. Conversely, to Maria, he'd have acted otherwise. Sly was not a word she previously would have ever associated with Josh, but she began to wonder if Josh hadn't been very sly indeed.

Though she had been very young at the time, she remembered the distress she'd felt at Maria's sudden and inexplicable disappearance all those years before. One day Maria had been there laughing and singing as she had bathed her and put her to bed, and the next day she was gone. Just gone. No warning. No explanation. Not understanding what had happened to upset her little world, Shelly recalled that she had cried herself to sleep for days, missing Maria's gentle presence and funny bedtime stories. Thinking about that time, it seemed she vaguely recalled that her parents had gone around tight-lipped for several weeks afterward and Josh had been sullen-faced and surly. The details weren't clear in her mind—she'd been lost in her own lonesome misery. Besides, she'd only been about four and it wasn't likely that she'd remember much from that age anyway. Putting the pieces together now, some thirty years later, it offered one explanation for Maria's disappearance—especially when she linked it now with Maria's return over a year later with a squalling, red-faced Nick in her arms and a husband—Juan Rios.

It must have been an awkward and uncomfortable time for Josh and her mother and father, Shelly thought. She had only a few memories of her father, but Catherine Granger had always been a cool, stiff figure in her memories, proud of being a Granger, conscious of her position in the community. Neither Catherine, nor her husband, for that matter, would have been pleased to discover their first grandchild had been conceived by one of the Mexican help. While not agreeing with them, Shelly understood some of the reasons behind her mother's actions. Catherine Vale had been born dirt-poor, and it was her fairy-tale marriage to Stanley Granger that had allowed her to live a Cinderella-like existence and put her past behind her. Once married into the family, she became more Granger than any Granger born to the name and was prouder and more fiercely protective of the Granger reputation than any Granger who had ever lived. Having climbed up from dirt, her mother had been, and Shelly acknowledged it with an inward sigh, a bit of a snob, and she would have been furious—to be fair, as much with Josh as with Maria—with the news of the pregnancy. Marriage would have been out of the question as far as Catherine and probably her husband, too, was concerned and Josh must have gone along with it—with everything, including Maria's banishment. They were, after all, Grangers, leading members of the community, and no more than his parents did Josh enjoy being gossiped about. But Maria had come back . . . and stayed. Wow! What she wouldn't have given to be a fly on the wall back then. Fascinating.

Oddly enough that was her reaction to the situation. Fascinating. Surprising. Looking at Nick with new eyes, she thought she could see a resemblance to her brother—to herself for that matter. Nick's eyes were not just dark as she had first thought, they were dark *green*, possibly the same dark green as her own, and the slightly almond shape appeared the same—a Granger trait, although not everyone in the family had it. Nick's height could have come from Josh, too—and that lazy grace of his. Certainly, now that she considered it, Nick had a way of moving that was not *un*like Josh's languid motions. Shelly might have reservations, but it never occurred to her to dismiss Nick's claim out of hand. She turned it over in her mind and found herself believing that Nick could very well be her brother's child. There could be other explanations, and she wasn't discounting them, but Nick's blunt revelation had a ring of truth about it.

Astounding all of them, including herself, Shelly suddenly thrust out her hand, and said, "Glad to meet you, nephew!" She smiled wryly. "Now would someone please tell me what the hell has been going on?"

Nick shook his head, a slow grin replacing his bitter expression. "You know, I always liked you—even when you were being a bratty teenager, but I think I like you even more now . . . auntie."

"You believe him?" Maria asked incredulously.

Shelly shrugged. "I'm willing to take his words at face value. I'm a little taken aback, maybe even stunned." She smiled slightly. "And curious, I'm not going to deny that. And when I've had time to consider it more, I'm sure I'm going to have a lot of questions."

Raquel let out a pent-up breath. "You're being very nice about this. Mom and I pleaded with Nick to keep his mouth shut." She shot him a look. "Tactful is not a word I would apply to my brother."

"Yeah, well, I'd rather be *un*tactful than tiptoe around the

subject. Even though Josh did his best to pretend the connection didn't exist, you can bet that in the valley everyone
suspected the truth. Better Shelly found out about it from me
than to have some well-meaning busybody spring it on her."

"I can agree with that," Shelly muttered, thinking of
some of the more sharp-tongued residents of the valley.
Glancing around at the three of them, she asked, "Is it really
a secret? Or am I the only one who doesn't know?"

"Doesn't know what?" Mike Sawyer asked, walking
back into the room, a small briefcase in one hand.

"That I'm no longer the only member of my branch of the
family," Shelly said, that thought having just occurred to
her. She liked the idea. Josh's child. She had a nephew. It
gave her a warm feeling, and while she knew that feeling
might not last, she accepted their relationship. She supposed
she should be traumatized by the news, or at least upset, but
she wasn't. She'd always liked Nick when they'd been kids
together, and Maria had always held a special spot in her
heart. In fact, she'd always thought of Maria as part of her
family, so why *shouldn't* she be happy with the situation?

Mike flashed Nick a glance. "I see. Nick just couldn't
keep from telling you that fantasy of his, could he? Not even
today."

Shelly's brow rose. "Fantasy? Are you telling me that
Nick *isn't* Josh's child?"

She glanced at Maria, who remained silent. "Is it true? Is
Nick my brother's child?"

Maria's lip trembled, and she shot her son an agonized
glance. "He believes it."

Shelly frowned. If it were true, why didn't Maria just say
so? Embarrassment? Maybe.

She would have pressed the issue, but Mike said coolly,
"This is hardly the time for this sort of subject. I have no
idea of Nick's parentage and quite frankly I don't care who

his father may or may not be." Ignoring Nick's snort, he went on, "And I am not going to discuss it. Your brother is dead—we just spread his ashes, and his secrets went with him."

"Wait a minute!" Shelly began. "You can't just pretend the situation doesn't exist. Besides, why would Nick lie?" She decided prudently not to mention Maria's reaction to Nick's claim, but it puzzled her—a lot.

"I think you've forgotten that there is a great deal of land at stake. You'd be surprised what people would do to get their hands on it."

Nick growled and started across toward the lawyer, but Shelly jumped up and put her slim body between them. Keeping Nick at bay with a hand on his chest, she glared at Mike, and demanded, "Let me get this straight. You're saying that Nick's whole purpose for claiming to be Josh's child is to get his hands on the estate?"

"You said it, I didn't."

Shelly gritted her teeth, wondering how she had ever thought she liked Mike Sawyer. Tightly, she said, "You implied it. Do you believe it?"

"My opinion in the matter doesn't count," he returned, apparently unmoved by the situation. "What counts is what your brother wanted. And I can tell you for a fact that he wouldn't have wanted you to hear this sort of wild, unsubstantiated claim on today of all days."

"Why not?"

Sawyer looked impatient. "My God, Shelly! You just scattered Josh's ashes—and I'm about to read you his will. You're bound to be upset and emotional. A perfect time for someone to play on your emotions." He flashed a black glance at Nick. "Nick can claim to be Josh's son all he wants, but there is nothing legally that supports his claim. I might point out that his mother is mute on the subject—

which should tell you something. And unless Nick's willing to go to court and drag you and the Granger name through the mud—and hope he can convince a jury of the relationship, you are your brother's only heir."

"But that's not right!" Shelly sputtered. "If he's Josh's child, he should be entitled to his estate."

"If," Mike said, and, putting the briefcase down on the table, began to open it.

"Hold it right there! Are you telling me that Nick is lying when he says that Josh was his father? And what about Maria? Wouldn't she know the father of her own children?"

"I'm afraid it would be a case of her word against a dead man's," Mike said dryly. "And as I pointed out—Maria has not endorsed Nick's claim. Your brother never publicly or legally acknowledged any relationship with her—or Nick." When Shelly's mouth opened indignantly, he raised a hand. "He did help Maria when her husband died—acts which could be construed as nothing more than kindness." Mike looked at Nick again. "And ten years ago, for pennies on the dollar, I might add, he leased Nick several cows from the Granger herd so Nick could start up his own cattle herd. At the same time he gave him a long-term lease at ridiculously low terms to the Bull Flat Ranch and house. I would remind you that these could be construed only as the acts of a generous man—which your brother was." Shelly glanced from Maria's averted face to Nick's strained one and back to the lawyer's. Something really weird was going on, but damned if she could figure it out. She'd tackle Maria later and get the truth out of her, but aloud she only said stubbornly, "If Nick is his child, he's entitled to his share of the family possessions."

"Ah, there is that word, if, again. As I mentioned, his claim to a relationship is based solely on his say-so."

"What about DNA?" Shelly hesitated. Her knowledge of

DNA was scant, but she knew enough to be aware that while *her* DNA could prove that she and Nick were related, it could *not* prove that Josh had been his father. In fact as she thought about it, she remembered vaguely having read a newspaper article a couple years ago about the Thomas Jefferson/Sally Hemmings controversy. There'd been something in the article about that, while it could be proven via DNA that the Hemmings' descendants had been fathered by someone in the Jefferson family, conclusive proof that they were in fact *Thomas* Jefferson's descendants could not be proven because Thomas Jefferson had left no male offspring. Shelly's eyes widened. "That's why he insisted upon being cremated." And then she said something she'd never thought to say about her brother, "Why that sneaky bastard!"

"Don't you think that you're overreacting?" Mike asked sharply. "You're jumping to conclusions. And, remember, Josh always intended to be cremated; it wasn't something that he just recently decided upon. Right now, you have only Nick's claim that there is any relationship. Are you going to put aside everything you ever knew about your brother simply because of something a young man you don't know very well says?"

Shelly glanced from one tense face to the other. Five minutes ago she had believed that Nick was Josh's child. Had it simply been because she *wanted* him to be? That she wanted some physical reminder of Josh still in this world? Was it possible that Nick was playing upon her vulnerability with an eye to gaining access to a fortune? She'd been away for seventeen years and she'd only been eighteen when she'd left. What did she really know about Nick—or his mother for that matter?

Shelly's head suddenly started to ache, and her throat felt tight. Jesus! She didn't want to deal with this right now.

Maybe Mike was right. Maybe she was jumping to conclusions. She looked at Nick again. OK, so he had green eyes, and she thought she saw a family resemblance. Maybe she was wrong. Nick wouldn't be the first person to turn greedy at the thought of a lot of money.

She stepped away, and, not meeting anyone's eyes, said softly, "Right now, I don't know if I ever even knew my brother."

❧

Alone in her room, Shelly lay down on the bed, trying not to think about the ugly ending of the day. She didn't want to think that Nick was claiming a relationship in order to cut himself in for a piece of the pie that Josh's estate represented. She wanted, she admitted, for Nick to have spoken the truth. She wanted in a way that astounded her for Nick to be her brother's child, her relative, but she couldn't discount Sawyer's words either. Nor could she reconcile the man who Nick said was his father with the open, generous, loving brother she had known all her life. If Nick were his child, why wouldn't he have told her? Oh, not when she was a child, but surely once she had grown up, what reason was there for him to keep it secret? Because he was ashamed and didn't want her to think badly of him? Well, yeah, maybe.

What bothered her most was the notion that if Nick had indeed been Josh's, he had never acknowledged that fact. Illegitimate or not, at some point, wouldn't love or pride have moved him to reveal his relationship? She sighed, trying to make what she knew of her brother fit with Nick's claim. If she understood the meager facts she had at hand, Josh had always maintained a distance, had always acted as if he were nothing more than Maria's kind, caring employer. He had never admitted the truth, if Nick's statement was true, to anyone, not even his lawyer. And Sawyer was right, damn him! The leased cows and land could be explained away as simply the generosity of a lonely man with no children of his own.

Round and round her thoughts went, Maria's reticence nagging at her. Why hadn't Nick's mother backed him up? Did Maria know he was running a scam and while unwilling to expose him, was not brave enough to give weight to his claim? She found no answers and eventually dropped off into an uneasy doze. She didn't know how long she had slept, but something woke her. Bleary-eyed, she gazed around the room, surprised to find that dusk had fallen, shadows filling the room.

She lay there a moment, trying to wake up. A tap on the door jerked her upright, and after fumbling for the switch on the lamp near the bed, she flicked it on. Soft, yellow light pooled near the bed, dispelling the shadows and spreading the sensation of warmth throughout the area.

Seated on the side of the bed, she yawned. There was another, more insistent tap on the door.

Rubbing her forehead, she called out, "Who is it?"

"Nick. May I come in?"

She hesitated, then replied, "Sure. The door's not locked."

Nick slipped into the room, a tray held in his hands. He walked up to her and put the tray down on the table near the bed. Grabbing one of the chairs, he pulled it up and sat down.

Shelly looked at the contents of the tray and couldn't help grinning. The total items were a big plate of Oreo cookies, a half-gallon carton of milk, and two tall glasses.

Picking up a cookie and taking a bite, she looked at Nick. "Did Maria tell you they were my favorite?"

He smiled uncertainly. "Nope, I remembered from when

we were kids." His smile faded. "Look," he said, "I want to apologize for what happened this afternoon. Mike was right about one thing—my timing stinks. I should have kept my mouth shut and given you time to settle in before I said anything. I'm sorry."

Pouring them both glasses of milk, she shoved one in his direction. Indicating the cookies, she mumbled around a mouthful, "Help yourself."

They ate cookies and drank milk in silence. It was a friendly silence. A comfortable silence, and Shelly remembered times from the past when she and Nick had done just as they were doing now, eating cookies and drinking milk in complete accord with each other.

Putting her empty glass down a few minutes later, she asked, "Your timing wasn't the best, I'll grant you that, but the problem doesn't go away." She looked him dead in the eye. "Was Josh really your father?"

He hesitated, took a deep breath, then said in a rush, "Yeah. I believe he was. He never admitted it, and Mom . . ." He looked puzzled and hurt. "She won't talk about it—but she and Juan were always open about the fact that Juan *wasn't* my father—even if I carry his last name." He sighed and glanced down at the plate of rapidly disappearing Oreos. "Whenever I questioned her about my father, Mom just said not to worry about him—we had a nice home and she had a nice job and we didn't need him. We were happy without him—besides, she was married to Juan. By the time I was old enough to really question her about him, I guess I'd just accepted her explanation and didn't think about it too much." He looked off into space. "I must have been about fifteen, sixteen, when I found out differently. Until that time, Josh had always just seemed like a really neat guy, you know. He was good to Mom, and he was great to Raquel and me after Juan died—in that easygoing, careless sort of way he had. I never suspected a relationship—even between them." He grimaced. "OK, I'll admit that now and then after Juan died I thought that it would be great if Mom got something on with Mr. Granger. But I never even once considered that your brother was my father."

"How'd you find out?" Shelly asked around an Oreo.

"Some wise-ass kid at school. It was at football practice, and I don't remember what happened exactly, but we got into it." He grinned. "All that young, male testosterone, I guess. Anyway, I damn near beat the shi—, uh, devil out of him, before his friends piled in, then my friends joined the fight." His eyes gleamed with remembered enthusiasm. "The coaches leaped in and pulled us all apart. We were read the riot act and three or four of us were benched for the next game. By then we had cooled down and thought we'd gotten off easy—we could have been out for the whole season."

Shelly raised a brow. "In St. Galen's? Where the entire high school can barely put together a full team? I don't think so."

Nick smiled. "Yeah, you're probably right. But Jim Hardcastle, the guy I'd been fighting with, started whining and complaining. He was always sort of a troublemaker and the coach told him that he'd make an exception for him: two games. That really set Hardcastle off. He started yelling that it wasn't fair. That I had started the whole thing and that I was nothing but a half-breed Mex and that if my father wasn't Josh Granger, I'd have been thrown off the team."

Shelly paused in the act of pouring another round of milk for the pair of them. "Wow! That must have been a shock."

"To say the least," Nick commented wryly. "I went at Hardcastle, calling him a liar, and punched him in the nose for bad-mouthing my mom." He made a face. "The adults separated us again, and I ended up being benched for three games—which for us, was most of the season. Coach ordered me home right then—wouldn't even let me finish practice."

"You sound more pissed off about that than finding out about Josh and your mom."

Nick grinned. "Well, in a way I was. Man, I hated getting benched! As for the other—I didn't really believe Hardcastle—I thought he was just being a blowhard and a pain in the ass. It wasn't until I got home and was in the kitchen—" he paused and winked at her—"cramming my face full of Oreos and milk, and spouting off about what a jerk Hardcastle was, and asking Mom how he thought anybody would believe such a damned lie, when I noticed her expression." He shook his head. "I took one look at her face, and my stomach dropped right to the floor."

Shelly stopped eating her Oreo and stared at him, sympathy in her gaze. "Must have been hard. What'd you do?"

"I tackled her with it right off, but I didn't get anywhere then or ever." He glanced away, his expression bleak. He took a deep breath, and, meeting Shelly's sympathetic gaze, blurted out, "You have only my word for it. Mom simply will not talk about it. Even now if I press her, she starts to cry, and says she promised. Says she swore never to tell anyone. But it's the tears that get me. She almost always bursts into tears . . . she cried a lot that first day." Nick's eyes dropped, his jaw working. "I never saw my mom cry before, and it shook me—bad. I was in a rage"—he smiled deprecatingly—"as only a sixteen-year-old-almost-a-man can be. Not at her," he added quickly, "never at her, but I resented the situation, and I was furious that they'd kept the truth from me. I was furious that they'd allowed me to find out in such a manner."

Shelly shook her head. "Knowing Oak Valley, you'd have thought that they'd have realized that someone was bound to put two and two together eventually. They should have told you—it was cruel and thoughtless not to. They had to know that you would find out sooner or later. Surely they didn't think you'd never find out?"

Nick shrugged. "Don't ask me. Mom keeps her mouth shut, just saying that your family was kind to her and that they supported her when she needed help. It's obvious she never expected more than what she got, and she was satisfied with it—that's the part that eats at my gut." The expression in his eyes hardened. "Your mother gave Mom money and paid for her to go back to Mexico . . . and stay there."

Shelly made a face. "Sounds like Mother. She really took her position in the valley to heart. She wouldn't want any slurs cast on the Granger name." She frowned. "But if your mom went away, never to return, what happened? She came back."

"Yeah, she did." Hurriedly he added, "And it wasn't because she wanted more money either."

"I would never doubt that. But why did she come back?"

He ran a hand through his dark hair. "I don't know if you knew, but Mom's father died when she was a child in Mexico and left the family almost destitute. She said that with her dad gone, they were practically living on the streets. Anyway, Abuela Ynez, my other grandmother, wrote to her only brother, Tio abuelo Oliverio. He had settled here and was working, for the"—he flashed her a glance—"Ballingers. When he received Abuela Ynez's letter begging for help, he sent for the entire family and helped them find jobs here in Oak Valley." He looked at Shelly. "This was Mom's home. She's lived here since she was eleven years old. She grew up here. She had her citizenship. Abuela Ynez, her uncle, her sisters, and a brother lived here. In Mexico there were just some cousins or something, and she was lonesome. So, when I was about six months old, she couldn't stand it anymore and she came home. To Abuela Ynez's—not to the Grangers'."

Shelly waved a hand. "I believe you. And I can guess the rest. Josh or one of my parents found out that she was here and they probably thought it would cause less talk if Maria came back to work for them than if they just pretended they'd never heard of her."

Nick nodded. "Mom never said, she can be pretty vague about stuff when she wants to be, but I guess it was something like that."

Shelly looked curious. "Doesn't she talk about it at all?"

"Not a word. You saw her today. Even for me she won't open up. She has some hang-up about breaking her word. If she had her way, we'd all just continue to pretend it never happened. She hates it when I bring up the subject." He grinned at her. "She really tore a strip off me this afternoon when we went home."

"The mind boggles at what the situation was like here— for them. *I* never suspected a thing."

"You wouldn't—you were a kid, just like Raquel and me. And by the time you were old enough to maybe notice something or ask embarrassing questions, you were gone— remember?"

Shelly grimaced. "I remember." She picked up another Oreo. Nibbling at the edges of it, she asked, "Did you ever face Josh?"

Nick took a deep breath. "Oh, yeah. And he just looked at me and said it was too bad that I listened to gossip." He flashed a wry grin. "I lied a little and said that Mom admitted it and he got that, I smell shi—, manure, grin on his face and told me that he couldn't be responsible for any tales his housekeeper might tell her son."

Shelly's eyes widened. "He actually said that?" she asked in a stunned voice.

Nick nodded and took a bite of a cookie. "Yeah. He said it. I should know—I was there. Jesus! I hated him at that moment. I wanted to pound him into the ground. Not so much for not acknowledging me, but for dismissing Mom that way—his 'housekeeper.' Needless to say, he and I didn't have very many friendly father-to-son chats after that."

"I guess not."

They chewed on the cookies for a few minutes in silence. Then Nick asked quietly, "Do you believe me? I don't have much proof." He laughed bitterly. "Hell, I don't have any proof—just gossip and a gut feeling. And green eyes. And a father my mother won't name."

Shelly sighed and put down her half-eaten cookie. "I find it hard to believe that Josh could be so cold and calculating and yet . . ." She looked at him, studied the lean, intent features across from her, and, for one dizzy moment, it was as if Josh stared back at her. She blinked, the resemblance vanished, and it was just Nick sitting across from her.

Did she believe him? It was a fantastic story and flew in the face of everything she knew about her brother, but there was something about it, something she couldn't just dismiss out of hand. And it wasn't improbable that young, pretty Maria would succumb to the charms of twenty-year-old Josh. This site, the site where they had lived in those days, was isolated. There were no near neighbors, unless you considered five miles down a winding twisting forest and brush-lined road near. They would have spent a lot of time here at the house when Josh had been home from college. They were worlds apart socially and financially, yet Maria was in his house, close at hand, day and night. . . . Shelly wrinkled her nose. The whole situation, if true, was nasty. It reminded her uncomfortably of the master/slave situation that had been so prevalent in the South and the *droit du seigneur* of old France. Had Josh considered making love to Maria his right? She thought about her brother, realizing that she'd always been aware, albeit vaguely, of his careless indifference to those he considered of a lesser stature than himself. He wasn't cruel. He just . . . Her mouth twisted. He just thought himself above the masses. He was, after all, a Granger. And not just any Granger, but a Granger of Oak Valley. It had been one of his less attractive traits, Shelly admitted, but he had always been so open and generous with those he liked and loved that one tended to overlook it. To forget about it.

Nick's touch on her arm made her jump. "Raquel's right—I am such a jerk sometimes." he said disgustedly. "Look, I came up here to apologize. That's all, honest. I really didn't mean to dump this ancient history on you right now." He smiled bitterly. "I just can't seem to help myself. It eats at me, you know. Not the land. The hell with the land! It's the fact that he could never bring himself to acknowledge me as his child. I don't even want the Granger name. I've been called Rios for as long as I can remember. Why would I want to change that? But I deserved his acknowledgment." His lips twisted bitterly. "He lived with me underfoot all those years, and he never *once* stepped down from his goddamn pedestal and acknowledged me. He should have given me that—even just privately. I want that, I *need* the recognition that I am his son—and to hell with everything else." He waited a second, then took a deep breath, and asked, "So do you believe me?"

Shelly's heart ached at the naked yearning in Nick's face, wanting desperately to tell him that she believed him. Instinct told her he was telling the truth . . . but instinct had played her false before. Sawyer's cautionary words drifted through her mind, and her lips tightened. Jesus! She hated this. Why couldn't things be straightforward? No doubts. No questions. Did she trust Nick?

Her gaze dropped to the demolished plate of cookies. A memory suddenly popped into her mind. She'd have been thirteen and Nick about nine. It had been June, and her mother was having her annual tea party. It was probably the only time of the year that most women of St. Galen's actually put on a dress. The tea party had been instituted decades ago by her great-grandmother. Shelly's nose wrinkled. Something, if she remembered right, to shove up the noses of the Ballingers. The Ballingers and their friends obviously were not invited. The annual Granger tea party had become a valley tradition and was one of the high points of the St. Galen's "season."

It was always held the first Saturday in June, and Shelly recalled the long tables covered with dainty sandwiches and delicate pastries that were set up outside underneath the oaks. Tables and chairs shaded by colorful umbrellas were scattered across the expanse of lawn. The ladies of St. Galen's, probably wearing dresses and nylons for the first time since last year's tea party, gossiped and laughed and enjoyed the elegant surroundings. For a while, the weather, the hay crop, the price of cattle or sheep, the setbacks and triumphs of the calving or lambing season, the timber harvest, fire season, the everyday worries that went with ranching and timbering, were put in abeyance.

That particular year, being a boy and nine and living in the country, Nick had started a collection of milk snakes. He'd caught two so far and kept the small white-banded black snakes in a huge old aquarium that Josh had found somewhere for him and had helped him set up in the barn. Nearly every Saturday morning Nick set out with a gallon pickle jar looking for snakes—and most of the time he came home empty-handed.

The adults had been busy with preparations, and Shelly remembered that she and Nick both had been told to behave and to stay out of the way. Nick had happily gone off looking for snakes and she, being above such childish sport since she had become a teenager, had been lazing in the hammock at the rear of the house, her nose buried in a *Seventeen* magazine.

The tea party was in full swing when Nick came up to her and shoved the pickle jar containing three writhing snakes in her face. She screamed, threw her magazine into the air, and fell out of the hammock.

Chortling, Nick had shoved the jar at her again, and the chase was on. Shrieking and running as if she had never seen a milk snake before, she had bolted for the front of the house, Nick hot on her heels. It was a game, and they both knew it. It was merely an excuse to run and scream and let loose some of that youthful exuberance.

Having forgotten the tea party, long coltish legs flashing in the sunlight, she ran smack into the middle of her mother's annual grand affair. Before she was spotted, she veered away and quickly skirted the crowd. Half-hidden behind one of the big oak trees, she waited, keeping an eye out for Nick and for the chase to continue. It never occurred to her that Nick wouldn't take the same evasive action.

Intent upon the game, he burst onto the scene and practically crashed into Mrs. Matthews, the grammar school librarian. Mrs. Matthews, a big, heavyset, brassy woman, was not a favorite of Nick's—he'd been sent to the principal's office by her more than once during the school year. Appalled to find himself in the middle of Señora Granger's party, he immediately tried to sidle away, but Mrs. Matthews stopped him.

"Ah, good afternoon, Nick," Mrs. Matthews said in her booming voice. "It's good to see you helping your mother this way." Smiling condescendingly down at him, she asked, "And what is this you are bringing to the table?"

He shouldn't have done it. Even he knew it. But the devil just took over, and he thrust the jar of snakes right up in her face. "Snakes!" he said with relish. Her reaction was everything he could have wished for.

Mrs. Matthews's heavy features contorted; she let loose a bellow that shook the ground and staggered backward wildly, bumping hard into the edge of one of the punch- and pastry-laden tables. Thrown off-balance, arms flailing, she scrambled clumsily to keep on her feet. It was no use: the table, the pastry, and Mrs. Matthews all went down in one loud thundering crash. Conversation ceased. Silence fell.

Horrified, Nick stood there, the jar of snakes clutched to his skinny chest, and stared at the scene of carnage before him. He was dead meat.

The expression on Señora Granger's face when she stalked up to him confirmed that thought. Her face stony, although he thought her lips twitched, she ordered him to his room. He was banished. Sent to bed without dinner. Worse, his collection of snakes was taken away from him. He was in complete disgrace. And not once, Shelly thought, as she studied the features of the man across from her, did he mention her part in the disaster—or for that matter ever blame her. And she'd been too much of a coward to come forth and share the blame. She grimaced. Cowardice seemed to be a trait of hers. But not, she reminded herself, anymore.

She glanced at the empty plate. That night, after everyone had gone to bed, she'd crept into his room at the rear of the house with a plate of Oreos and a half gallon of milk. They'd eaten the cookies in silence, drinking from the carton of milk. There were no words between them. He accepted her peace offering.

He hadn't betrayed her then, Shelly thought, and he could have. Most kids would have. And while the actions of a nine-year-old weren't a true test of the character of the adult, she decided it was good enough for her.

Slowly, she nodded. "Yeah, I believe you."

Nick let out his breath in a whoosh. "Thanks. I needed that."

They smiled at each other. "So," Nick asked, picking up the last cookie and taking a bite, "what do we do now?"

Chapter Four

It wasn't an easy question to answer, and Maria's stubborn silence only complicated the situation. Though she was determined to tackle Maria, Shelly didn't honestly believe that she'd have better luck than Nick had had getting the truth out of her. All she was likely to get from Maria was a better *feel* for the situation. They both agreed that since his ashes had just been scattered, obtaining a sample of Josh's DNA was impossible.

Tentatively, she offered, "We could use mine—the results would at least show that we're related."

"Yeah, that might be better than nothing." He grimaced. "But that wouldn't prove that Josh is dear old dad." He smiled wryly. "Thanks for the offer—I may get desperate enough to take you up on it—and while it would help, what I really want is something more tangible. Wish he'd conveniently left a blood sample lying around for us to find."

Shelly nodded. "I agree that's what we need for real, *legal* proof of parentage," Shelly said with a sigh. "Otherwise, we're just whistling 'Dixie.' "

His long legs stretched out in front of him, Nick nodded. "That part of it doesn't bother me." he murmured. "Right now, it's enough that you accept me." Huskily he added, "It's a good feeling to be able to talk to you about it; to have someone listen to me and *believe* me." His eyes hardened.

"And that you're not listening to that hypocritical bastard Sawyer."

"Yeah, well, that hypocritical bastard is just the sort of person we're going to have to convince if you want public recognition that Josh is your father," Shelly muttered. "It isn't going to be enough for me simply to say, 'Hey, everybody, I believe him!' And speaking of that, how are we going to handle that aspect of it? Take out an ad in the local newspaper?"

Nick laughed. "Nah. I won't put you through that. For the time being, let's just go with the flow."

Shelly simply looked at him, and he laughed again. "I know. I know. I want the recognition, but I feel like I've just jumped the biggest hurdle—you. Having done that, all of the other stuff suddenly doesn't seem important, or rather, not so urgent." He made a face. "Mom and Raquel are right—you really don't need to be burdened with ancient history at this point. You, we all need to deal with Josh's death right now, and you're going to have your hands full the next few months settling the estate. Once the estate is out of the way, then maybe we can put our heads together and come up with a way to expose the truth." He grinned. "Without, of course, causing a lot of talk."

Shelly snorted. "In this valley?" They exchanged wry glances, knowing the impossibility of such a thing. "I guess we'll cross that bridge when we come to it," Shelly said, suppressing a yawn.

Nick took the hint and, grabbing the tray, headed for the door. His hand on the doorknob, he looked back over his shoulder and grinned at her. "Nitey nite, auntie."

Shelly made a face at him. "Good night, nevvy."

Long after Nick had departed, she lay awake, thinking over the events of the day. In a way, she was almost grateful to Nick for springing the news of Josh's fatherhood on her:

it prevented her from brooding over Josh's sudden death and gave her thoughts a different direction. It didn't lessen her feeling of grief and loss, but it provided a distraction, and for the first time since she had learned of his suicide, that awful weight in her chest, that heaviness of spirit and the prickle of tears at the corner of her eyes was gone. Nick was right about something else, too: Until Josh's estate was settled she would have to put the question of his parentage on the back burner, and she was grateful that he was willing to do so.

———— ∞ ————

Shelly woke the next morning to rain. Not the fierce pounding of a major storm, but a heavy mist that blanketed the area and made it unpleasant to be outside. It was just as well; she spent the day going through Josh's office, trying to get a handle on his affairs.

The rain continued off and on for several days, never quite stopping long enough to make going outside for any length of time feasible or desirable. Shelly couldn't bring herself to drive into town; she wasn't ready to face the curiosity and the questions and exclamations her return was going to cause. She knew that the news of her return was already circulating; she'd made no attempt to hide it, but so far, beyond a few phone calls from the friends she'd kept in touch with over the years, no one intruded upon her privacy. And the weather gave her an excuse not to venture too far from the house. Maria took care of all the shopping and meals and housework, so there was no real reason to venture forth. She saw Nick nearly every day—he usually strolled in about dinnertime and allowed himself to be persuaded to stay and join her for a meal. By tacit agreement they didn't discuss Josh. Mostly, they were busy learning about each other and quietly reestablishing the childhood link between

them. Raquel was back in Santa Rosa, and Maria seemed
determined to pretend that nothing had changed: she was the
family housekeeper. Period. Shelly and Nick made faces at
each other when Maria stiffly refused the invitations to join
them, and the looks she sent her son as he sprawled at the
oak table in the kitchen alcove were full of disapproval.
Maria wasn't pleased with Shelly either; it offended Maria's
sense of what was proper to have Shelly eating meals in the
alcove rather than in the dining room, as Josh had always
done. And Maria was tight-lipped about any relationship she
might have shared with Josh. Shelly tried to introduce the
topic once or twice when she and Maria were alone, but
Maria's mouth remained firmly shut, and the resentment in
her dark eyes made Shelly decide not to push the issue . . .
at the moment. There would be time enough to breach those
walls in the future. She spent the majority of her time in
Josh's office and on the phone to Mike Sawyer. Her manner
was polite and professional with him, and he responded in
kind.

A couple of times, Nick had dragged her out into the
misty rain and they had hiked along the shaley mountainous
roads, the rainfall not heavy enough to make them muddy
and impassable. She enjoyed those walks. The cool, soft
mist on her face, the stretching of her muscles, the fast
pumping of her blood as they climbed a steep, twisting
track, and the wet scent of pine and fir in her nostrils, after
too many hours of sitting behind Josh's desk, were power-
fully invigorating.

April arrived and with it a glimmer of sunshine, and
Shelly knew she could not put off the short drive into St.
Galen's any longer. It was time. She'd been home now for
over two weeks and had grown comfortable in Josh's house.
Comfortable with her decision to remain in Oak Valley. A lot
of the initial work on the settling of the estate had been

done, and while there was still much to do, she could take a break from the paperwork with a clear conscience. She frowned. Going over the books, a troubling pattern of over-spending and dipping into capital was beginning to make itself apparent, and she suspected that she was going to have to dig deeper and demand some detailed answers from Sawyer. Worse, it appeared that Josh had turned his back on the Granger Cattle Company—the family's sole source of income. Unlike the Ballingers, the Grangers weren't wealthy in money; their wealth lay in the thousands of acres of land that they owned—and the fat cattle that roamed it. These days, the herd of registered Angus was decimated, the cattle either sold off or too old to breed. All that remained of a once huge and profitable herd was a twelve-year-old bull, Granger's Ideal Beau. It was depressing.

After lunch that day, Shelly stood up from the oak table, and, putting her plate on the counter, said casually, "I thought I'd drive into town today. Is there anything you need?"

Maria stopped her industrious scrubbing of the sparkling sink and looked at her. The expression in her brown eyes troubled, she asked, "Are you ready for all the questions? Everyone is going to want to talk to you about Josh's suicide. And your return. And your plans."

Shelly grimaced. "I know. I'm ready. I think."

It had been dark when she had first arrived, and she took her time driving down the steep crooked road that led to the valley floor, glancing around, trying to reacquaint herself with her surroundings. The shale-based road had been widened over the years and some of the worst curves taken out. Thickets of brush, manzanita, scrubby madrone, buck-brush, red-bud, already gowned in magenta blossoms, and wild white and purple lilac pressed close to the edges of the road, brushing the sides of the Bronco in some of the narrowest places. Seeing those impenetrable patches of tangled limbs and twisted trunks, she automatically thought of the fire danger they represented. Not even the wildlife could use some areas, they were so choked with brush, and if a fire ever started. . . . She shuddered. Everyone who lived in the country feared fire—especially in the summer months, when the entire area was nothing more than mountain after mountain, hill after hill of flourishing tinder just waiting for flame to strike.

When she hit the valley floor, she was pleased to see that there were few changes. The airport still looked the same; maybe a few more airplane hangars were there these days, but it still more resembled an open field with a strip of pavement running through it than an airport. It looked beautiful today, the golden poppies and blue lupine blooming their hearts out at this time of year. The grammar school, she noticed as she turned onto Soward Street, now had an attractive black iron fence around it—though there was no denying that the fence gave the appearance of a fortress. The high school was no longer painted a putrid green and the mural of a primitively drawn pinto mustang no longer hung over the entrance of the gym that she remembered from her youth. As she drove down the street toward the state highway, she realized that most of the houses had been painted or fixed up. There were still some weedy overgrown lots, and very few of the ramshackle places that had been around seventeen years ago remained, but she noted that there was still nothing ritzy or cottage-perfect about the street, and she was grateful for it. She would have hated to find herself driving down a street that looked Carmel-cute. None of the houses were alike, and since all had been built at different times, each was its own unique style, from the few small Victorian-style homes, to the more modern ranch-style and everything in between. The area looked like what it was, a street where average, hardworking families lived. Families who made every penny count—and then some. Some people might even find it a bit shabby, but to Shelly it was home, and it looked beautiful.

She had determined that her first stop would be Heather-Mary-Marie's. A smile tugged at the corner of her mouth. Heather-Mary-Marie's had been named for three sisters whose father had first opened the store around the turn of the century, and from things Josh had told her over the years, was still a fixture in the community.

In the beginning the store had been a small hole in the wall, supplying odds and ends to the ranchers and loggers who wrested a living from the land. The business had thrived and in due course, it had expanded, and all three sisters worked in the store right alongside their father, Graham Newell. The three sisters were considered spinsters, until Heather, the eldest, at the age of forty-five married the big, tough logger, Sam Howard. It had been according to local legend a stunning event. Another one was to follow: at the advanced age of forty-eight, Heather set tongues wagging again when she gave birth to a daughter. To no one's surprise, she promptly named her Heather-Mary-Marie.

These days Heather-Mary-Marie's was, Shelly supposed, as close to the old dry goods stores of the frontier West as you could get, although it was now called a gift shop. She was familiar with it since she had worked there summers from the time she had turned fifteen until she had left.

It had been Josh's idea that she take the job, and she could still recall the humorous patience in his gaze when he'd broached the notion. "Look kiddo," he had said, "I know you've just got home from boarding school and I know that you've got all sorts of things planned for the summer—working at Heather-Mary-Marie's not being one of them. But stop and consider this: You're gone from the valley almost all year, you're losing your contact with the valley—working at Heather-Mary-Marie's will give you a chance to meet a lot more people than the three or four special friends you have right now." At her mutinous look, he added, "Tell you what—you try it for two weeks, and if at the end of that time, you hate it, I'll let you off the hook." She smiled at the memory. After an initial resentful start, she *loved* it! And Josh had been right about meeting other people. Working at Heather-Mary-Marie's had kept her in touch with the community, had helped forge her bonds with the valley.

Working at Heather-Mary-Marie's had been fun, and she remembered her pleasure that last summer when Cleopatra, the owner, had allowed her to tag along to one of the trade shows and help select gift items for the store. But more than gifts were to be found in Heather-Mary-Marie's. A few books occupied the shelves; boots, socks, jeans, T-shirts and frilly dresses for little girls hung from the freestanding racks and the long rack against the far wall. Copies could be made on the Xerox. If you needed a new blouse or scarf, or a last-minute baby or wedding gift, there was just one place to go: Heather-Mary-Marie's. Coloring books, crayons, toys, kitchen and bath towels, clocks, glassware, signs, plastic-flowered funeral wreaths, cards, and a small selection of candy was always at hand. As a child, Shelly had thought it one of the most enthralling places in the world—better than Disneyland on a budget.

Ever since Shelly could remember, the store had taken up one entire end of a big, long, log building in the center of town. If you wanted the latest news and hoped for a fair amount of accuracy, Heather-Mary-Marie's was where you headed. Funeral notices were still posted on its doors, with the post office, Joe's Market at the south end of town, and MacGuire's, the biggest grocery store in the valley, being most of the other posting sites. If you went to town looking for someone, Heather-Mary-Marie's had to be one of your stops. Nearly everyone, it seemed, at one time or another, passed in and out of its swinging glass doors.

And if you wanted to announce your presence back in town, Shelly thought dryly, as she parked the Bronco in front of the log building, this was where you went. She sat there a minute after she had turned off the ignition, looking at the place. Nope, the building hadn't changed at all: green metal roof and gleaming windows and doors posted with various notices of coming events—bake sales, firehouse raffle, the FFA Mother's Day Parade and Rodeo, broke up the darkness of the logs.

She sat there glancing around, knowing she was wasting time, dragging her feet, putting off the awful moment. She sighed and, after pushing back a heavy fall of tawny-colored hair, forced herself out of the Bronco. Shoulders squared, she marched up to the front doors and walked inside, the old-fashioned bell over the door clanging to announce her presence.

A flood of memories washed over her. Racks piled high with goods, the same gray cement floor, and to her left, the glass counter crammed with jewelry—silver belt buckles, Black Hills gold earrings, bolo ties, and colognes, and, overhead, fluttery gleaming wind chimes hanging from the ceiling met her gaze. Delight speared through her. *Some things*, she thought, *just don't change.*

The woman behind the low, wooden counter near the front of the store looked up. She was tall, nearly six feet and buxom; her hair was an improbable shade of red, and she'd probably never see sixty-five again, although if the brilliant slash of crimson lipstick, penciled brows, and dangling silver earrings were anything to go by, she was fighting hard.

She stared at Shelly for a long minute. Then a smile,

huge, warm, embracing, lit her face. "Well, I'll be damned," she said in a voice like the clang of a tire iron on the bottom of a whiskey barrel. "It's little Shelly Granger, all grown-up! Come here, girl, and give us a hug."

Shelly fought back a sudden surge of tears, memories almost swamping her at the sound of Cleo's voice. Cleopatra Hale was the original Heather-Mary-Marie, until the age of eighteen, when she decided that her name was old-fashioned and legally changed it to Cleopatra. She claimed that Cleopatra sounded more glamorous and fitted her image better. Five husbands had all added their mite, with the last one about fifteen years ago being named Hale. Josh said that Cleo maintained she hadn't remarried since then because she'd decided that Hale went just fine with Cleopatra.

Arms outstretched, that huge smile on her plain face, Cleo came around the end of the counter and swept Shelly into an embrace. Shelly was overwhelmed, engulfed in a bear hug, the remembered scent of Charlie cologne and Kool cigarettes surrounding her.

They hugged each other a long time before Cleo finally pushed her away, and said briskly, "Guess that's enough sentiment for now. How in the hell could you have stayed away for so long? Without even a telephone call—let alone a visit?"

Misty-eyed, Shelly grinned at her. "Just happened. Can't tell you how. One day I was here and the next it was seventeen years later."

Cleo snorted. "Yeah. Right. Tell me another story." Her face softened, and she gave her a quick squeeze on the shoulder. "I'm sorry about Josh. It must have been hard on you."

Shelly nodded. "Thanks. It was—is—I still don't really believe it." She took a deep breath. "And I'm back for good. I won't be returning to New Orleans."

"Well, at least one good thing is coming out of Josh's suicide." Cleo shot her a considering glance. "You know that nothing else was talked about for days. In fact, it's only been the last week or so that talk has died down. Lots of speculation about you though—what you're going to do, when you'll show your face in town, how long you're going to stay, if you've gotten fat and hagged-looking after all these years—that sort of thing."

Shelly grinned. "And having seen me, what are you going to tell everyone?"

"Why, that you've changed . . . but not much." Cleo studied her, the bright blue eyes moving over her face and up and down her slender body. "And that all the changes are for the good." Cleo smiled. "My, my but Mrs.-Thinks-She's-High-and-Mighty Reba Stanton is going to be green with envy when she hears that you're just as pretty as ever . . . and staying. Believe me, it'll be my pleasure to tell her."

For a minute Shelly couldn't place the name. "Do you mean Reba Collier?" she asked.

"The very same. She married that nice happy-go-lucky Stanton boy, Bob, about eleven, twelve years ago. He ain't been so happy since."

The clang of the bell over the door made both women glance in that direction. Shelly braced herself to meet someone else from the past, someone that might not be as welcoming as Cleo. She relaxed when she realized that the slim older man who walked up to the counter was a stranger. He wore a red baseball cap, a white chef's apron over his jeans and Western shirt, and carried a small brown paper bag in one hand that he laid on the counter with a mocking half bow in Cleo's direction. Shelly studied him for a moment longer. He had a kind face, a comfortable lived-in sort of face, with bushy graying eyebrows and neat little gray goatee, and she was certain she had never met him before—

unless seventeen years had changed him all out of recognition. Intending to leave Cleo to her customer, Shelly turned away and began to edge toward the back of the store.

"Oh, no, you don't," Cleo said firmly. Grasping her by the arm, she led her back to where the newcomer stood. "Hank, let me introduce Shelly Granger. Shelly, this is Hank O'Hara, he and his sister, Megan, run the Blue Goose—it's new, not the building, just the restaurant, since you've been gone. They moved here about seven years ago and fixed up the old Stone Inn across the street." A gleam entered Cleo's eyes. "It's a fair enough place to eat."

Hank clutched his chest, his brown eyes dancing. "Ah, me darlin', you've fair wounded me mortal. 'A fair enough place to eat.' Oh the injustice of it." He grinned at Shelly and put out his hand. "Pleased to meet you. And let me invite you to try out one of our fine meals and see for yourself how this hornet-tongued witch maligns the Blue Goose."

"I'd rather be a hornet-tongued witch than a Blarney-Stone-kissing Irishman!" Cleo retorted with relish.

Hank grinned. "Oh, that's very good me darlin'. Very good, indeed. And here I am bringing you your lunch." He winked at Shelly. "Don't believe everything she says about me—or my cooking. The woman's in love with me and just can't help herself."

With amusement, Shelly noticed that Cleo's cheeks flushed pink. But the light of battle was in her eyes, as Cleo said, "And you can just march back across the street if you're going to start with that sort of nonsense." She fiddled with some papers lying on the counter. "Go on. Get. I'm busy." Adding under her breath, "In love with you, my ass. Now get!"

Hank chuckled and murmured to Shelly, "Isn't she just the loveliest sight when she's angry?" Cleo snorted, and he grinned. "Having completed my mission of mercy, 'tis back to the slave mines for me," he said. He looked at Shelly, and added, "If you give us a try, first meal's on me, Miss Granger." Shelly knew the moment he made the connection. His face fell ludicrously, and he muttered, "Granger. Granger. You're the sister who lives in New Orleans! Josh was your brother, wasn't he?" At Shelly's nod, he went on. "Oh, hey, listen. I'm sorry, real sorry about Josh's passing. He used to come into the Blue Goose three or four times a week for coffee and pie sometimes. We looked forward to seeing him—he was such a character—and kind, too. When Meggie and I first came to the valley, he was a one-man welcoming committee. Helped introduce us around and made us feel part of the community. He was a great guy. We'll miss him. Lots of people will."

"Thank you," Shelly said, a lump forming in her throat. Josh *had* been a great guy. Even, her conscience pricked her, if he hadn't always done the right thing.

Just as Hank left, a couple of customers wandered into the store, and while Cleo was busy with them, Shelly walked over to the wall of T-shirts. The bell rang a few more times, and as more people entered, she decided that she might as well forget about visiting with Cleo for now. Her hand riffled through the T-shirts and Western-style blouses one last time when she spotted a gold T-shirt with a snarling tiger on it that screamed "buy me." A T-shirt was the last thing she needed, since most of her wardrobe consisted of T-shirts and jeans, but smiling ruefully she took it down from the rack. Holding it against her body, she looked in the full-length mirror tacked on the wall outside the two miniscule dressing rooms crowded into one corner of the store. Not bad. And since there were days that she felt like a snarling tiger, the shirt would complement her mood. Still smiling, she swung around and found herself face-to-face with Sloan Ballinger.

He was leaning not six feet away against a counter of jeans and socks, his gold eyes locked on her. Her throat closed off, and her heart seemed to have taken up bungee jumping. Oh, Jesus. She wasn't ready for this. And, oh, damn, did he have to look quite so handsome? Quite so male? And, dammit to hell, why did she have to feel like melting into a puddle of warm honey, just because he was looking at her?

She stiffened as traitorous emotions tore through her. Oh, no. Not again. She wouldn't go through all that pain and disillusionment again—no matter how tempting the package. Her chin held high, with a smile that damned near killed her, she put out her hand. "Hello, Sloan. It's been a long time." She was quite proud of her voice. Not a quiver in it. Just a nice, pleasant, *polite* tone.

He pushed away from the counter, straightening to his full height, making her feel at once both threatened and fragile and very, very feminine. "Yeah, it has been," he said in that well-remembered whiskey-deep voice of his. And oh, hell, it still sent a warm, delicious tremor down her spine.

"You're looking well," he muttered.

The smile on her face felt as if it would splinter at any moment, but she kept it in place. "And I'll say the same to you."

Sloan ran a big hand through his black hair. "Uh, look," he said, "I'm sorry for your loss."

"But not," she replied evenly, "that Josh is dead."

He shook his head. "You know how I felt about him. And I haven't changed my mind. I never wished him dead, but just because he's dead, doesn't mean he's become a saint."

"I never said he was a saint. He was simply a man—a man with as many faults and virtues as the next person. You only saw his faults, never his virtues."

Sloan's face tightened. "I didn't come in here to start an argument with you—not about Josh, anyway."

"Well, then, I think this about covers our conversation, don't you? See you around."

His hand closed around her upper arm, and he jerked her around to face him when she would have pushed past him. Brought up next to his hard body, she was assaulted by memories of other times, other times when they had stood this close together, passion and need shimmering between them. Her knees grew weak as the memories swamped her, memories of passionate interludes, of nights spent in his arms, of afternoon trysts when they had made love under the hot summer sun. To her horror she discovered that her treacherous, treacherous body still responded to him . . . and his to her, if that blunt pressure growing against her stomach was what she thought it was.

He didn't try to hide his reaction, but his expression was rueful as he stared into her eyes. "It would seem that time hasn't changed much between us."

Shelly pulled her arm free and took a step away from him. "I'm afraid I don't know what you're talking about," she said frostily, ignoring the clamoring of her own body. "And there is nothing between us now. Whatever may have been between us ended seventeen years ago. Or have you forgotten?"

"I haven't forgotten a damned thing! Especially not that you believed that bastard's lies and ran out on me."

"He wasn't a bastard," she said from between clenched teeth. "And he didn't lie. I heard what you said that night. I saw you with her that night." She smiled sweetly. "By the way, where is your darling wife? Does she know that you go around accosting other women?"

His face took on a peculiar cast. "He didn't tell you?"

"Tell me what?"

"That my wife is dead," he said flatly. "Nancy died four years ago in a car accident."

The words slammed into her like a freight train. "Oh, Jesus! I'm sorry, Sloan," she exclaimed, her green eyes soft and full of pity. "I didn't know. Josh never said a word."

Sloan could have smashed his fist into the wall. The last thing he wanted from her was pity—especially pity for all the wrong reasons. Bitterly, he said, "I'm surprised he didn't tell you—his version of what happened anyway, but then your dear brother was good at keeping his mouth shut . . . when it suited him."

Shelly ignored the wave of anger, the urge to defend Josh that swept through her. "And here I believed you when you said you weren't going to argue with me about Josh." She smiled sadly. "Some things never change, do they?" When he would have replied she held her hand up. "No. Stop. I don't want to hear it. This is an old argument between us, and I didn't come back here to take up where we left off. Just leave me alone, and I'll leave you alone. Deal?"

Sloan shook his head. "No," he said quietly. "What was between us never ended—even if you want to bury your head in the sand and pretend otherwise. We have some unfinished business, you and I, and this time I want it finished."

"Well, you'll forgive me if I disagree," Shelly said, fear and anticipation curling through her at the threat . . . and the promise in his words.

He smiled, a smile that didn't reach the golden eyes that studied her so closely. "You can disagree all you want, honey, it won't change a thing."

"We'll just see about that," Shelly snapped, any idea of ending the meeting on a polite note vanishing. She took a deep breath, fighting to control her temper. Ignoring him, telling herself she wasn't aware of his tall, broad-shouldered body right behind her, she rehung the shirt, any pleasure she might have gotten from it erased by the exchange with Sloan. Turning around, she glared at him, and muttered, "You are still the most arrogant man it has ever been my misfortune to meet."

He grinned, the gold eyes crinkling attractively at the corners and making her heart lurch. "Yeah, I'm told it's part of my charm."

"Well, as far as I'm concerned," she said as she swept regally past him, "it's greatly overestimated. You shouldn't believe everything you're told."

Reaching the front of the store, not wanting to linger in spite of the fact that Cleo was now standing alone behind the counter, she waved at Cleo, and said, "I'll see you later—maybe you could come up to the house for coffee or something?"

"Sure thing. I'll call you, and we'll set up a time."

As if running from a fire, Shelly hit the swinging glass doors and was gone.

A disgusted expression on her face, Cleo shook her head when Sloan came strolling up to the wooden counter a second later. "You just don't learn, do you?" she scolded. "Couldn't you have left the subject alone? Or at least mouthed the conventional phrases?"

Sloan shrugged. "OK, I handled it badly. I didn't mean to start an argument . . ." He smiled ruefully. "Well, maybe I did. Having her angry with me is better than being treated to that frigid Granger politeness."

"I just don't understand the courtship rituals these days," Cleo complained. Glancing slyly at Sloan, she murmured, "In my day, used to be if a boy was interested in a girl, he was nice to her, polite, tried to please her."

"First of all, I'm not a 'boy,'" Sloan replied, his eyes

bright with laughter, "and second of all, I'm not 'interested' in Shelly Granger."

"Oh, is that so?" Cleo said, looking unimpressed. "Could have fooled me." She glanced down at her scarlet nails. "Josh Granger wasn't a saint—anybody who really knew the man would agree on that." When Sloan would have interrupted, she said, "Just a minute, then you can have your turn." She fixed him with a look. "Now I know that you have good reason to hate him, and I don't blame you one bit for feeling as you do about him, but Sloan, for your own good you have to let it go. Put it behind you. If you don't, it's going to eat at you and, in the end, destroy you. Do you want Josh to have that sort of power over you?"

Sloan made a face, feeling about ten years old. Worse, there was too much truth in what Cleo was saying for him to ignore. "OK. OK. I'll work on it. Will that satisfy you?"

"Might—if you work *real* hard." And as he turned to go, she added, "Something you should remember; he loved her. And whatever he did or didn't do, he did it for that reason. He loved her."

"Yeah," Sloan said grimly, "and so did I."

Chapter Five

~~~~~

Shelly raced from the store, intent upon putting as much distance between herself and Sloan Ballinger as possible. Fumbling for her keys, her mind on all the things she could have said to Sloan, she was rocked back on her heels when she slammed into an immovable object in the shape of a tall, broad-shouldered sheriff's deputy.

"Whoa. Whoa there. Where's the fire?" rumbled a voice that struck a chord of memory as a pair of big hands caught her shoulders and held her at a slight distance.

Embarrassed and shaken, Shelly gazed up what seemed like a very long way to a sun-dark face, the lower half concealed by an impressive black mustache. While the voice sounded familiar, she couldn't place it, and she didn't recognize him. But then, she thought, possibly only his mother would. The mustache was as effective as a mask, and the black-reflecting sunglasses and the cream-colored Western hat he wore hid the rest of his features. But there was something about him. . . . She was not a short woman, standing five-foot-nine in her bare feet, but the man before her was huge. Bigger, she decided, than Sloan, and he was, if she remembered right somewhere around six-four. Something about that voice and his size nagged at her. If he was someone she'd known in the past, that height and formidably muscular form should have made him unforgettable. An elusive memory slipped through her mind.

He grinned and it all came together. "Jeb!" she cried, delight obvious. "I didn't recognize you for a moment."

"Now that," he said in a deep voice, as he released her and removed his sunglasses and put them in his pocket, "just pains me no end. Not recognize your own cousin? Come on, Shelly. How many guys my size do you run into—in uniform and in St. Galen's?"

Looking up into those laughing black eyes, she grinned. "No excuses—between your size and the uniform I should have recognized you immediately." She held out her wrists. "So, wanna arrest me for a bad memory?"

He appeared thoughtful. "Nah—too much paperwork," he said with a twinkle in his eyes. Throwing his arms wide, he said, "Give us a hug, kid. It's been a long time. I've missed watching that sassy butt of yours."

Shelly smothered a giggle and launched herself into his embrace. Jeb Delaney had always been one of her favorite people, even if they had not known each other well. The ten-year gap in their ages had been one impediment. Jeb had been closer to Josh in age than to her. They were related through their grandparents; her grandfather and Jeb's grandmother, Anne, had been brother and sister. When Anne had married Mingo Delaney, it had caused no end of hard feelings—Mingo's mother had been a Ballinger, and the other Grangers had been appalled that Anne had chosen to align herself with one of the detested Ballinger clan. Anne had further enraged her family by defiantly naming her firstborn son, Jeb, after the original Jeb Granger. And Jeb Delaney, Senior, had followed through by naming *his* firstborn son, and the current holder of the name, Jeb. Shelly remembered Josh complaining about the high-handed way the Ballingers had stolen their family name. He had grumbled often enough that the name should have belonged to him—and not some shirttail relative of the Ballingers. Shelly had wisely not pointed out that Jeb Delaney was also a "ragtag" relative of theirs.

It had all seemed rather silly to Shelly, and it still did—you didn't *own* a name, and her parents could have named Josh Jeb, if they had wished. Laughing up into Jeb's face just now, she decided that now was as good a time as any to strengthen the easy friendliness that had always been there between them.

In a small town like St. Galen's, it was inevitable that their paths cross frequently, and despite the family estrangement, she and Jeb had made their own peace. He had teased her unmercifully at times during her youth, but he had also made certain that she knew that she could trust him. Probably one of the things she admired most about him was that he didn't give a damn about the family feud. "Hey," he'd told her once, "the argument was between York and Jeb—the originals—not me and not you. And if that stiff-necked brother of yours were as smart as he's supposed to be, he'd have realized that fact long ago. So, whadda you say that between the pair of us, we just pretend that the rest of the family is plain nuts?" Grinning, Shelly had agreed without hesitation. She'd been fascinated by this tall, handsome cousin, OK second cousin—as much because she'd been told to ignore him by her family, as his own appealing personality. Being warned against him, and all of the Ballingers for that matter, had had the opposite effect—at seventeen she had developed a terrific crush on Jeb and had mooned over him all summer until she had returned to boarding school that fall. He had her undying gratitude by never having acknowledged all her girlish attempts to catch his attention. Better yet, showing great restraint he had never teased her about it—thank God! Josh would have had a fit if he'd known how often that summer she'd thrown herself in Jeb's path. She felt herself blush even now as she remembered the ruses she had concocted to attract his attention. And if Josh had ever learned of it. . . . She shuddered. Josh had barely tolerated Jeb, and she wondered if there hadn't been something else between them, some other reason than just family legends for their mutual dislike.

They stood there grinning at each other for several seconds, then Jeb's face grew serious. Gently he asked, "Are you OK? Dealing all right with Josh's suicide?"

She nodded, her own face sober. "It's been hard—especially the shock of it . . . and living in his house—seeing constant reminders of him. . . . But, yes, I'm dealing with it." She smiled lopsidedly. "It's getting easier every day—I think."

He patted her clumsily on the shoulder. "That's my girl! Now tell me how long you're going to be around the valley, so I can figure out how many times I'll be sent out to break up all the wild parties you'll be holding."

Shelly grimaced. "You would remind me! Come on, Jeb, I was sixteen, and Josh was away for all of Easter week. I was up there by myself, well, except for Maria and her kids. All of my friends were on Easter break, and we were looking for something to do. What teenager wouldn't have thrown a party? And it wasn't that wild! If that old busybody Mrs. Matthews hadn't taken it upon herself to check up on me, no one would have known."

Jeb laughed. "I'd forgotten how much fun it is to get your goat. You take the bait so quickly."

"And you are no gentleman to remind me of one of my most embarrassing moments from childhood." She shook her head, smiling. "I'll never forget opening the door and there you were, looking just like the Terminator." She laughed. "My God, the panic you caused. Melissa-Jane nearly broke her leg climbing out one of the back windows and Bobba Neale gave himself a black eye when he ran into a porch post trying to get away."

"Hey, not my fault if you guys had a guilty conscience. Did I arrest anyone? Did I take anyone away? Nope. All I did was warn you to keep it down and to remember that it was against the law to be driving and drinking. Did I comment on the pyramid of beer cans in the middle of the living room floor? Which, by the way, was pretty impressive."

She smiled at the memory. "Yeah, it was."

"All kidding aside, how long are you going to be around?"

Briefly, Shelly explained her decision to return to Oak Valley for good. Jeb was pleased.

"I'm glad. You belong here. The ranch needs you. The community will be glad to have you back." He hesitated, let out a long breath, and said, "The past few years, Josh didn't seem to care much about what happened in the valley."

Staring at the shiny badge on his khaki shirt, she asked quietly, "Were you one of the deputies called to the scene?"

He sighed. "Yes, I was. I'm not stationed here anymore—I'm a detective these days, working out of the Willits substation. One of the reasons I was called to the scene. Don't see many violent deaths up here, but it's almost always someone I know. Never thought it would be Josh."

"I know. One of the hardest things for me to deal with has been that he committed suicide. I still have trouble believing it." There was just the faintest change in Jeb's expression, but she was on it in a flash. "It *was* suicide? No doubt about it?"

"That's what the coroner put on the death certificate," he replied in that neutral tone of so many law enforcement officers.

"You didn't answer my question," Shelly persisted, her eyes searching his.

Jeb sighed, pushed back his hat. "I didn't see anything at the scene that raised alarm bells, but like you, I knew Josh and suicide just didn't do it for me. Besides . . ."

"Besides?"

"Oh, dammit, sweetheart, I don't want to put ideas in your head or fill you with a lot of conjecture, but you might as well hear it from me as someone else." Jeb took a deep breath. "The last couple of years Josh was running with a bad crowd—pot growers, and not your home-garden variety either—the big guys—the guys who fund some of the little growers." Jeb paused, putting his thoughts in order. "Josh," he said eventually, "had always been a gambler, you know that, but about five years ago, with all the Indian casinos springing up all over the place, he really got into it. Lots of people from the valley saw him all over the place and carried back gossip of some big wins . . . and losses." He made a face. "You know the valley. You can't spit without everyone noticing and a half dozen people saying that it's raining—people notice and they talk and they don't always get their stories straight. Anyway, the nearest casino is outside of Willits on 20—they're scattered all up and down every major highway in the state. Hell, there's one north of Ukiah and a big one over in Lake County and of course, a lot of people from the valley enjoy a night out and the chance maybe to win a little cash." He smiled. "You know how it is—you can't leave the valley without running into someone from the valley—even as far away as Santa Rosa. And it wasn't like Josh was trying to hide it. He didn't. But my point is that just a few weeks before he started hanging out with the unsavory types, rumor had it that he'd taken some hard hits. Lost a *lot* of money. It could have been a coincidence that right after that, he and Milo Scott and Ben

Williams are suddenly the best of friends." Jeb grimaced. "I'm better acquainted with that pair of vermin than I'd like to be—the two of them are behind just about every dope deal in northern California, and when Josh started being seen around in their company . . . well, I'll confess it made me wonder."

Shelly frowned. "You mean, you think they might have lent him money? Did they do that sort of thing? Loan sharking?"

Jeb glanced around as if becoming aware that they were standing together right out in front of God and everybody having a very private, very serious conversation. "Look, I shouldn't have started talking about this right now—if ever. Let's just leave it that there are things that happened prior to Josh's suicide that didn't sit right with me." At Shelly's mulish expression, he said, "I know. I shouldn't have started if I didn't mean to finish. And I will. But not here. And not now." He glanced around, his gaze narrowing as he caught sight of a dark blue pickup truck pulling into the small gravel parking lot of the Blue Goose. "Oh, hell, speak of the Devil." He gave a faint jerk of his head. "There's Milo Scott getting out of his pickup at the Goose." His eyes on Shelly's, he said, "Invite me up to the house for dinner tomorrow night—I'd say tonight, but we're a little shorthanded right now, and I'm subbing for one of the other sergeants—the reason I'm in uniform and not in plain clothes. I still live up here, but I work out of the Willits office . . . unless someone dies violently. I don't mean to put you off—I promise, I'll tell you what I know." His mouth thinned. "Which is damn little. Deal?"

Shelly studied the wiry, sandy-haired man who slammed the door of the blue pickup and ambled into the restaurant. He looked nondescript, and she didn't recognize him. She turned her attention back to Jeb. "Deal. Come out about six-thirty tomorrow night," Shelly said. "And don't you try to wiggle out of it."

"I won't—honest. But don't fret over what I've told you and convince yourself there's some big mystery. Like you, I'm having trouble dealing with Josh's death, and I'm probably jumping to conclusions to keep from making the obvious one; he killed himself." His expression disgusted, he muttered, "Me and my big mouth. First time I see you in years, and I have to dump this on you."

Shelly forced herself to smile. "Tact was never your strong point."

Following her lead, he wiggled his eyebrows suggestively. "Honey, with my charm, I don't need tact."

Laughing, Shelly threw herself into his arms again, burying her face into his warm neck. "Oh, Jeb, I've missed you . . . the valley . . . everything. I can't believe I stayed away so long. Until I came home, I didn't realize that this is my real home, this is where I belong."

He dropped a kiss on top of her head. "I know, kid. You just had to have time to realize it yourself."

"How did you get so damned smart?" she muttered against his skin.

He hugged her tighter. "Just those Ballinger/Granger genes, I guess."

Neither was aware of Sloan pushing out of Heather-Mary-Marie's and walking past them until he said in arctic tones, "Afternoon, Delaney. Doing some private detecting?"

Jeb grinned and held Shelly firmly against him when she would have jerked away. "You bet. I'm a man who takes my work seriously."

Sloan snorted and slipped into the big Suburban parked next to where they stood. His mouth grim, he gunned the engine, reversed right smartly, and sped away.

"Brrrr." Jeb said. "Is it just me, or did you feel that glacial blast, too?"

"I felt it." Her mouth twisted. "Some things never change, do they? Simply because I'm a Granger, the Ballingers hate me."

Jeb chuckled. "Honey, that wasn't hatred that made Sloan all lemon-lipped and grumpy. I know a jealous man when I see one—I'm a detective, remember? And that was one jealous man. It's a wonder I'm still standing upright and not lying on the ground nursing a broken jaw. I thought he was going to take a swing at me, throw you over his shoulder, and gallop away. Whew! Sloan was pissed, no doubt about it."

"You're wrong. Sloan was just being Sloan."

"If you say so, kid."

Not wanting to discuss the matter, Shelly moved away from him, and muttered, "I've got to go now. I'll see you tomorrow night." She glanced at him. "Anything in particular you'd like for dinner, or should I just cook whatever comes to mind?"

He grinned. "Whatever comes to mind, darlin', will do just fine. I'm a bachelor—what more can I say?"

Shelly paused. "Again? Josh said something about you getting married a second time a couple years after I left."

"Yeah, well, you know me—I'm great at the chasing, but just can't seem to keep 'em when I catch 'em. About twelve years ago when my second wife left, I decided that marriage wasn't for me. Tried it twice and struck out both times, and I ain't looking to try it a third time."

Privately Shelly thought that his two wives had to have been crazy to divorce him. She'd known Ingrid, his first wife only a little, but had not cared for her—in fact few in the valley had liked the German baron's daughter Jeb had married so impetuously. The fact that the marriage failed within six months came as no surprise to anybody and had brought forth a collective sigh of delight from the female portion of the population—married and not. If his second wife had been anything like Ingrid, his second divorce was perfectly understandable. Keeping her thoughts to herself, she asked, "Josh never said, but any kids from the second marriage?"

"Now that's one mistake I didn't make," Jeb said with a hard note in his voice. "Guess I knew from the git-go it wouldn't last."

Shelly pressed a quick kiss on his cheek. "And maybe you just planned it that way. If your second wife was anything like Ingrid, I'm not surprised the marriage didn't last."

"Now don't you start. You're beginning to sound just like my mother."

Shelly grinned. "And how is your mother? No, never mind. You can tell me during dinner. If we start talking family, we'll be here the rest of the afternoon. I'll see you tomorrow night."

She waved to Jeb as she pulled out of the parking lot of Heather-Mary-Marie's, and since she didn't want to run the risk of running into Sloan again, she pointed the Bronco in the direction of home. As she drove the Bronco along the familiar road, she replayed the scene with Sloan in her mind.

She hadn't meant to argue with him. It had just happened. Seeing him after all these years, looking into that once-loved face, remembering the betrayal and pain of their parting and to still have her body reacting to his presence the way it had had just been too much for her to handle. She needed to put some distance between them and have some time to come to grips with the shock of seeing him again. She'd known that they would meet again, she just hadn't been prepared for it to happen the first time she ventured out of the house and into town. Nor had she counted on the leap her heart had given at the sight of him, the thrill that had coursed through her. Or the way her pulse had raced and her entire body had surged to life as she had stared at him. She'd been stunned. Aroused. Terrified. Looking at those blunt, hard features, seeing the broad shoulders and the way the black jeans had fit his muscular thighs she'd been eighteen again, and all her hormones had burst into the "Hallelujah Chorus" at the sight of him. *You'd think*, she thought disgustedly, *that at my age, I'd have better control of my emotions—and hormones.*

Shelly sighed. It was probably just as well, though, that the first meeting was out of the way. At least she didn't have to dread it anymore. And seeing Cleo again had been wonderful. Meeting Hank O'Hara had been fun. Running into Jeb had been great, too. She frowned, thinking about the things Jeb had said about her brother. Tomorrow night couldn't come soon enough for her, but she realized that Jeb had been right to suggest a more private setting. The more she turned over the conversation in her mind, the more troubled she became. Josh friends with dopers? That didn't sound right. And yet Jeb said that it had happened. The gambling sounded right . . . but not the huge losses. She caught her breath, suddenly remembering the odd entries in the account books. Maybe the valley gossip wasn't all wrong, maybe Josh *had* suffered some big losses and turned to this Milo Scott and Ben Williams for financial help. But that didn't sound right. Josh could have come to her. They could have dipped into the principal of the trust funds left them by their parents. She paused. No. Josh wouldn't have come to her—she was his baby sister and his first instinct would have been to protect her from anything unpleasant. And he wouldn't have been happy to reveal a flaw in his own nature to her. He wouldn't have wanted her to think less of him. She snorted. Men!

Reaching the house, she put on the brake and turned off

the ignition. She wasn't going to think about Josh's behavior any more today. Once she had talked to Jeb, she'd know more and could make a better assessment about what had really been going on in Josh's life these past few years. And if those events had led to his suicide . . . or something else . . .

She shook her head. She was being fanciful again. A rueful smile curved her mouth. As fanciful as Jeb Delaney thinking that Sloan had been jealous at seeing them together. Ha! That'd be the day.

———∞———

But Sloan was jealous. Fiercely. Savagely. Furiously. Jeb had nailed down his feelings exactly. When he had pushed out of Heather-Mary-Marie's and had seen Shelly standing in Jeb's embrace, Sloan had experienced a primitive emotion that had rocked him to his roots. It had taken every ounce of control he possessed to keep from yanking Shelly away from Jeb and strangling Delaney right then and there. He and Jeb had been friends for a long time, but this afternoon, as he pulled away from the store, Sloan's thoughts were murderous about his *friend*.

Even now, ten minutes later as he pushed a grocery cart down one of the narrow aisles of MacGuire's, his gut still twisted and his knuckles were white from the furious grip he had on the cart, imagining them around Jeb's neck. Bastard! Coming on to her before she'd been in town a half hour. Who the hell did Delaney think he was? Casanova?

The ridiculousness of the situation struck him and he grinned wryly. Ah, hell. Who was he kidding? He was just being a horny, jealous old goat. Jeb and Shelly had been friends in the old days, so why shouldn't he hug her? Sloan grimaced. God knows he'd had to fight against the powerful urge to pull her into his own arms and kiss her when she'd stood there before him in the shadows of the store. Of course, there wouldn't have been anything remotely *friendly* about his kiss. And if he hadn't been so eaten up with jealousy, he would have realized immediately that it was only a friendly embrace that the two had been sharing. Shelly had always been warm and generous in her affection, so why wouldn't she have been happy to see Jeb? His problem, and he admitted it, was that the sight of Shelly posing before the mirror in Heather-Mary-Marie's, that T-shirt held against her slender body, had aroused him and aroused emotions he'd thought long dead. And it wasn't like he hadn't expected to see her inside the store. He had.

As soon as he'd spotted the Bronco parked in the lot, he'd known whose vehicle it was. And had he continued on his original errand to the grocery store? Oh, no. He'd had to swerve into the lot and go looking for trouble. He snorted. And couldn't he have just said a friendly hello and left it at that? Not on your life! No, he'd had to go all stiff-necked over her brother. As much as he loathed the man, would it really have hurt him to say that he was sorry that Josh was dead? Probably not. God. Sometimes he could be such an asshole. You'd think he'd learn.

Muttering to himself he guided the metal grocery cart toward the meat counter. Pandora had let it be known this morning that she wasn't eating dry dog food another day. She was a predator, and she wanted meat. Raw. And lots of it.

Sloan bought a pound of calf's liver and the smallest beef heart he could find. He had a freezer full of meat from the steer he'd had butchered last fall, and even though he had doled them out judiciously, the organ meats had disappeared from Pandora's bowl months ago. Today's purchases would hold her for a while, and he'd be able to eat his own meals without having to endure her outraged stare. He'd planned to buy several other items, but the mood for shopping had left him the moment he'd spied Shelly's Bronco. He did take time to grab some milk and cottage cheese and some lettuce and onions before he headed to the checkout counter.

"Hi, Sloan. Didn't realize that you were in town. The big city finally got you down, and you had to come back to God's country, right?"

Sloan smiled at Debbie Smith, manning her familiar post at MacGuire's register. Well into her sixties, with her steel gray hair, pale blue eyes, pink, plump cheeks, and round little body, she looked like a Disney version of a grandmother. She had been at MacGuire's for as long as Sloan could remember and had started work behind the meat counter when the place had been nothing more than a tiny butcher shop tucked into the corner of Joe's Market, the oldest grocery store in the valley. As MacGuire's had grown and prospered, so had Debbie. She'd met her husband, Tom, at the store forty years ago; he'd been hired to stock shelves when the market expanded into its own tiny building, adding a few fresh vegetables, milk, and camping supplies to the meat counter. Those days were gone; MacGuire's was now a full-fledged grocery store, and Tom presently supervised the meat department and Debbie ran the freezer section and manned one of the three checkout counters whenever necessary or she felt the need to gossip. She could have retired long ago, but as she said often enough, "I like people. I like seeing what's going on in town. And if I retired, I'd be down here visiting with everyone anyway. This way, I get to visit, and I get paid for it, too!"

Glancing down at the liver and heart in Sloan's basket, she snorted. "You spoil that dog, you know that, don't you?"

Sloan grinned. One of the blessings and curses of the valley was that everyone really did know your business. "I know," he said easily. "Sometimes I wonder who owns who."

"If you'd get yourself a wife and some kids, that question

would be settled right quick," Debbie said as she rang up his order. "Your folks would love some grandkids, and with five kids, you'd think that one of you would have found the time to produce at least one member of the next generation."

"Yeah, well, you'd better talk to the others, because I tried marriage once, remember?" he muttered. With anyone else, he would have remained silent and simply frozen them with an icy stare, but Debbie treated everyone under the age of fifty as if they were one of her children—or grandchildren. Even as he wished she'd mind her own business, Sloan knew that her motives were kind.

Aware that she had strayed into painful territory, Debbie looked stricken. "Oh, Sloan, I *am* sorry. Me and my big mouth. I keep forgetting." But she couldn't leave it alone either. Her eyes on the task of bagging his groceries, she murmured, "Of course, it's been four years now. Time for you to move on. Tall, handsome fellow like you, shouldn't have any trouble finding a nice girl."

"Debbie, I haven't been interested in 'nice' girls since I turned sixteen. What makes you think I'm going to change now?"

"You're right about that! But since nice girls are out of the question, what's stopping you from finding yourself a bad one then? There's bound to be a half dozen floozies in town who would swoon if you gave them a chance to climb your bones. At least then you'd have some other female company besides that little rat of a dog."

"'Climb my bones'?" Sloan asked with mock incredulity. "Mrs. Smith, you have shocked me. Does Mr. Smith know that you pass out that sort of advice to young innocent men like myself?"

"Innocent?" Debbie snorted. "Go on, get out of here—and give Pandora a kiss for me."

Sloan grinned at her and hefted his bag of groceries and

walked out to the Suburban. His cabin at Hobb's Flat was ten miles away—six of it gravel and most of it snake-backed, but he'd driven it so often, he didn't have to concentrate on the road. He allowed himself to think about this afternoon . . . and the meeting with Shelly.

He'd envisioned seeing her again often enough. And he'd thought after having caught that glimpse of her in the car at Inspiration Point that night that he would be prepared for a face-to-face meeting. He smiled mirthlessly. But he hadn't been. He'd been blindsided at the emotional tangle she had aroused within him. He had been convinced that when they met again, that he'd be very cool and collected, that all he would feel for her would be contempt and something very close to hatred. Certainly he had never expected that he'd be glad to see her. He shook his head, as he turned off the main road and began to drive up the narrow lane to the cabin. He supposed that was what astounded him the most, the knowledge that for one split second he'd been deliriously, hell, ecstatically happy to see Shelly Granger.

The lust hadn't surprised him. In fact it would have surprised him if he hadn't reacted physically to her in some way. With everything else that had gone wrong between them, the sex had always been good. He grimaced. OK. Admit it, the best he'd ever had.

Pushing into the cabin, he avoided stepping on Pandora as she danced around his feet. Busy trying not to break a leg as Pandora scampered in and out of his legs as he tried to walk to the kitchen, he put thoughts of Shelly out of his mind.

There was a chill in the air, the hint of a storm, and after putting the groceries away and feeding a demanding Pandora half a slice of raw liver, Sloan made himself a small fire in the living room. It started to rain, and he stood staring bleakly out of the window, his thoughts straying toward Shelly.

An insistent pawing on his leg and a soft whine made him look down. Pandora, always sensitive to his moods, stared back, her little black eyes fixed on him. He smiled and picked her up.

"What's the matter, liver-breath?" he asked as he ruffled her ears. "Am I not paying enough attention to you?"

Pandora gave him a warm, wet kiss on the nose. Sloan blinked as he was enveloped in the odor of raw liver. "Whew! Haven't you heard of breath mints?" he scolded as he put her down. Pandora regarded him a moment, then, as if deciding she had lavished enough attention on him, she trotted over to the couch and jumped up onto her blanket and proceeded to make herself a nest. Curled up and comfy, she gave a contented sigh and made Sloan smile. It occurred to him, as he joined Pandora on the couch and propped his feet up on the low redwood table in front of it, that maybe Debbie was right. One thing was sure: Something was very wrong in his life when his only female companion was a dog who gave him liver-scented kisses.

Chapter Six

It was still raining on Wednesday night when Jeb came to dinner. Not a true rain, but a continuation of the misty drizzle that seemed to be the norm for most of the storms this year. Already there was talk of how dry the rainy season had been so far, and worries about the cost of hay and alfalfa had begun to creep into conversations around the valley. As for the feed in the hills, well, there wasn't much of that either and several ranchers had already driven their herds of cattle down to the valley floor—weeks, even months ahead of time.

Shelly had shooed Maria out of the kitchen as soon as she'd come home from shopping in town this morning. She had spent most of the day humming to herself as she had bustled about baking and cooking. She enjoyed cooking, but being single and living alone, it was something that she didn't do often, so she pulled out all the stops.

Working backward, she had started with baking a pecan pie, using a generous amount of the pecans she had sent along home in her Christmas package last year. It was a tradition, and the five pounds of shelled pecans were carefully doled out during the year in pies and cakes and cookies baked by Maria. Just as walnuts were plentiful in California, pecans were plentiful in the South and so walnut pies were common on the West Coast, pies made with pecans rare, while pecan pies held sway in the South. Jeb would, Shelly thought, appreciate the difference.

The pie baked and cooling on the long counter, the big prawns she had found in MacGuire's earlier in the day were cooked in a spicy court bouillon, then peeled and cleaned and put in the refrigerator to chill. She chose to make tiny cheese puffs for hors d'oeuvres, and once they were out of the way, she mixed up the remoulade sauce she would serve with the shrimp for an appetizer and then set about cooking the main course: chicken jambalaya. The scents in the kitchen were delectable, and Shelly had no doubt she'd gained three pounds just sniffing the fragrant air. The old-fashioned soaked salad she'd planned to serve was quickly mixed and set in the refrigerator to, well, soak. Fresh steamed broccoli and, she made a face, store-bought rolls would round out the meal. She'd have liked to have made some New Orleans French bread, but by three o'clock that afternoon, she was glad she had given in to practicality and bought commercial dinner rolls that morning. Now for the table.

She glanced into the walnut-paneled formal dining room and wrinkled her nose. It was handsome and grand and too big, too opulent for what she wanted. She decided that the oak table in the kitchen alcove would be just fine and would certainly make her serving task easier. Besides, she doubted Jeb would care where he ate as long as he ate. Some gaily patterned yellow-and-green place mats, matching napkins in brass holders, crystal goblets, and a dainty arrangement of daffodils from the garden completed her efforts. Now for a long shower and some comfortable clothes, she thought, as she climbed the stairs to her room.

At 6:30 P.M. almost on the dot, Shelly heard the sound of a vehicle in the driveway, and a moment later she opened the door to her guest. She smiled at Jeb, recognizing the St.

Galen's version of dress-up: Western-style jacket, a freshly ironed plaid shirt, clean jeans, and polished boots. Except for the loafers on her feet, she wasn't dressed all that differently, having chosen to wear a pair of hunter green corduroy jeans and a loose-fitting yellow sweater.

A big grin on his dark face, Jeb swept off the inevitable Western hat and thrust the two bottles of wine he held in his other hand at her. "Didn't know which kind to bring," he said as he stepped inside the house, "so I brought both."

Shelly glanced at the labels, her brows rising. "Impressive. When did you become a wine connoisseur?"

He chuckled. "I just went into a liquor store today in Ukiah and told the fellow behind the counter to give me a bottle of his most expensive white and do the same with the red." They both laughed, and the evening was off to a good start.

As the evening progressed, it was clear Jeb enjoyed every bit of her culinary efforts. Watching the amount of food he put away, from the miraculously disappeared cheese puffs to the dessert, she wondered seriously if one pecan pie would be enough. It was. Pushing back from the table, the few crumbs on his plate all that remained of his third piece of pie, Jeb gave a blissful sigh.

"If those paintings of yours ever stop selling, kiddo, you could get a job as a chef in a flash." He smiled at her where she sat across from him in the small kitchen alcove. "You could put me down as a reference."

Without comment she got up and poured them both another cup of coffee before settling once again at the table. Almost by tacit agreement they had spent the evening catching up with each other. She'd told him about her life in New Orleans, of her successful career as a landscape artist, and some of her plans for the future. He'd talked about happenings in the valley, filling in the pieces that Nick and Maria hadn't been able to. What they hadn't talked about was Josh.

Sipping her coffee, she gazed at him. "OK, I've fed you, and we've caught up on events here and in New Orleans. I think it's time that you sing for your supper and tell me what you know . . . and suspect, about Josh's death."

Jeb grimaced. "I'd kinda hoped to avoid that subject, but I'll play fair—or as fair as I can." He hesitated, looking down at his cup of coffee, the light overhead glinting on the silver strands that were mixed in with the black hair. Those silver hairs came as a shock to Shelly, as did the realization that Jeb was forty-five years old and no longer the cocky young deputy that she remembered so well. None of them, she admitted, were getting any younger—hopefully, they were wiser.

"First of all, I have to say that there is nothing in the coroner's report that isn't consistent with suicide," he said finally. "And my reservations are just that—reservations."

"But you *do* have reservations?" she asked, frowning.

"Yeah. I do. But only because I knew Josh and all the people involved. There was something going on between him and Milo Scott, but damned if I know what it was. The moment Josh started being so friendly with those two, Scott and Williams, I began snooping around, but I never caught them doing anything I could put my finger on—or at least arrest them for."

Jeb sat back, fiddling with his coffee cup. "You should know that part of my reservations come from the fact that there have been one or two suspicious deaths over the years in which Milo Scott was suspected of either killing the person himself or ordering it done." He made a face. "The problem was we could never prove anything. In one of the cases, we couldn't even prove it was murder—it had to be put down as accidental death. Suspicious as hell, but there you are." He sighed. "Mendocino County is a big county area-wise, but it doesn't have a big law enforcement segment. It's also one of the lowest paid sheriff's departments in the state, and except for lots of space, lots of trees, a gorgeous coast-line, and clean air, the county doesn't have as many ameni-ties as people from other areas have come to expect." He smiled crookedly. "It's just been during the last half dozen years or so that we even got a Walmart in Ukiah—and there was a huge fight over that. Willits only got a Burger King a few years ago. No doubt about it, Mendocino County *is* changing, growing, but the entire county is still pretty much small town, ranching and farming, and that sort of life doesn't appeal to everyone—a majority of people *expect* malls, pizza delivery, and six-theater complexes and fast-food places on every corner. Most of the time, after a new deputy gets some experience and can start to be of some real use, he—or she—usually ends up moving away for a higher-paid job, better career advancement—even if it's just into the Ukiah or Willits Police Departments. Which leaves us, the sheriff's department, constantly playing catch-up. De-spite the turnover we do a damn fine job, but there are prob-lems, and one of them is that there aren't many of us and there's a bunch of 'them.'" When Shelly looked puzzled, he added, "You've maybe forgotten that Mendocino is part of the Emerald Triangle and one of the largest marijuana-growing regions in the state. We're remote, have mostly rugged terrain, and we don't have much legitimate industry—or a big population. Logging, one of the biggest employers, has practically disappeared, and a lot of people, aging hippies and their offspring and the like who drifted in during the six-ties, don't think that there's anything wrong with growing a little patch of weed to supplement their income. Hell, a few years ago one of our county supervisors was campaigning for the legalization of pot—and he had tons of support.

We're not a rich area, and it can be hard to make a living here. There are cases where the pot patch is the only income for some people."

Shelly frowned. "You don't think that Josh—?"

He shook his head. "No. Not growing it. But it wouldn't surprise me to find out that he was paid to turn a blind eye to *others* growing it on Granger land."

Shelly sucked in her breath. "You mean, his gambling debts were paid off and for that he virtually leased the ranches for pot production?"

"Possible," Jeb said neutrally.

"But you never found anything like that, did you?" she asked sharply.

"Honey, you're forgetting how many thousands of acres your family owns, and where it is and how rough the terrain." He looked disgusted. "You could hide an army out there, and no one would find it—especially not with the number of men we have."

"So your reservations about Josh's death are mainly because of his association with Milo Scott and Ben Williams?"

"That and the fact that in the weeks prior to his death he gave no sign, that anybody noticed, of being suicidal. Besides, I *knew* the man. Not once during all the years I knew him did he even give a hint of being the type of person who would commit suicide."

Shelly grimaced. "Is there a type?"

Jeb sighed. "No, I guess not. I just can't accept the idea that he did it—even though all the evidence points in that direction. Call it my gut reaction."

"Mine too," she said softly. Those odd entries in the ranch books crossed her mind. Standing up, she said, "Bring your coffee with you. There's something I want you to see."

In Josh's office—she'd not yet been able to think of it as hers—Shelly walked over to the desk. Flipping through the account books that lay scattered across the top of the desk, she said, "Something strange was going on—he put down receiving fifty thousand dollars for some land, but I can't discover *which* piece of land. But what's really disturbing is that Josh sold off most of the herd, and while he claimed the money on his tax returns, the sums he received for the individual cattle were exorbitant."

Jeb frowned. "What do you mean?"

"Take a look at this." Her finger ran down the column in the small black book that had been underneath the account books. "Three years ago there was deposit of a hundred thousand dollars in Josh's account when he supposedly sold off ten cows with calves at side to a Rangemore Corporation. In fact all of the sales are to this same Rangemore Corporation. Now I haven't paid attention to cattle prices, but ten thousand dollars per cow/calf pair seems really, *really* high to me. And look at this—six months later is a deposit for more than double that amount—almost three hundred thousand. In the Granger Cattle Company books he claims the money—he didn't try to hide it, but there's no way he could have gotten those kinds of prices for the number of cattle he sold. Here's another one early last year for about the same sum, and the month before he died there's another one—which was when he apparently sold off the remainder of the herd. Most of it disappeared as fast as it appeared—that account currently only has about five thousand dollars in it. What really disturbs me, though, is that about four years ago Josh started selling off the stocks in his trust fund. Before these other amounts started appearing, he'd depleted his trust fund and begun to raid mine."

"Could he do that? Raid your trust fund?"

Shelly made a face. "Yes. I trusted him, remember? He had a power of attorney signed by me. I never questioned what he did. And probably never would have if he hadn't died and I had to go over the books. He could have always told me that we'd bought some bad stocks or whatever to explain the shrinking fund, and I would have believed him."

Jeb studied the notations, shaking his head, as if something had finally fallen into place. "The timing of the depletion of his trust is about right. Lots of rumors were flying around the valley at the time about his losses at the casinos. And it's about the time he suddenly took up with Scott and Williams." His finger following the questionable figures, he asked, "Is there anything left of the Granger Cattle Company herd?"

"He sold just about every head of cattle we own. The entire Granger Angus operation is down to one bull and four very old cows." She made a face. "According to the books, five animals is it."

Jeb looked shocked. Granger Angus were known all across the country. At one time, the Granger family had been the largest breeder of fine registered Angus on the West Coast. The family had been breeding cattle for generations and doing a damn good job of it. Granger stock was legendary for meat production and cow/calf pairs; the cows maturing early, calving easily, their bulls in demand all across the country, and their market steers finishing out lean and flavorful. He'd even bought several cows and a couple of bulls from Josh over the years to add to his own growing herd. It was hard to believe that Josh had decimated his own herd the way it appeared he had.

Jeb shook his head. "I'm sorry, Shelly. Your family had some excellent stock."

"And we will again," she said firmly. "The bull, Granger's Beau Ideal, is one of the best. He's old for a herd sire—pushing thirteen, but if I can get a couple of calf crops out of him, we'll do fine. Nick and I have discussed it—we're going into a partnership. Granger Angus will be small at first, and it'll be tough going, but we'll rebound. I'm a rancher's daughter, remember? And I come from a long line of cattle ranchers. Nick's got stock that goes back to Granger stock, and he's young, hardworking, and ambitious. I may have been gone for years, but don't forget, I grew up right in the middle of the cattle operation. I've forgotten a lot, it's true, but with some help and guidance, I can get this outfit going again. And I intend to."

His brows rose. "Do you really think you can do it?"

She grinned at him. "You bet your sweet ass!"

He laughed. "And to think that after all these years, I had you figured for a prissy city gal."

They smiled at each other, then almost as one, turned to look down at the account books. The light moment was gone.

His jaw set, Jeb said, "These entries don't prove anything. In fact, they could give a motive for suicide. It's clear he was in deep financial difficulties."

Shelly nodded. "I've thought of that myself."

"On the other hand . . . on the other hand, he was getting money from this Rangemore Corporation," Jeb said slowly. "Which is probably a dummy corporation for Scott and Williams. And they wouldn't give out that kind of cash without getting something in return. It's possible Josh balked at some of their demands and they, er, took care of business."

"You mean, murdered him," Shelly stated flatly.

"Yeah. I guess I do."

"But what would that have accomplished? I mean besides sending a signal to others or something. With Josh gone, control of the ranch and everything connected with it falls into my hands. And I'm sure as hell not going to play into their hands!"

"Chances are, knowing the Granger roots in the valley, they probably figured you wouldn't sell—at least not right away. The odds were in their favor that you'd stay nice and comfy in New Orleans and put the ranch in the hands of a manager—someone they could control or pay off. And if that had been the case, killing Josh was a smart business decision."

Her face tense, Shelly wandered over to where a large topography map of the area hung on the wall. "A business decision," she said tightly. "My brother might be dead because of a business decision?"

"Maybe. Maybe not," Jeb said as he came to stand behind her.

Together they studied the map. "Lots of land out there," Jeb said finally. "Lots of places to conceal some good-size marijuana gardens. And if Josh had been paid to look the other way and then changed his mind, or wanted a bigger piece of the pie . . ."

Shelly found it difficult to think that Josh had been murdered, and it was even more horrible to believe that he might have died so some pot growers could make a profit. Suicide had been hard to accept, but murder was almost impossible for her to connect with her brother. "Maybe it was a suicide," she said at last.

Jeb nodded. "Probably."

They sighed simultaneously and stared at the map as if the answer were somehow written on it. The valley itself lay in the center, the foothills and mountains rising up all around it. Some landmarks stood out; town, Town Creek, the abandoned Louisiana-Pacific Mill site; the high school, the airport and the sanitation pond, just beyond town. The Granger lands were all neatly outlined in blue ink, dotted with happy face stickers, the Ballinger lands were delineated in heavy black ink and skull-and-crossbones stickers pasted along the boundary lines—Josh's idea of a joke. A thick scarlet line ran through the north end of the Ballinger holdings, and, seeing it, Shelly smiled.

The Granger right-of-way. Grangers and Ballingers had been arguing over it since York Ballinger had first sighted the small valley through which it ran and had claimed it for his own. He had planned to dam the narrow end of the valley and create a hundred-acre-or-so lake, piping the lake water down to the valley floor to irrigate his fields of wheat, barley, and alfalfa. York had barely touted his plan before Jeb Granger, the original, had asserted a prior right to cross through the valley to reach some Granger land that adjoined the area. Jeb did have a document that attested to the fact that a right-of-way had been granted to him, but there had always been a question about *when* the document had been signed, before or after the sale to Ballinger. Through some misfortune that was never satisfactorily explained, the document had gotten wet and the date had conveniently smudged. The county records were equally and suspiciously unclear. The previous owner of the land, the town drunk, had averred that the deed of right-of-way had been given prior to the sale and was therefore valid. Of course that was when the Grangers were plying him with liquor. If the Ballingers were buying his drink of choice, his story changed dramatically, and he would happily admit that he'd signed the deed after he'd sold the land. It was a stalemate, neither side willing to go to court on the word of a drunk to settle it once and for all. The right-of-way remained a bone of contention.

"It's our poke in the eye," Josh used to say, "at the Ballingers. Can't let them have everything their way. They need to be reminded that they're not Lords of the Valley and that the Grangers were here first. They might be richer than we are, but we have more land than they do—and a right-of-way smack-dab in the middle of their land."

Shelly hadn't thought much about the right-of-way. It was seldom used anymore, although Josh had made certain that at least once a year they drove a small herd of cattle across it. "Just to keep my hand in," he'd said when she questioned him about it. "It's our duty to carry on the family traditions. Can't have old Jeb Granger turning in his grave." The twinkle in his eyes at variance with his solemn tone, he'd added, "Our family honor is at stake. The right-of-way must stay. All else is folly." She'd giggled, and the subject was dropped.

His eye on the Granger holdings outlined on the map, Jeb said, "One thing's for sure; if you're going to run cattle, you've got enough land for it. You've got a lot of timber and rough ground, but there's also some fine grazing land mixed in with it all." He traced a couple of areas with his finger. "Lots of prime grazing land."

Shelly nodded. "And it's been a long time since I've ridden over it." She smiled. "The weather is supposed to clear. I think I'll call Acey in the morning and see if he wants to give me a tour—reacquaint me with the area." She smiled. "Think I'll even keep up the family tradition and check out the Granger right-of-way."

"Uh, you sure you want to do that?" When she glanced at him questioningly, he looked uncomfortable, and muttered, "Well, uh, I mean, it's been a while since you've been riding—you might find it tough going. Steep country out there."

"Don't worry about me, I'll be fine—I rode some in New Orleans, so it's not as if I haven't been on a horse in years. There are just a few places I want to check out." She grinned. "Acey won't let me get lost."

Jeb left shortly after that, loaded down with plastic containers filled with leftovers. The rain had stopped, and Shelly had walked out to the car with him. Jeb slid into the dually one-ton red truck and turned on the ignition. Above the muted roar of the engine he said, "Go on, get back in the house. And thanks. The food and the company were great. Next time dinner is on me. The Steak House outside of Ukiah."

He watched until she was inside, and then, with a toot of his horn, swung the big truck around and headed down the road. The rain had been just enough to make the road slick and he concentrated on his driving until he reached the valley floor, then he hit the gas. His own place was on the other side of the valley, and it was only a few minutes later before he had parked the truck and was bounding up the steps to his house.

Jeb walked straight to the phone hanging on his kitchen wall. Though the hour was approaching eleven he was pretty sure Sloan would still be awake. He punched in the familiar numbers, and when Sloan answered, he said, "I just had an interesting conversation with Shelly. She's planning on riding out to inspect the Granger right-of-way tomorrow."

"Shit," said Sloan.

"Yeah. My sentiments exactly."

As had been predicted, the rain had moved on, and the day was dry, if chilly. Acey had agreed to accompany Shelly on her ride and had supervised as she had tacked up her horse. It wasn't really *her* horse; it was a horse, a quarter horse bay gelding, one of three or four that Josh kept in the small stables behind the house. Acey had picked out the gelding, saying, "I know you rode in New Orleans some, but you ain't rode regular, and I don't intend to be lugging you back here with a broken leg or some such nonsense because you got bucked off. Lucky is quiet and steady, and he don't get all spooked and snorty by a swaying branch or a covey of quail flying in front of him."

Shelly hadn't argued. She hadn't ridden *that* often in New Orleans, although she had been an intrepid rider in her youth. Like many in the valley, she'd practically grown up on a horse.

Despite the slight overcast and the coolness of the day, it felt good to be outside. Garbed in an old pair of Levi's, well-worn boots, her hair tucked under a faded baseball cap blazoned with the logo of the New Orleans Saints, and a jean jacket, she didn't look much different than she had seventeen years ago. Only the logo on the hat was different.

The Granger holdings were scattered throughout the foothills, with several tracts of land separate from the main holdings overlooking the valley. Since the area she wanted to ride across was some miles from the house, they trailered the horses for the first part of the journey, climbing up off the valley floor and into the mountains.

Forty-five minutes later, Acey's truck and the stock trailer they had hauled the horses in were parked off the side of the Tilda Road. Ten minutes after that, the horses were unloaded and they had mounted up and were heading into the brush and forestland. Acey's cow dogs ambled out in front of them.

Dragging in a lungful of the cool, pungent air, Shelly savored the scent of fir, pine, and the musty smell of the oak and madrone trees. She was happy, she realized with a start. Really happy. Perhaps for the first time in years. Her horse, Lucky, was a steady mount, and she could relax and enjoy the scenery, drinking it all in like a dying man finding a pocket of springwater in the desert. Again it dawned on her how much she had missed the valley. Missed the mountains and foothills.

Riding along through the open forestland, it was a thrill

to listen to the scolding of the blue jays, to spy overhead a gray squirrel leaping from branch to branch. Yellow and white trout lilies and bright pink shooting stars, pale blue cat's ears nodded their delicate heads as the horse's hooves brushed against them as they rode through small meadows and vales before entering the forests once more. They splashed through narrow, crooked creeks that burbled and sang over the rocks, the water clear and cold.

With each stride of her horse, memories came rushing back. Happy memories of her riding with Josh in this same manner, perhaps even along this very trail, crowded her mind. She smiled at Acey's trio of dogs—she and Josh had even had a pair of black-and-white cow dogs that had followed them. Memories, too, of teenage summers spent on horseback as she and her friends prowled this whole area flooded her thoughts. How could she, Shelly wondered, have stayed away for so long? And why had she allowed a silly, aborted love affair to drive her away? She shook her head. The only answer that occurred to her was that she had been a damn fool—and a coward.

As they rode, there was a companionable silence between them. Yet the world was not silent—the creak of leather, the muted thud of their horses' hooves harmonized with the sounds of nature all around them and created a joyous symphony. Some of the sounds Shelly recognized—the soft whistle of mountain quail, the screech of the ever-present blue jay and the chatter of the gray squirrels, but the small mysterious noises and rustles in the brush eluded her. Probably mice and lizards, she thought. She wrinkled her nose. And snakes. Once Acey pulled his horse up short and pointed. A smile on her face, Shelly watched as a doe, big-eyed and dainty, stepped across the trail in front of them. A moment later, the deer was gone, the slight waving of the fir branch the only sign of the animal's passing. Acey's sharp call to the dogs stopped them from chasing after the doe.

They'd been riding for over an hour when they began to climb up one of the hills that formed one flank of the valley through which the Granger right-of-way ran.

Acey halted his horse for a second and glanced back at her. "You talk to that Sawyer fellow lately?" he asked.

Shelly looked surprised and shook her head.

Acey grunted. "Didn't think so."

Without another word, he turned away and urged his horse up the rocky slope. Once they reached the ridge, the ground flattened out a little, and Shelly pressed forward eagerly. Just beyond the stand of pine trees on the far edge the terrain fell away, tumbling downward in a series of shaley ledges shaggy with manzanita and brush; a few pine and fir and the occasional oak or madrone tree clung tenaciously to the hills surrounding the valley.

Only there was no longer a valley there. Openmouthed, Shelly stared at the serene lake that lapped halfway up the hillsides and covered what once had been a small valley . . . and the Granger right-of-way.

Jaw set, eyes flashing green fire, she glared at Acey. "You knew about this, didn't you?"

Acey nodded. "Yep. Josh sold the right-of-way to the Ballingers about three, four years ago. Can't remember exactly when. Got a good price for it, too." He rubbed his chin. "Actually it was downright highway robbery, the damn thing probably wasn't worth more than a few thousand dollars, but Sloan would have paid even more—anything to get you Grangers out of his hair."

Shelly was stunned to feel hurt, and she was aware of a strong sense of betrayal that Josh hadn't told her, that she hadn't even discussed it with her. She was angry, too, for the same reasons. And she wondered again if she had ever really

known her brother. It was becoming increasingly difficult
to reconcile the understanding, generous, loving brother she
had known all her life with the man who had callously denied his own child. Her mouth twisted. A man who might
very well have struck a devil's bargain with a pair of notori-
ous dope dealers. But knowing how Josh had felt about the
right-of-way, it was almost easier to believe the other things
about him than to believe that he had sold it.

She'd always believed that there was an unhealthy ob-
session in the Granger family about that damned right-of-
way and privately, she'd thought that they should have
abandoned their claim to it a long time ago. That Josh had
actually sold it to Sloan seemed incredible.

Her face set, she asked, "Do you know what it sold for?"

"Sure do. It was a big secret—Sloan's orders—but Josh
couldn't help telling me—he had to tell someone. He got
drunk one night and blabbed to me. Said he'd soaked Sloan
for around fifty thousand dollars. He was happy as a lizard
with a bug on a board. Thought he'd really pulled one over
on the Ballingers." His gaze on the lake, Acey added, "I
never told anyone, as much because Josh swore me to se-
crecy, as the fact that Sloan would have taken a strip off of
Josh's hide and then come looking for me. Sloan's a fair
man, but he ain't someone I'd cross—I know when to keep
my mouth shut."

Well, that explains the land sale, Shelly thought to herself. *The time is about right.*

Staring down at the lake once more, she was surprised to
feel behind her anger and bewilderment a sense of loss. The
right-of-way had been part of her heritage, part of the lore
that surrounded the Ballinger/Granger feud. She would be
first to admit that they should have sold or given up the
right-of-way years ago. They didn't need it, hadn't for
decades—just before the turn of the century her great-

grandfather had bought a piece of land that connected the Granger land with the Tilda Road, eliminating the need for the right-of-way. Only contrariness and sheer perversity had kept the Grangers tramping across it all these years. She grimaced. Not exactly something to be proud of or to brag about. Uncomfortably she realized that deep inside she was prey to another emotion, not a very nice one at that. Try as she might, she couldn't help feeling resentful that the damned Ballingers had finally gotten their way—and never mind that any fair-minded person would have given up the right-of-way when it was no longer needed. She wasn't feeling very fair-minded at the moment.

She sent one last look at the lake and turned her horse around.

"Where're you going?" Acey called as he fell in behind her.

"Home. I've lost my taste for any more riding right now."

They rode several minutes in silence, then Acey piped up, "You gonna pout all the way home?"

Shelly laughed reluctantly. "No. It was just a shock. I'll get over it." And she would, she realized. Maybe it was best that the blasted right-of-way and the source of so much bad feeling over the years was no more. It was gone and in a way, now that she thought about it, she was *almost* glad. Over her shoulder she asked, "Are you sure of the amount Josh got?"

"Sure as I can be. Don't think Josh lied. But I sure as hell didn't go ask Sloan if he'd let himself be snookered out of fifty thousand dollars."

Another crime, Shelly thought bitterly, to be laid against the Grangers, and even she would have to agree that it *had* been criminal. Josh might as well have held up Sloan at gunpoint, she admitted, her sense of fair play digging painfully into her conscience. There was no other honest way to view it. Fifty thousand dollars! She squirmed in her saddle, feeling guilty and ashamed of Josh's greed.

"Thought you said you weren't going to pout," Acey said, bringing his horse beside hers as the trail widened.

She smiled crookedly at him. "I wasn't, I was just thinking."

"Well, don't think too much—it ain't healthy." He flashed her a shrewd look. "It isn't your fault what Josh did—or didn't do."

Shelly sighed. "You're probably right, I just can't help—"

"Thinking," Acey finished for her. "And what did I just tell you?"

She laughed, and together they both said, "It ain't healthy!"

Acey studied her expression a moment, then with a gleam in his eyes, he murmured, "It ain't healthy either for a woman your age to be alone. What you need is a man. Nice, young, strong man would keep you smiling all the time."

Shelly made a face at him. "No, I'm serious," he said. "You take my widow woman—before I come along, she was just pining away, lonesome for some red-blooded loving."

"But now, I suppose, with you in it, her life couldn't be better," Shelly said dryly.

"Damn straight."

"Acey, I hate to tell you this, but you're living in the wrong century."

He looked offended. "I'll have you know that I'm a modern man—I let her buy me dinner now and then."

"Acey . . ." she warned.

His features resembling those of a mischievous old monkey beneath his creased and worn cowboy hat, Acey murmured, "As a matter of fact, we're going out to dinner tonight." He wiggled his gray eyebrows. "Think I'll order oysters."

Chapter Seven

On Friday, Shelly's belongings from New Orleans arrived. She spent the weekend unpacking, her thoughts only half on what she was doing. She'd find herself stopping in the middle of her tasks, her mind on Josh, Sloan, and the fifty-thousand-dollar right-of-way. She couldn't even think of it anymore as the Granger right-of-way; it was, now and forever, the fifty-thousand-dollar right-of-way. She shook her head. She couldn't believe that Sloan had allowed Josh to take advantage of him that way. Dumping a sweater in the bottom drawer of the dresser in her bedroom, she tried to justify Josh's actions, tried to feel a sense of satisfaction that the Grangers had gotten the last laugh on the Ballingers, but somehow she didn't feel like laughing. What she *did* feel was guilty and ashamed—and disloyal to the generations of Grangers who had come before her for feeling as she did. It didn't help her conscience much to tell herself that Sloan could have nailed her brother with a glance from those glittering gold eyes of his and laughed in Josh's face. It wasn't, she argued, as if Sloan hadn't had a choice. He could have said no. He *should* have said no, she thought moodily. Staring blankly at the packing box on the floor, she wondered why Sloan hadn't done just that. And why the hell should it bother her?

When she discovered that she had unpacked and put her

coffee mugs in the medicine cabinet, she gave herself a shake and made an effort to pay attention to what she was doing. Fortunately, the boxes were all marked and after some poking around she selected the ones that held mostly clothing and art supplies. Everything else, with Nick's and Acey's help, she'd stashed for the time being in one of the storage sheds out behind the house. Acey didn't hang around. Looking sly, he climbed into his pickup, and said, "Got a hot date. That widow woman sure keeps me busy."

Shelly and Nick watched him drive off before wandering over to the stout corral near the barn that held a lone occupant: Granger's Ideal Beau. Beau was big, black, and beautiful, every inch a monarch. Leaning on the top rail of the corral, they watched him as he sauntered regally over to them.

"He knows he's really hot stuff, doesn't he?" Shelly said with a smile.

"He's got a right," Nick said. "Beau's one of the best bulls Granger's ever bred—or would have been if Josh had used him to his full potential. It's a damn shame he never bred him like he should have."

"Well, we're certainly not going to make that mistake, are we, partner?" Shelly teased.

Nick shot her an uncertain look. "Are you sure you still want to be partners? I mean, you could make it on your own—you don't really need me." He grimaced. "Actually, I need you a whole lot more than you need me."

Shelly laid a hand on his arm. "Nick, stop that. We've discussed this subject countless times in the last few weeks. I want this partnership. We need each other. I can't do it alone. I need your help." She grinned at him. "I really do need your young healthy muscles."

He smiled crookedly. "I know. And I know all the arguments why it's such a good deal for both of us. I know we both benefit and that pooling our resources only makes sense, it's just that . . ." He stopped and looked embarrassed.

"It's just what?" Shelly asked softly.

"It's just that I don't want you offering me a good deal because you feel sorry for me . . . or guilty . . . or something stupid like that," he said unhappily.

She smacked him lightly on the head. "Now that *would* be stupid," she said with exasperation. "I'm doing this because it makes sense. I'm not going to kid you, Nick—unless we can make this thing work, there's a good chance I'll lose the ranch. Literally. Except for the land, Josh depleted most of the Granger assets—I have to come up with a way to make it pay. I told you when I first broached the idea of a partnership, that we've got the land, Beau, your herd and, I think, I hope, enough money to get us started." She shook him slightly. "You're not looking at a rich little girl playing at raising cattle to amuse herself. I *have* to make it work, and I can't do it alone. I need you. And I don't feel one damn bit guilty about asking you to share my leaky ship either. We either bail out of this mess or we sink . . . together."

Nick's lips twitched. "When you put it that way, I guess all I can say is thanks."

"You're welcome. Although whether you'll be thanking me in six months remains to be seen."

Nick flung a friendly arm around her shoulders. Nodding in Beau's direction, he said, "Don't worry. We'll make it. With Beau as our herd sire, hell, we're halfway there already."

"He really is a great bull, isn't he?"

Nick nodded. "More importantly, without him, Granger Cattle Company would be screwed. Thank God, Josh didn't sell him. He's our future."

❧

By Monday the bulk of her clothes were stowed in her bedroom and the art supplies had been lugged up the stairs to the huge unfurnished room on the third floor. The area resembled a tower and like so many things these days, moving her belongings into it had been a bittersweet experience. Maria had shown her the incredible eight-sided room weeks ago, when she had first arrived, and had innocently knifed her in the heart when she'd said, "Josh mentioned once during construction of the house that if you ever came home again, you would need a place to paint. It even has an outside deck—I think now that he planned it for you."

A lump the size of Texas in her throat, Shelly had to agree. It was the perfect artist's studio, flooded with natural light from the skylights placed along the soaring, open-beamed ceiling and the tall windows that were interspersed throughout the room. She grinned when she spied the small glass-fronted woodstove in one corner. Josh and his fireplaces—how he had loved them, but she imagined that on rainy winter days, she might herself love the sight of a cheerful fire burning in the stove. Hauling the wood upstairs, she decided wryly, might take some of the pleasure out of it.

Stacking the last of her canvasses against one wall that Monday afternoon, she glanced around the room, thinking again that Josh couldn't have created a space that would have pleased her more.

The room had been thoughtfully planned, giving her just what she needed, privacy, space, views, light, even cupboards, some countertops, one with a sink in the middle of it, and closets for her supplies. Her eyes lit on the door at the far end of the big open room, and she smiled. Practical Josh—he'd even had a small utilitarian bathroom with a shower installed.

Despite its size and lack of furnishings, it was a welcoming room. The oak floors gleamed warmly in the morning light that poured in from the many windows, the scent of coffee from her coffeemaker on the counter wafted through the air, adding to the sense of welcome. A moment later, mug of coffee in hand, Shelly wandered around the room, touching things, familiarizing herself with her new domain.

A couple of easels had been set up near a pair of windows that overlooked the valley and the green-and-red-plaid couch she'd pilfered from Josh's office sat in lonely splendor in the middle of the big room. Protesting and swearing, Nick had helped her muscle it up the stairs last night. She'd need to see about some recessed lighting and a mini refrigerator—she wasn't hiking up and down two sets of stairs every time she wanted a cold drink or some real cream in her coffee. She eyed the couch. Maybe she'd splurge on a fake fur rug, too. It'd look great in front of the couch.

Sliding open one of the glass doors that led to the small east-facing deck, Shelly stepped outside. Breathing in the cool scent of the woods, she drank her coffee, her thoughts once more sliding to the fifty-thousand-dollar right-of-way. It wasn't her problem, she told herself. And if she were any kind of Granger at all, she'd be dancing with delight at having really stuck it to the Ballingers. Hadn't the two families spent the better part of the last 150 years trying to do just that to each other? And why, she mused, did it all seem so silly to her? Was it because she had moved away so many years ago? Because she hadn't spent the last seventeen years being steeped in the lore and legend of the Granger/Ballinger feud? She grimaced. If the truth were known, once she had left Oak Valley behind, the last thing she'd wanted to think about had been the Ballingers—especially Sloan.

Shelly closed her eyes, still not wanting to think about Sloan. But it was no use, behind her lids his dark, hard face swam in front of her. It wasn't a face easily forgotten, the rough-hewn features having a memorable attractiveness all their own. When Sloan Ballinger walked into a room, women looked and kept looking; the tough, masculine face with those striking gold eyes and that wide-lipped mouth at once mesmerizing and compelling. It didn't hurt that the body that went with the face was completely and utterly male. Shelly would bet that there wasn't a woman alive whose gaze wouldn't have lingered, even if only for a passing second, on his big, muscular body. Sloan dominated a room just by walking into it, something alive and vital, the promise of something exciting and feral entering with him. Just thinking about him, picturing him walking toward her, that mocking half smile on his lips, sent a flash of warmth spiraling through her, making her remember things she'd sworn to forget.

But Sloan was unforgettable—at least for her, she admitted bleakly. He'd been her first lover and for a precious few months, she'd adored him. To her cost, she'd discovered all too soon that he'd lied to her and betrayed her. She should hate him, some days she did, but to her distress, even when she was certain he was the most loathsome man alive, she still found him fascinating. Which showed just how much of a fool she was! And which, she reminded herself, did not change the fact that he'd paid an outrageous price for the right-of-way. It hadn't been a fair deal. She frowned. Was that why it bothered her? Because it hadn't been a fair deal? Or was it, whispered a sly voice, because taking advantage of Sloan the way Josh had only confirmed the Ballinger opinion that the Grangers were a bunch of thieving, crooked, underhanded bastards. Her mouth twisted. Of course, the Grangers had the same opinion of the Ballingers.

Having lost the desire for her coffee, she tossed the rest of it over the balcony and went inside. She had other things, she reminded herself firmly, to think about than Sloan Ballinger.

Shelly kept busy for several days, continuing to unpack some personal things from the boxes in the shed, handling the details as they came up in connection with Josh's will and generally settling into a new routine. The following week, she considered hosting a small, quiet party on Saturday night, but had hesitated about entertaining so soon after Josh's death. When she'd voiced her concerns to Cleo, Cleo had said, "Hell-all-Friday, girl! You know Josh. He'd have been the first one to tell you to throw a blowout. And it isn't as if he died just last week. Besides, I've got me a brand-new pair of black leather pants I want that Blarney-Stone-kissing Hank O'Hara to see me in. You have that party—and make certain you invite Hank and his sister."

With Cleo's approval and the support of her skinny-dipping friends from childhood, the ones she'd kept in touch with from New Orleans, Melissa-Jane McGuire, Bobba Neale, and Danny Haskell, the party had been scheduled. They'd been delighted to help organize the party and helped her with the phone invitations. In the end, the small party grew to be a rather large gathering, but the results had been gratifying: her first foray into valley society had been a re-sounding success. Moving among her guests, old-time residents and some newcomers, Shelly had found it amazing how easily she slipped back into the rhythms of the valley. It was, as she said later to Nick and Acey, both attendees at the party, almost as if she had never been away.

But if she had had a success on one front, she'd had no such luck with resolving her ambivalence about the right-of-way. Even involved in other things, it was there, lurking at the back of her mind. She brooded over it and finally, as April tumbled into May, decided to do something about it.

Mike Sawyer had been adamantly against the plan she

came up with to resolve the issue, and Bill Weeks, the family banker, hadn't been thrilled. They'd both been quite clear that her financial status was not the best—which she already knew—the Granger wealth had always been in cattle and land rather than actual hard cash—unlike the Ballingers. But their warnings had fallen on deaf ears and in the end, she'd gotten what she wanted.

She'd considered simply phoning Sloan and telling him what she planned to do, or writing him, that way avoiding a face-to-face confrontation, but neither idea felt right. For reasons she didn't want to examine too closely, she felt compelled to do this particular chore in person.

Dressing that Wednesday morning in the first week of May, it occurred to her that she had only leaped the first hurdle—the easy one. Nervous, her stomach fluttering, she picked through her closet and wasted a lot more time than the decision deserved on deciding what to wear. Finally wearing white Nike running shoes, a pair of close-fitting blue jeans, and a blue-and-white striped long-sleeve shirt, she looked at herself in the mirror and made a face. She looked so ordinary. But that was the point, wasn't it? This wasn't supposed to be a big deal. She stared some more. Well, maybe some lipstick and eyebrow pencil would help. And some blusher. Oh, and she had that new brown eyeliner. . . .

Fifteen minutes later, hating herself for having taken so much trouble with her appearance, she slammed shut the door to the Bronco and roared out of the driveway. When she hit the valley floor, she took a deep breath. She was really going to do this. She took another deep breath. Really.

The drive seemed all too short, and before she was aware of it, she had turned off the Tilda Road and was bumping along a rough gravel road that snaked into the forest. Not long after that, she was braking and turning off the ignition.

She sat there for several seconds in the large clearing, staring at the cabin, noticing the woodshed, corrals, and other outbuildings behind the cabin.

Her heart thumping, all the reasons why she shouldn't be here churning through her head, she finally grabbed her purse and stepped out of the vehicle. *Maybe*, she thought wildly, *he won't be at home.*

Her knock was met with a spate of hysterical barking, and a moment later Sloan opened the door, using his bare foot to hold at bay a small, yapping dog.

He had been braced for a confrontation with Shelly since the moment Jeb had told him she'd found out about the right-of-way. Every time he'd been in town lately, he'd discovered himself glancing warily around for sight of her, ready, he admitted cravenly, to duck and run. Knowing the Grangers, he didn't doubt that she was going to tackle him about the right-of-way and being a Granger, hold it against him for having bought it—even at an exorbitant sum. His mouth tightened. It still rankled that Josh had held the family up that way, but they'd wanted the Grangers out of their hair badly enough to bite the bullet and pay the money.

He'd been certain of two things, though: one, that Josh hadn't told Shelly about selling the right-of-way—there were lots of things that Josh hadn't told Shelly, he thought grimly—and two, that she would be infuriated about it when she found out. He didn't want to fight with her and had avoided town as much as he could. Town had been bad enough, but even in the cabin he'd been on edge—every time the phone rang, he'd approached it like he would a coiled rattlesnake. He'd known that there would be a reaction from her, that sooner or later, they'd lock horns; but what he had never expected was that she would show up on his front porch. OK, technically a deck. He also hadn't expected that the mere sight of her would leave him feeling as if he'd been sucker-punched. Hard. Right in the gut. Or that she'd look so damned tasty, he could have feasted on her for a week—and that would just be an appetizer.

They stared at each other for a tense second before Sloan finally found his voice. After admonishing Pandora to shut up, he said, "Uh, Shelly, hi. Didn't expect to see you out here." *Oh, brilliant, Sloan*, he thought wryly. *Bowl her over with your witty conversation.*

Shelly cleared her throat, wishing that her heartbeat would slow down and that her stomach would return to its normal position and get out of her throat. Standing in front of her in a pair of tight black jeans and a form-fitting yellow-and-green-plaid Western shirt, he looked so, so *masculine*—despite the dish towel he held in one hand and the puffball of a dog he kept from dashing outside with his feet. His black hair was mussed, a lock brushing across his forehead, and she fought to control the impulse to brush it aside and maybe, just maybe, lightly stroke his hard cheek. Her hand fisted at her side to keep it from acting on its own, she forced a smile, and said brightly. "Hi, Sloan. Hope I didn't catch you at an inconvenient time."

"No, no. I was just, uh, drying dishes," he muttered. He smiled lopsidedly. "Bachelor household."

Pandora, ignored long enough, managed to get out from behind Sloan's foot and shot out of the house to sniff excitedly at Shelly's Nikes.

"Pandy, get in here!"

Apparently, Pandora didn't find Shelly's Nikes interesting, because to Sloan's astonishment, she actually obeyed him and trotted back into the house, indifference in every movement.

"Cute dog," Shelly said.

Sloan smiled, a smile that made Shelly's knees go weak. "She can be—she can also be hell-on-wheels when the mood strikes her." The subject of Pandora had given him a chance to recover from the shock of Shelly's visit, and, stepping aside, he said, "Come on in. I just put on a pot of coffee—can I offer you a cup?"

"Sure."

She stood uncertainly in the center of the room while he disappeared into what she assumed was the kitchen. She glanced around the large room, liking the contrast of the cream-colored painted ceiling with the knotty pine walls. A couple of green-and-beige geometric-patterned rugs were thrown across the plain tiled floor, and a river-rock-faced fireplace with a wide oak mantel took up one corner of the room; a long, comfortable looking ox-blood colored leather couch was angled in front of it. To the left of the couch, two dark green recliners were separated by an oak table that held a brass lamp: the remaining surface overflowed with magazines and books, some spilling onto the floor. There was a small oak-furnished dining area behind the couch and a big rolltop desk and a chair against the far wall.

It was an inviting room, and a comfortable one, almost cozy, Shelly thought, trying to focus on something other than the reason she was here. She and Sloan had actually exchanged more than a half dozen words, and they hadn't started arguing yet. That was good. Keeping her fingers in a death grip on her purse, she walked over to one of the many windows. There were no drapes, just blinds that she supposed he lowered at night for privacy. Although, living out here in the middle of nowhere—the nearest resident was probably ten miles away—she doubted that he had any concerns about what the neighbors might or might not see.

The cabin sat on a small rise, and the windows gave wonderful views of the forest and the ascending foothills in the distance. She'd bet in the winter, with the firs dusted with snow, it was breathtaking. From what she could see, it was obvious that Sloan or someone had cleared a huge area around the cabin, leaving the nearest tree more than fifty feet away from any building. *Fire protection*, she thought automatically. Living in the wilderness, fire protection was always a concern, and smart people took seriously the need to keep the brush and trees well away from the structures.

"Here you go," Sloan said from behind her as he walked back into the room. He walked up to stand beside her, a mug of coffee in each hand. "As I remember, you take yours with a drop of cream. Sorry it's not the real stuff—I opened some condensed milk and used that."

Surprised that he remembered something so trivial, she smiled. "Thanks, condensed milk is just fine."

She looked around for a place to lay her purse, and Sloan said, "Just throw it on the couch."

Her purse taken care of, she took the mug from him. They sipped in silence a moment, then, indicating the outside with her hand, she said, "You have a great view. I'd like to paint it in winter. Would you mind?"

"Be my guest." He cocked a brow. "You planning on staying here that long? Until winter?"

Shelly nodded, taking another sip of her coffee. "Yes. I'm home for good." There was one thing about repeating a phrase often enough, she decided—after a while you could say it without thinking about it or giving it too much emphasis.

Sloan showed no reaction, his features just as unreadable as they had always been to her . . . except when he'd been furious or sexually aroused—*then* she'd had no trouble reading what was on his mind.

"Different sort of life in Oak Valley than you'd find in New Orleans—are you sure you won't get bored?" he asked quietly, his eyes on the view outside the window.

Shelly shrugged. "I know it'll be different, but I doubt I'll have time to be bored. In fact, I worry that running the ranch is going to take away time from my painting, and painting is my bread and butter."

He glanced at her, a frown wrinkling his forehead. "Run the ranch? The way I hear it, there isn't any ranch to run."

"There will be," she said stoutly. "Nick Rios and I are combining our operations. We're expecting a shipment of cattle in next week from Texas. There's a breeder out there who has many of the old Granger bloodlines. Most of Nick's stock is a couple of generations away from Granger stock, but we have Beau—the lone survivor of a long line of Granger bulls that we'll use—on his cows and these new ones. We figure if we can find one more bull with a different strain of Granger blood in it, we'll be on our way. Acey's offered to help me with the breeding program—and Acey knows his cattle. It'll take us a few years, but in time, we should have the operation up and running strong again."

It was the longest conversation they'd had in years, and while he was paying attention to what she was saying, his gaze was fixed on her soft mouth, and his thoughts strayed. He'd have liked it a whole lot more, if those sweet, tempting lips were saying something else, such as, "I've missed you. It was all a mistake. Let's start over again." Or better yet, "Make love to me."

Her scent, something light and flowery, drifted to him, and standing this close to her, he could feel the warmth of her slender body . . . a slender body he'd held in his arms and felt tremble and shake with passion. Passion that he evoked. And that mouth of hers, the things it had done to him. . . .

What had been a pleasant ache in his groin became urgent, and he didn't need to look down to see that he was hard as a rock and straining against the front of his jeans. Ah hell.

She was talking about breeding cattle, and all he could think of was breeding her.

Shelly knew she was babbling. She couldn't help it. She was enthusiastic about the cattle operation, and it was also a safe topic. Talking about the cattle prevented those uneasy silences and put off the moment she had to explain her reason for being here. Except she was too aware of him to think clearly, too aware of his eyes locked on her mouth, too aware of the heat of his body and that they were all alone. Together. In his cabin. In the middle of nowhere.

She swallowed. "Listen to me," she said nervously. "You should never have got me started on the cattle. I get carried away."

"That's OK. Get me started on horses, and you're liable to be here until you're old and gray." He took another sip of his coffee, cursing his inane tongue. But he'd rather have her think him inane than to realize how difficult it was for him not to give into the caveman urge to sling her over his shoulder and climb upstairs to the loft and make love to her for the rest of the day. And maybe the night. And the next day.

"Horses? Isn't Ballinger Inc. still raising cattle?"

Sloan shrugged. "My dad runs a few head, but we've pretty much gotten out of the cattle business." He smiled faintly. "We're fast leaving our country roots behind us and becoming big business."

"Oh. I thought. . . ." She groped for words.

"That things never change?"

She flashed him an uncertain look. "Yes. I guess so. Josh never said much, and I just assumed that your family was still raising cattle."

"We were already starting to get out of it when you left, remember? My degree, if you'll recall, was in architecture, and there sure as hell wasn't much of a future for me as an architect in Oak Valley." He put down his mug on the windowsill and took hers from her and set it next to his.

Shelly's heart was hammering when his hands closed around her shoulders and he gently turned her to face him. "Don't you remember, we talked about it," he said levelly. "We argued about it. Once we married you wanted to stay in the valley and I wanted to move away. Remember?"

Shelly nodded, not trusting her voice. She didn't want to remember, but she did. Especially that last terrible argument just before she'd found him in another woman's arms and heard him admit that he'd only been playing with her, that she meant nothing to him. Absolutely nothing at all.

She stirred in his grasp. "Look, I don't want to start arguing with you. The past is the past, and I'd just as soon forget the mistakes I made when I was eighteen. I was young and, I'll say it to you, an emotional little fool." She met his gaze. "I've grown up, Sloan, and hopefully learned from my mistakes. I've moved on, put the past behind me. What happened between us seventeen years ago is old history . . . and I don't want to rehash it. That's not why I came here today."

"Old history, huh?" he murmured, his eyes on her mouth. "Let's just see how old it really is, shall we?"

Before she could guess his intent, he pulled her against him and his mouth caught hers.

The instant his lips claimed hers, seventeen years vanished as if by magic, and she was eighteen years old again, her body clamoring for the touch, for the caress of this one man. She'd been mesmerized by him then, and she was terrified to discover that it wouldn't take much for her to fall into that same trap again. She tried to ignore the sensations flooding through her, tried to resist the lure of those knowing lips, but it was impossible. His mouth possessed hers, allowing her no escape, and the seductive sensation of his warm lips caressing and teasing hers made her brain go fuzzy, and every nerve in her body came singing to life. Her breasts ached and passion, a primitive passion she'd sworn she'd put behind her, twined and twisted low in her belly. His body was pressed against hers, and she could feel the hard wall of his chest against her breasts, could feel the blunt pressure of his erection pushing against her. But it was his mouth, the soft slide of his lips against hers, the hungry nip of his teeth on her bottom lip and the stark demand she sensed behind his kiss that sent her emotions spiraling out of control. He bit gently again and, shuddering with desire, she surrendered her mouth to him and her lips parted, giving him what he wanted.

But it wasn't enough. He kissed her deeply, his hand cupping her chin, holding her just where he wanted as he drank deep of the wine-dark sweetness of her mouth. Again and again he kissed her, each kiss more demanding, more explicit than the last. She was drowning in sensation, unaware of anything but Sloan, and the pleasure that plundering mouth of his was giving her. It had always been this way between them, she thought hazily. Always. He'd only had to touch her and she'd go up in flames. It seemed some things never did change. . . .

Suddenly conscious of where this would lead, she jerked out of his arms. Her eyes dark with passion, her swollen nipples peaking against her blouse, she stared at him.

It gave her small satisfaction to see that he was as aroused as she was. His face had that hungry, intent look she remembered so well, the glitter in the golden eyes making her heart pound frantically. As for his body . . . she'd already felt his readiness. Knew that all she had to do was lift a finger and that he'd make love to her. Right here. Right now.

Feeling as if she were fighting herself as much as him, she said, "I didn't come out here for this."

"Then why the hell did you?" he snapped, furious for his own loss of control, enraged to discover that she still had the power to arouse him more than any other woman he'd ever known. If he weren't a civilized man, he told himself, and this wasn't the twenty-first century, he'd grab her, tear off those tight little jeans of hers, and take her right then and there—on the floor, the couch, hell, it didn't matter. All that mattered was that he lose himself in that soft flesh of hers once more, and if he couldn't get them to his loft and the bed, the floor would do just fine. To his horror he discovered that a part of him was considering doing it.

He spun away and, staring grimly out the window, he growled, "Well? What was it that brought you here, if it wasn't for that?"

"You arrogant bastard! Do you really think I drove out here so we could take up where we left off? Are you crazy?"

He ran a hand through his hair and swung back to face her. "Yeah. Where you're concerned I've always been a little crazy." Cutting her off, he put up his hands in a gesture of surrender. "Forget it. I was out of line. Let's just bury this little incident with the past." He grinned crookedly. "Put it down to cabin fever. You're the first attractive female who's been out here in a while. Guess I got all excited and forgot my manners. Now drink your coffee and tell me why you're here."

"I don't want your damned coffee," Shelly said, her eyes bright and angry. She glanced over her shoulder, found her purse, and pounced on it. Opening it, she dug around and came out with a cashier's check. "Here, take this," she muttered, almost throwing it at him.

Frowning, he stared down at the check. It was made out to him in the amount of forty-eight thousand dollars. Puzzled, he looked over at her. "What is this for? You don't owe me any money."

Shelly's chin came up. "The Granger family does. That right-of-way isn't worth more than a few thousand dollars. Josh overcharged you. I'm correcting the error."

Sloan stared at her, stunned. He'd been prepared for her anger over the sale of the right-of-way, but he'd never considered that she'd try to refund part of the money. What game, he wondered, was she playing? Was she trying to renege on the deal? His face darkened. She couldn't do that. It was a done deal. And money, whatever her motives, was the last damned thing he wanted from Shelly Granger.

"By God, you're not!" he said, insulted. "My deal was with Josh. It had nothing to do with you. Take your money back."

He thrust the check back to her, but Shelly, her purse in her hand, had already turned on her heel and was heading toward the door. "No thank you. It's yours. Do what you want with it."

"Now wait just a goddamn minute—"

She spun around to glare at him, her eyes gleaming like emeralds. "No, you wait a goddamn minute! You overpaid for the right-of-way, and you know it. I'll say it for you: Josh screwed you. You know it, and I know it. All I'm doing is making things right and making certain that you damned Ballingers don't go around proclaiming what a tricky bastard he was." Her voice shook as she added, "I'm sick of this whole Ballinger/Granger feud. It's stupid and silly. Take the money and admit for once that all the Grangers aren't crooks or thieves."

"I never said that all the Grangers were crooks or thieves. Just some of them," Sloan said evenly, his temper cooling. She was upset, he could see that, and he could see that this was, for reasons that totally escaped him, important to her. "Look," he said, "why don't you sit down, I'll fix us a fresh cup of coffee and we can discuss this like adults."

"There is nothing to discuss," Shelly said from between clenched teeth. "The money is yours."

"And I don't want it," he growled, his jaw set.

"Too bad. It's yours, and there is nothing you can do about it."

"Wanna bet?"

"Yeah, sure, why not?"

And before her astonished gaze, he took the cashier's check and ripped it into confetti. He smiled, not a nice smile. "You lose."

Chapter Eight

❧

*T*he door slammed behind Shelly, and Sloan couldn't decide from the expression on her face as she'd run away if she had been astonished, appalled, or just plain furious with his treatment of the check. Probably all three, he thought with a shrug, letting the torn paper fall to the floor at his feet.

A nudge from a cold little nose on his ankle had him glancing down at Pandora. She regarded him unblinkingly. "What?" he asked. "You don't approve of my treatment of the lady? Let me tell you, kid," he said as he picked her up and suffered a wet kiss on his cheek, "that there aren't many men who throw away that kind of money." He looked down at the scraps of paper littering the floor and shook his head. "I can't believe I did that." He grinned at Pandora. "Hope it impressed the hell out of her—it sure did me."

❧

Shelly was not impressed. She was furious. *Leave it to a Ballinger*, she thought, *to turn a perfectly honest, sincere gesture into a farce.* She could strangle Sloan. Why couldn't he have been a gentleman and just taken the money? Even if he hadn't intended to keep it, he could have given it to a charity or set up a scholarship with it, or done *something* with it! He didn't have to rip it up.

She bit her lip. Now what did she do? She'd have to talk to the bank. A cashier's check wasn't like a regular check; she doubted she could blithely just go ask for another one. Her face burned. And explaining what happened to the first one was going to be almost as embarrassing as standing up naked on a Sunday morning in a packed church.

Shelly didn't let herself think about those moments in Sloan's arms. Didn't dare think about how right it had felt to be pressed against his big frame, didn't want to remember the sweet wildness in her blood, or the way her traitorous body had responded to his kiss. She forced herself instead to brood on the check and wonder what she was going to do next. Approaching the road to home, she decided that she wasn't going to go back to the house. She'd only wander around and dwell on Sloan . . . and the check.

Pulling up in front of the cheerful red-and-white steel building that housed McGuire's Market, she turned off the ignition. Hopefully Melissa-Jane would be in the store office.

She was, and answered Shelly's knock on the door with a frown. Seeing Shelly her expression changed, a wide smile replacing the frown. "Hi, Shell. What brings you here? Some hot gossip, I hope."

Shelly smiled back, shaking her head. "No. I thought that if anyone had gossip it would be you."

"Fat chance," Melissa-Jane said. "I'm usually the last one to know." She pointed to a chair next to one of the gray metal desks that crowded the area, and added, "Have a seat. I need a break anyway."

The office was small, almost a cubicle, and most of the floor space was taken up with either file cabinets, bookshelves, three desks, or other office equipment. A couple of short narrow aisles snaked through the clutter. Every conceivable surface was covered with brochures, advertising literature, and big red three-ring binders. The impression was one of disorganized order. There were two computers, a pair of large-screen monitors, a copy machine, fax machine, phones, and various other pieces of office paraphernalia scattered all over the place. A bank of security cameras hung from the ceiling near one wall and enabled anyone working in the office to keep an eye on the rest of the store. The room bordered on the claustrophobic, a small one-way window that looked out over the bread-and-bakery aisle the only thing that kept it from resembling a monk's cell. Lying on top of one of the file cabinets and completely out of place was a startling lifelike gorilla mask, the black lips pulled back in a ferocious snarl.

"What in the world," Shelly said, pointing to the mask, "is that doing in here? Last time I checked, Halloween isn't for months yet."

Melissa-Jane scowled. "Hang around long enough, and you'll find out." She glanced at the big round clock over her desk. "Yeah, he ought to be here in about a half hour."

Having made that cryptic statement, Melissa-Jane plopped down in the high-backed oak office chair in front of the middle desk and put her feet up on the rim of a black metal wastebasket. "So, how's it going?" she asked.

Shelly had known Melissa-Jane all of her life, and they had, until Shelly had left so precipitously almost seventeen years ago, been inseparable. Their parents had been lifelong friends, and there was only three weeks difference in their ages, Melissa-Jane, or M.J., as she preferred, having been born in late July and Shelly in mid August. They'd gone to grade school together and had endured the loneliness of private school when their parents had enrolled both of them in the same private high school. Only the presence of the other one had made the separation from family, friends, and the valley bearable.

The two women were opposites physically. M.J. possessed

a mop of bouncy blond curls, the blondness helped a bit these days by L'Oreal, and a pair of the biggest, darkest pansy brown eyes ever seen on a real live human being. She had a gamine face, a tip-tilted nose, and stood only about five-foot-three, to Shelly's commanding five-foot-nine, and while Shelly was on the lean side, Melissa-Jane was curvaceous— too curvaceous, she'd complained often enough. As teenagers, Shelly had envied M.J.'s small stature and generously endowed curves, and, naturally, M.J. had sighed over Shelly's tall slenderness.

Eyeing Shelly's long legs as she stretched them out in front of her just now, M.J. commented, "You know, I still don't think it's fair that you got the height and the slenderness. My boobs and hips would look a lot better on you."

"1 dunno," Shelly said with a grin. "I'll bet that even if we could switch body parts, we'd probably still think the other one got the better deal. You know—the grass always looking greener on the other side, or, you could say, the boobs always look greater on someone else's chest."

M.J. giggled, the same infectious giggle she'd had all of her life, and Shelly found herself giggling with her. That giggle, coupled with those big speaking eyes, were part of M.J.'s charm, and one couldn't hear that gentle gurgle of laughter without joining in, never mind that they were both approaching thirty-five years of age. Melissa-Jane's giggle was timeless.

M.J. glanced at the sliding window of the office and perked up. "Oh, would you look at that."

Another security feature, the one-way window only allowed those inside the office to look out and observe the interior of the store. On the other side, there was just a mirror, giving the inhabitants of the office total privacy.

Shelly turned her head and glanced out the window. "What?" she said. "It's only Jeb talking to some woman."

"Yes, but it's *who* he's talking to. Don't think you've met her yet, but that's Tracy Kingsley—the local vet. She came to the valley after you'd scooted off to New Orleans. Been around now, I guess, about ten years."

Shelly eyed the red-haired woman, laughing up at something Jeb had said to her. There was an air of familiarity between them, Jeb standing close to the woman, his hand resting on her shoulder. The woman was tall, probably about her height, Shelly estimated, and probably about the same build, maybe not quite as slim. *Bigger boobs*, Shelly thought gloomily. The other's woman's hair was pulled back in a ponytail and fastened with a plaid scrunchy, and she was garbed in typical valley wear—worn blue jeans, scuffed running shoes, and a comfortable shirt. A pretty woman, Shelly decided, taking in the even features.

"Vet, as in, veterinarian?"

"Yes. She's pretty good, too. When Jamie's dog, Rowdy, got kicked by a cow last summer and had his leg broken in three or four places, she patched him right up. Didn't charge an arm and a leg either. It was great not having to drive an hour down the St. Galen's road to Willits with a crying kid and a howling dog."

"How are Jamie and Todd?" Shelly asked, mentioning M.J.'s two sons.

M.J. tore her eyes away from the window and made a face. "Fine. They're with their father this semester. Since the divorce, he gets them about half a year and I get them the rest of the time. They've adjusted to the midyear change in schools pretty well, although their grades always suffer a little until they settle in. They'll be home around the end of July." Her features softened. "Can't wait. I miss them so much when they're gone—they're growing so fast. I can't believe that Jamie will be twelve in another month or that Todd, my baby, turned ten in February. Wait 'til you see them.

You'll never recognize them from the pictures I sent you at Christmas."

The divorce, final two years ago, ironically on Valentine's Day, had been hard on M.J. She had adored her tall handsome Highway Patrol husband, Charles Sutton, and she had been devastated when she'd discovered that a lot of those supposedly late-night assignments had been *assignations*, with various attractive young ladies he'd met during the course of his job. To discover, as she had done, that Charles had been cheating on her for years had been devastating. She'd been shattered by the betrayal, and the decision to end her marriage of twelve years, with the future of two small children to consider, had been painful and difficult. But as she'd told Shelly during one of their marathon telephone conversations during that dreadful time, "I can't trust him," she'd said, tears in her voice. "And if I can't trust him, there is no marriage." She'd given a bitter laugh. "Everyone in his unit, hell, half the county, knew that he was playing around on me. Worse yet, I've found out that he's been doing it practically the entire time we've been married. I can't forgive him, and if I can't forgive him, I can't stay married to him."

Shelly didn't blame her for feeling as she did. She and Sloan hadn't been married, but he had betrayed her in a painfully similar manner. Hearing M.J.'s sad, sordid little tale long-distance, all Shelly could do was weep with her and try to lift her spirits. The Valentine's Day when M.J. had gotten her final decree, she and Shelly had gotten pretty well smashed. They'd both bought a bottle of champagne in anticipation of the event, and when Melissa-Jane had called with the news, they had stayed on the phone for hours, drinking champagne and telling each other what bastards men were.

Once the house in Ukiah that M.J. had been so proud of had been sold, she'd packed up everything and moved back to Oak Valley. A good thing, too, she'd told Shelly. Her grandfather, the founder of McGuire's, wanted to retire—had wanted to for years—and since neither one of his two sons had ever shown any interest in the store, M.J. got tapped to take it over. "I think the only reason the crafty old devil dragged me into the store instead of one of my cousins was to keep me so busy I wouldn't have time to think about how miserable I was," she'd told Shelly last spring. "And you know what? He was right. I'm not going to say I don't still have my bad days, or that I'm not bitter about Charles, but I sure as hell don't have time to brood over it. Clever man, my grandfather."

Knowing how torn-up M.J. had been at the time, Shelly agreed with her statement. But Shelly had always suspected that Bud McGuire had chosen his oldest granddaughter to succeed him, not only to keep her busy during that painful time but also because M.J. was the only McGuire, besides Bud, who had ever cared about or shown an interest in the store. Until she'd been sidetracked by Charles Sutton fifteen years ago. M.J. had been well on her way to stepping into Bud's shoes when the time came. She'd grown up working in the store, and attending the junior college in Ukiah, she'd been taking marketing and business classes, readying herself for the future.

M.J. squealed, distracting Shelly's thoughts. "Look! Look! He kissed her."

Shelly looked. "On the cheek," she said dryly. "Jeb does that to every female he meets. Doesn't mean a thing."

M.J. sighed. "Yeah. You're right. I'd forgotten that."

"Why are you so interested in Jeb's love life anyway?" Shelly cocked an eyebrow. "Is it possible that you've changed your mind about all men being lying, cheating, penis-brained Neanderthals, and you've set your sights on Jeb?"

"Good God, no! You know his reputation. He's left a trail of broken hearts from Santa Rosa to the Oregon border and beyond. Our boy gets around, and Jeb's the last man I'd be interested in." Melissa-Jane sniffed. "*If* I ever get interested in another man in *this* life. After Charles, scum-sucking lowlife bastard that he is, men aren't high on my list."

Thinking of Sloan, Shelly nodded. "Can't disagree with that."

"So. What brought you to town today? Just slumming or are you bored?"

"Not bored or slumming, I just didn't feel like hanging around the house by myself today. I needed a break."

M.J. studied her. Shelly's words were just a little too careless to be taken at face value. "The estate coming along OK? No problems?" she probed.

"Everything's fine. It'll be six months or so before everything is finally taken care of, but for now, most of it is just stuff that Sawyer can take care of."

"Sawyer-the-Lawyer," M.J. said in a singsong chant. "How is he to work with? I've finally convinced my grandfather that we ought to have an attorney on retainer, and I've been asking around."

Shelly hunched a shoulder. "You could do worse. He seems all right."

"Not a glowing recommendation. Don't you like him? Josh liked him pretty well. They were good friends."

"Maybe that's part of the trouble," Shelly admitted. "Sometimes, I feel like he's Josh's lawyer, not mine."

M.J. started to say something, but a glance out of the one-way window had her leaping to her feet and grabbing the gorilla mask. Shelly stared as M.J. jerked on the mask.

A look out of the window showed Danny Haskell, all decked out in his sheriff's office uniform, strolling down the aisle. When Shelly had left Oak Valley, Danny had been a gangly, big-eared, clumsy teenager, his feet too big for his growing body. Over the years she'd been gone, M.J. had sent pictures of herself and her family, as had Bobba, but Danny had not, and seeing him for the first time a month after she'd arrived back in the valley had been a shock. He had matured into a very handsome man and the fumble-footed, awkward, not-particularly-good-looking friend of her childhood was gone forever, replaced by the attractive man walking toward the office.

Broad-shouldered but slimly built, Danny sauntered closer with a loose-knit grace, his olive complexion and black hair and eyes the only outward heritage of his Indian great-grandmother. His badge was pinned on the front of his khaki shirt; his narrow waist ballooned with all the various accoutrements required by the sheriff's office. He was bareheaded, his unruly hair brushed back from his brow, and he had a goofy smile on his face—*that* hadn't changed one bit.

Shelly watched openmouthed as M.J., wearing the gorilla mask, chortled evilly and positioned herself in front of the window, one hand ready to slide the glass open.

Shelly rose and, peering over M.J.'s shoulder, saw Danny glance around, then hustle up to the mirrored window. He tapped it and thrust his face against it, contorting his handsome features into a horrible, ugly grimace, wagging his tongue and wiggling his fingers on either side of his head.

Startled, Shelly stepped backward; at that same instant M.J. gave a savage roar, flung back the sliding glass, and stuck her gorilla-masked head out the window.

Nose-to-nose with a snarling gorilla, Danny's eyes bugged, his mouth went slack, and he shot back from the window as if he had been fired from a cannon. He flew backward so fast that his feet tangled and he lurched sideways, his arms flailing wildly. Desperately, he grabbed, but his fingers could find no purchase on the slick metal shelving, and his gyrations sent boxes of cookies and loaves of bread flying. A rack of potato chips was his undoing, his own momentum slamming him into it. With a crash he hit the floor in a heap—chips, cookies, and bread half-burying him.

M.J. ripped off her mask. "Gotcha!" she cried gleefully, grinning from ear to ear.

"Jesus H. Christ!" Danny said from his position on the floor. "You scared me half out of my wits."

"Considering you only have half of them anyway, what's the big deal?" Melissa-Jane asked sweetly.

The sound of the crash brought several people running to the site, including Jeb. Hands on his hips, he surveyed the scene. Shaking his head, he glanced from Danny lying supine on the floor to Shelly's and M.J.'s laughing faces in the window.

"I should have known," Jeb said, a twinkle in his eyes. He shook his head again. "I don't even want to know what went on."

He turned and walked away.

"Hey," yelled Danny, a good-natured grin on his face, "there's an officer down here. Aren't you going to help me?"

Jeb kept on walking, saying over his shoulder, "Run along now, children, and try not to play too rough."

Danny looked over to Shelly and M.J. "Good one, Milly," he said as he stood up and began to pick up the scattered bags of chips. "I owe you—big-time."

"No. And don't call me Milly. You know I hate it. We're even now. You've been creeping up and scaring me for months. You deserved it."

Danny laughed. "I guess I did, but that doesn't let you off the hook." His face twisted maniacally, his hands formed claws, and in a deep, threatening voice, he intoned, "You'll never know a moment's peace from this day forward. Be warned—when you least expect it, I'll strike."

Melissa-Jane wrinkled her nose at him. "Go away. Some of us have work to do. And clean up that mess you made."

Grinning, she slid the window shut and slumped down in her chair. "Wasn't that great? Did you see the expression on his face? God! I thought I'd die laughing."

Shelly chuckled, nodding. "I know. I haven't seen him move that fast since we stirred up that nest of ground hornets when we were ten."

M.J.'s expression grew wistful. "We had some good times when we were kids, didn't we?"

"Yes, we did. And if today's exhibition is any indication, I'd say that some of us haven't put childhood far behind."

M.J. laughed. "Ain't it grand? I've been racking my brain forever to come up with a way to even the score, and Saturday, when I was in Ukiah, I happened to park in front of this party-supply place. I noticed that they had costumes, and when I spied the gorilla mask . . ." She grinned. "The rest is history."

They talked for a few minutes longer, then regretfully, Shelly stood up, and said, "Well, I'd better let you get back to work."

M.J. made a face, and Shelly felt a pang of guilt. Running the store took up an exorbitant amount of time, and M.J. had mentioned once that a ten-hour day was considered a short day for her. As for a day off . . . ha! She often worked twelve- and fourteen-hour days and had forgotten what a weekend was like. M.J. tended to grab an hour here or there and it had been one of the reasons, Shelly knew, that she'd been glad of her visit.

"You're probably right," M.J. admitted. "I've got a ton of stuff to do." She brightened. "Things have been a little slow lately though . . . maybe I could sneak off for a couple of hours or leave work early. You want to get together and go out to dinner Saturday night? I could introduce you to the nightlife of St. Galen's."

"What? Drinks at the only bar in town and then dinner in

one of the two greasy spoons? Or were you thinking of hitting Joe's Market for Mexican food or the Burger Place for burgers?"

"I'll have you know that we at McGuire's now offer fine take-out dining. You can choose from a selection of fried chicken, fried burritos, fried wontons, fried potatoes, and whatever else the meat department has fried up this week."

"Er, has the word *cholesterol* entered the vocabulary of any of Oak Valley's residents?"

"Probably, but some of these old cowboys would die before they admitted that they actually watch what they eat. Seriously, these days the store does a great roast chicken, and on Friday nights, we've even done a prime rib and some tri-tip roasts. Oh wait. I have an idea. I could get off Saturday afternoon, grab something for us to eat, and we could take it with us and go for a ride up to the old homestead." The telltale flicker of pain in Shelly's eyes made M.J.'s face fall. "Oh, Shell, I'm so sorry. I forgot. That's where he did it, wasn't it?"

Shelly forced a smile. "Forget it. I think that it would be an excellent idea to ride up there. I have to go up there sometime. Why not Saturday afternoon?"

"Are you sure? It won't give you the whim-whams or anything?"

"Listen, if spreading his ashes didn't bother me, at least, not as much as I feared, going to the cabin shouldn't be so terrible. Besides, like I said, I have to go up sometime, and seeing it with a friend might make it easier." Shelly frowned. "Although I better check with Maria to see what condition the place is in." A thought occurred to her. "I wonder if the sheriff's office is through with it?" She looked troubled. "Maybe the cabin isn't such a good idea. If it hasn't been touched since Josh . . ."

M.J. gave a delicate shudder. "I agree. He wasn't my brother, and it'd freak me out to walk in there and see blood-

stains or the chalk marks outlining where his body fell."
Aware that she had put her foot in her mouth again, M.J. said
wretchedly, "Oh, shit, Shelly. I am so sorry. Me and my big
mouth. I didn't mean to conjure up all the ugliness." She grimaced. "I was trying to make it better, and I only made it
worse."

Shelly smiled, albeit with an effort. "That's OK. I have to
get used to it. And I am dealing with it. I can talk about him
now without bursting into tears—most of the time, but it's
still hard." She shook her head. "Sometimes, I wake up at
night and think that it's all been a bad dream and that Josh is
going to come through my bedroom door with a mug of coffee in his hand and tell me to get my lazy rear out of bed."

Melissa-Jane groped for the right words. She hated seeing
that tragic look in Shelly's eyes, she didn't know what to say,
but she couldn't stand the awful silence either. Rushing into
speech, she said, "I know. I couldn't believe it when I first
heard the news. He just never seemed like the kind of guy to
do that sort of thing, and at the cabin at that. But then again
maybe it isn't so strange he did it there. It's just *when* he did
it that got me. I mean, if he'd done it right after—" Appalled
at where her rambling tongue had led her, M.J. stopped in
midsentence, her face the picture of appalled guilt.

Shelly regarded her fixedly. "Go on. 'If he'd done it right
after—' what?"

Melissa-Jane dropped her head on her desk. Pulling her
hair, she muttered, "Oh God! Why can't I learn to keep my
big mouth shut? Why am I cursed this way?"

"We'll worry about that later," Shelly said grimly. "Finish
your sentence."

M.J. raised her head, her big brown eyes distressed and
swimming with tears. "I don't suppose," she asked miserably,
"that we could just forget we had this conversation? That we

could go back a couple of minutes in time and simply decide upon a nice place to have our picnic?"

"Melissa-Jane, if you don't tell me what you know, and right now, I swear that I'll snatch you bald-headed. Tell me, dammit! You're supposed to be my best friend, and now I find out that you're keeping secrets from me."

"I didn't mean to," M.J. said tearfully. "Danny, Bobba, and I just didn't see any reason for you to know. Jeb agreed with us, and so did Maria and Nick. It wouldn't change anything and . . . and," she muttered, "if you force me to tell you, it'll only make you unhappy."

"Tell me," Shelly said through gritted teeth.

Not meeting Shelly's eyes, she fiddled with some papers on her desk. "Josh was having an affair with Nancy when she died four years ago," she finally blurted out. "They used to meet at the cabin—Nick caught them once, and Maria knew what was going on—Josh didn't hide it from her."

Shelly rocked back on her heels, her face white. "Nancy? Sloan's Nancy? Sloan Ballinger's wife, Nancy?"

M.J. nodded. "Yes. I guess they'd been carrying on for several months, secretly at first, but getting bolder and bolder the last few weeks before she died."

When she would have stopped, Shelly flashed her a look. "Go on. Tell me all of it. Don't leave out anything and, for God's sake, don't make me beg for details."

M.J. sighed. "OK, here's what I know. The night Nancy left Sloan she crashed her car and died. Several neighbors of theirs in Santa Rosa had heard them arguing, 'violently,' as the newspaper reported, before Nancy drove off from their house. One even said that he'd heard her yell that she was going to her lover, Josh Granger, and that she'd take Sloan for everything he owned. It was ugly, made more so by Sloan's loose-tongued neighbors. It would have been a lot better for everyone if the papers hadn't gotten ahold of the story. For a while, until it was determined that the crash really was accidental, there was a lot of public speculation that Sloan might actually be arrested for murder." M.J. grabbed a tissue from the holder on her desk and blew her nose. "It was just terrible. Even when Nancy's death was declared accidental, we couldn't just forget about it—there was fear that Sloan would come after Josh. Ross, you remember Sloan's brother, don't you?" At Shelly's curt nod, she rushed on. "Well, Ross, Jeb, all of us loosely banded together to keep an eye on Sloan, or rather to keep Sloan away from Josh." She grimaced. "Considering everything, it wasn't hard to imagine the pair of them shooting away at each other on Main Street."

Shelly sank down into the chair near Melissa-Jane's desk. She couldn't seem to get her thoughts straight. Josh and Nancy. Sloan's wife had been having an affair with her brother. Jesus! The thought made her sick. No wonder Sloan had torn up the check. It was amazing he'd even let her in his house. Josh had stolen his wife, plunged him into an ugly scandal, then sold him a right-of-way worth about two thousand dollars for a small fortune. It was a wonder she had escaped from Sloan's place with her head still intact.

Melissa-Jane peeped over at her. "Are you very angry? We didn't do it to hurt you. It was just that it happened four years ago, and if Josh hadn't told you, none of us felt that you needed to know. Your knowing wouldn't change anything, and no one, even Jeb, thought that Nancy's death had anything to do with Josh committing suicide—at least not four years after she died." Unhappily, she added, "We weren't exactly trying to hide anything. We just didn't think Josh's affair with Nancy was something you needed to deal with right now. We were trying to help." M.J. bit back a sob. "Oh, Shelly, please don't hate us . . . me."

Shelly wanted to be angry. She wanted to punch something, to stand up and scream and throw things around the office, to rail and shout at her friend, but she knew that Melissa-Jane spoke the truth. They had been trying to help—all of them in their own way trying to protect her. Their motives had been kind and honorable, but their kindness left her reeling with a sense of betrayal and a nasty taste in her mouth. They were her friends. She'd trusted them, and they had hidden the truth from her. It made her squirm to think of all of them knowing what had happened and letting her blithely go on her way. Didn't they realize that she was an adult? Didn't they understand that they did her no favors by hiding the truth? If she was ever to understand the man her brother had really been, she needed to know everything. Her mouth twisted. Even the ugly and the sordid.

Wearily, Shelly said, "No, I don't hate you. I'm hurt, probably angry, but I'll get over it."

"Are we still friends?"

Melissa-Jane's voice wobbled, and Shelly couldn't help responding to the misery she heard. She looked at M.J.'s tear-streaked face. "Yeah. We're still friends—always will be. Just don't . . . don't protect me anymore. It's been hard enough dealing with Josh's death, without some misguided friends tiptoeing around the fact that my brother seems *not* to have worn the halo I'd always put on him. If you know something, tell me. OK?"

Melissa-Jane nodded. "OK." She sniffed and wiped her eyes. "So," she said brightly, "we going on that picnic or not?"

Chapter Nine

⤞⤝

They never did decide on a date for the picnic. A quick look at the calendar revealed that M.J.'s schedule was a whole lot busier than she'd first thought.

"Damn!" she'd said. "Looks like we can't get together anytime soon—certainly not this weekend. Next Sunday would work, but that's Mother's Day and the FFA Parade and Rodeo." She beamed suddenly. "I get the boys that weekend and, friend that you are, I still wouldn't give up *that* time for you. Maybe we'll just leave it in the air and see what develops?"

Shelly concurred, and a few minutes later she drove away from McGuire's. Her thoughts were troubled as she considered what she had just learned about Josh . . . and her friends. Looking at it objectively, as objectively as she could, she didn't really blame Melissa-Jane and the others for keeping their mouths shut. They had been trying to help, she'd grant them that, and faced with the same situation, she probably would have done the same thing. Which didn't, she admitted grimly, make the hurt and feeling of betrayal go away completely. It would, she knew, in time; but at the moment, she was feeling raw and bleeding. And yet . . . and yet, she had now discovered another piece of the puzzle that added to her knowledge of Josh. Only weeks ago, she would have been outraged at M.J.'s story and leaped fiercely to his defense, but knowing about Nick, or rather believing in Nick, and some of the other things she had learned recently had made acceptance easier.

In her heart, she'd known that Josh wasn't perfect. She'd been aware for a long time that he'd always been a bit of a womanizer, but she'd excused it, telling herself it was just that he hadn't met the right woman yet. Maybe. She'd give a lot to know the motives behind Josh's affair with Sloan's wife. Nothing excused it—adultery was adultery, but she'd be able to understand it if it had been one of those tragic and unfortunate instances where love really had been blind and had struck willy-nilly. If the woman had been any other than Nancy Ballinger, she might have been able to convince herself that love alone had been the driving force behind the affair, but when it came to Josh and the Ballingers. . . . She sighed as she pulled up in front of the house.

Pushing away further speculation, she got out of the Bronco and climbed the steps to the house. Not in the mood for conversation and afraid she'd end up pumping Maria for more information about the affair, she stuck her head inside the kitchen doorway and let Maria know she was home and that she would be upstairs in the studio.

Alone in the studio, she wandered around, stopping now and then to stare out of the windows. What a disaster the day had been! If she'd known about the affair, she'd never have approached Sloan. Her mouth drooped. Especially not with money. *No wonder he tore up the check. He'd probably been furious. Try insulted, too*, she thought wryly. Knowing what she did now, she didn't blame him for tearing up the check—she'd have done the same thing. But why, she wondered bleakly, had he kissed her? Perhaps he'd been seeking a little revenge of his own?

And why had Josh started the affair with Nancy? He had to have known it could only end badly. Maybe he hadn't cared. She could almost see her brother deciding that an affair with Sloan's wife, bedding his enemy's wife, would be one more victory for the Grangers in their ongoing feud with the Ballingers. He certainly couldn't have foreseen Nancy's death, but maybe he'd been hoping for a violent confrontation with Sloan. She shook her head in mystification. To her, the crimes committed by her ancestors against the Ballingers and the Ballinger retaliations had been the stuff of legend—the stories made for interesting tales, but they had little to do with her life. For Josh it had been different. He believed in the feud. She'd once seen him cross the street to keep from meeting Sloan's father, Mark. And when he'd discovered her romance with Sloan. . . . She wiped back a tear. He'd been wonderful, comforting, helpful, but he had never understood how she had allowed herself to be taken in by a Ballinger. Probably, she decided moodily, because he had grown up steeped in the tradition of Granger hating Ballinger for no other reason than the fact that they were Ballingers. Had Josh embarked upon an affair with Sloan's wife intent upon perpetuating the bad feeling and mistrust that had started 150 years ago?

The thought made her ill, but she couldn't ignore it. Having an affair with another man's wife was tawdry enough, but to do it solely to cause trouble . . . Guilt flashed through her. How could she think such thoughts about Josh? He was her brother. She loved him. No, she had adored him, and here she was making him appear petty and vindictive . . . and he hadn't been. She couldn't deny that Josh had been impulsive, careless, sometimes selfish, but he'd also been generous, kind, and thoughtful.

But maybe he'd *really* loved Nancy. Maybe, right or wrong, Nancy Ballinger had been the one woman who had captured his heart. Maybe he couldn't help himself. Maybe the attraction between them had been too strong for either one of them to resist. Could he have been so despondent over Nancy's death four years earlier that he couldn't bear the loneliness anymore and had killed himself? It was feasible. And it wasn't as if he would have been obvious and open about his grief for another man's wife. Her brother had been a private man. Maybe he'd mourned and suffered in private until he couldn't stand the pain of Nancy's loss any longer and had ended it.

Feeling despondent herself, Shelly gave herself a shake. Whatever the reasons behind his death, it didn't change anything, and she wasn't doing herself any good standing around brooding about it. There was something she could do, however, and with a determined step she walked to the wall phone she'd had installed in the studio.

A telephone call to the bank in Ukiah put her mind at rest. A new cashier's check could be issued—in a few weeks— and a stop payment would have to be put on the original check. She did that and putting the phone down, felt a little better.

How she was going to get Sloan to keep the money still remained a problem, but her biggest worry about replacing the check had been relieved. And, she thought with a twist to her mouth, she had a little time to come up with a solution.

She had just turned away when the phone rang. Answering it, her mouth went dry when Sloan's voice came over the line.

"Shelly, is that you?"

She nodded, then realized he couldn't see her actions. "Yes, it is," she said, hating the breathless note in her voice.

"I got your number from information," he said. "Glad that it wasn't unlisted. Listen, I want to apologize for what happened today."

Shelly's mouth fell open, and she stared at the phone as if it had turned into a fudge cupcake. "You do?"

Sloan laughed, albeit wryly. "Yeah, I do. Look I appreciate the offer, but the deal was between Josh and me. Leave it alone."

Her fingers tightened on the receiver. "So you can continue to think that the Grangers are all crooks?"

He sighed. "I never thought that all the Grangers were bad . . . just certain ones, and you can't blame me for that—there are certain Ballingers that *your* family doesn't hold dear to their hearts either."

It was a valid point and an old argument between them. Even at the height of their love affair, they'd disagreed about whose family was to blame for all the bad feelings that existed. A sharp reply was on the tip of her tongue when she discovered that she didn't have the taste for continuing to fight ancient history anymore. *Maybe I've grown up*, she thought ruefully.

Relaxing slightly, she said, "OK, I'll agree to that."

"I beg your pardon? You're not going to take up the fight and come after me with tooth and nail?"

Smiling, she said, "Nope. Not this time." It seemed so normal to be teasing with him that Shelly found herself slipping into the easy familiarity that had once existed between them. "I'll concede that there were wrongs on both sides. Happy?"

"Stunned is more like it."

She laughed. "Well, enjoy the moment. It won't last."

"Do you realize," he said softly, "that we've been talking together for almost a minute and neither one of us has slammed down the phone?"

"Must be a record for us," she muttered. She had always found him hard to resist, and that seemed to be one thing that hadn't changed.

"You're wrong there. I seem to recall several occasions that we got along for hours at a time without arguing. . . ."

"That was a long time ago, Sloan. Don't go there."

He hesitated. "All right," he said slowly. "In the interest of our continuing, uh, peaceful relationship, I'll let it alone. For now."

There was almost a threat in those last words, and Shelly frowned. Deciding to get out while they were still treating each other like humans, she said politely, "Thank you for calling. And I accept your apology."

Sloan chuckled. "My, my, how formal we've suddenly become—but I guess it's better than having you throw knives at me."

"Good-bye, Sloan," she said firmly, and hung up the phone.

She stood there staring at the phone for a few minutes after she'd hung up on him. Wow. Who would have thought it? Sloan had actually called her and apologized. Even more amazing, they'd had a conversation, sort of, that hadn't ended in anger and recriminations. Of course, it didn't change her objective, she reminded herself. She *was* going to pay him for that right-of-way, but his telephone call left her feeling optimistic. They'd talked like two reasonable, adult human beings. Wow. Would miracles never cease?

Her spirits lifting, she left the studio, and a discreet rumble of her stomach reminded her that she was hungry. Wandering into the kitchen she wasn't surprised to find Maria serving Acey a cup of coffee. Greetings were exchanged and Shelly raided the refrigerator to find the makings for a sandwich. Maria reseated herself at the end of the table and just watched, but Shelly could tell she itched to push her aside and make the sandwich for her. They'd had a few mild tussles during the weeks since she'd come back home, but Shelly had gently got across her point that Maria didn't have to wait on her. Difficult to do without making Maria feel pushed aside and unwanted, but she'd managed, so far, to walk that fine line between doing for herself yet not offending Maria's sensibilities.

Shortly, a tuna, dill pickle, onion, and lettuce sandwich sitting before her, she took a place at the table across from Acey, who was eyeing her sandwich with revulsion. She grinned at him and took a bite.

"I offered to make one for you," she said after she swallowed that first tasty bite.

"I'm a baloney man, myself," he said. "The only thing from the sea that I eat is oysters, remember?"

Maria snorted, and Shelly rolled her eyes.

"Jesus, Acey," Shelly said, "give it a rest. We know how virile and sexy you are—you tell us every chance you get."

"Man can never be too sure the message is getting across," Acey said with a twinkle. "Don't forget advertising is what it's all about these days. And I believe it definitely pays to advertise."

Maria looked innocent. "*Sí*, this is true," she said straight-faced, but Shelly caught the teasing gleam in her dark eyes, "but I have also heard it told that there is much false advertising these days. The television and magazines and radio are always trying to sell us things that turn out to be duds."

"Yeah, that's right," Shelly piped in, laughter not far away. "Lots of advertising wasted on products that don't work."

Acey put his cup down and stood up. With great dignity, he said, "I'll have you know, I ain't no 'dud.' And I don't stay where I'm being insulted either."

Maria gasped, and Shelly's mouth fell open. Before their astonished gazes, he turned on his heels and marched out of the kitchen.

"Well, what was that all about?" Shelly asked bewildered. "Acey's the biggest tease I know, and he's always taken as good as he gets. He *likes* the zingers sent his way. I can't imagine what set him off today." Shelly took another bite of her sandwich. "Something sure didn't sit well with him."

"You don't think we hurt his feelings, do you?" Maria asked, her expression anxious.

"I hope not—I wouldn't hurt his feelings for the world. Surely he knows we were only teasing?"

"It's very strange. I have never known him to act in such a manner. Nick always gives him a bad time, calling him 'grandpa' and 'old man' and teasing him, and he never takes offense."

Shelly shrugged, thoroughly mystified by Acey's abrupt departure. Finished with her sandwich and the glass of milk she'd poured, she carried the plate and glass to the dishwasher. Thinking to find out what was bothering Acey, she hesitated. Cutting her eyes in Maria's direction, she considered the situation. This was too good an opportunity to miss.

She sat down across from Maria and taking a deep breath, she said, "Speaking of Nick. . . ."

Maria's face closed up, and she started to move from the table. Shelly's hand closed around her wrist, and she said, "Don't you think we should talk about Nick—the problem isn't going to go away."

"There is no problem," Maria said fiercely, jerking her arm from Shelly's grasp.

"That's not true, and you know it. Doesn't it bother you that Nick, your son, is suffering? You could end it by telling what you know."

Maria stood up, her face dark and angry. "This is none of your business! How dare you pry and probe. Leave it alone."

"Maria, we have to talk about it," Shelly said carefully.

"No, we do not." Maria leveled a cold look at Shelly. "I have nothing to say, and I will not say anything. You keep digging away at this, and I shall leave. I repeat, it is none of your business."

"What about Nick? Doesn't he deserve to know the truth?" Shelly said hotly, frustrated and angry at Maria's stubborn refusal.

Maria drew herself up stiffly. "Nick is none of your concern. He is *my* son, and I will not have him hurt."

Stalking away, Maria dragged on a sweater hanging by the door and said, "I'm going home. I'll see you tomorrow."

She exited the door, slamming it behind her.

Shelly winced. It seemed to be her day to upset people. Deciding that at least she'd try to make her peace with Acey, she got up and walked out of the kitchen.

Shelly left the house and walked out to the barn behind the house. Acey had worked for the Grangers off and on as long as she could remember. He had a small home and about a hundred acres of land at the edge of the valley, where he ran some cattle of his own, but she remembered he used to spend most nights sleeping in the small upstairs apartment in the barn. It was, he'd declared, his home away from home, and Shelly had grown up with Acey always somewhere nearby. He was an excellent cowboy and while he had his own herd and occasionally worked for other ranchers, the Grangers had first call on his time and loyalty. Josh said Acey should have retired years ago, and, in fact, Acey had been receiving a small annuity for about eight years from the Granger Cattle Company. But the old cowboy persisted in hanging around, always ready to lend a hand and give some blistering advice if needed—sometimes when not needed.

Her feet dragging, Shelly approached the barn. Acey had commandeered the apartment since she returned home, telling her that he didn't like the idea of her being alone at night in the house up here. She hadn't argued with him, liking the knowledge that he was somewhere around after Maria went home about two o'clock most afternoons. The apartment had originally been built as a place to stay when watching over or dealing with sick stock, but over the years it had become known simply as "Acey's pad," since he used it almost exclusively. It consisted of a large room with a kitchenette and cabinets in one corner, complete with an apartment-sized refrigerator and stove, and off to one side, a bathroom not much bigger than the closet right next to it. She remembered from her youth that the floor was covered by a hideously colored vinyl of uncertain vintage; the walls were knotty pine paneling; one window, over the sink, gave a view of the back of the house, the other, inside the barn, overlooked a large stall and the barn alleyway. A red Formica-topped table with four matching chrome chairs, a hide-a-bed in dark blue Naugahyde, a small square pine table with a nineteen-inch television, and a couple of cheap end tables with lamps that didn't match comprised the furnishings. It was certainly less than grand, but Acey always said the apartment in the barn suited him to a T. No mess, no fuss. He liked it that way, he'd said more than once over the years.

Climbing the stairs to the apartment, Shelly considered ways to ease into the conversation. Standing outside on the tiny landing before the shut door, she made a face. No easy way to handle this. She'd just have to come right out with it.

She sighed and knocked.

The door opened, and Acey stood before her, and for the first time, it really dawned on her that he wasn't a young man anymore. Acey had always seemed timeless, but just now, she realized that there was a small slump to his shoulders, that he looked almost frail. With his ready smile gone, his eyes without their usual glint of amusement and his face somber, he looked all of his seventy-three years.

Acey appeared startled to see her. "What's the matter?" he asked, anxiety in his voice. "Nothing's happened, has it? Maria's OK?"

She smiled. "No, nothing's happened and Maria's fine. I was just concerned about you."

"About *me*? Jesus, girl, I'm a grown man! You're the one who needs a keeper"—that sly smile of his lurked at the corners of his mouth—"or a man. Yep. A man. That's what you need. A big strong man like . . ."

"Acey, you'd better leave it alone," she warned, glad to see that his odd humor had vanished. "Besides, I think you're the one who needs a keeper."

"Now don't you start. It's bad enough that Nick hovers over me like a hen with one chick. I sure as hell don't need you doing it, too." He wiggled his eyebrows. "How can I chase the ladies if you two are going to start shadowing me. Bad for my reputation."

Whatever had set him off in the kitchen didn't seem to have had a lasting effect, and, relieved to see him his usual self, she decided not to press the issue. Still, she wanted to do a little probing. "I wanted to talk to you about that load of cattle that should be arriving sometime after the middle of the month, but you left before I had a chance to bring up the subject."

A faint tinge of red brushed across his cheekbones, but that was the only indication he gave that he'd acted oddly. "Well, yeah," he said, "sure. Come on in."

Since he didn't seem inclined to offer an explanation, Shelly followed his lead and entered the apartment.

A quick glance confirmed the same knotty pine walls, but the ugly vinyl floor of her youth had been replaced with a tough beige-and-brown indoor/outdoor carpet. The hide-a-bed had been re-covered in a bright blue plaid, the television was newer and bigger, but everything else looked pretty much the same. Acey, or someone, had added a black leather recliner and a round oak coffee table, and now that she took a closer look, Shelly could see that the counter was new and that the kitchen chairs, though still red, had been reupholstered.

Seated at the red Formica table, she watched as Acey made a pot of coffee in the coffeemaker on the counter. She smiled. There was a time when he'd sworn that no coffeemaker would ever replace his battered coffeepot, but it appeared he'd finally given in to modern conveniences. Hiding a smile, she noticed a microwave oven, sitting right next to a shiny chrome-and-black four-slice toaster oven and, lo and behold, there was even a small portable dishwasher tucked into one corner of the kitchenette. Looked like Acey was grudgingly entering the twenty-first century.

Coffee on, he joined her at the table. "Now what's this deal on the cattle."

She'd only used the cows as an excuse to see him, and for a moment her mind went blank. "Oh. Well," she mumbled, "er, I was wondering if you'd be around to help unload when they arrive. Nick'll help, but I'd like an extra pair of hands, ah, handy."

"That so?" Acey sent her a look—the same look he'd used in the past when he'd caught her shading the truth about having done chores, or where she'd been and who with and, as she had done then, she squirmed in her seat. He knew a red herring when he saw one, but he let it go by, adding mildly, "Yeah. I can help. Got any idea when they'll be here?"

"Not a sure date, but they're supposed to be leaving Texas toward the end of next week—the seller will let me know when the hauler picks them up. Once I know they're on the road, I'll have a better fix on the arrival date."

"So how many did you buy?" he asked as he got up and grabbed some cups.

"Thirty head—all I could afford."

He cocked a brow. "Lot a steak on the hoof." Putting a white mug of steaming coffee down in front of her, he sat down again, bringing his own mug of coffee with him from the counter.

Shelly grinned. "Not these babies. These babies are going to be the basis of the new and improved Granger Cattle Company."

Acey snorted. "Lot of money and work, girl. You'll be starting practically from the ground up. And you're female—don't forget that. I know, I know," he said at the expression on her face, "but you'd best face facts. Lot of redneck cattlemen out there who still think a woman's place is in the kitchen and bed." Hastily, he added, "Not me, of course. Honey, there'll be resistance and prejudice simply because you're a woman, doing what used to be called 'man's work.' You'll have to deal with it as well as the cattle operation itself, and raising cattle today ain't like it used to be. Lot of paperwork, lot of data required, lots of records to keep. It don't matter how fine your stock is, what bloodline you've got, if you don't have the paperwork to back it up, they won't count for squat—unless you're just raising for the slaughter market—then there's no reason to bother with purebreds." He took a sip of his coffee and glanced at her. "I assume you're going to want to stick to what Grangers always were—a cow/calf operation?" Shelly nodded, and he added, "That's a hard market, kid, takes time to build, make contacts, and while you'll have the Granger reputation to give you a little boost, you're gonna have to prove yourself to some hardheaded, tight-fisted old cattlemen. It ain't gonna be easy, and it ain't gonna happen overnight. You can't start this thing, and then six months from now hightail it back to New Orleans because the excitement's worn off. You sure you're in for the long haul?"

Shelly's chin came up. "I'm home for good, Acey—I told you that. I'm not going back to New Orleans. And as for being in it for the long haul, you bet your bony ass, I am. So will you help me?"

"Well, hell, girl, I was wondering when you were gonna get around to asking me. Nick's all fired up about it, says you two are partnering up. Have to tell you, I was beginning to feel downright left out."

Delight washed through her at his words. She'd never doubted that Acey would help her, but it was great to have him confirm it. She did have some concerns though, and bending toward him, she asked, "What about your own herd? Besides, aren't you supposed to be retired? Seems to me when I was going over Josh's papers, I saw that both you and Maria are receiving income from an annuity my father set up years ago as a retirement plan."

"Yep. I know. Josh insisted I take it when I turned sixty-five, but dammit, Shelly, retirement is for sissies. What the hell would I do all day? Cattle and horses are my life—there ain't nothing I'd rather do." He grinned. "'Cept, of course, chase wimmen."

Shelly rolled her eyes. "What about your cattle?" she persisted.

"Ah, hell, honey, they're just a bunch of ornery range cows I keep for amusement—cutting, roping and such. Been thinking about selling 'em off and leasing the pasture to my next-door neighbor."

"Acey, I'll be honest, I can't afford to pay you a big salary. Josh left things in a mess, and maybe a dollar above minimum is about as much as I can pay you."

He looked insulted and for a moment Shelly feared that he'd stomp out of the room. *Touchy old devil*, she thought affectionately. *Proud, too.*

"I'm already getting a pension from Granger Cattle Company," he growled. "If you want to pay me more, I won't argue with you, but why don't we settle on me moving permanent into this here apartment. You'll have to let me use your washer and dryer for my clothes, and I'll have to build a kennel for my dogs. I've got a cat I like, and there's my horses, but you let me move in and I'll only charge you three bucks an hour for any work I do."

Shelly considered arguing with him about the money, but the look on his face told her she'd better leave it alone. Having Acey living on the ranch wasn't a problem at all, in fact, it sounded like a good idea to her. She frowned. "But what about your house?"

"I can rent it. Got a fellow's been after me for months— city type—wants a long-term lease. I like my house, but it'll be there when I decide climbing the stairs to this place is getting too hard." He grinned at her. "Figure that'll happen about the time I get too old to notice a pretty girl."

"That'll never happen," Shelly said with a laugh.

"So, we got a deal?"

"You betcha!"

❧

The next days flew by. Acey became the self-appointed foreman of the small operation, and Shelly found herself, at his orders, rising before dawn and meeting him in the kitchen for breakfast. The first morning she'd staggered downstairs and found him at her table eating the scrambled eggs and ham Maria had cooked, she asked grumpily, "It's bad enough I have to get up while it's still dark outside, but did I agree to this? I mean feeding you, too?" Acey studied her sleep-rumpled features, a hint of smile lurking under that big white handlebar mustache. "As I recollect, you never were a morning person. Looks like you haven't changed— still cranky and crabby when you first get out of bed. As for feeding me . . . seems sort of foolish, for me to gulp down some coffee and toast, all alone in my place in the barn when there's company and Maria's fine cooking just a few steps away. Of course, if you don't want me to . . ."

Shelly had snagged herself a mug of coffee and after taking the first ambrosia-like sip had grinned at him. "Shut up, Acey. You know you're welcome."

He grinned back at her. "Yep. Just like I figured." He shot her a teasing glance. "Can't say you're at your best when you first wake up, but never figured you'd deny me a meal."

That morning meeting worked out very well, and Shelly was surprised she hadn't thought of it. Lingering over the remnants of Maria's cooking, with the occasional tart comment from Maria, who had returned to her normal self, and joined now and then by Nick, they had a chance to discuss the progress or lack of it every morning before the day's work began. She looked forward to those morning meetings, liking the homey feeling of the kitchen, the scent of bacon or ham and coffee lingering in the air, the give-and-take of exchanging ideas with the others, the strong sensation of having really returned home. Josh might be gone, but the mornings with Acey, Maria, and Nick gave her a sense of having a family.

Acey might tease and joke, but he was no gentle taskmaster. The work was hard, backbreaking, and physical—tearing out old fencing, mainly around the barn, and replacing it with strong, new material. The cattle chute had to be completely rebuilt, as well as new holding pens and, on the back side of the barn, a feeding area, complete with shelter and manger. On Acey's advice, Shelly had hired a couple of young men in the valley who were skilled in that kind of work, but she still did her share of lugging material to and fro and digging fence posts and stretching fence. Nick was there as often as he could be, and Shelly was thankful for the added power of his young muscles.

By the time the Mother's Day weekend rolled around, a week and a half later, Granger Cattle Company seemed to be almost a reality. The cattle from Texas were on their way and scheduled to arrive on Monday. Acey had moved lock, stock, and barrel into the apartment. A good-size kennel holding his three cow dogs had been constructed at the side of the barn; his horses occupied three of the eight stalls in the barn, and his truck and trailer had taken up residence next to the kennel. His cat, Mouser, a bright calico, was proving her worth, rustling around in the barn and grounds looking for prey, when she wasn't winding around someone's feet expecting a pat on the back. Shelly liked Mouser, she just wished the cat would stop presenting her with little gifts consisting of dead mice and gophers. Ugh.

They'd worked straight through last weekend without stopping, but Acey had declared they all needed a break and dismissed everyone about four the previous afternoon, declaring they'd best be back at eight o'clock sharp on Monday. Despite not having to get up at the crack of dawn this morning, to her astonishment, Shelly had found herself rolling out of bed, not too much after 6:00 A.M. Putting off her shower, she'd thrown water in her face, brushed her teeth, and, after dragging on an old flowered wrapper, wandered downstairs. Maria had weekends off, and the kitchen seemed lonesome without her bustling around. The coffeemaker had been left set up, and a few minutes later, the fragrance of fresh coffee filled the air.

Sipping her coffee, Shelly wandered outside, her feet automatically taking her to the barn. She prowled around the barn, viewing the results. She was walking stiffly this morning—and had been for the past week. She ached in places she hadn't known *could* ache, and she had discovered muscles she'd forgotten she had. A couple of Tylenol had become a nightly ritual, but it was worth every twinge, every creak, and every ache when she looked at what had been accomplished so rapidly.

The once-dilapidated cattle chute bristled with new lumber, and the long manger was finished, only the roofing of the cover of the feeder area yet to be completed. Stout new fencing had sprouted up all around, and several tons of early grass hay had been delivered and, covered with big blue tarps in case of a late rain, was waiting to be stacked in the barn. She grimaced. Monday's first chore.

There was so much more to be done, Shelly thought with a sigh, more fencing, more sorting pens, a new bull pen, although Beau seemed perfectly happy in his current quarters, and before the cattle could be turned loose they'd have to rebuild all the broken-down fences. First on the best pasture, then farther afield as time and the operation allowed. Acey had been right—it *was* going to be a long haul, a long, hard, tough haul. But even knowing what lay in front of her, her joyous feeling of satisfaction couldn't be tamped down— there was still a ton of work to do, but the most immediate needs seemed to be taken care of—she hoped.

Smiling, she grabbed a flake of alfalfa and walked over to Beau's pen. At her approach, he let out a bellow of welcome and trotted right up to the fence. She threw him the flake and even reached through the rail and gave his glossy black hide a pat. He was an Angus bull, it was true, but he had become such a pet during the past weeks that Shelly didn't fear him—at least, as long as she was on this side of the fence and he was on the other. She watched him toss the flake around and laughed at his antics. Thank God they had Beau. There was some concern about his fertility, but no one doubted that they'd get at least one calf crop from him. But they *had* to get that one crop from him. It was vital and could make the difference to whether Granger Cattle Company reestablished itself . . . or not.

Acey ambled out of the barn, looking spiffy in a red-and-blue-plaid shirt, a scarlet bandanna tied rakishly around his throat, and new dark blue jeans, a smart crease running down the length of the legs. His black boots gleamed, and he was wearing his best hat—a black Stetson with wide scarlet hatband.

"Jesus, girl," he exclaimed when he took in her attire. "Don't tell me *that's* what you're wearing for the parade?"

"Parade?" Shelly asked, her expression blank. "What parade?"

"Now you ain't been gone that long—you can't have forgotten this is the Mother's Day weekend and the FFA Field Day. Parade. Junior Rodeo. Dance. Remember?"

"Oh, wow. I did forget," she confessed, wondering how that had happened. How could she have forgotten one of the most important social functions in the valley? Even M.J. had mentioned it, but with everything else on her mind, the Mother's Day events had gone completely out of her head.

St. Galen's hosted three big community events a year. The Mother's Day FFA Field Day was the first, followed on the first weekend in August by the Blackberry Harvest and ending with the Labor Day Rodeo. To outsiders, it all might look rinky-dink and small-time, but in the valley each event was eagerly planned and looked forward to by the entire community. Relatives and friends who lived all over the state planned their vacations and trips home around those dates, and those weekends would find the valley flooded with smiling, laughing visitors reestablishing bonds of friendship and family. If St. Galen's had a social season, it started with the Mother's Day weekend and culminated with attendance at the Oak Valley Rodeo on the Labor Day weekend. The only other busy time was deer season, and for the week before it opened, the highway into the valley would see a steady stream of pickup trucks and campers, mostly strangers, passing through on their way to the Mendocino National Forest. The hunters did provide increased business, and their arrival was happily greeted by the merchants each fall.

"Jesus, Shelly! Forget the FFA Field Day?" Acey shook his head. "You've been away too long, my girl. Now go get prettied up—I'm taking you and Maria to the Cowboy Breakfast at the Masonic Hall." He wiggled his eyebrows. "You won't want to miss it—think that red-haired widow I've been seeing is one of the cooks this year. You and Maria can check her out—see if I'm getting in over my head. I've got the day all planned. Breakfast, parade, rodeo, and then the dance."

Shelly smiled, shaking her head. "Gee, I didn't know you were also my social secretary."

"Somebody's got to be, girl. Left to your own devices, you'd never find a man. You ain't getting any younger, you know. Time's a passing. You don't want to end up a lonely old maid, do you?"

Shelly made a face. "Acey . . ."

"Now don't start. Been thinking a lot about you, woman alone and all that stuff. I know it's old-fashioned and don't fit with all the newfangled Women's Lib crap, but I'm telling you straight: You need a man. Not just any man, even I know that. You need a good man, one with strong ties to the valley. But he's got to be flexible. Got to understand that you're an independent woman with a mind of your own." He grinned. "Someone like me—only younger. Lot younger. And maybe more handsome, but that'd be hard to imagine."

Shelly snorted. "Acey, I appreciate your concern, but trust me on this—if I wanted a man, I could find one."

He glared at her. "Then why haven't you? Fine-looking young heifer like you. You ought to be married, but to the right man. I worry, girl. I worry that some slick-talking dude's going to slide into town and sweep you off your feet while you're all vulnerable and such. Like I said, you need a man, but it's got to be a man who can be trusted to do right by you."

"And I suppose you've found this paragon for me?" she said through gritted teeth.

Acey grinned like a cherub. "Yep. He's meeting us for breakfast. Sloan Ballinger."

Chapter Ten

Shelly wasn't certain how it happened, in fact she'd been certain that she'd grow old and gray before she stepped one foot off the place in order to meet with Sloan Ballinger, but forty-five minutes later, she was riding with Acey and Maria on their way to the Cowboy Breakfast. Acey had let her say her piece, then he had looked at her, and asked simply, "You want everyone in town to think you're afraid of meeting him? The fact that he's joining us for breakfast isn't a big secret. Lots of people be interested in how that turns out. Want 'em to think you're a coward?"

"Damn you! I'm no coward. And I'm sure as hell not afraid of Sloan Ballinger."

"Couldn't prove it by me," Acey drawled. "I can only think of one reason you're acting all skittish and such." He looked thoughtful. "Probably what everyone else will think, too. Including Sloan."

She'd thrown him a furious glance. "Has anyone ever told you that you are an interfering, manipulative, old devil?"

Acey rubbed the side of his jaw. "Now as I think on it, Sloan said something about me being a meddling old bastard." He grinned at her. "Sloan's not as polite as you are."

Shelly choked back a laugh. "You're impossible," she said as she started toward the house. "And yes, I'll go with you to the damned breakfast. Can't have the whole town

think that there was ever a Granger who backed down from
a meeting with a Ballinger. Let me get showered and dressed,
then I'll be ready."

"Take your time, I've got to hook up the trailer and load
my horse—I'm riding in the parade with the Oak Valley Riding Club. Part of the color guard."

Once they reached town, they detoured down Main Street,
where Acey left his trailer alongside several others owned by
various members of the Oak Valley Riding Club. The street
was crowded with vehicles, horses, dogs, and people of all
ages getting ready for the parade. There were a couple of
homemade floats, some members of the fledgling high
school band, a half dozen feathered Indian dancers and an interestingly arrayed contingent from the St. Galen's Women's
Club. It was their fond wish that they represented blackber-
ries, promoting the Blackberry Harvest held in August, but in
their purple tights and interestingly lumpy costumes, green,
leaf-shaped hats on their heads, they looked more like grapes
to Shelly. Ripe grapes, plump and fully packed. More participants were arriving by the minute, and it took Acey a bit to
break free of the swelling ranks.

All too soon for Shelly's liking, they were parking near
the Masonic Hall and exiting the truck. Nervously, she
smoothed down her black jeans. They were made of a butter-
soft suede and fit her like a glove. A tight glove. She had
paired the jeans with a long-sleeved emerald green shirt that
intensified the green of her eyes. The material flowed snugly
over her breasts before disappearing into the waistband of
her jeans, where a narrow black belt with a Black Hills gold
buckle emphasized her small waist and slender hips. The
shirt was open at the neck and a green-and-black-checked
silk scarf was tied jauntily around her throat, gold earrings
winked through her cloud of tawny hair, and she wore a pair
of black Justin Ropers on her feet. *City meets cowboy coun-*

try, she thought wryly as she followed Acey and Maria into the pink cinder-block building that housed the Masonic Hall.

They entered the large room set aside for the Cowboy Breakfast. Portable tables and metal folding chairs had been set up; syrup, butter pats, salt, and pepper were set in the middle of each table. About two dozen people were scattered around the tables, laughing, talking, and eating. It was a large room with a utilitarian beige vinyl floor, and was capable of holding ten times as many people as were present without overcrowding. A row of high, narrow windows in the opposite wall allowed plenty of natural light. In one corner, near the serving window at the far end of the room, there was a table holding a pair of coffee urns; Coffeemate, packets of sugar, styrofoam cups, paper napkins, and plastic spoons lay nearby. Looking over the waist-high counter of the wide serving window, she could see several local people bustling around in the small kitchen as they cooked the usual fare: pancakes, scrambled eggs, and link sausages.

Shelly had told herself that she'd dressed so carefully with the knowledge that she'd be meeting people she hadn't seen in years, and it was for them that she had taken such great pains with her makeup and clothing. The moment Sloan uncurled his long length from behind the table where he'd been waiting for them, and their eyes met, she knew she'd deluded herself. There had been nothing public-spirited behind her actions. She'd dressed for one man and one man alone. Sloan Ballinger. Dressed deliberately and provocatively to remind him of all that he had thrown away seventeen years ago. *Eat your heart out, you two-timing bastard.*

There was an electric silence as their eyes met and clashed. Acey and Maria were standing right beside her, but she knew that the charged atmosphere had nothing to do with the presence of the others. Her heart was banging like a steam hammer, and her pulse was racing as she and Sloan stared at each other, the air between them seeming to crackle and hiss with sexual energy. For a split second, everyone stopped what they were doing to take in the scene of Ballinger confronting Granger, then the moment passed and Sloan was smiling and crossing the room to greet them and everyone went back to what they had been doing before their arrival.

They exchanged greetings, Sloan shaking Acey's hand and dropping a kiss on Maria's cheek. Shelly steeled herself to act casually, but when Sloan moved in front of her and smiled down at her, her mind went blank. The warmth of his big body hit her first, then the scent that she had always considered uniquely his tangled in her nostrils. The next second, his hands were on her shoulders, and his mouth was taking hers.

It took her a second to react, then she stiffened and jammed her hands between their bodies. "Let me go!" she hissed, furious.

"Easy, easy," Sloan whispered against her mouth, the taste of the coffee he'd been drinking lingering on her lips. "Everyone's watching. Don't want to give the good folks something to talk about, do we?"

She pasted a smile on her face. "Point taken," she said through clenched teeth. "But if you don't let go of me, in about ten seconds, I'm going to show you . . . and the good folks, of course, what a well-placed knee can do to a conceited son-of-a-bitch like you."

Amusement glittered in his eyes. Prudently taking a step back, he said, "Believe me, I don't doubt it for a moment. Truce?"

She shrugged, aware of the covert looks being sent their way. "Why not? I think I can behave myself long enough for us to eat breakfast."

"Well, that'd be a first," he said, as he guided her to stand in line behind Acey and Maria.

Ignoring him, she picked up a napkin and plastic utensils from the table near the serving window.

"Why bless my soul," said a familiar voice. "Acey said that he was going to bring you along this morning, but after all that fine New Orleans food, I didn't believe you'd settle for pancakes and sausage." The words were said kindly, and there was a gentle twinkle in the blue eyes of the tall, bald-headed man who smiled at Shelly.

"Mr. Smith! I didn't expect to see you here," Shelly exclaimed, an answering smile on her lips. "I thought for sure that you'd be busy at the store."

"And miss slaving away over a hot stove for the Chamber of Commerce?"

Shelly chuckled and shook her head. "No, I guess not." Tom Smith, McGuire's longtime butcher and manager of the meat department, had cooked at the Cowboy Breakfast for as far back as she could remember. He was one of those individuals who always volunteered to help the community, or anyone in need for that matter, and he belonged to just about every service organization that Oak Valley supported. He worked hard for all the different clubs, whether it was the Lions Club, the Masonic Lodge, the Chamber of Commerce, the Oak Valley Riding Club, or the Oak Valley Rodeo Committee to name a few; Tom Smith could always be relied upon to lend a helping hand. Shelly had always liked him, and his wife, Debbie, but she had a particular soft spot for Tom. For a moment she remembered those childhood days when he seemed always to have time for a friendly word and a Tootsie Roll to press into a small, grubby hand.

They talked for a few moments as Tom deftly turned pancakes on the wide black iron griddle on the stove. She recognized two of the people busy cooking up the other food

items. Dell Hatch, another old-time resident, a cattle rancher
nearly as round as he was tall, and his wife, Sandy, who
flashed Shelly a friendly smile as she scrambled eggs. There
was also a younger couple, a dark-haired woman and sandy-
haired man, in the kitchen, and an older woman helping with
the breakfast; Shelly didn't recognize any of them.

Greetings, introductions, and conversation kept her dis-
tracted until her plate was heaped high and she was standing
in front of the coffee urns. She had poured her coffee and was
following Acey and Maria to one of the tables when it occurred to her that someone had been missing in the kitchen.
As they sat down, Acey and Maria on one side of the table,
Shelly and Sloan on the other, Shelly said, "1 didn't notice
any redheads in the kitchen. Didn't you say your widow was
going to be cooking?"

Acey looked innocent. "By golly, you're right! She wasn't
there, was she?" He shook his head. "Women. Can never
count on them to keep their word."

Sloan choked on his coffee, and Maria snorted and poked
Acey in the ribs. "On the other hand, most women," Shelly
said sweetly, "are not sly and sneaky like some people I
know."

Sloan put down his coffee and advised, "You know, Acey,
if I were you, I'd leave that one alone and just eat. Scrambled
eggs and sausage taste a whole lot better than crow."

"Figure you're right," Acey said, a gleam in his eyes.
"After all, you've eaten so much of it."

Shelly ducked her head, hiding a smile.

Sloan grinned. "Now that's one that *I'm* going to let lie
right there."

"Acey Babbitt, shame on you!" scolded Maria. "Sloan is
your guest. You're being rude."

A slight flush stained Acey's cheeks. "Aw, Maria, we were

just funning. Sloan can give as good as he can take. Don't
you worry none about him."

Maria sniffed and dug into her pancakes. Everyone else
did the same, and it was then that Shelly noticed the little
Tootsie Roll lying on the side of her plate. A small burst of
warmth went through her, and she glanced over toward the
serving window. Tom Smith looked up just then, and, catching her eyes on him, he grinned and winked.

"I have one, too," Sloan said beside her, as he twirled one
of the familiar red-and-white-wrapped chocolate rolls under
her nose.

"I'd think," she said primly, "that you'd be too old to have
gotten Tootsie Rolls from Mr. Smith."

"Hell, honey," he murmured, "I'd lay odds that there isn't
a person in this valley under the age of fifty who hasn't gotten Tootsie Rolls from Tom Smith at one time or another."

Breakfast took a while. Several people already seated and
eating knew Shelly from years ago and wandered over to
welcome her back to the valley. As others who recognized
Shelly came strolling in for breakfast, it was inevitable that
they, too, stop at the table and exchange greetings. Not by
one lifted brow or startled expression did anyone let on that
there was something unusual about a Ballinger and a
Granger sitting side by side. They might not have indicated
it, but Shelly knew that she and Sloan were going to be the
main topic of quite a few conversations today . . . and
tonight . . . and next week and probably even next month.

Less than a half dozen people in the valley knew the details of their long-ago relationship, and for that she was
thankful. Had it been common knowledge, speculation
would have been rampant, and it was bad enough knowing
that everyone was watching them and wondering about them.

She had enjoyed the meal and she had enjoyed renewing
old acquaintances, but she'd have been lying if she hadn't

admitted that she was glad when the four of them rose to leave. Being the object of covert looks, even kind ones, had never appealed to her.

After dumping their plates and cups in one of the big lined plastic garbage cans set against the back wall of the room, head held high, Shelly allowed Sloan to escort her from the building. Outside, she turned to bid him a polite good-bye, but was immediately forestalled when Acey said, "Hope you'll excuse Maria and me—Maria's part of the judging committee, and I've got to get my horse unloaded and readied for the parade." He pulled out a battered stainless-steel pocket watch and muttered, "Parade'll start, if we're lucky, only an hour late."

Before Shelly's startled gaze, Acey and Maria turned away and hustled on down the street. She could have sworn that she heard Acey smother an evil chuckle as they walked away. Maria had the decency to glance back, but then she bent her head toward Acey and giggled at something he said.

"I think," Sloan said thoughtfully, watching the departing pair with mingled emotions, "that you have been rather cavalierly handed off to me for the day."

"And I think not!" Shelly muttered. "Don't worry about me, I can find someone to run me back to the house."

"And miss the parade? After Acey went to such lengths to get you here and provide you with an escort?" Sloan asked, his hand clasping her arm and holding her at his side. He might not care for Acey's heavy-handed tactics, but he sure as hell didn't mind taking advantage of them.

"Even after that," she said, a note of near panic in her voice. If there was one thing Shelly had learned over the years, it was to recognize a dangerous situation and either defuse it or get away from it.

She'd thought she was over Sloan, but even if her mind was convinced of that fact, her treacherous body was not. All through breakfast she'd been conscious of Sloan sitting right beside her, conscious of the warmth of his body, of his size, of his powerful masculinity. It wasn't anything that he did, he was just *there*, and just the sight of his long-fingered hand reaching for a cup of coffee, the sound of his whiskey-rich voice, the brush of his arm against hers had sent a shaft of heated excitement through her. She tried to tamp it down, tried to ignore it; but she was unbearably aware of every move he made, every breath he took, and aware of her own body's response in ways that worried her. Glumly she admitted that she'd been humming with plain old carnal attraction from the top of her head to her toes curling in her boots since the moment their eyes had met this morning.

She sighed. Oh, hell. Now what should she do? It was dangerous to stay, but the temptation to do so was overwhelming. She'd been so sure, so positive that time and her own maturity would have lessened his appeal to her, but she discovered she was wrong. Dead wrong. In spite of all the years between them, the hurt, the lies, the mistrust, the old attraction was still there. She didn't know how to defuse the sexual awareness that simmered between them, didn't know if she wanted to, so that left getting away from temptation her only option.

Forcing a smile, she glanced at him. "Look, I know that Acey dragooned you into this—just as he did me. We had breakfast together and we didn't kill each other or even start a fight. Let's quit when we're ahead, OK?"

The expression in his eyes was hard to read. "Don't tell me you're afraid?" he taunted, pulling her closer. "A Granger afraid of a Ballinger?"

Her chin lifted. "Being afraid has nothing to do with it— and for the record, I'm not. I'm sure, however, that you have other things you'd rather do than drag me around with you all day."

He grinned. "Is that so. Figured that out all by yourself?"

Her teeth ground together. "I'm trying to be polite, but you're making it damned difficult."

"Polite? Honey, you haven't been polite to me since the first day we met and you threatened to break my head open with that lug wrench of yours. Why start now?" Eyeing her mutinous expression, he said gently, "Shelly, it's only a damned parade."

Put that way, her objections seemed silly. But it wasn't the parade that gave her pause; it was the simmering sexual awareness between them that had her ready to hightail it back to the house and away from temptation. She'd said she wasn't afraid of him, but she was lying through her teeth. The power he seemed to wield over every nerve in her body was terrifying. And mesmerizing. And exciting. Dammit!

He gave her arm an impatient shake. "Come on, Shelly, what do you think is going to happen if you spend the day with me? We'll be in full view of most of the population of Oak Valley." His mouth twisted. "Believe me, it's highly unlikely that I'll do something rash like attack and ravish you with so many witnesses around." He didn't know why it had become so important that he keep her at his side, but it had—vitally so. He'd been furious with Acey for manipulating the meeting, but now that it had happened and the world hadn't exploded, he realized that he'd be a fool not to take advantage of the opportunity Acey had handed him. He *wanted* to spend the day with her. He grimaced. *Ah, hell, face it, Ballinger*, he thought, *you just want* her . . . *any way you can get her.*

"OK," Shelly said abruptly. "Let's go watch the parade." She flashed him a look. "But I'm warning you, Sloan, don't get any ideas. I still hate you."

Sloan laughed and, pulling her along with him, walked toward the highway that ran through the center of town. It was a short walk; the Masonic Hall fronted on the highway, and the area they'd been in, at the rear of the building, was only about a block away.

The parade route was short. Probably not more than a quarter of a mile long, as it ambled down the highway, heading north. It started at the corner of Main Street, just south of McGuire's Market, and traveled straight through the main part of town to Soward Street, where it turned right and worked its way back to Main Street, where it had all started. There was nothing commercial about the parade. It was just a group of hometown residents dolled up and strutting their stuff for friends and neighbors.

Shelly enjoyed the parade. One of the big red fire trucks from the volunteer fire department led the parade, and she recognized Bobba Neal behind the wheel. He recognized her, too, and a large smile crossed his face. Next came the Field Day Sweetheart, a tall blond teenager on a skittish bay horse, her rhinestone-studded crown gleaming in the sunlight. It was fun to see the silly float the local feed-and-hardware store had put together on the rear of the large flatbed truck that they used to bring in goods from outside the valley. It was rigged to look like a jail and a half dozen prominent members of the community hung out the barred windows, yelling greetings and insults as the truck slowly made its way down the highway. With delight, she saw that Danny Haskell was one of the convicts. He spotted her, waved madly, and grinned. The high school band came next, drums a-banging; grinning members of the 4-H and Future Farmers of America marched behind the band; then came the Indian dancers, hooting and whooping as they moved down the street; another float, this one sponsored by McGuire's Market, followed. The float was made up to resemble a saloon and had a bunch of gamblers and saloon girls prancing around. One of the saloon girls, she saw with a smile, was M.J. And she hooted with laughter when she realized one of the other women was Cleo, looking racy in a low-cut, skintight, red satin gown that clashed garishly with her bright red hair. The Women's Club entry strolled past, laughter and catcalls following them. The ladies returned it all with interest. A towheaded little boy in his finest cowboy duds rode by on his spotted pony, then a pair of young girls dressed as angels, or fairies, Shelly couldn't decide which, came by, their chestnut horses bedecked with pink ribbons. They were followed by a couple of small metal carts decorated with purple-and-white crepe paper pulled by fat little ponies, their proud drivers not more than ten years old. Next was an old farm wagon freshly painted a bright blue, and some ranchers and their wives waved to the crowd lining the highway. A fancy black-and-gold vis-à-vis, a pair of mules pulling it, rolled by. The Oak Valley Riding Club was the next-to-the-last participant, Acey riding tall in the saddle, the California flag held proudly at his side. Shelly didn't recognize the other two members of the color guard, but she thought she saw a couple of friends she remembered from her youth riding along with other members of the club. The last entry was the manure sweepers and laughter and friendly gibes followed them as they swept and cleaned up after the horses.

Throughout the parade, Shelly and Sloan had stood near the judging stand in front of the old St. Galen's Hotel and had had a good look at each entry as it had stopped before the judges to receive its awards. Hank O'Hara had manned a scratchy and imperfect loudspeaker and he had kept the crowd laughing with his comments as he announced the winners. Another teenage girl, probably the runner-up in the Sweetheart contest, handed out the ribbons.

Shelly had forgotten the genuine enjoyment the community took from the parade. Looking at it through sophisticated eyes, it was probably pretty rinky-dink and small-time, but she loved it. Certainly it bore no resemblance to the fabulous Mardi Gras Parade in New Orleans, but she wouldn't have traded the experience for a handful of diamonds. What made it so unique and fun was that, besides her friends, she recognized half the participants and realized that just about every spectator lining the short route had a family member or a friend in the parade. There was a sense of community pride in the air. The affection and delight everyone felt was almost palpable. It left her feeling proud and glad and, in an odd way, as if she really had come home.

The parade might have held most of her attention, but she hadn't been unaware of the looks she and Sloan had gotten. Some of the looks were just plain curious, some were startled, several were friendly, a few were disapproving and tight-lipped, and several more were openly speculative. Sloan had chosen a very public place for them to watch the parade, and Shelly wondered if he'd done it on purpose. More importantly, she wondered how much longer she could stand here appearing relaxed and at ease when she was so painfully conscious of Sloan's big body at her back. His heat seemed to envelop her and every time he leaned over, which had been frequently, to point out something of interest, the brush of his warm lips against her ear had been excruciatingly erotic. Her entire body was tingling, her breasts were heavy and aching, and she knew that her lower body was in exactly that same state—aroused and ready.

It might have comforted her, if it didn't terrify her, to discover that Sloan was in precisely the same state. Maybe worse. He had managed to keep his hands off her during the parade, but he'd had to fight continually the urge to drop his arms around her and pull her back against his hungry body. Every time she moved, she brushed against him, and the scent of her perfume, Red, teased and tantalized his senses. That cloud of tawny hair tickled his nose, and it was all he could do not to grab her and bury his head in the gleaming strands. Oh, yeah, and when he so politely leaned over to point out some facet of the parade, he'd wanted to nip that little ear of hers so badly that he was damn near ready to howl when the parade finally ended. He was heavily, painfully aroused, and if she moved that tight butt of hers against him one more time . . . well, he wouldn't be responsible for what happened. He either had to put a little distance between them, he decided grimly, or get her someplace private where he could at least have her in his arms and snatch one kiss before she slapped him. He took a deep breath and tried discreetly to edge his swollen organ away from the zipper of his jeans, where it was digging into him. Jesus he was in a state.

The crowd was thinning, and Sloan turned her and began to walk back toward Soward Street, where he had parked his vehicle. "How about if we check out the rodeo? That's where just about everybody is heading now that the parade is over."

Shelly didn't look at him. She was afraid if she did, he would see the desire and longing in her eyes. She had to get away from him.

"Uh, if you want to drop me off at the house, that'd be all right," she muttered. "It, um, isn't that far out of your way."

Sloan's mouth tightened and his fingers dug into her arm. "Do you have to fight me every step of the way? You enjoyed the parade, didn't you? Even if you have to put up with me, you'll enjoy the rodeo—if you'll let yourself."

She tried to jerk her arm away from him, but it was no use, and, swearing under his breath, he frog-marched her over to where he had parked the Suburban.

"Damn you, Sloan! Let me go. I want to go home. Now."

He glared at her, threw up his hands, and muttered, "Fine! I'll take you home. You can sit there by yourself and sulk all day while everyone else is out enjoying themselves."

He flung open the door and roughly bundled her into the

vehicle, frustration and anger in every movement. He was on the point of slamming the door behind her, when a voice called out, causing him to spin around.

"Sloan! Wait! I need a ride to the house."

Shelly bent her head around Sloan's big frame and watched as one of the most beautiful women she had ever seen in her life came rushing up to him. The newcomer was breathtaking, model-slender in a pair of form-fitting blue jeans, chiseled cheekbones to die for, shoulder-length curly black hair that gleamed like polished ebony, and a pair of the laughingest golden eyes she'd ever seen. Her bright red mouth was generous, softly curved, a mouth that automatically made 90 percent of the male population think of hot, steamy sex. She looked familiar, but Shelly couldn't place her.

The enchanting creature threw her arms around his neck and brushed a kiss against his jaw. "Hank said you were somewhere in town. I'm glad I caught you before you left."

Sloan smiled, his affection obvious as he returned the hug. "Hi, sweetheart, when did you get in town? Couldn't have been too long ago—I haven't heard of any insurrections, stampedes, earthquakes, or tornadoes . . . yet."

The other woman made a face. "Come on, that's not fair. Can I help it if things just sort of seem to happen when I'm around?"

"Probably not. And yeah, hop in, I'll run you out to the house." He opened the back door of the vehicle, and asked, "What happened to your ride? You had to get into town some way." He glanced down at the impractical high-heeled boots she wore. "I know for damn sure that you didn't walk into town wearing those ankle breakers."

She wrinkled her charming nose. "God no! Roxanne actually walk instead of taking a limousine? I'd never live it down. Darling, you know I'm far too indolent to do anything remotely strenuous. I drove my car in today, but the battery in the damn thing died. It's at Western Auto now, but they won't have the right-size battery for it until tomorrow." She grinned. "That simply divine Mr. Harris who owns the glass place is bringing one in from Ukiah for me tonight. Such a darling man."

Shelly started at the name Roxanne. Of course. Sloan's sister. No wonder she had looked familiar: Roxanne was one of the most famous models in the United States. Her face regularly appeared on the covers of *Vogue, Mademoiselle*, and the like, although not as often the past two years. The list of her lovers and would-be lovers was made up of the A-list celebrities and some of the wealthiest, most powerful men in the country. A Victoria's Secret model also, she was the fantasy of half the world's males.

Sloan laughed. "Have you ever met a man who wasn't a darling?"

Her eyes narrowed. "As a matter of fact, yes. And the jerk is walking toward us at this very minute. Punch him in the nose for me, won't you, Sloan dear?"

Shelly tore her gaze off Roxanne's fascinating face and followed the direction of the other woman's eyes. To her astonishment, she saw Jeb strolling toward them. Jeb a jerk? Well, yeah, maybe.

"'Morning, Sloan," Jeb said as he stopped by the vehicle. Spotting Shelly in the front seat, he grinned. "My God. I need to mark this day down in history. A Granger accepting a ride from a Ballinger? Or is he holding you at gunpoint?"

Shelly shrugged. "Acey abandoned me, and Sloan offered to give me a ride home. Don't make too much of it, OK? I don't intend to make it a habit."

Roxanne seemed to notice Shelly for the first time. She frowned. "Aren't you Josh's little sister? Sheila or Sharon or something?"

"Shelly is her name," said Sloan quietly. He bent a look at his sister. "Be nice. I don't think I could handle a catfight this morning, and I should warn you that Shelly is a worthy opponent. She draws blood. I should know—she's done it often enough to me."

The look in Roxanne's eyes was speculative as she studied Shelly's face. "Is that so?" she drawled, one elegant brow rose haughtily, then she ruined the effect by grinning at Shelly. "Good for you, girl! My sisters and I have been trying for years to do that very thing, and so far he's escaped our claws. Glad to know someone can get the better of him. He can be such an arrogant prick." Her gaze slid to Jeb. "Speaking of arrogant pricks, don't you have somewhere else you have to be? Catching lawbreakers or something? Shouldn't you be browbeating criminals or whatever it is you do?"

Jeb took a long, lazy appraisal of Roxanne's slender form. "Nasty, nasty, princess. At least I wear clothes when I do my job." Ignoring her gasp of rage, he glanced at Sloan. "I'll leave you to it. Looks like you have your hands full." He looked once more at Roxanne, and something flickered briefly in those black eyes of his. "Don't envy you a bit."

Sloan slammed the back door before his sister could reply and just as hastily shut Shelly's door. "Thanks a lot. Now she's going to be in a snit all day," he said to Jeb.

Jeb shrugged, the expression on his face unreadable. "Not my problem. See you."

Sloan watched him walk away. Both his sister and Jeb were effortless charmers. They both could charm the socks off a mannequin, and yet when you put the two of them together, they were like a pair of cats with their tails twisted and tied together . . . Sloan smiled. It was downright . . . interesting.

Chapter Eleven

⸻

$\mathcal{S}$helly had expected the drive to the Ballinger mansion to be silent, stiff, and uncomfortable. To the contrary, Roxanne proved to be not only charming, but voluble as well. Learning that Shelly had been living in New Orleans, she immediately started extolling the wonderful food for which the city was famous.

"Oh, man, I just *love* jambalaya, gumbo, and pralines!" Roxanne laughed, and added, "But after two weeks of that kind of food, it's back to celery and tuna and carrots—that's the downside of your body being your fortune. Of course, one of the good things about being a model is that you get sent to marvelous locations—Hawaii, Mexico, the Caribbean and, last but not least, New Orleans. Never tell my agent, but I'd go there on a shoot for half my fee. How could you bear to leave it?"

"It was easier than I thought it would be," Shelly answered. "And I guess it was just a case of missing home."

Sloan slanted her a look. "Yeah, right. You missed home so much you stayed away for seventeen years."

Shelly glanced sideways at him. "I didn't," she said coolly, "realize that you were counting."

The Ballinger mansion was situated on Adobe Road, as the crow flies not more than three or four miles from the center of town, but by vehicle it was almost double that distance. In the winter when the north end of the road was flooded, from town it took even longer to reach the mansion because of the almost circular pattern that had to be driven.

As they turned onto Adobe Road and headed south toward the mansion, Shelly wondered, as she often had, why it hadn't been renamed "Ballinger Road" a long time ago. The narrow, almost one-lane road ran parallel to and about four miles east of the state highway, and there were thousands of acres of flat, fertile, oak-dotted land that lay between the two roads—land mostly owned by Ballingers.

In view of the situation between the Grangers and Ballingers, Shelly had never been to the Ballinger mansion. And since it sat about a mile off Adobe Road, half-hidden by the huge sprawling valley oaks that were sprinkled across the landscape, she was curious to see for herself the fabled house. Anticipation built as Sloan drove down a gently winding gravel road lined by magnificent redwood trees that were nearly 150 years old. In places the limbs of the huge trees touched overhead, dappling the road here and there.

Sloan guided the vehicle around a curve, and Shelly's breath caught in her throat at the sight of the Ballinger mansion. It really *was* a mansion, she decided, as she took in the three stories of the house and the sheer breadth of it. It had been built at York Ballinger's direction in the 1870s and looked like it belonged somewhere near New Orleans. The half dozen or so native, massive oaks that guarded it increased that sensation, but it was the style of the house itself and the ten huge Doric columns across the front of it that shouted Deep South. It was certainly, Shelly mused, no Victorian, which is what one would have expected. Trust a Ballinger to do the unexpected.

The house was at once bold and charming. Two more columns had been used for the portico in the middle of the house; a pair of circular freestanding staircases seemed to float downward from the second story to the ground and gave the structure a fairy-tale air. The two upper stories had iron-railed galleries that ran the length of the house, those galleries continuing partway back along each side of the house. The slate roof was gently hipped, the expanse broken by four tall brick chimneys, jutting skyward. The building was painted a soft green, and the iron banisters were just a few shades darker. It was, Shelly thought, a gorgeous place.

Sloan pulled the Suburban to a stop at the front of the house. "Don't say I never did anything for you," he tossed over his shoulder to Roxanne.

Pushing open the door, she grinned back at him. "You can be a prince sometimes . . . when you're not being a bastard. See you."

The stiff, uncomfortable silence she had expected earlier filled the vehicle as Sloan sped away from the house. She endured it for half a mile, then, clearing her throat, she said, "Your sister is very nice."

"When she's not being a royal pain in the ass—which is most of the time." The underlying affection in his voice took the sting out of his words.

Silence fell again. Shelly shifted in her seat, too aware of Sloan's nearness for her own liking . . . too aware of the confines of the vehicle, the intimacy that was inescapable. At least, she thought wryly, they weren't in some little stick-shift two-seat sports car where every time he shifted, his hand would brush her leg. A shiver went through her at the idea of Sloan's hand on her body.

She bit her lip. And that was precisely why she didn't want to spend one minute longer than she had to in his presence. Keeping her face averted and forcing herself to concentrate on the passing countryside, Shelly stared out of the window.

Sloan cast her a glance or two, but all he saw for his efforts was the back of her head. *And you should be damned glad, too,* he berated himself. *You don't need the kind of trouble Shelly Granger represents*, but even as he thought that, his eyes slid over the thrust of her breasts beneath the green shirt and the long, sleek length of her legs. His body reacted instantly, the aching need to touch her flooding through him, his penis standing up boldly beneath the zipper in his jeans.

His lips thinned, and he stepped on the gas. The sooner he got rid of her the better off he'd be. Mindful of that fact, he kept the Suburban at a good clip even when the pavement ended and they hit the shaley road that curved up into the foothills. With his foot steady on the gas, like a bad-tempered cat the vehicle shot up the twisting road, rounding the curves with a speed and a snarl that sent gravel flying. It was only when they reached the turnoff that led to Josh's house that Sloan's speed slackened. The narrow drive leading to the Grangers' place was one stretch of road he'd never traveled before and not even to rid himself of Shelly Granger would he speed down an unfamiliar road.

The silence between them hung thick and heavy and Shelly sighed with relief when the driveway widened and Sloan pulled to a stop in front of the house. He shut off the vehicle and sat there staring at the log-timbered house.

"Nice place," he said. "I wasn't home when the original house burned. When I returned, it sure seemed strange to look up here and not see that big white Victorian looking down at the valley. It was quite a landmark. I was sorry when it burned down."

Shelly nodded. The original Jeb Granger had chosen this large fir-covered knoll as the site for his home, and once the area had been cleared around it, the house had been visible from just about anywhere in the northern end of the valley. The valley had never been wealthy, and most homes had been smaller and more utilitarian; consequently, the grand house, at a distance looking almost like a castle, had been pointed out with pride to visitors.

"It was a shock," she said as she pushed open her door and stepped outside. "When Josh called me with the news, it took him several minutes to get me to believe that it was gone. I'm used to the new house now, but when I first—" She stopped, the noise of another vehicle coming from the back of the house catching her attention.

The driveway split in two directions, one part angled off to the front of the house becoming part of the circular drive where she and Sloan were parked, while the other continued on around to the back of the house, ending at the barn. Visitors to the house used the circular driveway, stock and barn visitors continued on along the side of the house to the outbuildings at the rear.

A second later a dark blue pickup slowly nosed out from beside the house. At the sight of the Suburban, the driver braked, seemed to hesitate and then turned into the circular drive and brought the pickup alongside Sloan's vehicle.

Sloan recognized both the truck and the driver. Now this was damned interesting. What the hell was Milo Scott doing creeping around the Granger place when no one was home?

Deciding he wasn't in such a hurry to abandon Shelly after all, Sloan stepped out of the vehicle and nodded to Scott, as the other man exited the truck.

"Afternoon, Scott. What brings you here?" Sloan asked.

"I think that's my line," Shelly muttered under her breath as she walked around the vehicle and came to stand beside Sloan. She didn't think Sloan had heard her, but he obviously had; he grinned and gestured for her to take over.

Having only gotten a glimpse of him once that day with Jeb, she wouldn't have recognized Milo Scott if Sloan hadn't given her a clue. And she didn't know that she was exactly thrilled to find the local drug dealer on her doorstep. And yet supposedly, he'd been a friend of her brother's and, if Jeb was correct, might even have had something to do with Josh's death. . . . It gave her a shock and a small thrill of horror to know she might be facing a murderer. Her brother's murderer. Her throat closed up, and for a second her mind went blank. With an effort she focused on Milo Scott, wondering if he had indeed played a part in Josh's death. She could hardly ask him about it, and even Jeb admitted that the evidence surrounding Josh's death was consistent with suicide. She pushed further speculation away and since she'd never been officially introduced to him she stepped forward, and, extending her hand, said, "Hello. I don't believe that we've met. I'm Shelly Granger, Josh's sister. And you are?"

"Milo Scott," he said easily, smiling at her as he took her hand and shook it. "Sorry if I intruded, but I, er, wanted to, um, have a word with . . . ah, Acey."

Ignoring the soft snort Sloan gave behind her, she said, "Oh, I'm sorry but you've missed him. He rode in the parade this morning and isn't home yet." Deliberately she'd left out that he'd be gone all afternoon helping at the rodeo. She'd just as soon that Mr. Scott didn't know she'd be here alone. "If you leave a message, I'll see that he gets it. Unless there's something I can do for you?"

"No. I appreciate it, but this is something I need to talk to Acey about. Guess I'll catch up with him at the rodeo." He hesitated. "Sorry about Josh. He was a friend of mine. A lot of people will miss him."

Shelly made a polite reply, wondering what Milo Scott needed to talk to Acey about—if that had been his real reason for being here. She doubted it and even if she hadn't known about his drug connection or the possibility that he'd had something to do with Josh's suicide—if it had been suicide— she wouldn't have liked him. There was something furtive and sinister about him, something that made her happy she was confronting him in daylight and not alone—maybe Sloan did have his uses. Milo Scott wasn't a big man. He was slim and not much taller than she; with his even features and a mop of sandy blond hair, he could be called handsome. Certainly there was nothing overtly intimidating about him, and many people would have found him attractive. She did not. She was wary and mistrustful of him. Jeb's influence, she thought wryly. Whatever the reason, there was no denying that there was something about the man, something in his flat blue eyes that made her increasingly thankful that Sloan was very big, very tough, and standing right behind her.

"Uh, guess I'll be on my way," Scott said awkwardly. "It was nice meeting you. See you around, Sloan."

He turned and walked back to his truck. His hand on the roof of the cab, he paused and looked across at her. His fingers tapping on the cab, he said, "Don't know if anybody has mentioned it or not, but Josh and I did business together. We, um, had some agricultural ventures we were partners in—when you have time, I'd like to discuss them with you."

"Now I find that very interesting, Mr. Scott," Shelly murmured, Jeb's suspicions and those large deposits uppermost in her mind. "In going through Josh's papers, business or otherwise, I've seen no reference to you or any, ah, agricultural ventures that Josh was involved in. Perhaps you're mistaken?"

Scott's mouth thinned. "No mistake. Josh and I were good friends, very good friends. Buddies you could say. Mostly we did business the old-fashioned way: We decided on the terms and sealed it with a handshake."

Sloan stepped closer to Shelly, his hands falling onto her shoulders. There was possessiveness and something distinctively territorial about his stance. His eyes on Scott's, he said, "That's really too bad, Scott. Verbal agreements are really a bitch to prove in court. Of course, if you feel strongly about it,

I suggest you see a lawyer about your chances of making any, ah, agricultural agreements with Josh stick."

"Yeah. I'll do that," he snapped, wrenching open the door to his pickup. He sent Shelly a hard look. "This isn't over. I'll be getting in touch in with you." A sneer entered his voice. "When your boyfriend isn't around."

"Well, that was certainly entertaining," Shelly said, as she and Sloan watched Scott's pickup disappear down the gravel road.

"You could say that," he agreed. "But before I leave I want to check things out and make certain that he didn't leave any surprises around."

Shelly turned and looked at him. "What sort of surprises?"

He shrugged. "With Scott you never know." No reason to frighten her unnecessarily. And it would frighten her, he thought grimly, if he mentioned the trashing of Cleo's place, the prized colt of his he'd found with a smashed foreleg, or the young bull that Nick had lost under suspicious circumstances. Just before her house was broken into and vandalized last summer, Cleo had caught Milo sneaking around on her property and had had him arrested for trespassing. The other two incidents had happened a couple of years ago—just after he had pithily refused to lease some remote land to Scott and Nick's cattle had accidentally wandered into a marijuana patch being cultivated in a far corner of the Mendocino National Forest. Coincidence? Neither he nor Nick thought so—and Cleo had always been certain—and vocal about Scott being pond scum. Having his own ideas of the extent of Scott's viciousness, he'd feel better once he knew that Scott hadn't left an ugly scene for Shelly to find.

Shelly stared at him. His expression might be bland, but she sensed that he was holding something back. "What aren't you telling me? I hate it when I'm treated like a child. If there's something I should know, tell me," she demanded. "I'm a big girl now."

Sloan grinned, his eyes traveling appreciatively over her. "I'd sort of noticed that. Be hard not to with those butt-hugging jeans of yours and that slinky blouse you're wearing . . . but that was the whole point, wasn't it, honey? To make me notice?"

Shelly's cheeks flamed, and she spun around. Damn him! Suddenly wishing that she'd worn a burlap sack this morning, she stalked to the house.

Still grinning, Sloan ambled after her, his mouth watering at the view presented by those same butt-hugging jeans.

Just as she reached the first step, he caught her arm, and said, "We'll save the house for last. He came from behind the house, so let's start there."

She threw off his hand and glared at him. "And what makes you think that I'm going to help you? Why should I?"

"Because you're curious?"

Muttering under her breath, she led the way to the back of the house. Hands on her hips, Shelly watched with growing irritation as Sloan walked around the new construction, glanced at the huge stack of hay under the bright blue tarp and examined the interior of the barn.

Satisfied that Milo hadn't wreaked any obvious havoc in this area, as he walked out of the dim interior of the barn, Sloan said, "All those new corrals and pens and chutes, for the cattle operation?"

"Not that it's any business of yours, but yes." Pride and excitement had her blurting out, "I'm expecting a shipment of heifers sometime tomorrow that carry some of the old Granger bloodlines. We'll be using Granger's Ideal Beau on them—which gives us a head start on rebuilding. Beau's our linchpin."

Sloan glanced to the pen where the big black bull was

drinking from the water trough. "He's a great-looking animal—he should do well for you. I always thought it was a shame that Josh had pretty much dispersed the herd. Granger's had some good Angus at one time."

"And will again."

Sloan smiled at her confident tone. Walking over to the new kennel where the dogs barked and wiggled when he stopped in front of them, he asked, "Acey's dogs?"

"Yes. I told you Acey is living here. In the apartment upstairs—the apartment you insisted upon seeing. Remember?"

He shrugged. They went through the other outbuildings and, convinced that Milo hadn't done any damage here, Sloan turned his attention to the house.

Entering through the back door, after passing through the spacious mudroom, they walked into the big kitchen. Shelly forced herself to be polite. After all, she told herself, Sloan was just making sure everything was OK—she'd figured that much out all by herself—and she should be grateful, not crabby and annoyed. Attempting to make amends, she crossed to the refrigerator, opened it, and asked, "Do you want something to drink? There's soft drinks and beer."

"A beer'll be fine," he answered, his gaze traveling around the pleasant kitchen. He might have detested Josh, but he had to admit the man had good taste, liking the cheerful colors and layout. Sipping from the cold bottle of beer Shelly had handed him, he continued his inspection of the house, feeling more and more like a voyeur as time went by. It was obvious that whatever reasons Scott had had for being here, it hadn't been to deface or destroy. Maybe Scott really had been looking for Acey? Sloan frowned. Didn't seem likely. Acey had no use for a man who didn't put in an honest day's work and Scott had never done an honest day of anything in his life.

Shelly found it unsettling to have Sloan roaming through the house. Watching him prowling through it like a tiger on the hunt made her feel vulnerable and resentful. Resentful because she hadn't flatly refused to let him do so and vulnerable simply because it was Sloan invading her privacy. He was low-key about it, so damned polite, for Sloan, that she wanted to smack him.

"Next floor?" he asked after he'd finished a cursory glance at the main floor. His original reasons for conducting the search had vanished. There was no sign that Scott had ever been inside the house, or if he had, he hadn't left a trace of it, but Sloan was loath to leave. He was, to his irritated amusement, enjoying her presence—even if her body language told him she wished him in Hades. He grinned. If he'd been a decent sort, he'd have apologized and left. Problem was, when it came to Shelly, there wasn't one damned decent bone in his entire body. Everything's fair in love or war, he thought. So which was it? Love or war? He couldn't wait to find out.

"Look," Shelly said bluntly, "this has gone on long enough. Whatever you were searching for, it's apparent you're not finding it."

Having him in the house was bad enough, but just the thought of Sloan sauntering around her bedroom made her breath catch and her knees go weak. Feeling as she did, being in the same room alone with Sloan and a bed was just plain dangerous. And foolish. And dammit! Oh so tempting.

"There's absolutely no reason for you to see any more of the house," she said.

"What's up there?" he asked, waving a hand toward the staircase.

"There's nothing," she said between gritted teeth. "Just bedrooms and bathrooms and on the third floor, my studio."

"Ah, the place where the famous artist creates, huh? Don't want it contaminated by the prying eyes of the philistines."

"Precisely!" Turning away, she added, "Now if you'll follow me, I'll show you out."

"Afraid to show me?" he taunted softly.

She spun around, her hands fisted at her sides. He hadn't moved. He was still standing at the base of the stairs, challenge in his gaze. "Fear has nothing to do with it," she snapped, aware that fear had everything to do with it. "There's just no reason for us to continue."

He shook his head, his expression marveling. "Never thought I'd see the day. A Granger running from a Ballinger."

She rose to the bait, just as he had known she would. "Fine! I'll show you the whole damned place." Brushing past him, she started up the stairs. "You know, I really hate you sometimes," she snarled. "And after this you're leaving. Do you hear me? You're gone. Outta here."

Grinning, Sloan followed, his fascinated gaze on those lovely pumping buttocks only inches in front of him.

Reaching the top of the stairs, Shelly stopped in the wide hallway. She flung out a hand and, with an exaggerated bow, said, "Please, be my guest."

Sloan smothered a chuckle and entered the first room he came to. It was huge, probably Josh's, he thought, glancing at the sable suede bedspread on the king-size bed and the comfortable, distinctly masculine furniture scattered about the room. Since he'd insisted upon seeing this floor, he made himself go through the motions, but he didn't expect to find anything. And he didn't.

By the time they reached her bedroom, Shelly was all nerves and apprehension. If he just gave her room the same sort of swift look he'd given everything else, she'd be fine. She could keep her composure, politely escort him from the house, then faint with relief that he, and all the temptation he offered, were finally gone. But if he lingered . . . if he dared to kiss her as he had at his cabin . . . She swallowed. He hadn't even touched her, but she wanted him to—and would have died before admitting it.

Sloan sensed the moment he entered the room that it was Shelly's. Looking back over his shoulder at her where she stood in the doorway, he asked, "Yours?"

She nodded, her mouth dry, her body tense. It might seem silly to hover uneasily in the doorway to her own bedroom, but she wasn't, she told herself, stepping one foot inside it until Sloan was safely out of the damned house.

He took his time wandering around the room, peeking into the closet and bathroom before he sat down on the side of her bed. "Nice room."

The sight of him on her bed was thoroughly unnerving; images of the two of them making love popped instantly into her head. Hastily pushing the image aside, she said tightly, "If you've satisfied yourself, I suggest you leave. Now."

"Honey, I haven't even begun to be satisfied," he muttered. "And if you'll just bring that sexy little body of yours over here, we can see about changing that."

Across the width of the room they stared at each other, the sudden, stark hunger in Sloan's eyes making her nipples swell and damp heat flood her lower body. "Don't!" she cried out in a tortured voice. "Don't start, Sloan. Get out."

He hesitated, then, with a shrug, stood up and began to walk toward her. A lopsided grin on his face, he said, "You don't know what you're missing."

The strident ringing of the telephone by her bed interrupted the rude comment that sprang to her lips.

Sloan stopped his progress midway across the room and glanced from her to the ringing phone. "Want me to answer it?"

"No. No. I'll get it. Just go. Show yourself out."

"In a hurry to get rid of me?" he mocked.

"Yes, dammit! Now get out of here so I can answer the damn phone."

He grinned, not budging. "Nothing's stopping you. Answer it."

Unable to ignore the insistent peal of the phone, Shelly scuttled into the room, keeping well away from him. Snatching up the phone, she barked, "Yes! Who is it?"

A voice like warm brandy flowed through the phone lines. "Now, sugar, is that any way to talk to your favorite cousin?"

A delighted smile curved Shelly's lips. "Roman! It's so good to hear from you." Waving a dismissal to Sloan, she sank down onto the side of the bed and prepared to let Roman's Southern charm soothe her shattered nerves. "How is everything in New Orleans?"

"Dull as dust without your charming company. Tell me, please, that you have changed your mind about living in that little jerkwater community and that you're coming back soon to bring joy and light into my life once more."

Shelly laughed. "Surely, you exaggerate, kind sir. If I remember correctly, there are any number of nubile young ladies eager to bring joy into your life. You don't need me to add to your harem."

"Ah, *ma belle*, you wound me. As if one of them could take your place."

She laughed again and absently began to unlace her ropers. "Well, one of them is going to have to—I'm staying right where I am."

"Then I am afraid that you leave me no choice—I must join you in your wretched exile from all that is worth living."

"*What?* You're coming out here?"

"Hmm, yes. Will it be all right?"

The thought of the ever-elegant and urbane Roman strolling arrogantly down the streets of St. Galen's was mindboggling. Leaving off struggling with her bootlaces, she demanded, "Are you serious about this?"

Sloan decided he had been ignored long enough, and he

walked over to where Shelly sat. Dropping down to one knee, he took her foot in his hands and deftly began ridding her of the boots.

Shelly yelped at the first touch of his hands on her foot. Lips parted, eyes wide she stared down into Sloan's features, Roman forgotten.

"Something wrong?" Roman asked.

"N-n-no," Shelly stammered breathlessly, as Sloan slid off first one boot and then the other, his hands lingering warmly against her skin as he completed his task. She snatched her foot away from him and, covering the phone with one hand, hissed, "Go away."

Sloan smiled, a slow intimate smile that made her heart turn right over in her breast. He stood up and to her outrage and horror, settled himself comfortably on the bed behind her.

Twisting around, she glared at him. "Did you hear me?" she hissed again. "Go away."

"Is someone there with you, *ma belle*?" Roman laughed huskily. "Never tell me that I have called at an inopportune moment? Can it be that some tough, swaggering cowboy has stolen your heart?"

"Absolutely not! And no, no one is with me," she said, throwing daggers at Sloan before turning her back on him.

"Now that's downright rude, honey," Sloan murmured, and, pleasing himself, he ran a finger along that stiff spine of hers. Shelly tried to wiggle away from him, but he thwarted that action by the simple expedient of sitting up, putting his hands around her waist to hold her still, and dropping a soft kiss just under her ear.

Her breath left in a whoosh the instant he touched her. Worse, his hands showed a distressing tendency to wander, and his teeth were nibbling at the side of her throat. "Roman," she said hastily, "I have to go now. I'll call you back. I promise."

She slammed down the phone. Heart hammering, she tried to calm herself. She had to be cool. She had to be firm. Common sense had to overcome her treacherous body. That treacherous body that wanted nothing more than to offer itself to the one man that could break her heart. Had broken her heart, she admitted bleakly.

Having accomplished his purpose, Sloan had lain back down on the bed, ready to outwait her. The next few minutes, he mused, should be . . . interesting.

She took a deep breath and half swung around to face him. *Oh, God*, she thought helplessly as she stared at him, *I'm in big trouble.* He looked so right lounging against the pillows of her bed, his hands behind his head and that mocking smile on his lips, the half-shuttered eyes full of sensual promise.

"We have to talk," she said levelly, holding on to her churning emotions by a thread.

"No, we don't," Sloan said. Before she realized it, she was caught and dragged across the bed. "Talking," he muttered against her mouth, "always seems to get us into trouble. But never this. Never this."

His lips took hers in a kiss that sent her senses spinning. Too well did she remember the power of his kiss; too well did she remember the hungry thrust of his tongue, the demand of his lips, the sting of his teeth. He used them all, teeth, tongue, and lips, to arouse, and her body responded as it always had, the world around her exploding in a fireball, leaving behind only the fierce ache of wildly spiraling desire.

Hands on either side of her head, he held her still and kissed her a long time, the drag of his lips against hers, the stroke of his tongue deep within her mouth coaxing and demanding at the same time. Denial was impossible. She gave him everything he asked for, her lips parting fully for his exploration, her tongue mating with his and her arms closing hungrily around his shoulders.

He was half-lying on her, the warm weight of that muscled length familiar and yet not. It had been a long time since she'd made love, and it had been an eon ago, a lifetime ago since she had lain in Sloan's arms, a very long time since she had felt passion this overwhelming, this primitive.

When his hand swept down and fondled her breast, she arched up, the brush of his thumb against her nipple sending spears of pleasure through her. His lips followed his hand, and the sensation of that insistent, tugging mouth made her breath catch and her heart pound. But it was the touch of his hand between her legs, the subtle slide of his finger against her damp aching center that startled a cry of need from her. Even with the barrier of clothing between them, the caress was potent, turning her brain to cinders.

The sexual tension had been building between them all day, and that soft cry destroyed Sloan's restraint. With a low, frustrated growl he began to strip her, his fingers fighting with buttons and zippers as he sought to expose all the naked beauty that had haunted him for years. Shelly was no better. She had fought to avoid precisely this situation, but it had been a futile battle. She wanted him. She ached for him, wanted desperately to feel the power of that big body moving over hers. Every cell in her body was clamoring for the sweet completion she would find in his lovemaking; her body was screaming for the blunt invasion of his, and having lost the fight with herself, she wasn't going to be denied satisfaction.

In a frantic fumble of hands and seeking mouths they dispensed with clothing. Sloan sat on the side of the bed, cursing as he fought free of his boots and his jeans and briefs, holding on to just enough sanity to grab the foil packet from his wallet. It took him an agonizing second to prepare himself, then he came back to her.

On their knees they met in the middle of the bed and the sudden sweet shock of naked flesh against naked flesh was almost more than he could bear. Her arms twined around his neck, and they kissed deeply, hungrily. His hands were everywhere, exploring, caressing, his fingers leaving trails of fire wherever they touched.

Shelly indulged herself, rubbing her breasts against his hard chest and squeezing her thighs against his heavy, swollen organ where it lodged between her legs. Mouths and bodies molded together, they rocked gently, his thick penis sliding against her damp throbbing flesh, arousing a frenzy of desire. Aching, frantic for more, her hands swept down his back and squeezed the taut flesh of his buttocks. She'd always had a fondness for his butt and apparently still did—his skin was warm even here, the flesh smooth and resilient.

Precariously close to the edge, Sloan tore his lips from hers and bent his head to find her breasts. As his lips closed around a tight, sweet nipple, Shelly shivered in his arms. When she touched him a moment later, when those exploring fingers closed around his penis, he writhed, and blind, primal need consumed him.

"I can't wait," he muttered. "I want you . . . *now.*"

Sultry green eyes met his. "No one's stopping you," she said breathlessly.

Half-laughing, half-growling, he pushed her down into the bed and fell upon her like a starving man at a feast. For wild seconds, his mouth and hands were everywhere, her throat, her breasts, her flat trembling belly, then his lips were on hers, his tongue delving deep. His hand slid downward, seeking the heat between her legs. Finding that heat, he cupped her, a feral smile crossing his face when she shuddered. Parting her, he inserted first one finger then a second into the damp welcoming heart of her. Her hips arched, a mewling sound escaping from her as he stroked deep within her, and finding the swollen nub in the midst of her folds, he brushed it, once, twice with his thumb. His mouth hard on hers, he captured the scream that erupted from her as her body jerked and pulsed and she climaxed.

His control shattered, Sloan jerked her thighs apart, and, sliding between them, he buried himself inside her. Jesus! He'd forgotten the fire, the sweet tightness of her body. She fit him like a hot glove, the satiny walls clinging and dragging him helplessly under. Driven, racing for that final convulsing pleasure, he thrust urgently into her, his hips moving like pistons as he slammed into her again and again.

Shelly climaxed again, her body stiffening and jerking as the scalding wave took her; Sloan followed seconds later, his fingers digging into her hips and a cry, half snarl, half shout was torn from him as he drowned in ecstasy.

For a long while they lay there, both too boneless with pleasure to move. Eventually Sloan fell away to lie beside her, but he kept one hand on her hip, almost as if he feared she would disappear.

She didn't want to think about what had just happened, about what it might mean. *So I had sex with him*, she thought defensively, *big F deal. Leave it at that. Treat it like that. I shared the simple act of sex with him. So what?* It wasn't a crime. They didn't hurt anybody. They were adults. He'd worn a rubber. A half-hysterical giggle rose up through her. They'd even practiced safe sex.

Next to her, Sloan turned on his side, his gaze moving over the tempting, delicious length of her. Between his legs his sex twitched, and he grimaced. Why wasn't he surprised? She'd always had that effect on him. No matter how often they'd made love, he never seemed to get enough of her sweet passion. His lips thinned. And he wasn't sharing it either.

Tugging on a strand of her hair, he forced her to look at him. Unsmiling, he met her wary gaze.

"So do you get rid of the guy on the phone, or do I break his neck?"

Chapter Twelve

For a moment Shelly didn't have a clue. Then realization hit. Roman. He was talking about Roman.

"I think that Roman would have something to say about that and, knowing Roman, I suspect you'd find breaking his neck beyond even your capabilities," she said, sliding away from him. Grabbing a pillow, she clutched it in front of her, suddenly modest.

"Get rid of him," Sloan said flatly. "I'm not in the habit of sharing."

Her mouth tightened. "First of all, there is nothing to share, and second of all, Roman is my cousin—and even if I was inclined to do so, which I'm not, I'm hardly likely to tell him to take a flying leap on your say-so."

"Your cousin?" He frowned. "If memory serves me, you don't have a cousin named Roman."

"Yes, I do." She smiled sweetly. "He's a descendant of the branch of the Granger family that remained in Louisiana after the Civil War. The relationship may be distant and many times removed, but he's definitely my cousin."

Sloan wasn't quite certain what to make of that information, but since this Roman guy was actually related to Shelly—even if distantly—he admitted that he wasn't going to be able simply to break the guy's neck to get him out of her life.

"You and, er, Roman close?" he asked cautiously.

"Yes. Very."

Ignoring Sloan's scowl, pillow still clutched to her chest, she scooted from the bed and, after scrabbling around on the floor, found the green shirt she'd been wearing earlier. Shrugging into it, she was grateful for the extralong tails that fell halfway down her thighs. Once it was buttoned, she didn't feel quite so vulnerable.

Brushing back her hair, she looked at him, and said, "I think that about ends our conversation, don't you?" When Sloan simply stared at her, she added, "Shouldn't you get dressed . . . and leave?"

"Just like that? A quick screw, and now you're throwing me out?"

"I'm sure that we both agree that what just happened was a mistake. It shouldn't have happened, and it certainly doesn't change anything between us."

Sloan considered her for an unnerving second, then, jaw rigid, he got off the bed. Grabbing his jeans and shirt, he disappeared into the bathroom. He came out a couple of seconds later, wearing his clothes, the shirt unbuttoned and the tails hanging out.

Shelly had used the time to scramble into her own clothing, suspecting that Sloan wasn't just going to leave. She was right.

The moment he walked out of the bathroom, he said, "You can't pretend it didn't happen. And it does change things between us."

She shook her head. "No. It doesn't. I won't let it. You're still the same lying bastard I ran away from seventeen years ago."

"I never lied to you," he snarled. "You left me, lady. One minute you were swearing you loved me and wanted to marry me—the next you're gone. Poof. Vanished. Without one god-damn word of explanation."

Shelly glanced away from the golden fury in his eyes. Her throat felt raw, and all the pain and betrayal she'd felt that terrible night came rushing back. Struggling to keep her emotions under control, she said, "You didn't deserve an explanation. Not after what you did."

"What the hell did I do except fall in love with you?" he asked, anguish in his tone. "That's all I ever did—love you."

Her fingers digging into the palms of her hand, she fought against responding to the desperate note in his voice. He was very good at this, very good at turning it all into her fault.

"No, that's not all you did," she said bitterly. "At the same time you were, ah, loving me, you were also loving Nancy Blackstone." At his startled look, she demanded fiercely, "Did you think I wouldn't find out?" A mirthless laugh escaped her. "It's really funny when you look at it. I left you that last afternoon, determined to do as you'd been begging me to do for weeks. It was difficult, but I finally gathered up my courage and told Josh all about us—that we were in love and that we wanted to get married."

Sloan swore under his breath. "I knew his name was going to come into it sooner or later."

"You wanted me to tell him!" she shouted, fists at her sides. "You'd been badgering me for weeks to tell him."

"I didn't expect you to face him alone," he said through gritted teeth. "If you'll remember I was pushing for us to do it together, figuring that if he turned ugly I could take you away right then. I wanted to be with you. I told you that. But did you listen? Oh, no, you had to barge in and confront the bastard all by yourself."

"Don't you dare call him a bastard! He loved me! And all he ever wanted was to protect me—and he did!"

"How?" Sloan sneered. "By filling your head with lies about me?"

"No. By letting me find out for myself just what a deceiving, double-crossing, cheating, lying son of a bitch you really were."

Unconsciously Sloan reached for a cigarette, biting back a curse when his fingers found only an empty shirt pocket. He really needed a cigarette—or a drink, a stiff drink at that.

"Double-crossing? You want to explain that?" he finally asked.

"Do you really want me to cross all the t's and dot all the i's?"

His eyes hooded, Sloan said, "Yeah, I think I do. I've waited seventeen years for this, and I don't want to miss one little iota. Please go on."

He wasn't the only one who had waited, she thought furiously. She had dreamed about this moment. It had haunted her, and in the beginning she had dreamed constantly about tossing his lies right back in that handsome face of his. Of course in her dreams, she did this right after he'd declared his undying love for her—she threw that back in his face, too. The situation didn't quite live up to her dreams, but it was probably as close as she was going to get. She sighed. Reality was like that—it seldom bore close resemblance to dreams.

Taking a deep breath, she said quietly, "When I got home, I found him in his office. Maria was gone for the day, so I knew we wouldn't be interrupted. He was in a relaxed mood—he even teased me about never being home much anymore. It seemed too good of an opportunity to miss. I didn't give myself time to think, I just blurted out that I loved you and that we wanted to marry and leave the valley." She glanced away, remembering that moment, remembering the stunned expression on Josh's face. It had been hard for him to

accept what she was telling him, hard enough for him to accept that she wanted to marry a descendent of the man who
had been reviled and hated for generations. She swallowed. It
had been harder still for him to accept that his baby sister
wasn't a baby anymore. Pushing away memories of Josh's an-
guished, angry face, she admitted, "He was furious, shocked,
and astonished, too—which wasn't surprising, since he'd had
no idea we'd ever even met, much less fallen in love. Naturally, he was hurt and disappointed that I'd kept our relationship a secret. But in the end he said he understood why we'd
felt the need to hide the truth. He was very kind and sweet
about it."

"I'll bet he was," Sloan said dryly. "I can see his face even
now, all full of compassion and brotherly concern for his baby
sister."

"Look, do you want to hear this or not?"

Sloan grimaced, and with one hand gestured her to continue.

"Anyway, he took it very well. We talked for a long time—
he had a lot of questions, and he needed to be convinced that
I knew what I was doing." She smiled faintly. "He wasn't real
enthusiastic about any of it to begin with—I won't kid you
about that! To be truthful he was furious and dead set against
us, but after a while, a *long* while, he finally conceded that
even though you weren't the man he'd have chosen for me, if
I really loved you and wanted to marry you, he wouldn't stand
in our way. After all, he said, our families might have been at
each other's throats, but there was no denying that marrying
you would give me social prestige, not only here in Oak Valley, but in the county, too. He admitted that while he wasn't
thrilled at the notion of a Granger marrying a Ballinger, he
could see the advantages and if I loved you . . . well, he
wouldn't argue—he wasn't happy, he thought I was making a
mistake, but if that's what I really wanted . . . We even drank

a glass of champagne together and he gave a toast to the new Mrs. Sloan Ballinger. When I left him and went upstairs to my room that afternoon I was floating on air." She grimaced. "I was such a besotted little ninny—all I could think of was how happy I was and how happy you'd be when you found that I'd told him about us." She stopped, lost in the past, remembering what it had been like to be eighteen and wildly in love.

"And that's it?" Sloan growled, breaking into her thoughts. "You told him, he was kind about it. Aren't you leaving out a few things?" His face twisted and he gave her a little shake. "One minute I was the happiest guy in the world. I loved you. You swore you loved me. And then poof! You're gone. No explanation. No word. *Nada*. You're just gone. Vanished." His voice thickened. "Your leaving like that blindsided me, and I went half-mad trying to figure out what I'd done that made you just up and leave—without one damn word. One clue as to what had gone wrong so suddenly between us. What I'd done that was so terrible you couldn't even face me with it. I still don't know. So, I repeat, aren't you leaving out a few things from your explanation? Such as *why* you left me."

She glared at him. "No, I'm not forgetting anything. I'm just telling you that you were wrong about Josh. You'd thought he'd forbid us to see each other, that he'd try to tear us apart—well he didn't! He had accepted the fact that I was going to marry you . . . at least at first."

"Ah, now, we're getting to it, aren't we?"

"Will you stop being so sarcastic?" she snapped. "You never believed that Josh loved me and that all he ever wanted was for me to be happy. I don't blame him for making some telephone calls to his friends to try to find out what they knew about you. He didn't really know that much about you other than what I had told him and the usual valley gossip he'd heard over the years. You'd have done the same thing if your sister had suddenly sprung it on you that she wanted to marry a member of a family that had been at odds with yours for decades. You know you would!"

Sloan's gaze narrowed. "Tell me about the phone calls. Who did he talk to?"

Shelly threw her hands up. "I don't remember. I don't even know if he told me. I only know when I came down that evening for dinner, he said that he wanted to speak with me. He admitted that . . . that he'd done some checking up on you." She made a face. "I was furious with him. I couldn't believe that he had done such a thing. I wouldn't listen to him— I tried to get away from him, but he begged me to listen, pleaded with me. I was so angry with him, so hurt, but I finally sat down and listened to what he had to say." She flashed him a look full of condemnation. "He told me everything, Sloan. Everything."

"Really?" he said with a raised brow. "Well, I, for one, would be very damned interested in hearing what that 'everything' was."

Staring at him with dislike, she declared angrily, "This is all a big joke to you, isn't it?"

"Oh, yeah," he said with a mirthless laugh. "I've been laughing my head off for years."

"He told me about Nancy Blackstone," she said quietly, ignoring the stab of pain that even now went through her, remembering another girl, another time when she had been full of dreams and anticipation and that they had all been shattered in an instant. "Apparently, your affair with her was common gossip in the valley. That and the fact that you were still seeing her." Her lip curled. "When, of course, you weren't sneaking around behind her back screwing me blind."

Sloan reached for the phantom pack of cigarettes. Cursing his own weakness, he met her accusing eyes and admitted, "Before you showed up that summer, I won't deny that Nancy and I had been seeing each other—and that it was pretty serious for a while. You could say that we were considered quite an item—I'm sure all the busybodies in town, male and female alike, had our wedding all mapped out. They only made one miscalculation—I wasn't planning on marrying Nancy. That was her idea."

Shelly walked away from him to stand in front of the glass sliding doors. Staring blankly outside, she muttered, "I'm glad you admitted—it wouldn't have done you any good to deny it: I saw you together in the gazebo at her parents' place. She was in your arms, and you were kissing each other like you'd never let each other go. I heard what you told her that night—that you were just passing time with me. That she didn't have a thing to worry about, that I was just a mere fling." She sighed. "After that there was no reason for me to remain in Oak Valley. Josh had waited in the car for me, and when I returned he knew from the expression on my face that I had discovered for myself just what a lying, cheating bastard you were. He never once said 'I told you so.' He helped me pack and got us on a flight to New York that night. Later, after I finished art school, he helped me start again in New Orleans." She swung around to look at him. "I heard you, Sloan. I saw you kissing her, and I heard you tossing away my love for you as if it were nothing more than last night's garbage."

"I see," he said slowly, his expression hard to define. "Let me see if I've got this one point straight—it was dear Josh who arranged for you to be there at the Blackstone place at that particular time, wasn't it?"

"What the hell difference does it make?" she blazed at him. "Oh, never mind. You're just going to take it as one more crime committed by him—but yes, he did arrange for me to be at her parents' place that night." Painfully, she admitted, "I didn't believe him about your involvement with her—even though he'd told me that numerous people in the valley had confirmed the affair. I told him they were lying or mistaken, but that it just wasn't true." She laughed bitterly. "You loved me, I told him. You wouldn't treat me that way. I wouldn't listen to him—I, lovesick fool that I was, believed in you. Even when he said that Nancy had told a girlfriend of hers that she was meeting you that night, that Nancy suspected you were seeing someone else and that she was going to have it out with you, I still didn't believe him."

"Did he happen to mention the name of the girlfriend who just happened to have all this useful information? Or, even more interesting, how he found out about the girlfriend and what inducement he used to get her to tell him about Nancy's plans?"

"What do you mean?"

"Didn't it ever occur to you just how very convenient everything worked out for Josh?" he asked grimly. "You drop a bombshell in his lap and a few hours later he knows all about my affair with Nancy. Hell, he knew about it when it was going on—he and Nancy always had some sort of weird relationship even then—for your information, *they'd* been an item before I showed up—more amazingly, at least to me, they were still friends. When we had our affair, she was always tossing Josh's name in my face. At that time, I could never figure it out, but I'll bet he never called any of his friends to check me out. He knew all he needed to. But more importantly, doesn't it strike you as odd that he just happened to know when and where Nancy was going to meet with me to, er, have it out with me? Doesn't that seem just a little coincidental? Doesn't it smell like a setup to you? A nifty little plan concocted by two people, each with their own interests to serve?"

"Jesus! I don't believe you. Caught red-handed in your own lies, now you're going to try to tell me that it was all Josh and Nancy's plotting. I thought better of you—my mistake."

Her eyes glittering like emeralds, she walked up to him

and poking him in the chest with one finger, she said, "I don't want to hear any more. Just tell me one thing: did I or did I not hear you tell Nancy Blackstone, your future wife, that I was just a mere fling? That it was nothing serious, just a summer romance?"

"That's two things," he pointed out.

"Goddamn it, Sloan! Did you say it or not?"

He studied her angry face for a long moment. "You said you were there," he replied coolly. "So you heard what I said as well as anybody."

Shelly had thought she was immune to the pain, thought he couldn't hurt her any longer, but his words were a knife to her heart. "Get out," she said softly. "Get out of my house and out of my life."

He smiled crookedly. "Normally I'd do anything to please a lady, but not this time." He grabbed her and crushed her lips with a punishing kiss. Lifting his head, his golden eyes dueling with hers, he said softly, "I'll get out of your house for now. But not out of your life. You believe what you want about that night, but just remember this: Sometimes things aren't always what they seem."

⎯⎯⎯∾⎯⎯⎯

Shelly was so mad she could have spit nails. Why couldn't he, she wondered furiously several minutes later as she stood under the shower, just take defeat gracefully? Would it have hurt him simply to admit that he'd done wrong? She didn't understand how he could still try to blame her brother for what had happened. He was the one who had been at fault, not Josh! He was the one who had been screwing around behind her back. She grimaced. Or was it Nancy's back? At any rate he'd been screwing around behind *someone's* back. Why couldn't he just admit it? It wouldn't change anything, but maybe, she thought wistfully, if he'd admitted he'd been wrong, they could build a new relationship. Her lower lip drooped. Who was she kidding? There wasn't any way she'd ever completely trust him again. She'd believed him once, and look where that had gotten her.

It was almost six in the evening when Acey and Maria arrived back at the house. Shelly was in the kitchen finishing up a tuna sandwich and a glass of milk when they walked in.

Acey frowned. "Didn't think I'd see you back here until after the dance tonight. Where's Sloan?"

Shelly shrugged. "I have no idea. He brought me home after the parade and left." And that, she thought to herself, was an understatement if she'd ever heard one.

"He didn't take you to the rodeo?" Maria asked. At the negative shake of Shelly's head, she murmured. "What a shame. You missed a really great time. The kids are so much fun to watch. They are all so serious about competing and such good little riders and ropers." She chuckled. "Today's sheep ride was one of the funniest things I've seen in a long time. The sheep were really bucking, and those little kids were hanging on for dear life." She patted Shelly's hand. "Don't you worry—we'll go tomorrow again—you can come watch with Acey and me. You'll enjoy it. Especially at the end, when they turn the youngsters loose with an arena full of baby pigs, goats, chickens, ducks, you name it. The kids can keep whichever critter they can catch with their bare hands. It's a hoot—the best part of the rodeo as far as I am concerned."

Acey was still staring at Shelly, the frown firmly in place. To distract him, she said, "By the way, when Sloan and I came home, Milo Scott was here looking for you."

Acey's frown got blacker. "Scott, huh? Wonder what that dizzy bastard wanted—not anything good, that's one thing you can be sure of." Acey pulled on one side of his luxurious mustaches. "Don't like the fellow, never have, never will. I sure as hell don't like the idea of him nosing around here— especially when no one was home." He shot her a sharp look. "Did you check the place out? See if everything was OK?"

"Sloan did that before he left. What is it with you guys and Milo Scott?"

"He is a bad man," Maria chimed in. "I know that Señor Josh was friends with him, but he is bad news."

"Who's bad news?" demanded Nick, strolling into the kitchen from the mudroom. "Certainly not me."

"That's debatable," Shelly said with a laugh. "Were you at the rodeo all day?"

He nodded and, tossing his hat onto the coatrack near the back door, said, "I worked the chutes all the day—hot, dusty work, even if it's only sheep and calves and not bulls and broncos. I'm dying of thirst. Is there any beer in that refrigerator?"

"Of course. Help yourself."

"I intend to," he said, grinning, and proceeded to do just that. A moment later, slumped bonelessly in a kitchen chair with a tall cold bottle of Carta Blanca in front of him, he sighed blissfully. "Now this," he said as he took a long swallow, "makes it all worthwhile."

"When Shelly came back from the parade Milo Scott was here," Acey said as he seated himself across the table from Nick. Maria placed a bottle of beer in his hands and, snagging one for herself, joined the others at the oak table.

Nick jerked up as if jabbed with a cattle prod. "What did he want?" he demanded grimly.

"He said," Shelly repeated patiently, "that he wanted to talk to Acey. He also mentioned that he and Josh were good friends and that they often did business together—*mostly* based on nothing more than a handshake."

Acey snorted. "That fellow can't say more than a dozen words without there being at least three lies in them. Why the hell Josh thought so highly of him still escapes me." Shaking a finger at Shelly, he said, "You don't have no truck with him. He's a liar, a thief, and ten miles of ugly road. You ever find him on the place again, you get a gun and throw him off. Don't listen to a word he says—it'll all be lies or half-truths."

"You check the place out after he was gone?" Nick asked.

"Yes. Sloan did that." Her gaze moved from Nick's face to Acey's. Frustration in her voice, she demanded, "Is someone going to tell me what's going on? What is it about this guy that sets you all off? I mean aside from the fact that he's a known drug dealer? Sloan acted like the Gestapo and insisted upon checking the whole place out."

"Sloan was here?" Nick asked, curiosity gleaming in his green eyes. "Sloan, as in Sloan Ballinger? Hated enemy of the Grangers?"

"Yes. Sloan was here. He escorted me home from the parade." She shot Acey a dark look. "Acey set it up, and I didn't have much choice in the matter."

Nick whistled and glanced around the room. "Well, the place is still standing." He grinned at Shelly. "I thought for sure that we'd all hear the crack of doom and the world would end if a Ballinger ever stepped foot in this place."

"Tell me about Milo Scott," Shelly said, not about to be diverted.

Nick looked at Acey and shrugged his shoulders. "Not much to tell," he said slowly. "He's connected to the marijuana trade in the area—some say he's also a source of crack in the valley, and rumor also ties him to hard drugs in other parts of the county, maybe statewide. He pretty much keeps to himself and other like-minded people." Nick grimaced. "Even here we have an element we could do without, and I'm not talking about your backyard grower. Lots of people grow marijuana in this area, but it's mostly for private use—a few people probably grow enough to pay their property taxes or put some extra groceries on the table, but nothing big-time. Scott is changing that, and, worse, he's got a nasty streak. If things don't go his way, accidents and bad things seem to happen to anyone who crosses him." Briefly he related the loss of his bull, Sloan's colt, and the trashing of Cleo's place, as well as a few other incidents. "Of course, you can't prove anything, and that suits Scott just fine. I don't like him, I don't trust him, and he's probably more dangerous than anyone realizes."

"Jeb already told me some of that, about the drug connection, not about the vandalizing or the loss of animals," Shelly admitted, "but he told me enough to make me understand that Milo Scott wasn't the sort of man Josh would normally have had as a friend."

"I figure," Acey said, "that Scott paid off some, if not all, of Josh's gambling debts in return for that supposed friendship of theirs."

"Why would he do that?" Nick asked, frowning. He made a face. "Never mind. I got it. The land. All those remote parcels of Granger land just perfect for growing lots and lots of little patches of marijuana." He smacked his forehead. "Jesus! I should have put it together and tumbled to it sooner. When you put Josh's friendship with him in that context, it all makes sense."

Shelly's gaze moved around the kitchen table, studying the intent faces. These people were her family. Oh, perhaps not by blood, except for Nick, but they were her family nonetheless. They had blindly thrown in their lot with her, and they deserved honesty from her and needed to know just how deep a hole Josh had dug for himself. Taking a calming breath, she plunged right in, telling them everything—the huge deposits, the sad state of the Granger finances, and the suspicion, slight though it was, that Scott might have had something to do with Josh's death . . . that it *might* not have been a suicide.

There was heavy silence when she finished speaking. Nick stared at his beer bottle; Maria studied the flat top of the table, and Acey looked off into space, pulling absently on his left mustache.

Acey started nodding a moment later. "Yep. That explains a lot. I knew things were bad, but not that bad. You don't worry none about paying me a salary—I got enough laid by to take care of my needs." He glanced at her from under beetling brows. "And don't argue with me."

"Listen, I don't have a lot of cash available—I've put most of it into my herd and equipment, but if you need it," Nick said, looking at Shelly, "it's yours." He smiled bitterly. "Looks like Josh will get his money back in the end."

"I, too, have a little put aside," Maria said quietly, reaching out a comforting hand to Shelly. "It is yours."

Tears clogged her throat and burned her eyes, but she was smiling, albeit shakily, as she looked around the table. Her fingers tightened in Maria's warm hand. "Thank you," she managed, "you don't know how much your offers mean to me, but our situation is not quite that grave. I'm not broke—yet. First of all, the land is owned outright, and for that I'll be eternally grateful to Josh, that he didn't mortgage it to Milo. The money, however, is pretty much gone, but there is still enough, I hope, for us to get Granger Cattle Company up and running—provided we don't run amuck and buy Cadillac pickups!"

"And here I had my heart set on just that very thing," Nick teased. "A bright red one, with white leather interior. Yeah, the cows would have liked that."

Acey snorted, but laughter gleamed in his eyes.

Maria looked reprovingly at her son. "Always you joke and laugh," she said.

"Better than crying," Nick said, and took a swallow of his beer.

"Nick's right," Shelly chimed in. "We should be laughing. The land is debt-free, and after the cost of the Texas cattle is deducted, there's enough money to keep it running"—she made a face—"for a while without resorting to taking out loans from a bank." She grinned at them. "And don't forget that I am, I'll have you know, an artist—people actually pay me money for my paintings."

"What? Ten bucks a pop?" Acey growled, not being much for the arts.

"Hmm. Yes, that's about right," Shelly admitted, her eyes dancing.

"Well, that sure as hell ain't going to add much to the coffers," he muttered.

"Ten, Acey," she murmured, "as in thousand . . . ten thousand."

It took him a second to work it out. "Are you serious?" he finally managed, his expression thunderstruck.

She nodded. "Yes. I am. Believe it or not, there is a demand for my work. I've made a very nice living selling three or four pictures a year. Not a fortune, but enough."

He leaned back in his chair. "Well, then," he said, "if that's true, I don't see why Nick and I both can't have one of them red Cadillac pickups."

———⁂———

Several hours later, as she was sitting at Josh's desk, she thought of Acey's comment and smiled to herself. She'd love to see the expression on that old devil's face if she were ever able to present him with such a thing as a Cadillac pickup.

Imagining his reaction to such an extravagant gesture, she chuckled and reached for the file she'd left lying on the corner of the desk a few days ago—too lazy to put it in the file cabinet at the time. It was a very thin file, and from what she had seen, had just been a place where Josh had stuffed odds and ends like magazine renewals and memberships in various organizations. As she picked up the file, intending to put it away, a sheet of paper fluttered out, landing on the floor beside her chair. Bending over, she grabbed it, and before shoving it back in the file, glanced at it, her eyes widening as she read the contents.

Well, well, she thought, as she laid the document down in front of her. *Scott may have claimed that* mostly *he and Josh settled things with a handshake, but this document proves that they also put things in writing.* And it hadn't been there a couple of days ago when she'd first gone through the file—she'd swear on it. Which explained, she decided sourly, Scott's presence at the house today—he'd chosen a time when no one was likely to be around to place the document in a file—or rather place it in the file in such a manner that it would come to her attention.

She scanned the sheet of paper again. It was a copy of a simple lease agreement, stating that for the nominal sum of one thousand dollars, Josh Granger leased to Milo Scott, for ten years, several parcels of land adjoining the Mendocino National Forest. Her gaze dipped to the bottom of the page. *Josh's signature was notarized,* she thought, *but I see nothing on the document that indicates it was recorded in the recorder's office.* She studied Josh's signature and the date. Her heart began to thump. Josh had signed it the day before he committed suicide . . .

Chapter Thirteen

The date Josh signed the lease could just be a coincidence, Shelly told herself, biting her lower lip. But she didn't believe it. She couldn't at the moment see how the lease alone could have precipitated Josh's suicide, if it had been a suicide, she reminded herself for about the thousandth time. Unless, Josh had somehow reneged at the last moment . . .

The marijuana industry was huge, and in Mendocino County, it was probably the largest cash producer, earning more, all of it illegal, than timber and cattle combined, the two main legitimate industries. If Scott had been depending upon that land in the lease to plant a crop of pot . . . and Josh had backed out at the last moment . . . She swallowed. Thousands of dollars could have been at stake and could have provided a motive for murder. But had it? Maybe everything had just come crashing in on Josh, she thought sadly. Maybe signing the lease with a drug dealer had made Josh realize just how far he had fallen. Maybe the lease had been the final straw and had pushed him over the edge.

The lease in her hand, she stood up and paced around the office. She could speculate endlessly and accomplish nothing. The first thing she needed to know, she decided, was if the lease was legal. *The signature was notarized, so that gave it some legality, but the fact that it had not been recorded. . . . Maybe that gives me some wiggle room.*

She needed to talk to her attorney. Then she needed to let Jeb know what she had found. And dammit! It was nine-thirty on a Saturday night! Fat chance of reaching Mike Sawyer until Monday morning. Jeb would probably be at the dance tonight, but at the thought of searching through the mob at the recreation center trying to find him, she quailed. Sloan might be there, and, coward that she was, she admitted that she wasn't about to run the risk of bumping into him so soon after what had happened between them this afternoon. She sighed. It looked like she'd just have to wait to find out if the lease was significant or shed any light on Josh's death.

Despite all the activities going on in town, for Shelly, Sunday dragged. She smiled and clapped at the rodeo, cheered for the kids, laughed at the clown, and ate barbecued steak with some of Tom Smith's special spicy beans. No Oak Valley affair would have been complete without Tom's beans and Debbie Smith's Jell-O-and-fruit salad that they concocted for every community occasion (Tom was working this day at the rodeo grounds, having relinquished his spot in the kitchen in town). Tom had winked as he had served her a spoonful of the beans, and she had grinned when she spied the two tiny Tootsie Rolls he had slipped onto her plate. He was such an old dear. Having left a message for Jeb on his answering machine that morning, she kept her eye peeled for his big frame all day, but never saw him—or Sloan. For which she was grateful, she reminded herself firmly.

Keeping to the normal routine, before daylight Monday

morning she staggered downstairs to the kitchen. Acey was standing at the kitchen sink staring out the window. Mindful of the telephone calls she needed to make, she begged off from starting work until midmorning.

"It'll probably be after ten o'clock before I finally join up with you," she said, grabbing a mug of coffee.

Acey regarded her with a beady eye over his mug. After letting her squirm for a second or two, he grinned and said, "After the weekend, I don't think anybody's in a hurry to get started. Take your time, we'll manage without you. Besides, we've got everything just about ready."

It was well after 10:00 A.M. when Shelly finally reached Mike Sawyer at his office. As soon as the polite chitchat was out of the way, she said, "Listen, this weekend when I was going through some of Josh's files, I found a copy of a ten-year lease he signed with Milo Scott. Josh kept the grazing rights, but the lease doesn't look as if it was recorded. Do you know anything about it?"

"Not a great deal, but I seem to remember that Josh mentioned something about leasing some remote parcels to him. It was, I think, shortly before Josh . . . ah, died."

Telling herself not to read anything in Mike's hesitation, she asked, "Do you know if it was recorded, or doesn't that make any difference?"

"It would be best if it was recorded, but I have no specific knowledge if either one of the two parties involved did so. But to answer your question, if the lease has been executed properly, recorded or not, it's valid. Of course if you sold the land, and the lease wasn't recorded, then Scott would have to hope that the new owner would honor the lease, but he wouldn't have to."

"So you're saying that Milo Scott has a ten-year lease on several parcels of Granger land."

Sawyer cleared his throat. "Well, I haven't seen the document, but based on what you're telling me, yes, it would appear that he does."

"Can the lease be broken?"

He chuckled. "Shelly, you're talking to a lawyer, remember? Of course the lease can be broken, but do you really want to do that? It'll cost more in attorney's fees and court fees than it would be worth—especially if Scott wants to fight you. Why not let the lease stand?"

"Because I think that Scott intends to grow marijuana on those parcels. And if he were caught, wouldn't the land fall under the forfeiture laws?"

There was a pause, then he said, "Hmm. That's a possibility. Or at least it might be tied up temporarily in some sort of legal action until you were cleared of any connection to any illegal action."

"Sounds to me like reason enough to break the lease," Shelly said.

"Er, yes."

"Then do it," she said grimly, and hung up the phone.

The phone rang just as soon as she put it down. She eyed it for a moment. Probably Sawyer. Damn lawyers, always wanting the last word. Snatching up the phone, she said, "I meant what I said. Break it. I'm not going to argue with you about it either. If you won't do it, I'll get a lawyer who will."

"Why don't you tell me what it is I'm supposed to do first?" drawled Jeb.

"Oh, Jeb." Shelly said with a laugh. "I thought you were someone else."

"Obviously. You want to tell me what's going on?"

Succinctly she did. When she stopped speaking, Jeb murmured, "Interesting. But it doesn't prove a damn thing—nor is the lease illegal."

Feeling deflated, she muttered, "But if Josh tried to back

out of it, doesn't it provide Scott with a motive to, uh, you know . . ."

"Could. *If* Josh tried to back out, and we don't know that and have no way of finding out. For now, it's just . . . interesting."

Shelly snorted. *Interesting, my ass*, she thought, hanging up. Irritated and annoyed that her big find was turning out to be a dud as far as anyone else was concerned, she wandered into the kitchen and helped herself to another cup of coffee. Maria smiled a greeting from her position in front of the stove, and Shelly returned it before walking over to the kitchen table.

Nick was seated at the table finishing up what had been a big plate of scrambled eggs, fried potatoes, ham, and biscuits. Taking the chair across from him, Shelly eyed his rapidly emptying plate, and said, "I know we're partners, but I didn't know feeding you was part of the deal."

Nick grinned at her, his eyes dancing as he broke a biscuit and buttered it. "Don't worry, I won't eat up our profits. At least not much."

"I didn't think you'd mind," Maria began, an anxious expression on her face.

Shelly waved her away. "I don't. I'm just grumpy this morning and wanted someone to pick on."

"Why grumpy?" Nick asked with a raised brow.

She told him about the lease, but didn't mention any bearing, or not, it might have had on Josh's death.

"Good thing you told Sawyer to break it. Those forfeiture laws are a bitch, and innocent people sometimes get caught up in them."

"Yes, well, I just don't like the idea of Scott or anyone else having a say in what's done on Granger land."

"Spoken like a true Granger. Why I could just close my eyes," he drawled, "and hear your dear sainted brother saying those very same words. Everyone knows that Grangers hold Granger land sacrosanct for their exclusive use. Since Josh doesn't have a grave, bet your daddy would turn over in his grave if he knew that a shirttail relation like me was leasing some of his precious dirt. For pennies on the dollar, too."

"Oh, shut up," Shelly said, but she was smiling. "And don't slander my daddy—you were, what two—three when he died? You can't remember anything about him."

"True. But you'll have to admit it sure did sound like something one of your, our, dearly departed ancestors would have said."

"Probably." Looking around, she asked, "Where's Acey? And isn't it kind of late for you to be eating breakfast?"

Nick hooted. "Breakfast? This is my midmorning snack—I ate breakfast hours ago. As for Acey, he ran into town for some groceries. Said he'd be back shortly."

"If he doesn't run into some of those gossipy old men he likes to hang out with," Maria said darkly. "If he hooks up with them, we won't see him until noon."

"I don't think he'll waste any time this morning," Shelly said. "The cattle are due to arrive sometime today, and he wouldn't want to miss it."

As if to give credence to her words, the back door slammed and, after depositing his hat and jacket in the mudroom, Acey ambled into the kitchen. "Nasty day out there, cold, gray, some drizzle coming down," he said as he grabbed a mug and poured coffee. "Could have wished the girls were arriving in better weather."

"Hey, it's only California's liquid sunshine. They'll love it," Nick teased.

———❧❧———

Watching the sleek black cows some five hours later as they slipped and scrambled out of the shipping trucks, Shelly couldn't tell whether they appreciated California liquid sunshine or not. It wasn't really raining, it was more of a heavy mist, and she was grateful that it wasn't blazing hot as it could have been. She'd checked each animal off as it had left the truck, able to identify it by the numbers printed on the big yellow tag in the right ear. Her heart swelled as the corral filled with bellowing, milling cows. It didn't matter that it was gray and cold or muddy—Granger Cattle Company was in business again.

She glanced across at Nick and knew the smile on his face matched the one on hers. Acey looked as if he'd just won a bull-riding contest, his grin stretching from ear to ear. *Yep*, she thought, *Granger Cattle Company is back.*

The truckers were paid and sent on their way. Maria had joined them at the corral, and the four of them, oblivious to the dampness, leaned against the stout boards and stared at the constantly shifting black mass of cattle. They were a stirring sight, all gleaming, coal black hides, big brown eyes, wide nostrils, wonderful straight backs, and long loins. They were taller and longer than the old-fashioned Angus, and, having been bred to meet a changing market, they produced leaner, less fatty meat these days than a couple of decades ago.

"They are so beautiful," breathed Maria as she leaned on the corral, her hands clasped under her chin. "Your father would be so proud of you. He loved the cattle."

"How many did you say were already bred?" asked Acey.

"Hmm, just a second, let me look," Shelly said, leafing through the sheaf of papers she still held in her hand. "Ten— the older ones. The other twenty are open, and a few are yearlings—I'd have to check their registration papers to know for sure."

"Fall calves?" Nick inquired, eyeing the bigger cows.

"The ten? Yes. I have their breeding dates here some-place, but when Samuels and I made the deal, he said they had been bred to calve in late October, early November."

Acey nodded. "That's when most of the local cattlemen try to have their calf crop, some as early as September. Get those calves on the ground and up before bad weather hits; they nurse on their mamas all winter and about the time the spring grass comes along, they're ready to chow down on something besides Mama's milk."

Shelly frowned. "Everything is so ugly and yellow and dusty in the fall, and there isn't hardly any grazing at all—except on the valley floor. And this year, it's been so dry no one expects there to be much grass in the hills. I know that Dad and Josh always had fall calves, but is there any prob-lem with having some spring calves?"

"Nope. Just have to feed 'em more and longer, which can cut into your profits. But remember we've got those subirri-gated fields on the valley floor. Unlike a lot of the others, Grangers can breed whenever they want to—you've got the land and the pasture. But since we're not raising for the slaughter market, probably doesn't make much difference whether it's spring or fall," Acey replied.

"So, you gonna hold over the open ones and breed in Jan-uary for fall calves next year?" Nick asked, glancing at Shelly. "If that's the plan, let me tell you it's a long time to feed a cow with no return," he said.

"I know—before I made the deal, I factored in the cost of holding them over if I had to, against the cost of buying older heifers—it was a case of six of one, half a dozen of the other. So I compromised and bought some older heifers we can breed in June/July and then some yearlings we can breed in January. It was cheaper that way." She hesitated, thinking of the money it would cost to hold the yearling heifers over until January. Hesitantly, she said, "I know some cattlemen breed their yearlings."

Acey shook his head. "Bad idea. Cow ought to be sixteen–eighteen months old at a minimum—less calving problems. By breeding young, over the life of the cow, you *might* get one more calf out of her, but you also might lose her and the calf first time out of the chute."

Shelly and Nick nodded. "Well, it's settled then," Shelly said. "The yearlings wait until January. The others we'll be breeding to Beau in a few weeks."

Acey rubbed his chin. "Even with the poor grass this year, you've got enough land to feed this bunch or more for that matter without having to worry about putting up a lot of hay. You'll have a crop this fall from the ones that are already bred and come January, February, you can breed all the open ones and get ready for your spring crop. Sounds like a plan to me: fall calves *and* some spring ones—covers all the bases."

Shelly nodded slowly. "I knew I couldn't accomplish anything overnight, but it's just sort of dawned on me that it's going to take *years* to rebuild the Granger herds. When Dad ran the place, we had hundreds of cattle. This lot and Nick's are all we've got—and we'll be selling off a certain percentage of the crop each year, so that'll cut down on our increase." She made a face. "And, of course, we can't count on a crop of just heifers either."

"Told you, it wasn't something you could just start and then drop. Takes commitment. Planning—long-range planning—you've got to be thinking three, four years down the road. You'll be building up your herd one calf crop at a time. There'll be disappointments, and, if you've done your homework, there'll be successes, but it ain't something that happens overnight. It's gonna take a lot of luck and years of hard work." Acey grinned and gleefully rubbed his hands together. "Sounds like job security to this old cowboy."

They all laughed.

After seeing that the cattle had a salt lick, hay, and water, and were beginning to settle down, they walked to the house.

"Are you going to have the ten preg tested?" Maria asked, as they reached the house.

"Be a smart thing to do," Nick said, holding open the back door for them. "The trip probably stressed them out, and it's not likely any of them aborted, but it'd be good to know."

"Smart idea," Shelly said. "We'll give them a week or so to settle in, then we can do it." She glanced at Acey. "Which vet would you recommend? The one here in the valley or one from Willits or Ukiah?"

"Tracy'll do you a good job. She's mainly into horses, but Nick has used her for the past couple years"—he slanted her a sly glance—"and of course, everyone knows that Sloan thinks she's the cleverest thing since sliced bread. She does all the AI work on his fancy cutting paints."

"From my observation, Jeb also thinks rather well of her," Shelly returned dryly, remembering Jeb's easy manner with the tall red-haired vet.

"That's a fact," Acey said. "Just about everyone likes Tracy. She's a good vet . . . for a woman."

Shelly snorted, and Maria sent him a look. He grinned. "Just kidding, ladies, just kidding. Tracy Kingsley is a great vet."

"She really is," said Nick. "And while she specializes in horses and does some small animal stuff, she knows her way around a cow—or a bull for that matter."

"I'm sure she is particularly knowledgeable about bull,"

Shelly said. "Working with Neanderthals like you, she'd have to be."

Acey snickered, and Nick just shrugged and smiled.

Several days later, watching Tracy Kingsley's smooth action around a chute full of unhappy, bawling cows, Shelly had to agree that the woman did indeed know her way around cattle. So did Sloan, she thought sourly, staring as Sloan, astride a big black-and-white paint horse, urged several cows into the catch pen. He and Nick were both on horseback and while they could have done the work on foot, it was faster and safer on the back of a horse.

Shelly had been looking forward to meeting Tracy Kingsley in person, but she had been taken aback when the vet had shown up at the barn forty-five minutes ago and she had caught sight of the big Suburban pulling up behind the vet's green pickup. Shelly noticed that behind Sloan's vehicle was a white two-horse trailer. The reason for the horse trailer became apparent when, with a polite nod in her direction, Sloan had exited the vehicle and walked around to the back and began unloading a pair of horses. The second horse, a leggy buckskin-and-white gelding, was for Nick, and her eyes narrowed when she saw the friendly way Sloan and Nick greeted each other. Well, well. Funny that Nick had never mentioned that he and Sloan were such good buddies.

A smile on her face, her hand outstretched, Tracy had said, "Hi, I'm Tracy Kingsley, and you must be Shelly Granger." As the two women shook hands, Tracy added, "It's nice to meet you in person. Josh spoke of you often, and I enjoyed talking to you on the phone the other day when you set up the appointment."

There were a few minutes of polite conversation between the group of five; Nick, Sloan, Acey, Tracy, and Shelly. Despite Sloan's disturbing presence, Shelly found herself relaxing and liking the vet—and determined to ignore Sloan.

Garbed in worn blue jeans, a green-checked shirt, and comfortable leather boots, her red hair caught back in a ponytail, Tracy had a friendly, competent air about her. She looked to be in her mid-to-late thirties, and while she wasn't a beauty, she was very attractive with her slim build, intelligent blue eyes, and smiling mouth. When the conversation turned to the cattle, it was obvious that while horses and small animals might be her specialty, she was very knowledgeable about cattle, too. The easy give-and-take among the others also told Shelly that they were no strangers to each other.

"You been out to the Broken Spoke lately?" Nick asked Tracy with a grin. The Broken Spoke, Shelly knew, consisted of thousands of acres of wild and rough mountainous terrain that had been owned by the Bransford family for several generations. The ranch was remote—being about twenty-five miles out on the Tilda Road—and since the Tilda Road had all the curves of a snake's back and was graveled to boot, remote meant *remote*.

Tracy grimaced and shook her head. "Nooo thank you. Once was enough."

Sloan laughed. "Don't tell me old Bransford had you out there to actually doctor something?"

Even Shelly remembered that the Bransfords were known for their cut-and-dried attitude toward their animals. Sick or hurt, cow, horse, or dog, except for some basic tending, it got better, died, or was shipped to slaughter. "Got no truck with this wasting time and fussing over critters crap," old Ted Bransford had been heard to exclaim on more than one occasion. "They're *animals*, for Christ's sake!"

Tracy grimaced at Sloan's question. "Yes, he did—seems he had this expensive cow dog he'd bought last year and he wanted me to look at it."

Nick snickered, and Tracy's lips quirked. "He told me that the dog had just been lying there out back doing nothing for a couple of days, not eating or drinking, and he thought as how I might take a look at it, considering how much money he had paid for it. I suggested that he bring the dog into the clinic, but he informed me that he was a busy man and didn't have the time and wasn't about to take the time. I was a mobile vet, wasn't I? He had a point, and I was concerned about the dog, so I drove out all twenty-five miles of wretched road to his place." She shook her head disgustedly. "When I got there, the dog was dead."

"Oh, what a shame," Shelly said. "Too bad he hadn't called you earlier."

Nick burst out laughing and Tracy muttered, "He would have had to have called me a *lot* earlier. The dog hadn't just died, Shelly—it had been dead for three or four days. Good thing it was cold weather, or it would've been crawling with maggots." At Shelly's look of incredulity, Tracy nodded, and added, "Yes, I mean dead. Dead. Dead. Stiff as a board and deader than a doornail. I told him as much, and he just looked down at the dog, and said, 'Guess that explains why he wasn't moving around much.'"

"Are you serious?" Shelly demanded, torn between shock and amusement.

Tracy nodded. "Yes, indeedy. A real caring, observant soul is Mr. Bransford."

"Just be glad there aren't too many like him around," Sloan said.

Tracy snorted. "Yeah, right. There's too many for my liking—believe me, I could tell you some tales that would make even your hair stand up."

Pulling on his mustache, Acey said, "OK, that's enough jawing. We got work to do and I'd like to get it done today, if you all don't mind. This ain't no tea party."

Shelly and Tracy exchanged a grin. Her bright blue eyes dancing, Tracy said, "Well, don't get your shorts in a twist, Acey. We'll get your ladies all sorted out in no time."

And true to her word, they did. Riding their horses, Nick and Sloan herded the cattle into the catch pen and Acey prodded them toward the squeeze chute. Once caught, Tracy wormed, shot, and preg tested when necessary and Shelly acted as her assistant, handing wormer, plastic gloves, lubricant, or syringe as needed, and kept track of the paperwork. The work progressed smoothly and swiftly.

To Shelly's relief the ten pregnant cows were indeed pregnant. Sloan and Nick had cut them out from the herd first, and Shelly hadn't envied Tracy the job in front of her. Preg testing a cow was dirty, messy work, and the cows protested vigorously when Tracy eased her hand and arm, as far as her elbow, into their rectums to check for pregnancy. Shelly didn't blame the cows for bellowing at the insult. Manure flew, and by the time they were finished, Tracy's blue overalls, which she'd put on to protect her clothing, were ready for the wash. Smiling at Shelly as she slipped off the dirty, long plastic glove that covered her from fingertips to shoulder, Tracy said, "Unless I miss my guess, come October, November, you should have your first calves on the ground and be ready to rebreed your next crop." She motioned to the cows. "Now let's get the rest of these babies done."

Watching Nick and Sloan work the cattle in the big pen was fascinating, and Shelly found her gaze lingering on Sloan often and more than she liked. He looked very tough and virile in tight-fitting Levi's and a blue, long-sleeved chambray shirt open at the neck. His face was half-hidden by the brim of his black Stetson, and his concentration was all on the cows. The day was hot, and staring at a streak of sweat as it trickled down his dark cheek, she was conscious of a tingling in her breasts, and her breath quickened. That thin liquid line down the side of his face seemed to mesmerize her, and she imagined the taste of it, the scent, the saltiness of his skin if she were to kiss it away.

Almost as if he could feel her eyes on him, Sloan pulled on the reins and brought his black-and-white paint to a halt. Pushing back his hat, he stared at her across the width of the corral. His gaze fastened on her face, and Shelly flushed and looked away.

"My God, that's the first time I've ever seen that!" Tracy remarked, a sweaty grin on her face.

"What?" Shelly asked, glancing over at Tracy.

"A man eating a woman with his eyes. If you were a T-bone, I'd say Sloan was a starving man with a voracious appetite."

"You're mistaken," Shelly said swiftly. "There's nothing between us."

"Uh-huh. Sure. You just keep right on believing that."

Shelly made a face. "OK. There *is* something between us, I just don't know what—and I'd give anything in the world if there wasn't."

Shelly tried to keep her eyes off Sloan after that; it was difficult, but she managed. Sort of. It was impossible not to stare as Nick and Sloan seemed effortlessly to move the cattle right where they wanted the animals. It didn't take her long to realize that they had some sort of contest going on—or that they were pitting the skill of their horses against each other. First Nick and then Sloan would point out a particular cow, then aim his horse at it and just sit back in the saddle and hang on as the horse expertly cut the cow from the herd and worked it to the catch pen. The horses' skill was breathtaking as they stopped on a dime, whirled, and, ears pinned to their skulls, crouched like cats, to prevent a stubborn cow from going in the wrong direction. Their movements were fluid and smooth, the sun making their coats glisten and, with ears laid back, heads held low, it was clear they meant business as they kept each animal moving precisely where they wanted.

Tracy stopped for a minute to watch the show. "Sloan's got some of the best cutting horses in the industry, and what you're seeing is an example of why."

"The horses are really something, aren't they? It's like they can outthink the cow, that they know just what it's going to try next," Shelly breathed, as Nick's buckskin, with no noticeable guidance from Nick, shot off after a cow that had tried to make a break for it.

They finished up just after noon, and Shelly invited Tracy to stay for lunch. Removing her filthy overalls, Tracy said, "I'd love to." Washing her hands with the warm water from the tank she carried in the vet pack at the rear of the pickup, Tracy nodded to the cows. "You've got some fine animals there. How do you plan to breed?"

Nick and Sloan dismounted and after giving the horses a drink of water from the trough, tied them to the side of the trailer. Walking up to where Tracy and Shelly were standing and hearing Tracy's question, Nick said, "Shelly has an older bull that Josh didn't sell—he's got some great old Granger bloodlines. Granger's Ideal Beau is sound and fertile. We'll use him to breed our own bulls. Beau has several crosses to Beau Granger, and we're excited about reestablishing the bloodline."

Beau Granger had been one of the best-known Granger bulls ever bred, and his fame had been nationwide. His get had commanded top dollar at Angus sales all across the

United States, and nearly thirty years after his death, many of the top stock of today traced back to him.

"Didn't most of your cows carry a lot of the same blood?" Sloan asked, looking directly at Shelly. Except for that one brief moment, she'd ignored him all morning, and he was getting tired of it. Volunteering to help had seemed a good idea last Sunday when he and Nick had met at the recreation center to help with the cleaning up after the dance Saturday night. The pair of them and a half dozen other volunteers, Tom Smith in charge of the crew, had made short work of emptying trash cans, putting the folding tables and chairs away, and sweeping out the huge cement floor building. Someone else had already taken down the red, white, and blue crepe paper decorations from the ceiling. Four or five women, Debbie Smith and Cleo among them, had been in the kitchen, making certain that it was in order. When the job was done, Nick and Sloan had stopped to talk a minute about a mare Nick had bred to Sloan's buckskin-and-white paint stallion the previous month. The mare had been confirmed by Tracy to be in foal, and Nick had just happened to mention the arrival of the cattle. Since he was at loose ends and had been racking his brains for a way to insinuate himself back into Shelly's presence, it had seemed a heaven-sent opportunity. "I'll be glad to lend a hand when you get around to shots and worming," Sloan had said casually. "I can even bring along Cognac for you to try out with the cattle. You can see how much cow he has in him."

Cognac was a paint gelding that Nick had been thinking about buying, and he had leaped at the idea. "Great! I'll call you once the cows arrive and I know when Shelly wants to have the vet over."

Sloan had known that Shelly wouldn't be well pleased to see him, but he figured, ah hell, he didn't know what he'd figured. He grimaced. Which was about par for his relationship with her. Still, he'd caught her looking at him, and from the look on her face, it hadn't been difficult to see what had been on her mind. He'd gotten a boner that would have done a stallion proud and had almost forgotten where he was. Something else she seemed to do to him whenever they were together.

At Sloan's question, forcing herself to be polite, Shelly glanced at him. And wished she hadn't. God! That dark, intensely masculine face, the blue chambray clinging in damp patches to his chest, the scent of horses and cows all around them made the most lustful images fill her mind.

Jerking her gaze away, Shelly said, "Yes, they did. Grangers always did a lot of line breeding. That's part of the reason I bought these particular cows—Granger Cattle Company didn't breed them, but they do carry several of our lines."

Nick chimed in, "We're going to try to intensify those lines by doing as much line breeding as we can." He looked discouraged. "It's going to be hard. My herd is small—not more than twenty cows, and I've only got two bulls—neither one a Granger direct."

"Which is all the bull you need," Acey said tartly. "Now come on, let's get out of the sun and go get some chow. I'm starving, and I need my vittles." He glanced at the two women. Wiggling his eyebrows, his wise old eyes dancing, he murmured, "Fresh women and hot vittles keep a man young, don't you know."

Chapter Fourteen

❧

$\mathcal{A}$s they walked inside, the house was cool and inviting after the heat outside, and the scent of baked chicken and apple pie was floating in the air. Stopping in the mudroom, everyone washed up in the big old deep porcelain sink by the back door before trekking into the kitchen. As they spied the pile of food that Maria had laid out on the table, there was a collective moan of pleasure. Anticipating their arrival to within minutes, Maria had just put out tall frosted glasses for the pitcher of iced tea on the counter and taken an apple pie from the oven. Bliss.

Smiling over her shoulder at them as she placed a big blue bowl of potato salad on the table, she said, "I was watching for you. After this morning's work, I figured that you'd all be hungry as bears."

Giving her a hug as she walked to the table, Shelly said, "Maria, don't ever even *think* of retiring. This is wonderful!"

Maria laughed. "I *am* retired, child, but I knew if I left the food to you and Nick, you'd all be eating peanut butter sandwiches."

Sloan stopped before Maria, and, taking her hand in his, he kissed it extravagantly. "Madame, I thank you. My mouth thanks you. My stomach thanks you. We all thank you." He glanced at Shelly. "Peanut butter sandwiches?"

Shelly shrugged. "Hey, I may be a modern woman, but

you can't expect me to work cattle all morning *and* cook up a feast for lunch." She grinned. "What I need is a house husband."

Nick and Sloan groaned.

"You know that isn't a bad idea," Tracy said as she sat down next to Sloan at the table. "I think I'll get me one. Be nice to come home after a hard day of wrestling cows and nasty mares to find a warm meal and handsome face waiting for me."

Acey winked as he reached for the platter of baked chicken. "Sweetheart, you say the word, and I'll be happy to apply for the job."

This sally provoked some ribald comments about old men and young women. Lunch was a raucous affair.

Toward the end of the meal, when they were all digging into Maria's tart apple pie, Tracy looked from Shelly to Sloan, and said, "I don't want to start anything, but aren't you two supposed to kill each other on sight? Ever since I came to the valley, I've heard tales about the Granger and Ballinger feud. Are you telling me it isn't true?"

Sloan and Shelly exchanged glances. There was an awkward pause, then Sloan said, "The feud was at its worst before the turn of the century—the rest of us have just sort of . . . kept up the tradition." He made a face. "Ballingers and Grangers just naturally seem to find themselves on the opposite side of any question. In a place this small and remote, it creates bad will and tends to keep the old feuds going."

Tracy looked from one to the other. "But you're here today—helping a Granger I might add. And Nick and Acey are both here." She glanced at the two men. "Unless I'm mistaken, haven't both of you worked for Ballingers *and* Grangers from time to time? Isn't that a no-no?"

Acey snorted. "No, it ain't a no-no. Grangers and Ballingers might rub each other the wrong way, but the two families had to face the fact that the other residents had to be able to deal with both of them without reprisals, or the area would have been split right down the middle—and that wouldn't have been good for anybody."

"The Ballinger/Granger feud," Nick added, "is the stuff of legends, and like most legends, it all happened a long time ago." He made a face. "Which isn't to say the families are the best of friends today." He glanced over at Shelly. "Wasn't it in the seventies sometime that there was that plan to bring in a wood-burning electrical plant?"

Shelly nodded, wondering what Nick was thinking. This was his family, his history that they were talking about, and yet he had to pretend otherwise. From the expression on his face, she couldn't tell anything, but there was a look in his eyes that made her suspect the conflict inside of him. "Yes, that's right," she said with an uncertain smile at Nick. "I was just a kid, but I remember all the yelling and shouting that went on."

"That was the most recent time," said Acey, "and it left a lot of hard feelings in the valley."

Playing with his empty glass, Nick declared, "It's hard to explain to an outsider. There are several people in the valley related a generation or two back to both Ballingers and Grangers—and they tend to walk a careful line, not taking either side if they can help it." He grimaced. "In fact they tend to not want to claim either family, since both sides disowned the sinners that dared to cross the line between Ballinger and Granger. These days for most of them the feud is just an interesting family footnote. Sloan and his family and Shelly and . . ." He stopped, looked at Shelly with bleak eyes, then muttered, "Shelly's the last of the valley Grangers, and when she marries or dies, hopefully as a very *old* lady, that'll probably be the end of the story."

"Oh, I don't know about that," Sloan murmured. He

glanced at Shelly. "What about Grangers from New Orleans?"

"Roman? He's a Granger all right, but a New Orleans Granger." She stared challengingly at Sloan. "So I *am* the last of the Oak Valley Grangers."

"Not a very prolific family," Sloan said dryly.

"Just because we don't breed like rabbits"—she smiled sweetly—"like some families. . . ."

Hastily, Acey said, "Well, there you have it, Tracy. In the over a hundred years since the Ballingers and Grangers first laid eyes on each other, all of us in the valley have learned"—and he shot a dark look at both Sloan and Shelly—"to get along."

"OK, I can understand that," Tracy said, pushing aside her crumb-scattered plate, "but what about the principals—actual Grangers and Ballingers." She pointed to Sloan and Shelly. "Like those two." Despite Acey's intervention, the interplay between Sloan and Shelly hadn't escaped her.

Sloan made a face, and Shelly wiggled uncomfortably. How *did* one explain about her and Sloan? Shelly wondered. She didn't understand it herself. She peeked at Sloan—he didn't appear to be willing to offer an explanation either. There was a small silence, but before it became awkward, with a rueful smile, Shelly said, "It's a weird relationship— I'd be the first to admit it, but not *every* Granger or Ballinger is at the other's throat. As Nick mentioned, there have been cases of Grangers and Ballingers marrying—also, as Nick said, usually causing a lot of teeth gnashing and disapproval from the two families. Jeb Delaney's maternal grandparents are an example. When they got married, from what I've heard, it brought all the ugly feelings out in the open again and for a decade or two, emotions ran strong again."

"Of course," Sloan said, "you have to remember that Jeb's grandmother, a member of the New Orleans branch of the

Granger family, was engaged to Shelly's grandfather's brother at the time. When my great-uncle, Matt, ran off with her—just days before the wedding, I might add—it caused a huge scandal. And you can't just blame the resulting uproar on the Ballinger/Granger feud—any family would have been outraged." His gaze rested on Shelly's face. "I know I'd be out for blood if someone stole my bride—unlike Shelly's great-uncle, I'd have hunted good ole Matt Ballinger down and killed him . . . and taken my bride back."

"Whoa. You're telling me that a Ballinger stole a Granger bride and the world didn't tip on its axis?" Tracy asked, looking impressed.

"Hell, honey," Acey answered, "Ballingers and Grangers have been stealing each other's brides and grooms since the very beginning—that's what caused so much of the bad feeling." He scratched his chin. "And one or two other things that I'm too polite to mention in front of ladies."

Tracy stared. "Let me get this straight." She pointed to Sloan and Shelly again, who both looked as if they would have been more comfortable having open-heart surgery—without anesthesia—than sitting right here. "You two are actually related—way back?"

Sloan shrugged. "Way back, yeah."

"Way, *way* back," Shelly added. "So far back it almost doesn't count."

Maria, who had been silent during most of the conversation, rose to her feet. After picking up several empty plates, as she walked to the sink, she said, "Well, I think the whole thing is all very silly. Ballingers and Grangers have always acted like spoiled little children—they each want what the other has simply because the other has it."

No one argued with her, and the subject was dropped. Leaping to their feet, they all helped clear the table and would have remained under Maria's feet trying to be of use if she hadn't shooed them out of the kitchen like a bunch of pesky flies.

"Go. Go," she ordered. "You will only slow me down."

After thanking her for lunch, they meekly followed orders and trooped outside. Since the work was basically done for the day, in a very few minutes, thanks and good-byes said, with a friendly wave, Tracy pulled away. Nick, Acey, and Sloan loaded the two horses, Sloan lingering to talk to the two men. Shelly, intent upon putting some distance between herself and Sloan, wandered to the barn, to the office, giving the others the excuse that she wanted to file the paperwork on the cows.

Standing in the doorway to the barn office, Shelly stopped and looked around, a feeling of nostalgia winging through her. The barn office had been her father's sanctuary, and despite her mother's repeated request that he move it into the house, he'd insisted upon keeping it right where it was. She smiled. All his old cowboy cronies didn't think twice about stopping to jaw a while when he was out in the barn office, but they'd have hesitated to do so in the house—one of the reasons, she now suspected, he'd clung so stubbornly to it. There had been an old kerosene heater to knock the chill off on winter days, and the high roof and the heavy timbers of the barn kept it cool in the summertime—although she remembered that there'd also been a couple of fans kept handy for blistering August days. The office was spacious, and a big pot of bitter black coffee had always been kept simmering on an ancient hotplate. An old refrigerator just outside the door usually had some beer or soft drinks in it for anybody who dropped in.

Her father's office had been a casual meeting place for many of the local ranchers. Often, when very young, she'd come out here and found the place full of bewhiskered, tobacco-smoking or -chawing men wearing battered cowboy hats, faded blue jeans, and manure-stained boots, all of them sitting around and talking about the hay crop, the calf crop, the weather, someone's new horse or cow dog. She clung to that memory, as she did to one of the few other clear recollections she had of time spent with her father. The memory of skipping out to the barn office and peeking around the doorway to watch him work at the massive oak desk that still sat at the far side of the room drifted through her mind. He always seemed to sense her presence, and he'd look up from whatever paperwork he was doing and, with a big smile, call her in to visit him. She'd climb into his lap and prattle away about her doings, or listen rapt as he told her some funny little story about the cattle. Sometimes he'd hand her the crayons he'd kept in his top desk drawer just for such visits. "Draw me a cow," he'd say, a smile in his voice. "A real, real purty one. Just for Daddy."

She didn't know how many cows she'd drawn for him during the short time she'd had him, but it must have been a bunch, she thought with a bittersweet pang. Josh had found a stack of them in the bottom drawer of the desk after their father's death and had given them to her when she had been about sixteen. The first budding of my artistic talent, she mused wryly . . . and her father had treasured them.

Swallowing the lump that rose in her throat, she walked into the office and sat down behind the desk. Laying aside the paperwork she carried, she ran a caressing hand over the smooth surface of the desk. Her dad's desk. She felt close to him here, and if she closed her eyes, she'd swear that she smelled the faint scent of tobacco that had surrounded him and heard the deep rumble of his voice. Tears welled in her eyes, and she wondered what he'd think of her plans. He'd approve, she was confident of that much, and she figured he'd probably be pleased that his old office wasn't abandoned, gathering dust and cobwebs anymore.

Ignoring work that needed to be done with the rest of the barn, during the last couple of weeks, she'd spent every spare moment she had in the office, cleaning it, painting it, stocking it, going through files, making it hers. A good used refrigerator had replaced the old one just outside the doorway; a coffeemaker and a microwave now sat on the bank of new almond-colored metal cabinets. The pertinent files were in pristine order in the two oak filing cabinets her father had used, the wood dark with age. After their father's death, Josh had moved everything into one of the rooms in the old house that he had made into an office—who knows how much history of Granger Cattle Company had been lost when the house had burned down. Josh had been able to save some things, though, and through the Angus Association had been able to get duplicates of the most important papers—those he had placed in his office in the new house. She grimaced. And she had just spent a couple of days carting many of those same papers back out to the barn office. Guess she was more like her dad than she realized.

She glanced around, liking what she saw. The walls were painted white, and the floor was varnished pine. The wide window that looked toward the back of the house and driveway was framed with new blue gingham curtains; a narrow bookcase she'd swiped from Josh's office sat underneath it. Nick had picked up four wooden chairs in various designs from a used furniture store for her in Ukiah the last time he'd been down there, and they had been placed about the room. She'd ordered a small brown Naugahyde sofa from the JC Penney catalog—it should arrive next week at the Penney's store in Ukiah. A new Angus magazine and several pamphlets and cattle supply catalogs lay scattered across the top of an oval table she'd raided from one of the extra bedrooms. She'd also absconded with a couple of lamps and a nightstand. The office, she decided with satisfaction, looked pleasant and efficient. She frowned. She'd need a computer and would have to get hooked up to the Internet during the next month, and before winter she'd have to do something about heat, but at least that was one decision she could put off for a while.

Her mind on all the other things she'd need to do soon, she rose to her feet, picked up the papers she'd brought in with her, and crossed to the filing cabinet. It only took a few minutes to file the papers, and she made a face at the half-empty drawer before she slammed it shut. The one file cabinet was empty, and this one didn't have much in it either. But it would, she promised herself. Granger Cattle Company was going to grow. She had big plans for it.

She turned away and stopped, startled to see Sloan standing in the doorway, his black cowboy hat in one hand dangling near his knees. How long had he been standing there? It gave her a funny feeling to think of Sloan watching her when she was unaware of it.

Ignoring the leap in her pulse, she smiled politely, and asked, "Can I do something for you?"

As soon as the words left her mouth, she knew that they were a mistake. Sloan's slow, distinctly carnal smile told her exactly what he was thinking. Her chin lifted, and her eyes narrowed, daring him to say what was on his mind.

Sauntering into the office, Sloan murmured, "Honey, you really should be careful what you say. There are some men who might take that as an invitation . . . for oh, just all sorts of things."

"But since you're not one of those men," she said, one hand resting on her hip, "I really don't have anything to worry about, do I?"

"Don't push your luck."

"Come on, Sloan—what is it you want? We've said good-bye, and I can't think of one thing we need to talk about—I certainly don't have time to play games."

He stared at her, thinking she looked good enough to eat—even in stained blue jeans and a smudged oversize purple T-shirt. The jeans fit just as they should, cupping her butt and sliding slimly down her thighs, and despite its large size, the T-shirt did nothing to disguise her breasts. She wore a bra under the shirt, and he had some dark thoughts about the gentleman who had invented that confining garment. The image of her swelling breasts and raspberry-hued nipples swam into his mind, and he felt his own body's instant response. Since it was unlikely that she would welcome an advance at the moment, he quelled his unruly instincts, trying to act in a civilized manner.

Smiling ruefully, he asked, "Why do I have to want something? Maybe I just came in to say thanks again for lunch. Did you think of that?"

"Did you?"

He scratched his check. Amusement gleaming in his eyes, he admitted, "Nope. I came to ask you out to dinner on Friday night."

Shelly looked astonished. "As in a date?" she asked cautiously, curiosity in her gaze.

"Yeah. Why not?"

"Because it would be a waste of both of our times," she muttered. "Look, I know that what happened Saturday might lead you to think that I have ball-bearing heels, but let me assure you I don't. And if you're looking for an easy lay—I ain't it."

His face darkened, and he walked up to her, crowding her back against the file cabinet. "Honey, you're overestimating your charms—if all I wanted was to get laid, believe me, there are enough women out there who would be willing to share my bed with damn little encouragement from me."

"Modesty isn't your strong suit, is it?" she said, her breathing rapid, sexual excitement welling up inside of her. He'd always had this effect on her, and she hated herself for her response—and him for being able to create the almost irresistible urge to fling herself into his arms. Again.

He grinned. "Nope. Ballingers have always known their worth." He ran a lean finger down her cheek. "And you know something else? We've always known exactly what we want . . . and more times than not, we get it."

"And that's supposed to mean something to me? I should take heed, or warning or something?" she asked, an open taunt in her voice.

Sloan crowded up closer, his hard body pushing into hers, trapping her between the file cabinet and his bulk. "Yeah, honey, you really should take warning." He bent his head, his breath caressing her ear. "I want you, Shelly. Saturday changed nothing between us." His lips trailed light as a butterfly's touch across her jaw. "In fact, you might say, Saturday clarified things for me. Made me realize *precisely* what it is that I want—you."

Shelly had trouble breathing, her heart was hammering in her chest and her blood simmered, racing in her veins. His mouth was so close, so temptingly close . . . She fought the impulse to throw her arms around his neck and crush her lips against his. "Is that so?" she managed to croak.

He lifted his head and smiled down at her. "Yeah, honey, it is. So, you gonna have dinner with me Friday night?"

Fighting back a laugh at his pure male arrogance, she shoved him hard in the chest. "Get out of here, Sloan. Like I said—I don't have time to play games."

He let her push him backward. Turning his hat in his hand, he said quietly, "No games, Shelly. Let's start over. Let's just shuck all the baggage from the past and see what happens this time. We're not kids anymore. We're adults, and we should be able to act like it." He grinned. "At least most of the time."

She smiled faintly, but she was shaking her head. "Starting over doesn't solve anything for us. I can't forget the past—not when I know you lied to me and were seeing another woman, telling her you loved her at the same time you were telling me the same thing." Her smile faded and her eyes searched his. "I'd never trust you—I'd always wonder if you were stringing me along again."

A muscle twitched in his cheek and his eyes darkened. "I never strung you along, goddammit! I loved you, and I meant it when I said so. What happened with Nancy was—"

"Was what?" she asked when he stopped. "A mirage? Something I dreamed up? Something I imagined I saw?"

"No, you saw it all right, and you heard what I said just fine, but suppose I told you it was all a setup?" he demanded, anger bubbling just below the surface. "Suppose that Nancy and Josh put their heads together and created a little play that night—I was the lead and you were the audience, only neither one of us knew the act was especially written for us—that its whole purpose was to bust us up."

Disgust filled her. Turning away, she said bleakly, "You know, I'd have a lot more respect for you if you'd just admit the truth instead of trying to lay the blame on someone else."

Sloan reached for his shirt pocket, then remembered he didn't smoke anymore. Cursing under his breath, he said, "I'm not blaming them—they had their own agenda—Nancy never made any bones about wanting to marry me, and Josh, despite what he may have said to you, would have rather seen you in a damned convent than married to me. I'd be the first to concede that they did a great job. We both fell into their hands like ripe plums—and it was all a sham—a wellconstructed scene with Nancy pushing my buttons to get me to say exactly what you needed to hear to convince you that

I was a liar and two-timing cheat." He gave an ugly laugh. "And you bought it, lock, stock, and barrel, just as Josh knew you would. But just to make certain, he whisked you out of the state and away from me so damned fast you couldn't have changed your mind if you wanted to—and I was never allowed to explain to you my side of the story. Did it ever occur to you that I might have been trying to throw Nancy off the scent? She could be vicious when she didn't get her way—and she was older, far more sophisticated—you'd have been no match for her. If she'd thought for one second that you had something that she wanted, in a thousand ways she'd have made life hell for you—and I wasn't about to allow that to happen."

Something in his voice made her look at him, really look at him. His expression was bitter, the gold eyes icy and grim. *He believes everything he's saying.* His words and expression shook her. Was it possible that she had misinterpreted what she had seen and heard that night? She had believed the opposite for so long that it was difficult even to consider an alternative point of view. But. But she couldn't pretend that his take on Nancy wasn't correct. If Nancy had thought for even one second, had even suspected, that Sloan wasn't in her thrall, she'd have come after the competition with fangs bared and claws outstretched. Shelly swallowed. These days Nancy's words and actions would be more irritating and infuriating than hurtful, but at eighteen. . . . At eighteen, unsure, not totally confident with herself, Shelly realized how vulnerable she would have been, how devastating having Nancy as an enemy would have been. Nancy had been older, smarter, infinitely crueler, and more selfish, and would have known a dozen different ways to annihilate her, to destroy her confidence, her belief in herself, even her belief that Sloan loved *her* and not Nancy. And Sloan . . . One thing about Sloan that she had never doubted—he would always protect his own. . . . Everything he said made a painful sort of sense to her. Her heart clenched. Despair swept through her. Had she completely misunderstood what she had seen that night? She shook her head. But he *had* to be wrong! Josh wouldn't have— Her thoughts crashed to a halt. And it occurred to her again that Josh had done a lot of things she wouldn't have believed possible until recently. She bit her lip. Maybe . . . maybe there was some kernel of truth in what Sloan was saying. She wanted to believe him, but believing him would mean that Josh had . . . Jesus. This was crazy. Why was she listening to him? *Because her heart wanted to believe.* Cool logic might reject everything he said, but her heart; ah, her heart had a mind of its own.

Her gaze fell to her dusty boots. "Where would we go?" she asked, scaring herself at how easily the words came.

Sloan's breath sucked in, his heart pounding with thick, hard strokes. "Ukiah," he said, glad to hear that his voice sounded normal and not stunned. "There are a couple of good restaurants there. Not world-class, but good."

She risked a glance at him. Smiled almost shyly. "OK. What time?"

"Uh, the drive'll take an hour and a half, how 'bout I pick you up about five-thirty?"

"OK. Five-thirty Friday afternoon."

Wearing a smitten smile, Sloan floated away, hardly able to believe his luck. He had a date with Shelly. *Hot damn!*

Unaware that she was wearing a smile similar to his, Shelly watched him leave. She was crazy. Absolutely raving mad. Sloan was probably the best liar she'd ever met. Worse, he was a Ballinger, and she was a Granger. If she dared to believe one word he said, she'd have to admit that her brother, a man she had respected, trusted, and loved all her life, had lied to her and tricked her in the cruelest way possible. She didn't want to think about it. Didn't want to examine too deeply what might or might not have happened on a certain night seventeen years ago. *Sloan is likely just spinning me a line. Maybe not. And oh, God, I'm looking forward to Friday night.*

Wrenching her mind away from Friday night and a certain summer night seventeen years ago, Shelly spent the rest of the afternoon upstairs in her studio, painting. In the time since she had returned to Oak Valley, she had been so busy with Josh's affairs, Granger Cattle Company, getting the barn office ready, as well as her studio, reacquainting herself with old friends and meeting new ones, that she had spared little time for her art.

Creating a dreamy, otherworld landscape had always soothed her, and this afternoon, standing before a blank canvas, she was relieved to discover that putting brush to canvas still pushed everything out of her mind but the gradually appearing subject in front of her. She painted all afternoon, deciding that tomorrow she really must call the gallery in San Francisco that her New Orleans dealer, Madame Fournier, had recommended. She sighed. A trip to the city was probably called for—she'd need to introduce herself and take along a portfolio of some of her works. The glowing letter from Madame Fournier would help, as would copies of the art reviews she'd received. She made a face. It was probably the list of her sales that would turn the tide. And she reminded herself, she *was* fairly well known . . . in certain circles.

Dusk was falling by the time she cleaned her brushes and felt relaxed enough to wander downstairs. No one seemed to be around and, grabbing a banana, she peeled and ate it as she ambled to the barn.

She discovered that Nick was in the loft, throwing down hay to the cows. Calling to him, she climbed up to join him.

He was just tossing down that last flake of hay, and she said, "Thanks for feeding. I was just thinking of doing it."

Nick grinned and, sitting down on a bale of hay that overlooked the manger, patted the place beside him. "Come on over and sit. To my way of thinking this is one of the best parts of the day."

"What about your stock? Don't you have to get home and take care of them?"

He shook his head. "Mine are on pasture—such as it is— just like yours will be in a few weeks."

Shelly joined him on the bale, and together they watched the cows as the purple-and-gray edges of twilight crept around them. The cows pushed and butted each other in their greed and eagerness for the hay. Some lowed to each other, the calls soft and oddly soothing and appealing. As the minutes passed and each cow found her place at the manger and nosed through the hay for the choicest morsel, the gentle rhythmic sound of contentedly eating cows drifted upward to where Shelly and Nick sat.

Shelly looked at Nick and smiled. "It's great, isn't it? That sound? Makes me feel connected to the past."

He nodded. "Like I said, this is my favorite part of the day. There's something about them shuffling through the hay, the snuffling and lowing . . . I don't know. It gets to me. Makes me glad I'm a cattle rancher—or trying to be."

"Me too." She grinned. "Of course, you've been a rancher longer than I have."

They talked softly for several minutes, enjoying the quiet, the sound of the cows, the deepening twilight. Even though he seemed his usual lighthearted self, Shelly sensed a somberness, a sadness about Nick tonight that troubled her.

Keeping her gaze on the gray shapes of the cows below them, she asked gently, "Did it bother you today? When we were talking about the family? The Grangers?"

Nick kept his eyes on the cows. "Yeah. It did. It's hard to talk about them like a disinterested outsider. Something wells up inside of me, and I want to stand up and shout: Look at me—I'm a Granger, too." In the gloom, he flashed her a twisted smile. "Silly. I should be happy being Nick Rios. That's what Raquel says—but then there's no question that Rios was her father. I just have his name. Not his blood. You know the really queer part—I don't want to change my name, I don't want to become Nick Granger, I just want. . . ." He dropped his head. "I guess I just want people to know who I really am. I don't want it to be a dirty little secret anymore. And I guess more than anything. I want to know the truth. Mom is no help. She won't talk about it. She just ignores me when I start pestering her."

Shelly's heart ached for him. He reminded her of Josh in so many ways—or at least the Josh she'd thought she'd known, and in her mind, there was no doubt that he was Josh's son. She felt closer to Nick than she did to anybody else in the world. There was a bond and a trust between them that she couldn't explain—not even to herself. Some of it, she knew, came from their shared childhood, but some of it . . . well, there just wasn't an explanation for it. They understood each other. And, she thought with a wry smile, they shared a dream—Granger Cattle Company. But Nick had another dream, she admitted painfully. A dream that somehow she had to help him obtain—impossible though it seemed right now.

Shelly reached over and gripped his arm. He looked at her, his features barely discernable in the growing darkness.

"I don't know how we're going to prove the truth, but I promise you one thing," she said fiercely, "we will do it. Whatever it takes."

Chapter Fifteen

❦

Wednesday Shelly drove into town to pick up M.J. at McGuire's for lunch at the Blue Goose. It was a late lunch—after 2:00 P.M., but it was the only time M.J. could escape from the demands of the store.

M.J. was waiting at the front entrance. The instant she spotted Shelly's vehicle, she came running up. Climbing into Shelly's Bronco, she said, "Step on it—before they discover I've escaped." Shaking her head, she added, "Man, if anybody had ever told me how hard it is to run your own business, and a grocery store at that, I'd have run screaming to the hills."

Shelly grinned. "Liar. For as long as I can remember, running McGuire's has been your dream."

M.J. made a face. "Which will just teach me to be careful what I wish for. But, you're right, it *is* what I've always wanted to do. It's just that sometimes. . . ."

"Sometimes, it gets a little complicated?"

M.J. nodded. "Lots of things to keep track of and anticipate. And the help situation is terrible. No one wants to work—having the reservation in the valley with half its inhabitants on welfare doesn't help. And when I do get someone, they never last for very long. You hire someone, just get them trained so they know what they're doing, and bang! They're gone, or they're having a baby or they're getting married, or moving away. Any one of a dozen reasons why the six, eight months you've invested in them is wasted. If I could just hire and *keep* reliable help, it would eliminate one headache."

"What sort of wage are you paying? It's amazing how loyal money can make an employee."

The Blue Goose was less than two blocks from McGuire's Grocery, and M.J. shot Shelly a dark look as she pulled into the gravel parking lot at the side of the restaurant. "Are you being sarcastic? Everyone knows that McGuire's only pays minimum wage—can't afford to pay more."

"Well, that's understandable and only fair for beginning, untrained help. They have to start somewhere. It's the pay of your experienced employees you need to look at—pay them enough, and maybe they won't be so inclined to leave."

"I know. And I don't disagree with what you're saying either," M.J. muttered as, like Shelly, she pushed open the Bronco's door and prepared to get out of the vehicle. "It's my grandfather—he still keeps a hand in the store, and every time I try to explain that paying more to trained help is just good business and could actually *save* us money in the long run, he nearly has a heart attack. When he found out that I was paying Tom and Debbie Smith, who have worked at the store *forever*, a wage comparable to what they could earn in Willits, I thought that Granddad would bust a gut—or drop dead right in front of me. He's still stuck in the fifties somewhere when it comes to wages, and I can't get him to understand that you got to give a little to get a little."

Over the hood of the Bronco, Shelly sent her a commiserating smile. "Nothing's easy, is it?"

"Not in this lifetime."

Shelly had not tried the charms of the Blue Goose yet, and she was looking forward to lunch. The small, squat building had undergone quite a bit of renovation in the years since she had left the valley. Seventeen years ago, it had been a dilapidated wreck falling into decay, with a leaky roof, plywood-boarded windows, peeling paint, and some god-awful stonework around the windows. These days it was painted a crisp blue and cream, sported a new roof, a covered walkway around two sides of the building, and the tacky stonework had disappeared from around the windows. A dozen or so redwood half barrels filled with pink petunias, blue pansies, and white ageratum were scattered in front and along the parking lot side of the building. There were five or six other vehicles besides her own in the parking lot, which in Oak Valley constituted a crowd and a sure sign that the place was popular.

M.J. went first, stepping from the gravel onto the cement walkway. Looking back over her shoulder at Shelly, she said, "I hope that Megan has cooked up a great special for your first time." Hand on the handle, she pushed on the door, expecting it to open, but the opposite happened; her arm crumpled and she slammed full force into its unyielding surface. Stunned, she stared at the heavy wooden door. She gave it a shove, but it remained shut, resisting her efforts to open it.

M.J. tried again, this time putting all of her slender weight into it, but the door didn't budge. Impatient, she jiggled the handle. "I don't know what's going on—I know the damned place is open." She really put her shoulder to the door this time, thinking it was stuck, and pressed down hard on the latch. Zip.

Puzzled, she stepped back and glanced at Shelly. Just as puzzled, Shelly shrugged.

Looking at her watch, Shelly said, "They're supposed to be open—the sign says until 3:00 P.M. and it's just 2:10 P.M. now. And there's all those vehicles in the lot . . ."

The door swung open, and Sally Cosby stood there grinning at them. "Don't blame me," she said. "It's that bunch of yahoos at the big table in back. One of them locked the door when they saw you coming."

Even from where they stood they could hear the guffaws and laughter coming from inside the building. Both women peered around the edge of the door and caught sight of several males looking ridiculously pleased as they sat around a long table in the rear of the small room.

Recognizing Danny Haskell, Jeb Delaney, Bobba Neal, and the others, M.J. shook her head and walked the rest of the way inside the restaurant. "I should have known." Hands on her hips, M.J. said, "Very funny. Don't you dickheads have anything else to do than to harass poor hardworking women?"

"Ooh, she's talking dirty," Danny said, his eyes dancing. "Don't you just love it when she does that? Makes my little ole heart go pitter-patter."

"I know, I can't hardly stand it," Jeb said, clutching his chest, a big grin on his handsome face.

All of them, except for Jeb and Bobba, were in uniforms of some sort—Danny in his sheriff's office khakis, the other three wearing the green of the Forest Service. Everyone wore a grin. Shelly thought she recognized two of the others—Rick Hanson, who'd been a couple years younger than her crowd, and Mingo Delaney, Jeb's younger brother, who was just about three years older than she was. The other man, about Jeb's age, had a sprinkling of gray at his temples and looked sort of familiar, but she couldn't place him. Probably a friend of Jeb's.

Wiggling his eyebrows, Danny teased, "Are you gonna spank me for being a baaad boy?"

M.J. put a finger to her bottom lip as if she were considering it. "I might," she said, "if I can remember where I left my whip and chains."

Hoots and catcalls greeted this sally, and, chuckling, Shelly took M.J.'s arm and said, "Leave them alone—you'll only encourage them. Come on, let's find a table."

Waving her fingers in their direction, M.J. allowed Shelly to guide her to a table in the corner. Once they were seated, Shelly had a chance to look around.

The entire restaurant was not large, and at this time of day, except for Jeb and the others, there was just one couple, a dark-haired man and a blond woman, sitting at a table at one side of the rectangular room. The eating area only held about ten tables, most set up for four occupants, a couple for just two—the table where Danny and the others sat was the only one big enough to hold more than four people. The tables were made of thick slabs of redwood finished with a gleaming coat of urethane. The chairs varied from barrel-shaped covered in rust-colored Naugahyde, to spindle-legged steel framed with bright blue-and-rust patterned seats and backs. The walls were white, with strutting blue geese stenciled around the top and around the windows and door; white lace curtains hung at the windows, and the carpet on the floor was a short pile in electric blue tweed. The far wall behind the table containing Jeb and the others was made of an imitation stone in shades of russet; a squat, black, wood-burning stove stood on a stone hearth. Through the wall of glass separating the restaurant and the kitchen, Shelly recognized Megan, Hank's sister, as the cook. They'd met at the party Shelly had held when she'd first come back to the valley. She watched as blond-haired Megan glanced up at the paper order tabs above her head and slapped something on the big black grill with its huge, equally black hood. That task completed, Megan turned to face the room and began to put together something on the counter in front of her.

"Well, what do you think?" M.J. asked, having watched Shelly's inspection.

"It's . . . nice," she said, still looking around, noticing the pitchers of ice water on each table as well as the other condiments and ketchup and Tabasco sauce. "Rustic, cozy, yet with touches of sophistication."

They looked at each other and burst out laughing. "Wow," Shelly said. "Did I ever sound like some sort of snobbish food critic."

"That's OK—just as long as you know it."

Sally walked up and laid two menus on the table. Her brown eyes smiling, she said to Shelly, "Welcome back. Sorry I couldn't make your party. I wanted to come in the worst way, so did Tim—he's heard tales of our wicked past and was looking forward to meeting you." She grimaced. "But girls both had a flu bug, running a fever, achy and miserable—we just wouldn't have felt right leaving them home alone while we went to a party. Even *your* party. Heard we missed a good time." She grinned. "So are you adjusting? Bet everything seems really different after living in New Orleans."

Sally Adams, as she had been then, had been part of their crowd, and her parents and grandparents had been friends with the McGuires and Grangers for years. Sally hadn't changed much over the intervening years: a sprinkling of freckles still dusted her nose, her cinnamon brown hair was still cut short with a curly perm, and her sturdy shape hadn't expanded by as much as one pound. From M.J. Shelly knew that Sally had married a local logger about fifteen years ago and was the proud mother of a pair of twelve-year-old twin girls. Smiling back at her, Shelly said, "It's different, but it's wonderful to see how little the town has changed." She made a face. "I'd have hated it if there had been a McDonald's or Burger King in the valley."

Sally laughed and shook her head. "That isn't likely to happen—they need a big population. As it is, there's barely enough business for the three restaurants in town and the Burger Place and Rolle's. And you gotta keep track of everyone's hours of operation or you'll starve—we only serve breakfast and lunch—same as the Inn. They're open seven days a week, though; we're closed on Sunday and Monday. River Bend, I think it was called Hunter's Meet when you lived here, is only open for dinners Wednesday to Saturday." She grinned. "Don't even think of going out to dinner on Sunday, Monday, or Tuesday nights. Never happen."

"I'll keep that in mind," Shelly replied, glancing at the menu. It consisted mainly of sandwiches, some cold, some hot, like chicken and steak. Nothing jumped out at her, and she asked, "What would you suggest?"

"The special today is pretty good—Megan makes a mean wrap—ham, turkey, lettuce, tomato, onion, and guacamole—she's not stingy with the guacamole either. It's filling—you might want to split one. Comes with soup or salad; today's soups are tomato basil or creamy potato—both equally yummy. Or you can choose a salad from the refrigerator case near the cash register—macaroni, potato, green, carrot-and-raisin, and bean are the usual, but I think Megan made a couple of new ones for everyone to try out. If you want a sample, just let me know."

After a brief consultation, M.J. and Shelly decided to split a wrap and each ordered a green salad.

After their salads had been served and Sally had left them to their meal, M.J. said, "So, how's it going? I saw you at the parade with Sloan. Want to tell me about *that*?"

Subtle was not a word that applied to M.J. Digging into

her salad, Shelly mumbled, "There's not much to tell—Acey blindsided me." Honesty made her add, "Sloan too. We were kinda stuck with each other. Nothing much happened."

"Oh, yeah. I believe that. This is me you're talking to, remember? You and Sloan could never be within five yards of each other without spontaneous combustion. I remember the few times I saw you together." M.J. waved a hand like a fan in front of her face. "Hot. Hot. *Hot*. Now give."

Shelly chewed on a mouthful of spring greens, trying to think of a way to sidetrack M.J. Nothing occurred to her. And she certainly did not want to mention the date coming up on Friday night. Just as had happened seventeen years ago, she wanted whatever was happening between her and Sloan to proceed without the avid, eagle-eyed interest of everyone in the valley.

As she fumbled for some sort of an answer, the front door opened and Hank ambled in, a red baseball cap on his head and a white apron around his waist. Spying Shelly, a wide smile crossed his face. "Ah, me darlin', you finally came in." Rubbing his hands together, he walked to their table. "Now tell me, what did you order?"

"The special," Shelly said with a laugh, delighted to see him, not only for his own sake but also for the distraction he provided.

"A good choice. Too bad this isn't one of the days when Megan has whipped up something really exotic. Everyone seems to like the wrap, so we have it often. We try to keep the menu simple and easy, but sometimes, Megan'll pull all the stops—like a turkey dinner or roast pork with all the trimmings." He winked at her. "Saturday morning is when you should come in—that's the day I get to create, and I modestly admit that I have come up with some tasty offerings."

M.J. piped in, "Not to make his head swell any bigger

than it is, but he does these special potatoes and a spicy omelet with jalapeño jack cheese and ham and onions and green peppers—great stuff."

"I'll remember that," Shelly said. She indicated the interior. "The place looks great—not at all what I remember. When I was a kid the place was an eyesore and all boarded up—I never even had any idea what it looked like inside."

Hank laughed. "It looked like a rat's nest when we first bought it. Took us months of painting and cleaning before we could even think of furniture or equipment—your brother was a great help. See these tables?" At Shelly's nod, he continued, "He found them somewhere near San Francisco and haggled a good deal for us. Helped finance the place, too, and when we opened, sang our praises to everyone in the valley. I don't think we would have been as successful as quickly as we were if Josh hadn't badgered nearly everyone in town to give us a try. Megan and I owed him a lot."

"You're not the only one either," M.J. said, pushing aside the remains of her salad. "Josh was willing to help just about any legitimate new business get started in St. Galen's. And if he didn't finance it himself, he'd go sit on the bank manager's desk until the necessary loan was approved." M.J. smiled softly. "When I first took over the store, and things would get me down, he was always there to hold my hand and tell me what a great job I was doing. I miss him."

Swallowing the lump that rose in her throat, Shelly said, "I do, too. He was always just, Josh, my big brother—sometimes I forget that he helped a lot of people. I know he was always trying to think of ways for St. Galen's to prosper. The poverty in the valley bothered him—I remember him trying to think up ways to make the valley more profitable without changing the very things that make most of us love it. It troubled him that the young people have to leave the valley to find a job that pays a decent wage."

"Still do," M.J. said glumly.

"Of course," Hank said, with a gleam in his eyes, "being one of the biggest employers in the valley, if McGuire's would pay more . . ."

M.J. snorted. "Talk to my grandfather—you're one of his cronies."

Hank shook his head, grinning. "Not a chance, me darlin'—he'd swat me down like a pesky fly. Very opinionated, your grandfather. I respect and admire him, but there's no denying higher wages is a sticky subject with him. I don't envy you trying to bring him into the twenty-first century."

The door opened, and M.J., who was seated facing it, glanced over to see who was coming inside. Her gaze dropped almost immediately, and she said under her breath, "Oh, damn. Just our luck that she'd come in today. Brace yourself. Here comes Reba Stanton."

Hank looked over his shoulder at the new arrivals. Glancing back at M.J. and Shelly, he murmured, "The Queen Bee and her lady-in-waiting have arrived. Excuse me while I go ingratiate myself." Ever the affable host, he left M.J. and Shelly to their salads and walked up to the two women who had just entered the restaurant. "Good afternoon, ladies," he said. "Your timing is perfect, the rush is over, and you have your choice of tables."

"Oh, we're not here to eat," Reba said. "I noticed Shelly Granger's vehicle outside, and since I haven't had a chance to say hi since she returned, Barbara and I thought we'd stop in."

"Lucky you," M.J muttered sotto voice, hearing Reba's words.

"Barbara?" Shelly mouthed, leaning across the table.

"Jepson—used to be Babs Denman," M.J. hissed. "Remember?"

Shelly crossed her eyes. Indeed she did. Nancy Blackstone, Reba Collier, and Babs Denman, as they had been known in those days, had comprised the trio from hell. Older by six or seven years, they had lorded it over the younger women and perfected to an art the ability to make them feel like gauche, feeble-minded, mud-spitting children. At seventeen, eighteen, no matter how great they felt about themselves or how proud they were of some accomplishment, all it had taken was a look, an arched brow, or a drawled comment from one of the terrible trio to send their self-esteem crashing to the ground.

Shelly's lips tightened, remembering the year Sally had been crowned Field Day Sweetheart. They'd been seventeen that year, and she and M.J. had been home from boarding school for the Field Day festivities. Sally had been an intrepid horsewoman, able to rope and ride rings around anyone in their crowd—even the boys. Sally's incredible riding abilities had been one of the reasons she had won the title of Sweetheart—that and the fact that she was a pretty, always smiling, eager-to-please young woman. Sally had glowed at having won the title over the other three contestants. Shelly recalled how proud she and M.J. had been of her and how thrilled they had been to bask in Sally's reflected glory. She and M.J. had been helping Sally get ready for her grand entrance into the rodeo arena, giving Sally's palomino mare a final brush and checking that Sally's crown was pinned on securely, when the trio had strolled up and stopped to watch.

Six feet away, hand on her hip, looking gorgeous in form-fitting black Sassoon jeans, high-heeled boots, and a clinging scarlet sweater, Nancy had murmured in that condescending tone of hers, "Oh, my, the little Sweetheart and her cortege—aren't they just too cute? Do you remem-

ber when we used to think that being the Field Day Sweetheart was such an honor? Hard to believe, isn't it?"

"I know what you mean," Reba had answered. "It seems
so ridiculous now, doesn't it? I mean St. Galen's Field Day
Sweetheart . . . who cares beyond the valley?"

"Oh, well," Nancy had drawled, "let the girls enjoy themselves. They'll find out soon enough that what seems important in St. Galen's doesn't mean squat anywhere else."

"Now, now Nancy," Babs had scolded, "remember this
will probably be the highlight of their lives." The three had
snickered, and Babs had exclaimed, "Ugh! I'd hate to think
that Field Day Sweetheart was *my* crowning moment."

Having delivered their poison, they had wandered away.
The glow on Sally's face had dimmed, and, as she shook
with rage, Shelly's hands had curled into fists. Under her
breath, M.J. had snarled, "Bitches!"

Putting aside the memory, Shelly couldn't help wondering if Reba and Babs would be any less bitchy today than
they had been in the past.

"Shelly!" cried Reba as she came up to the table, "how
wonderful to see you again."

A polite smile on her face, Shelly glanced up. "Reba.
How nice . . . it's been a long time, hasn't it?"

"Don't remind me," Reba replied, her gaze running as-
sessingly over Shelly's slim shape in her simple pink
pullover and neatly pressed blue jeans. "Time has just flown
by, hasn't it?"

"Well you know what they say—when you're having
fun. . . ."

"Oh, I envy you—New Orleans . . ." Babs breathed, avid
brown eyes pricing to the penny the cost of Shelly's clothes.
"Doesn't the valley seem boring and too, too country after
New Orleans?"

"No, not at all," Shelly replied. "After the noise, congestion, and crowding there, the slow pace of life in the valley is great. I feel lucky to be back."

Babs stared at her. "Really? Why, I would have thought . . ."

Reba laughed, but there was an edge to it. "Oh come on, Shelly—you're just teasing, aren't you? We've imagined for years that you've been living this really wild and decadent life, while we've been stuck raising babies and listening to conversations that revolve around nothing more exciting than electing the next school board—or the hay crop. Don't disillusion us."

Babs and Reba were both just over forty, and they reminded Shelly of a pair of sleek Angora cats—smug and superior. The years had not treated them *un*kindly, but despite the careful makeup, hair, and clothes, they both looked, well, matronly. Attractive, undeniably, but definitely matronly. Very well fed matrons, Shelly decided, tongue in cheek.

Replying to Reba, Shelly said, "New Orleans *is* exciting. Every day there's something new going on, but it can't hold a candle to the things that make Oak Valley such a great place to live: space, tranquillity and . . . I don't know . . . a feeling of having stepped back in time, I guess. The valley has its share of problems—problems with drugs, teenage pregnancies, and husbands who still beat their wives; but there's also a sensation of having escaped to a place where life is easier, simpler. Things that are scoffed at now still mean something in the valley—loyalty, reputation, honor, a man's word, family—all those old-fashioned qualities. And there's not so much pressure and need to rush, rush here and there." She grinned. "I mean, let's face it—there's no place to rush *to*. Life moves at a slower pace, and while it *does* revolve mostly around cattle, hay, and timber, there's something terrific about that. If you don't know what I'm talking about, it's hard to explain." She glanced at M.J. "You've lived out of the valley, don't you feel the same?"

M.J. nodded. "You couldn't pay me to live anywhere else—even if we don't have a Round Table Pizza or a mall just down the road. Nope, I like Oak Valley just fine."

Reba looked down her nose at them, and murmured, "Well, you both were always a little strange. I guess there is just no telling about taste, is there?"

"Yeah, I guess you're right," said M.J., a gleam in her eyes. "Bob married you."

Shelly choked and glanced hastily down at her salad.

"Jealous?" Reba purred, brushing back a lock of silvery blond hair, a hard gleam in her sapphire blue eyes.

"Excuse me, ladies," said Hank, walking up to the table with two plates. Ignoring the frosty silence, he slipped a plate in front of M.J. and Shelly. "Sally got to visiting with you and forgot to ask what kind of dipping sauce you wanted, so I brought out both honey mustard and ranch. If you want something else—like blue cheese, let me know, and I'll go get it."

"Er, no, this is fine," said Shelly, eyeing with anticipation her half of the rolled flour tortilla stuffed with thinly sliced ham, turkey, lettuce, and tomato that spilled out onto her plate.

"Well, you need anything," Hank said, "you just give me a holler." With a nod at Reba and Babs, he strolled away, whistling.

"We'll leave you to eat your lunch," Reba said. "We just wanted to welcome you back to the valley and say hello. I'll call you next week, and maybe we can arrange to have lunch together." She smiled, but it didn't reach her eyes. "We can discuss old times and all that."

"Oh, yeah, sure, that'll be fine," Shelly said, thinking that she'd have to have ready a half dozen or so excuses to decline when Reba called—if she called.

The door shut behind Reba and Babs, and Sally popped out from wherever she had been in the back room. She made a face.

"Sorry I deserted you, but I just didn't want to get into it with Babs. Her oldest boy, Gary, he's about eleven, was giving some of the younger kids a bad time at the rodeo Saturday afternoon—he was making fun of them, so Jane and Jean, my girls, roped him, tied him, and dropped him off in the center of the arena. Babs was *not* pleased."

M.J. chuckled. "I heard about that. Served the little jerk right—Todd was one of the kids he was picking on. Good thing Jane and Jean got to Gary before I did—I'd have probably done a lot worse and gotten into a fistfight with Babs."

"You?" Shelly asked, her eyes dancing. "Nah, never happen, not sweet, shy, ladylike you."

The three of them laughed.

"I'm so glad you're back," Sally said to Shelly. "Seems almost like old times. Only thing different is that it's the terrible twosome now, instead of the terrible trio." Sally clapped her hand over her mouth. "Ah jeez, I didn't mean to speak ill of the dead. I never would have wanted anything bad to happen to Nancy."

"You know what?" M.J. said, looking up at Sally. "You're too nice. You always were. You need some meanness, girl."

"Don't listen to her," Shelly said. "She's got enough meanness for all of us. You stay just as you are—let M.J. be the bad girl."

"And what are you? Miss Prim? The voice of reason?" M.J. asked dryly, taking a bite of her wrap.

"Well, I do try," murmured Shelly. She grinned at M.J. "Except when I lose my temper. Remember that time I blacked Danny's eye because he'd brought me that box of chocolates? Only it wasn't chocolates?"

"Oh, God, I'd forgotten that," M.J. said, her mouth puckering. "I can't remember, did you actually eat one?"

"No, at first I just thought they were funny-looking chocolates. He'd done a good job of picking up the right-shaped ones and putting them neatly in that Sees candy box, but when I got close enough to smell I recognized what they were right off."

In unison, all three said, "Chicken shit."

"Must have taken him weeks to find just the right, er, droppings, in the chicken pen to fill that box," Sally commented. "What a little devil he was." They all glanced over at the table where Danny sat with the others drinking coffee. "And to think," she marveled, "he's now one of our resident deputies. Scares you when you think about it."

In between other tasks, Sally continued to stop by their table, the three of them reminiscing and recalling happy times from their childhood. Shelly had just finished the last bite of her wrap when Hank reappeared, this time with small, blond-haired Megan.

Megan looked much younger than Hank—over twenty years, Shelly guessed. Hank had to be in his sixties, which meant that Megan must be somewhere in her early forties. Seeing the speculation in Shelly's gaze, Hank said, "Megan's my *little* sister—not only in size, but age, too."

Shyly, Megan said, "Hank's mother died when he was fifteen. It was five years later that his dad met my mum and they got married. Hank was twenty-one when I was born." She smiled. "He acts more like a father than an older brother—I can't seem to convince him that I'm all grown-up and don't need a keeper anymore." She indicated her petite frame. "Being small doesn't help."

"I know what you mean," M.J. commiserated. "Everyone

thinks that because you're small you don't have a brain in your head." She looked at Shelly. "You don't know how lucky you are to be tall—people take you seriously. When I say something, even now, they're more inclined to pat me on the head, and say, 'There, there, little girl, don't worry about it.' Drives me nuts."

"You're wrong," Shelly argued. "Believe me, cute-and-small wins every time. I remember thinking once that it just wasn't fair—when we were twelve you still got chucked under the chin, but everyone expected me to act wise and mature."

M.J. grinned. "Yeah, there was that."

Their meal finished, after complimenting Hank and Megan on the food and a few more minutes of conversation, they got up and paid at the cash register. They were exchanging a last word with Sally after she'd given them their change when the door to the restaurant flew open.

A man in his fifties stood in the doorway breathing hard. He wore stained jeans and a faded blue T-shirt with the words "Eat shit and die" written in white letters across the front; there was a dirty gray baseball cap on his head, and his weathered face bristled with a salt-and-pepper beard. His gaze swiftly scanned the inside of the room.

"Holy shit, Danny," he roared when he found the deputy, "where the hell have you been? I've been lookin' all over the damn town for you. You gotta get over to Mary Wagner's place right away. That goddamn Buffalo of the Indians is tearing up the whole north end of the valley. The son of a bitch tore down old Mrs. Finch's fence, ripped Nora Allen's wash off the line, and shit in the church driveway. You get your ass out there now and shoot the motherfucker!"

Shelly looked at M.J. "Does memory fail me, or is that 'Profane' Deegan?"

M.J. grinned. "You got it. Wanna go watch the show?"

Chapter Sixteen

❦

Like floodwater shooting through a glory hole, they exploded from the restaurant, Danny and Jeb leading the pack, Shelly and M.J. following behind. There was a mad scramble into the various vehicles, then, with siren shrieking, Danny headed the procession out of town.

"Does this happen often?" Shelly asked, as they tore down the state highway in swift pursuit.

M.J. nodded. "A lot lately. Most of the time everyone forgets about the buffalo herd the Indians own, but recently there's a young bull that's been walking through fences like they're made of butter. And when he gets out, he goes where he wants. He isn't vicious or anything like that, he just wanders around walking under, over, and *through* anything in his path." She grimaced. "He's caused considerable damage to property, and folks are getting tired of it—especially the whites. Tempers are short and bad feelings between whites and Indians are rising. A half dozen men have threatened to shoot the bull, which only enrages the Indians."

Shelly shook her head. "It seems so weird to hear those words 'whites' and 'Indians.' Makes me feel like I've stepped back in time 150 years."

"Well, yeah, I know what you mean, but I suspect that it's used commonly anywhere within twenty miles of any reservation—here or in Texas, New Mexico—you name it. It just seems weird to you because you've been gone for so long."

Even without Danny's screaming siren to guide them, it wasn't hard to find the site of the bull's latest infractions. Five miles and a couple of turns later Shelly pulled the Bronco to a stop and parked on the grassy side of the road. The narrow road was clogged with haphazardly parked vehicles and men, women, children, and dogs were roaming in and out: the air was punctuated with the sound of laughter and the murmur of voices. No one seemed worried or afraid; there was almost a carnival air about the scene.

"Looks like half the valley is here," Shelly commented as she climbed from the Bronco.

"Well, you know St. Galen's," M.J. said with a grin. "It takes so little to amuse us."

Shelly laughed.

As they walked down the road, they saw signs of recent carnage. A white picket fence looked like a pile of kindling, and a rope clothesline, still bravely waving the wash that had been hung on it, was draped over bushes and sagging barbed-wire fences. As they approached the crowd, they could hear the sound of whistles and the snap of a whip and a moment later caught sight of several people on horseback. Shelly recognized Acey, Nick, Tom Smith, Vivian Adams—Sally's mother—and Rob Fenwick, another cattle rancher in the area. Through breaks in the crowd, she saw the darting forms of a pair of black-and-white cow dogs that were helping the horseback riders herd the recalcitrant bull toward his pasture. Nick spotted her and flashed a smile.

The whole affair became anticlimactic. Surrounded by horsemen, harassed by the nipping dogs, the bull trotted down the road and almost meekly went into the pasture he had left such a short time ago to wreak havoc. A cheer went up from the watching spectators as the massive bull, his short black horns gleaming in the sunlight, ambled through the gate. Excitement over, the crowd began to disperse.

Their task done, Nick and Acey and the others were busy loading up their horses in the various trailers—it wasn't a time to stand around and talk. Shelly waved a good-bye when Acey looked up, and she and M.J. strolled toward the Bronco.

At the side of the road, Danny and Jeb were in conversation with three or four Indians. It was obvious the Indians did not like what they were being told. Their expressions were angry, voices were raised, and there was some wild gesticulating. Time and again, Danny and Jeb appeared to calm them down, only for the temperature to rise once more.

"Come on," M.J. said, "I've got to get back to the store, and the excitement is over anyway."

Jerking her head in the direction of the Indians, Shelly said, "I don't know. Looks to me like those guys would like to punch out somebody."

"Yeah, well, I don't want it to be me. Besides, Danny and Jeb know how to calm down tempers—they've had a lot of experience in that department. And they have plenty of backup—look over there, Mingo and Rick are waiting by the trucks."

Reluctantly Shelly agreed, and a few minutes later was turning the Bronco around and heading back to town. After dropping M.J. off at the store and making plans to meet for lunch again soon, she drove home.

When she arrived home Maria was just leaving.

"Did you have a nice lunch?" Maria asked, standing by the side of her red compact truck.

"Yes, indeed," Shelly replied, smiling. "Had some excitement, too—a buffalo bull got out and was terrorizing the neighborhood at the north end of the valley. Nick and Acey and some others showed up and got him safely back in his field."

"That bull was loose again?" At Shelly's nod, she added, "If they'd fix the fences, they wouldn't have this problem, but you can't tell them anything. I know one thing, though, something's going to have to be done because if it isn't, somebody is going to get hurt or some hothead is going to stop making *threats* and shoot that animal—and then we'll really be in the soup."

Shelly nodded again and made a face. If the bull *was* shot, the Indians would be furious and the whites would be righteous—not a good situation.

On Thursday, Shelly finally contacted the art gallery in San Francisco that had been recommended to her. It was a pleasant conversation; the owner, Samuel Lowenthall, had seen and knew of her work. He was eager to hang some of her landscapes in his gallery. They discussed the possibility of a show in the future. Shelly was flattered. She made arrangements to UPS overnight the letter of introduction from the gallery owner she had worked with in New Orleans, and they set a date to meet for lunch and for her to bring in her portfolio of recent work.

Hanging up the phone, Shelly made a face. Her recent output had been damn little, but she still had two canvases that she had brought with her from New Orleans and she had just about completed another painting. Going up the stairs toward her studio, she scolded herself. *You're going to have to concentrate, my girl, get your mind off of Josh, cattle, Nick . . . and Sloan.*

Nick's situation troubled her. He needed closure. He needed proof, and she just didn't see how they were ever going to be able to *prove* that Josh had been his father. Her doubts about his parentage had been settled long ago, and she knew in her heart her DNA would show they were indeed relatives. She believed that he was her brother's son, and if right now she was relying on little more than intuition, so what? She believed. Maria was no help. Whenever the subject was broached, and Shelly had tried her hand at it a time or two, Maria's friendly face closed up, her lips flattened, and she'd turn away. Maria simply would *not* discuss it. Ashamed? Shelly wondered. Didn't she realize what her silence was doing to her son? And yet, even if Maria said, yes, yes, it's true, Josh is Nick's father, it wouldn't solve the problem. It would help. But Josh's DNA, she thought bitterly, would have given them a concrete answer—and they had cremated Josh, cremating his precious DNA with him.

She struggled with all sorts of schemes and scenarios but couldn't see a solution. At least not today, she told herself, and tomorrow was another day. One thing was clear though—she'd have to talk to someone knowledgeable about DNA testing. Maybe they could point her in a different direction.

That afternoon she drove into town and picked up her mail. There was a letter from Mike Sawyer in the box, and she read it before she even pulled away from the post office. Sawyer was following her instructions and attempting to break the lease with Milo Scott. He'd had, he informed her in his letter, a recent meeting with Mr. Scott, but he could not say that there had been much progress. Mr. Scott's position was that he had signed a valid lease, and that he did not want to break it. Mr. Scott had, however, indicated that for a price, he might consider giving up the lease. Mr. Sawyer feared that the price Mr. Scott would demand to break the lease would be high. It might be better if she allowed the lease to stand.

Shelly snorted. Better for whom? Folding the letter, she put it back in the envelope and returned home. It was just after 2:00 P.M., and she took a chance and called the lawyer's office. Sawyer was in.

After some polite chitchat, Shelly said bluntly, "I want that lease broken—and if we have to go to court to do it, then we will. I'd be willing to pay him a nominal sum—something in the range of what he paid for the lease in the first place, but I'm not going to be held up."

"Well, I can't tell you what to do, but I would *advise* you to just let sleeping dogs lie and leave the lease alone. Mr. Scott doesn't want to give it up, and I can't see him doing so without ample compensation—and a fight."

"It's just not that simple," Shelly said, "Mr. Scott is a reputed drug dealer in this area. I can't prove it, but I'm fairly certain that he intends to, or may have already, planted marijuana on that acreage. I don't want to run the risk of running afoul of the forfeiture laws should he do so. Besides," she added, inspired, "I intend to run several head of cattle on that land this summer, and if Mr. Scott *did* plant an illegal crop, my cows would probably eat it or trample it—he runs the risk of having his crop destroyed. He'd lose money. Look . . . tell him I'll pay him double the pittance he paid Josh for the lease in the first place—but not one penny more. Talk to him."

Grumbling and not holding out hope for any success, Mike Sawyer agreed.

Friday morning, she woke with a curious mixture of excitement and unease curling in her belly. Tonight was her date with Sloan, and she couldn't decide whether she was acting like a fool or a woman in love. Her mouth twisted. Sometimes it was hard to tell the difference.

The day passed. At times it dragged, other times the hours flashed by. She'd tried to paint, but thoughts of Sloan kept breaking her concentration, and by early afternoon, she gave up.

She wasted more time than the situation warranted trying to decide what to wear. Dinner in Ukiah. Nothing too dressy, yet she didn't want to wear jeans and a blouse. After agonizing over her closet for far longer than she should have, she finally decided on a simple sheath sewn out of a silky copper-and-bronze-colored fabric. The scoop neck and fitted three-quarter sleeves made the garment look almost medieval, but the flirty flip of the hem just at her knees was pure twenty-first century. A pair of stylish mid-heeled shoes in rusty suede, a short bolero-style jacket that nearly matched the bronze color in her dress, pearls around her neck and at her ears, and a small green fabric purse completed her attire.

Uncertainly she eyed herself in the full-length mirror in her bedroom. She'd washed her hair earlier, and it waved around her shoulders like a tawny cloud of spun gold. A coppery red lipstick was on her mouth and the bronze-and-green eye shadow she wore made her eyes look big and mysterious. Was she overdressed? Underdressed? She bit her lip. Maybe she should dump the pearls? She touched the single strand of pearls. No. They were all right. She was fussing too much.

A touch of White Diamonds cologne, and she was ready. She took a deep breath, ran a nervous hand over her hair, and went downstairs. She paced the big living room, reminding herself over and over again, that hey! It was *only* a date . . . with the only man she had ever loved—the man who had broken her heart and played her for a fool.

When Sloan drove up five minutes later, a ball of butterflies seemed to have lodged in her stomach. The sight of him bounding up the steps looking unbelievably handsome in dark slacks, a long-sleeved mauve-and-burgundy-patterned shirt, and a close-fitting black leather vest made her forget about the butterflies and concentrate on making her heart behave. It was leaping in her chest like a frog on a hot rock.

She opened the door and smiled at him. He stopped as if he had run into a brick wall, his expression stunned. He swallowed. Stared. Stared some more. "Do you realize," he finally said in a husky, almost reverent tone, "that this is the first time I've ever seen you in anything other than jeans of some sort? You look gorgeous!" He patted the region of his heart, a killer smile on his lips. "You should warn a guy— my heart's beating so fast and hard, I'm afraid I'm gonna have a heart attack."

Shelly laughed, delighted. She ran a teasing finger over the knot of the black-and-burgundy-striped tie he was wearing. "That makes two of us. You look quite, quite handsome, Mr. Ballinger."

His eyes darkened, his gaze fixed on her mouth. "I think you'd better hold the compliments—without much encouragement, I'll have you on the floor and that lovely dress of yours up around your waist."

Shelly's heart leaped, and a flash of pure carnal longing streaked through her. Uh-oh, she was in trouble. Maybe going out with him tonight wasn't such a good idea, after all. Well, she'd known that from the git-go, she reminded herself grimly, and despite appearances to the contrary, where he was concerned she did *not* have ball-bearing heels. She just had to prove it to herself.

Her chin went up. "I believe that I would have something to say about that. Now are you going to feed me or just keep me here making indecent proposals?"

Sloan laughed. "I'll feed you. And as for the other . . ." He grinned as he took her arm. "Let's just see how the evening goes, shall we?"

The drive to Ukiah took about an hour and a half, Sloan taking the curves with the ease and speed of someone fa-

miliar with every crook and angle of the road. Shelly had
been worried more about the long drive to and from than the
actual date, but Sloan put her at ease, introducing relatively
safe topics—her plans for the cattle operation, his paint
horse program, and even the saga of the rogue buffalo. By
the time he pulled into the parking space in front of the Café
on State Street, she was relaxed and looking forward to
dinner.

The Café had not been in existence when she had left for
New Orleans, and she was pleasantly surprised at the welcoming ambience of the place. The dining area was a big
room with old-fashioned high ceilings and a soft blue-green
plush carpet. Antique wooden cabinets scattered discreetly
around the room displayed a colorful collection of old china,
pottery, and crystal. Green linen napkins, a slender vase of
fresh flowers, delicate columbine and ferns, and a white vo-
tive candle adorned each of the tables. A dark green table-
cloth added a touch of elegance, and the soft lighting was
inviting.

Once they were seated, a basket of warm yeast rolls and
a glass dish of butter were placed before them. The menu
was limited, but Shelly had no trouble deciding on the spicy
chicken and cajun sausage in cream sauce over pasta. Sloan
ordered something with shrimp that sounded almost as
good. They both opted for the spring greens salad with the
house honey-mustard vinaigrette—delicious. After checking
with Shelly, Sloan selected a nice white Zinfandel from the
Napa Valley to drink with their meal.

Ordering and eating filled in any awkward moments that
may have arisen, but in fact, Shelly found Sloan's company
easy to take—too easy. She shrugged that thought aside, unwilling to let suspicion and mistrust ruin what might be a
new beginning. She hadn't forgotten the past, but enough
doubts had been raised in her mind about Josh's character

that she wasn't willing just to dismiss Sloan's implications about Josh's fine hand in what had happened that final night. But neither could she pretend that she wasn't suffering some guilt, feeling that she was being disloyal to Josh—and all the Grangers who had come before her. But was she? She didn't know the answer, and she settled back in her chair prepared to enjoy herself . . . for tonight.

To her surprise, conversation flowed effortlessly between them, but then it shouldn't have surprised her—they shared a common background and knew many of the same people, places. Sloan kept it light, and they spent most the meal catching up on each other's past. Shelly told him about her life in New Orleans, more of her hopes and dreams for the Granger Cattle Company, and Sloan spoke of his decision to leave the family development business and concentrate on raising champion reining-and-cutting paint horses. Whether by accident or design, they both skirted any mention of topics that might cause a rift in their evening.

They finished their meal, both passing reluctantly on the chocolate mousse torte offered for dessert.

"Too rich for me," Shelly said with a laugh. "But I wouldn't mind a cup of coffee."

"I'll have the same," Sloan said.

Their coffee had just been served when Sloan, who was seated facing the doorway, said, "Uh-oh. We've been spotted—and by one of the worst gossips in St. Galen's. Brace yourself."

Shelly shot him a curious glance, tensing a second later, when Reba Stanton's tinkling voice came to her ear. Damn. A little bit of Reba went a long way, and Wednesday hadn't been that long ago. Not nearly that long ago.

"Why, isn't this the most amazing sight I've ever seen," exclaimed Reba as she swam up to their table, her pale blue

eyes full of speculation. "A Granger and a Ballinger breaking bread together and not over each other's heads."

Attractive in a slim-fitting black dress, her silvery
blond hair swept up, and rhinestone earrings dangling
from her ears, Reba smiled at them like the cat that ate the
canary. "Oh, my, never say that I am interrupting a secret
rendezvous?"

Innately polite, Sloan had stood up as she approached,
and a second later found Reba in his arms as she greeted him
effusively. Only by a quick turn of his head was he able to
escape her kiss landing on his lips. Wiping away the smear
of red lipstick he knew was at the corner of his mouth, he
said, "Hello, to you, too, Reba. And as for the other, if we
had wanted it to be secret, it certainly won't be for long, now
will it?" He took a step backward, putting some distance between them.

Reba shook a finger at him and laughed. "Naughty,
naughty."

Reba had always rubbed Shelly the wrong way, but she
had been genuinely startled at the surge of green-eyed jealousy that had flowed through her at the sight of the other
woman in Sloan's arms. That Sloan looked like he wished to
be anywhere else but in Reba's arms was the only thing that
made her remember that she had been born a lady and that
ladies did not leap up and scratch out the eyes of other
women . . . at least not in public. Maybe she was imagining
things? She didn't think so—there was something about the
way Reba looked at Sloan—very much like a rattlesnake
spying a plump rabbit—that made her uncomfortable. Had
Reba grown tired of her perfectly nice husband and was now
on the lookout for Number 2? Or was she just looking for a
little action on the side and had decided that Sloan would
suit her needs? If that was Reba's plan, it looked like the
other woman was in for a fight. From what she could see, it

appeared that Reba was the one sending the signals and that Sloan was desperately trying to duck the broadcast. She grinned. Poor Sloan. The price he paid for being irresistible.

Reba's husband walked up to his wife's side just then. Grinning down at Shelly, Bob Stanton said, "Hi kid. You're looking good. New Orleans must have agreed with you."

"Bob!" Shelly cried, springing to her feet. She hugged him and said, "How great to see you. I'd heard you married Reba—congratulations."

Bob Stanton had always been one of Shelly's favorite people. He was one of the good guys—always ready to lend a hand or a sympathetic ear to anybody; he was highly regarded in the community and very well liked by everyone, young and old alike. If she had her facts right, he was probably pushing fifty, and these days he was a successful cattleman, but Shelly remembered him as a sandy-haired stripling working for her father, and then later for Josh. He had shared many an orange Popsicle with her on hot summer days and hadn't been above squirting her unmercifully with the hose when she got pesky on those same hot afternoons. Bob wasn't exactly handsome, but his features were even and pleasant, laugh lines crinkling attractively at the corners of his hazel eyes, a ready smile on his wide mouth. The years had added a few pounds to his sturdy build, but he still looked fit and active.

"Well, now," Bob drawled as he put Shelly from him and glanced her up and down. "If I'd a known that the snaggletoothed kid who followed me around all those years ago was going to grow up into such a beautiful young lady, I might have been a bit nicer to her."

They all laughed, and if Reba's laugh was a bit forced, no one paid any attention to it.

Sloan reached across, and he and Bob shook hands.

"Nice to see you," Sloan said. "Heard you got some good prices for your bulls at the Turlock sale last month."

Bob nodded. "Sure did. Was a nice surprise after the way the cattle market has been the last few years. How's your folks doing?"

They spent an enjoyable time talking about cattle, Shelly's Angus venture, Sloan's luck with his horses, the lack of rain, and generally catching up with each other's news. Reba's expression became more and more bored and irritated with every passing moment. "Oh, that's enough!" she finally said. "I thought we came down here to get away from St. Galen's—and cattle and hay and horses."

Bob grinned ruefully. "Guess we did, sweetheart. Sorry. Sloan's and my path hasn't crossed too much lately, and I haven't seen Shelly since she came back." Putting his arm around Reba, he kissed her on the cheek. Looking back at the others, he said, "Since I was lucky enough to marry the prettiest girl in the valley, have to keep her happy." He waved a hand at them. "Talk to you all again. Maybe we can meet for lunch or something?"

Shelly and Sloan both nodded and made affirmative noises.

"Call me a cat if you want, but he's much too nice for her," Shelly muttered as soon as Bob and Reba were out of earshot.

"Won't get an argument out of me. No one, except maybe Reba and her family, was thrilled when she nabbed him. I thought Cleo was going to have a fit when she heard the news—she always had a soft spot for Bob and never cared much for Reba—which about sums up the general opinion in the valley." Sloan grinned at her. "There's just no accounting for taste when it comes to love."

Their check arrived just then, and, a few minutes later, they were walking out of the restaurant to Sloan's vehicle. A moment after that they were on their way back to St. Galen's.

Shelly had enjoyed herself—more than she had thought she would. She had worried unnecessarily, she thought dryly. So far they'd avoided controversial topics, and sex hadn't raised its disturbing head—yet. Sloan had been a perfect gentleman . . . of course, he would be when they were out in public, but what would happen when they reached her house and it was time to say good night? If Sloan took her in his arms and kissed her . . . Shelly swallowed, sudden heat swirling insidiously through her lower body. Desperately, she wrenched her thoughts away from thoughts of Sloan's hot mouth on hers, his hands striking fire wherever they touched her body. They'd had a pleasant evening, she reminded herself, and she didn't want to ruin it. As long as they both stayed on their best behavior everything would be fine. Yeah, right.

It had still been daylight when they had left the valley, but night had fallen while they were eating, and everything looked different as the Suburban sped through the darkness, the headlights spearing through the blackness—trees and brush took on fantastic shapes as the road rushed up to meet them.

There was less conversation on the way home than there had been on the drive out, but the silences that fell were comfortable. The sight of a deer caught in the beam of the lights would occasion a comment and once as they rounded a curve a fat black-and-white skunk waddled off to the side of the road, and they both laughed.

"So when are you going to meet Lowenthall?" Sloan asked a few minutes later.

"I don't know—probably not for a couple of weeks. I need to gather up a bunch of stuff first, and I'd like to finish the painting I'm on now before I see him." She sighed.

"Since I've been home, work has been the last thing on my mind."

"You've had a lot to deal with—settling an estate, even a small one, is time-consuming—and then there's the sense of loss you feel." He slanted her a glance. "I might not have the fondest memories of your brother, but I know that he meant the world to you."

Shelly nodded. "He did—he practically raised me. I remember more of him than I do my father." She sighed. "Up until a couple of months ago, I would have sworn that I knew everything there was to know about Josh . . . but sometimes I now wonder if I ever knew him. It's like the Josh I knew and the Josh who lived here were two different people." To her astonishment, she found it easy to talk to Sloan about Josh. Maybe it was the intimacy of the vehicle, the blackness of the night pressing in, isolating them almost as if they were the only two people alive, that made the words come forth so easily.

"How do you mean?"

Relaxed, slumped comfortably in the seat, the slight buzz from the wine they'd had for dinner loosening her tongue, she told him about Scott, about the deposits, the gambling, Josh's pilfering of her trust.

Sloan whistled under his breath when she finished. "I'd heard rumors that Josh had dropped some big bundles at the Indian casinos, but I never suspected the extent of his gambling—or that Scott had gotten his hooks into him. Mostly Scott is an annoyance, but he's caused some people some serious trouble." His eyes on the road, he asked lightly, "How bad is it?"

Shelly sat up and laughed. "Not as bad as it could be. I'm not in any danger of having to sell the ranch or hock the family valuables—yet. There's still enough money to act as a safety net, but between you and me and the gatepost, the great Granger fortune of legend and lore, which I should point out was never as great as local rumor, ain't no more."

"Ah, and being a big, bad Ballinger I should now try to work that fact to my advantage, shouldn't I?"

She glanced at him, his strong features shadowed, his gaze straight ahead, his hands effortlessly guiding the heavy vehicle down the road. "Will you?" she asked curiously. "Take advantage of the situation?"

Sloan shot her a look. "Honey, if you really think you have to ask, you shouldn't have told me."

Shelly bit her lip. "You're right, and though I know that Grangers are turning over in their grave, even with all the old family history between us, I trust you." She glanced at him again. "Most of the time."

He smiled. "I'll settle for that."

The Suburban swooped down onto the valley floor, and Sloan stepped up the speed, the vehicle's lights slicing through the night, barbed-wire fences and electrical poles flashing by. They were about two miles from the center of town when they noticed that they were fast coming up on several flashing lights and flares.

Sloan slowed and as they came closer they could make out vehicles, a fire truck, the volunteer-operated ambulance and a sheriff's office Bronco, all with their red-and-blue lights blazing, and a white pickup truck and a small blue car. Flares were scattered up and down the highway, the car rested drunkenly in the ditch, the driver's side door open, its front end caved in by the carcass of a black cow. In the Suburban's headlights and the lights from the other vehicles, Shelly could see more bulky dark forms moving around and the silhouettes of a half dozen or so men trying to shoo the cattle off the road. Two or three other people stood at the rear of the open doors of the ambulance.

"Oh, no," she cried. "Someone's cows have gotten loose. I hope no one was seriously hurt."

Cows, or even horses, roaming loose on the roads were not a common hazard, but it did happen from time to time, especially in the fall, when the cattle were driven to the hills. Sometimes the cows would try to come home a couple times before they stayed in the mountain winter pastures, or they got separated from the main herd and wandered around the valley floor until someone noticed and started calling around trying to find out who owned them. With horses, it was usually an unlatched gate or a downed fence. But either animal presented a real danger. There was nothing worse than having a four-legged, half-ton-or-more apparition appear without warning in the middle of the road. In the dark of night, a black animal was almost impossible to see until too late. And as had happened here, it was usually fatal for the cow or horse.

Sloan pulled the Suburban off the road and parked. He and Shelly both got out and walked toward the fire truck. Spying Bobba's compact frame, Shelly wandered over to him, while Sloan stopped to talk with Doug Simpson, the owner of the white pickup, whose place was just a quarter mile down the road. Bobba was at the side of the fire truck radioing some information back to the firehouse when Shelly walked up. He grimaced at her and finished his call. Putting away the handset, he said, "Good thing you weren't fifteen, twenty minutes earlier—it could have been your vehicle wearing that bull, instead of Mrs. Matthews' car."

"Our Mrs. Matthews?" Shelly asked, "The librarian?"

Bobba nodded. "Former librarian—she retired about five years ago."

"Was she hurt?" Shelly asked, concerned.

"Shook up, but she's OK. The tecs checked her out and once Brannigan, the deputy on duty, got her statement, he sent her home with her husband. You just missed them." He grinned at her. "For a moment we were more worried about him—old Ted's got a heart condition, and he was pretty upset. We got him calmed down and once he learned that Thelma wasn't hurt, he was fine. They're both fine. Her car is another matter. It looks totaled to me. And as for the bull. . . ." He shook his head, his freckled face angry. "I just hate this sort of thing—Mrs. Matthews is an old lady—she might have been killed or hurt badly." He glanced over at the blue car. "At least this time," he muttered, "the bull was killed outright, and we didn't have to have the deputy shoot the animal to put it out of its misery."

Of all of her childhood friends, Bobba had always had the softest heart; he had cried the most when in sixth grade the class mascot, a guinea pig, had died. He loved animals— he had even raised a litter of orphaned ground squirrels, considered vermin, to be shot on sight by almost everyone else. All through the years, his shoulder had been there for anyone who needed one to cry on. He just couldn't say no to someone—human or animal—in need. Looking into his guileless blue eyes and open, friendly face, Shelly wondered how he dealt with the tragedies, big and small, that he must see often in the course of his duties. She would never have expected him to become a fireman, much less the chief of St. Galen's volunteer fire department, all volunteer, except for his position, which was paid by the county. And yet if she thought about it, maybe his becoming a fireman wasn't so out of character. Hadn't everyone, at one time or another, seen a picture of a gallant fireman climbing a tree to rescue a frightened kitten? That was Bobba Neal—a hero in his own understated way.

The slamming of the ambulance doors jerked her attention away. As she watched there was a flurry of activity and then the long white-and-red vehicle pulled away, driving back in the direction of town.

"Any idea who owns the cows?" she asked, turning back to Bobba.

"Not yet—we're just now starting to check that out."

She and Bobba walked toward the blue car, where Sloan and Deputy Brannigan were examining the dead animal, looking for a brand or ear tags, something to identify ownership. The other cattle were momentarily being shooed down Cemetery Lane to get them off the state highway.

Sloan's face was grim as he climbed out of the ditch where the car had landed.

"What?" Shelly asked. "Can't identify it?"

Sloan took her arm. "Let's walk over here." Puzzled, Shelly let him guide her to the edge of the road, away from the deputy and Bobba. "There isn't an easy way to say this, honey . . . the dead bull is Granger's Ideal Beau—I recognized his ear tag. I suspect that the others are your cows from Texas."

Chapter Seventeen

❧

Shelly blanched. She glanced again at the black shape of the bull, her spirits sinking. Oh, God, if it were Beau . . . If it were the old bull, a lot of dreams and hopes for the future had died with him. She blinked back tears, watching the dark shapes being herded down Cemetery Lane by a couple of men on foot with flashlights. Sloan had made a mistake, she thought stubbornly. He was wrong. They couldn't be *her* cows! It wasn't her bull lying dead over there.

She shook her head, her voice full of disbelief, and said, "It's impossible!" She pointed to the foothills to the east. "The ranch is up there, four, five, six miles away. I didn't check, but I know that when we left Beau was in his pen; so were the cows—there's no way they could have gotten out." Desperately, she added, "And if they did get out, they wouldn't have ended up down here on the highway—you know they wouldn't have. They'd still be hanging around the barn or wandering in the foothills."

"Shelly, honey, they're your cattle," Sloan said gently. "I don't know how they got down here, but they did."

"It doesn't make sense," she muttered, almost to herself. "The corrals are brand-new. The gates have new latches, and all of us know to double-check the gates. We just rebuilt the corrals. They couldn't just have gotten out."

"I don't disagree with your reasoning," Sloan said evenly,

his big hand rubbing up and down her arm, his eyes compassionate. "But the fact of the matter is that they did end up down here, on the highway, and if it wasn't an accident . . ."

Her eyes widened. Almost in a whisper she said, "You think it was done deliberately?"

He sighed and pulled her into his arms. "It's a possibility, honey—but before we go down that road, let's make certain that we're not jumping at shadows." He urged her toward the Suburban. "There's probably a logical explanation for what happened."

Opening the door of the Suburban, he reached across the seat and picked up the cell phone lying on the console. "Does Acey have a phone in his quarters?"

"Yes." And she rattled off the number.

His eyes on hers, he punched in the number and waited as the phone rang endlessly, no one picking it up. He glanced at the gold watch on his wrist. It was after 1:00 A.M. Acey should have answered. He redialed just to make certain. Again no answer.

"He's not answering his phone."

Fear for the old cowboy speared through her. If the cattle had been turned loose deliberately and Acey heard a suspicious noise and went to investigate . . . "We have to get to the ranch. He could be hurt."

"Acey?" Sloan said with a reassuring smile. "I'd put my money on that little old Banty rooster every time. What do you want to bet that if there *was* any funny business, that Acey is presently holding the culprits at gunpoint? He's probably too busy swearing and cussing at them for interrupting his sleep to come to the phone."

Shelly tried to take comfort from Sloan's words. She was, she reminded herself, probably just running down the road to meet trouble. Acey was fine. And if there had been trouble, she had confidence that the old cowboy could handle it.

Tonight's events were just one of those tragedies that sometimes happen when dealing with animals. They did get out—
even out of the best fences. They did wander where you
would never expect. There was a simple explanation, and she
needn't go looking for boogey men to discover it.

She glanced down Cemetery Lane, biting her lip, thinking.
"Let me call Nick."

Nick answered on the tenth ring, his voice grumpy and
thick with sleep. By the time Shelly finished telling him what
had happened, including the news that Acey was not answering his phone, and what was needed, he was wide awake and
any irritation at being awakened, gone. "I'll be there as soon
as I can."

Shelly broke the connection, looked at Sloan, and asked,
"What about B-b-beau? Isn't there someone I'm supposed to
call to get the . . . body removed?"

"I'll take care of it. Don Bean runs a lot of equipment in
the valley. He'll have a loader and truck to haul it away for
you. There's no need to wake him right now—the body's off
the road, but I'll get hold of him first thing in the morning."

The California Highway Patrol, dispatched out of Lay-
tonville, arrived and took in the scene. Sloan knew the officer.

"Hi, Frank," Sloan said, walking up to the side of the
black-and-white patrol car. "Haven't seen you up here in a
while."

The young man grinned, his teeth flashing beneath a trim
blond mustache. "You guys have been behaving yourselves
lately—hasn't been any need. And between you and me," he
said as he exited the vehicle, "I'd just as soon keep it that
way."

Frank Hilliard's handshake was strong when he and Shelly
were introduced, and Shelly liked his open, friendly features.
He spent just a few minutes with them, then went in search of
Brannigan, the officer who had been first on the scene.

It took a while, but eventually Nick arrived hauling a two-horse trailer behind his pickup. To Shelly's surprise, Jeb was riding in the truck with him.

Sliding out of the cab, Jeb smiled at her and said, "Nick called me. He figured you'd need another pair of hands, since Acey appears to be playing hooky, and at this hour of the morning, I was the only one he could think to call who wouldn't hunt him down and murder him."

"Thank you," Shelly said simply, hugging him tightly.

One of the men who had been herding the cattle down Cemetery Lane walked up. Shelly recognized him: Bill Tanner, a local cowboy who had worked for the Ballingers for years. After greeting everyone and telling Shelly how sorry he was about her bull, he said, "We found a gate open on that vacant 160 acres of Sanderson's at the end of the lane, near the cemetery. That's probably how they got here. I guess they came down out of the foothills, cut across the east end of the airport, then most likely, considering the state of Sanderson's fences, found a break on that side and just ambled on across and out onto Cemetery Lane." Pushing his brown baseball cap back on his head, he looked at Sloan and asked, "You want me to get my horse and help herd 'em back?"

Sloan shook his head. "No. Nick brought along a couple of horses, and he and I can drive them. Jeb and Shelly will see to it that the vehicles get back to the ranch." They shook hands. "Thanks, Bill," Sloan said. "We appreciate your help."

Bill's sun-wrinkled face cracked a shy smile. "No thanks needed—we've all had troubles—glad I was around to lend a hand."

Ten minutes later, Sloan and Nick were disappearing down Cemetery Lane on the horses and Shelly was following Jeb in the Suburban as he drove Nick's truck and trailer. It would take Nick and Sloan a while to herd the cattle home—there wasn't much of a moon, just a thin sliver, and they would have to travel slowly to make certain they didn't leave any animal behind in the dark.

Jeb parked at the back of the house, and Shelly pulled in beside him.

"You want to check out the house first?" Jeb asked after they had both exited their vehicles and were standing at the rear of the horse trailer.

"No. I want to know why Acey didn't answer the phone."

Jeb shined the big flashlight Nick kept stashed in his truck around the area.

On the surface the ranch looked serene. There was nothing out of the ordinary, except, Shelly noticed with a start, that the halogen light over the wide double doors of the barn was out. Most ranches had a couple of them scattered around outbuildings—the lights came on automatically at dusk and remained on all night.

She touched Jeb's arm, whispering, "The barn light isn't on . . . and it should be."

"Could just be burned out," he said quietly, but he handed her the flashlight and reached behind his waist for his gun.

"You wait here," he ordered. "Let me check this out." He looked at her strained features and smiled. "There's probably a simple explanation for everything. Now don't go getting all hysterical on me, OK?"

She sent him a watery smile, nodding.

"Flick off the flashlight and let me see how much of my sneaking and slipping around I remember. And stay here." He waved the gun under her nose. "This is loaded, and if I have to shoot it, I want to know that it's the bad guys I'm shooting at—not you."

Shelly remained rooted to the spot, her gaze locked on the last place she'd seen Jeb's big form. It was eerie standing in the darkness, only the sound of her own breathing coming to her ears, the buildings and trees creating spooky shadows in the thin silvery moonlight. The minutes dragged, but before her imagination had a chance to run away with her, Acey's dogs started to bark and Jeb hailed her.

"Over here, Shelly," he called from the shadows near the kennels. "I've found Acey—he's hurt, but not bad. Bring Sloan's cell phone with you."

Shelly rushed to the Suburban, snatched up the phone and, the flashlight guiding her way, ran to the end of the barn, in her haste almost turning an ankle because of her dressy heels. Her breath caught in her throat as the light fell on Acey's slumped form, blood staining his white hair red.

"Acey!" she cried, kneeling beside him. "How bad is it?"

Fierce blue eyes glared up at her. "Not as bad as the dizzy bastard who did this to me is going to feel once I get my hands on him."

With Jeb's help, Acey stood up. He was steady on his feet and seemed more outraged by the incident than hurt. He touched the gash at the back of his head and winced. "At least my hat'll hide it." Taking in Shelly's anxious face, he grinned. "Glad they didn't hurt my pretty face. Got a date with that redheaded widow woman Sunday night—wouldn't want to scare her."

Shelly smiled perfunctorily and pointed to the house. "If your feet are working as well as your mouth, I suggest you march right over to the house. You can tell me all the details of your love life after I've had a look at the wound."

In the kitchen, Shelly and Jeb both examined the cut on Acey's head. It wasn't as bad as it had first looked—head wounds always bled profusely. After Shelly had cleaned it out with a mild disinfectant and wrapped a length of white gauze around Acey's head, she admitted that Jeb and Acey were right about the lack of need for stitches—or an ambulance.

"You're sure you feel all right?" she asked for the tenth time since they'd come inside. "No dizziness? No blurred vision? Are you positive you don't want a doctor or one of the med tecs to look at it?"

Acey made a face, looking rather rakish wearing his white bandage. "Shelly, I'm fine. I've suffered worse than this, believe me. I know when I'm hurt. Nothing is hurt right now, but my pride." He touched the spot and winced again. "And maybe my head is a trifle sore, but it's nothing. All I need are a couple of aspirin and that coffee you promised. I figure we're gonna need it."

Once the coffeemaker was burbling away, she sank down on the chair next to Acey. Jeb was seated in a chair at the table across from them.

"What happened?" Jeb asked.

"I don't know what woke me, but I woke up sudden-like. I heard some four-wheelers in the hills not too far away and figured that it was them racing around, gunning their engines that woke me. I kinda drifted off and the next thing I know the dogs is raising a fuss. I thought a raccoon or skunk was sniffing around, riling 'em up. They kept barking and yelping and after a while I decided I'd better take a look. Didn't think much that the barn light was out, figured the bulb was bad. Anyway, I walked around the side of the barn and was checking out the back of the kennels when I heard a sound behind me." He grimaced. "And that's the last thing I knew until I woke up with a hellacious headache, just a few minutes before you found me." He looked from one to the other. "If I remember correctly," he said slowly, "Shelly had a date tonight with Sloan . . . not you. Now that I've told my story, you suppose you want to tell me what's going on?"

The air turned blue from Acey's curses when the full extent of the trouble was explained to him. When the worst of his rage had abated, he took one of Shelly's hands in his. Her fingers tightened around his gnarled hand. "I failed you," he said in a pained voice. "It's my fault old Beau is lying down there dead on the highway. If you want me to move out, I'll understand, and I wouldn't blame you a bit—without Beau, the Granger breeding program is damn near ruined."

Shelly smiled and kissed his bristly cheek. "Don't be silly. We're in this together. What happened was an accident. You can't blame yourself. And the loss of Beau is tragic, but we'll just. . . ." She took a deep breath. "Granger Cattle Company will just have to go in another direction. It might even be for the best."

Neither she nor Acey believed that, but they were both putting on a brave face. Jeb let them brood for a moment, then he said, "If you're feeling up to it, Acey, let's take a look around. See for ourselves if it was an accident . . . or mischief."

"You damn well know it was mischief," Acey snarled, getting up from the table and walking toward the door. "I sure as hell didn't hit myself in the back of the head!"

The three of them went out together. It didn't take long to discover how the cattle had gotten out: The gate to Beau's pen was wide open, as was the gate in front of the area holding the cows.

Slamming Beau's gate shut, Acey growled, "Might as well leave the other one open for when the cows show up. They can drive them right on in—and if we fill the mangers with alfalfa, they might just go on in without darting all over first."

The mangers overflowing with sweet-scented alfalfa, they walked back to the house. As they entered the kitchen, Acey muttered, "There's no way what happened tonight was just bad luck. Even if you try to make out that, maybe, it was just someone pilfering around that hit me on the back of the head, them cows getting out weren't no accident. You could argue that, maybe, I'd a been careless latching one gate—and I wasn't. But there's no way in hell that I'd mess up with two gates. And them cows wouldn't have ended up on the highway unless someone herded 'em down there."

Solemn-faced, Shelly had poured coffee for them all. "But who? And why would anyone do such a thing?"

"Plain old meanness, pure and simple," Acey said. "And if you think about it, Shelly, there's only one person it could have been—Milo Scott."

Shelly gasped, her thoughts tumbling. "Of course," she said after a moment. "It has to have been him. He's the only person who had a reason to cause us harm."

"If I might add a word of caution," Jeb said lightly. "Before you go off half-cocked, you'd better make sure of your facts. And if Milo Scott is responsible, you'd better have proof—and let the law take care of it." He shot Acey a hard look. "Prove it to me, and I'll arrest him tonight."

Acey swore some more—none of it complimentary to Jeb or the sheriff's department. "You know goddamn well, I can't. And I'll even bet if you was to go check out that lying, sneaking son of a whore, he'll have an alibi for tonight a mile long."

Jeb raised a hand. "I know. And I don't disagree with your assessment, but without some sort of proof, there isn't much that I can do."

Acey glanced at Shelly. "I ask you—what's the point of having a lawman in the family if they can't do you any good?"

"Acey, I can't break the law," Jeb said patiently. "I want to nail the bastard who did this as much as you do, but we have to do it legally or else we'll end up on the wrong side of the law and in jail ourselves."

Acey puffed up like an adder. "You'd arrest me? But not that son of a bitch Scott?"

Jeb sighed. "Let's leave it lie, OK? I don't need you getting beaten up and then thrown in jail because you tackled him. And you know I'm right."

Acey shot him a furious look, then bent his head and concentrated on his coffee. An uncomfortable silence fell. To break it, Shelly asked, "How long do you think it'll take Nick and Sloan to drive the cattle back here?"

Jeb glanced at the big round chrome clock on the kitchen wall. "Hmm, it's been over an hour since we left them—even if they push the cows right smartly, it'll probably be at least another hour before they reach here."

"Then I'm putting one of Maria's pies in the oven," Shelly said, jumping to her feet. "She's got about a half dozen apple pies in the freezer, and I think this calls for one."

Acey brightened up. "Good idea. Apple pie, mischief and coffee at 3:00 A.M. Makes a good combination."

Shelly laughed and, deciding that it was safe to leave Acey and Jeb alone, excused herself and ran upstairs to change into a pair of jeans and boots. When she came back downstairs it was to find Jeb and Acey with their heads together, almost whispering. She couldn't hear what they were saying, but she was certain she caught Sloan's name and Scott's. . . .

Hands on her hips, she stood in the doorway, and demanded, "OK, what are you two planning that you don't want me to know about?"

They both jumped and turned startled faces in her direction. Jeb recovered first. Leaning back in his chair, he smiled and said, "Now, Shelly, what makes you think we're up to something? We were just going over things."

"Yeah, that's all," chimed in Acey. "It was a real intense conversation. But we weren't planning anything."

Shelly didn't believe them, but she knew that further probing would get her nowhere. But it bothered her. Linking Sloan's name with Scott's made her heart sink. Surely, they didn't think Sloan had hired Scott to turn the cows loose? She found it hard even to consider much less believe. The shades of all her ancestors rose up in her mind, each one berating her foolishness in trusting a Ballinger. She sighed. It was foolishness all right—foolishness to think that Sloan would be that underhanded.

She had just taken the pie from the oven and the second pot of coffee had just finished perking when the sounds of hooves and lowing cattle drifted inside the kitchen. As one, the three of them dashed outside, skidding to a halt as the first of the cows came ambling past them.

Almost as if they had done it for years, first one cow and then another meandered through the open gate and into the pen they had left hours ago. The last cow in, Acey shut the gate as Sloan and Nick dismounted.

After seeing to the horses, they all walked back to the house. The pie and coffee were appreciated, and if one didn't know better, it would have looked like they were having a celebration. In a way, it was. Acey was relatively unhurt and the cows were back safely in their pen. Everyone was aware of how much worse it could have been. No one wanted to talk about the blow that Beau's loss had given Shelly and Nick's brave new venture, and they stepped carefully around that subject. Milo Scott's name came up more than once, but Jeb reminded them, his gaze locked on Sloan's, that there was no proof.

Sloan leaned back in his chair, his tie gone, a couple of buttons of his mauve-and-burgundy shirt undone and a lock of black hair brushing across his wide forehead. Acey and Nick were heated about the subject, but Shelly noticed that Sloan hadn't said much—which made her wonder why Jeb was directing most of his warnings to him.

"Don't you think Scott is guilty?" Shelly asked, her eyes on Sloan's face.

"Oh, he did it, all right," Sloan said carelessly. "I knew that, just as soon as I realized that it was Beau lying there on the hood of that car." He smiled crookedly. "I'm no psychic, but it wasn't more than half an hour earlier that you'd told me

about your lease problems with him. It was a simple jump."
His mouth grew grim. "I'd already decided that he'd probably
try something, I just didn't figure he'd move so quickly."

"So what are we going to do?" Nick demanded, his green
eyes bright with anger.

Sloan smiled lazily. "There's nothing legally that we can
do," he said, taking a sip of his coffee, his gaze on Jeb's face.
"After all, just like the big guy says, there's no proof."

Acey and Nick were vociferous in their disdain for that argument, but Shelly put an end to the discussion. Picking up
some of the empty plates, she walked to the counter. "It's
late," she said, putting the plates in the sink. "We're too tired
to think rationally right now anyway. I suggest we call it a
night."

They followed her lead, Sloan lingering by the back door,
as the others said good night and walked out into the night.
Shelly had accompanied the men, and in the faint light from
the kitchen she looked up at Sloan.

A half smile on her mouth, she said, "Seems our date had
a little more excitement than I planned for, how about you?"

His fingers brushing her cheeks, he murmured, "This certainly wasn't how I expected it to end . . . although the hour is
about right. And I had hoped that it would prove to be *very*
exciting."

Shelly's heart banged into her ribs. "Sloan . . . I don't think
that this is a good idea."

His mouth teased hers. "You think too much," he said
against her lips. And then he kissed her, his arms drawing her
close to his long body.

It was several minutes later when he finally lifted his head.
Both of them were breathing hard. Shelly's arms were around
his neck, her lips already missing the warmth of his, her body
aching for completion. She was aware that all he'd have to do
was take her hand and lead her upstairs for her to follow him.

He touched her lips with one finger. "Keep my place for me, will you?"

Helplessly, she nodded.

A moment later he was gone.

Whistling softly, Sloan walked to the Suburban and slipped inside the big vehicle. A moment later the vehicle slid smoothly past the house, its lights making shadows jump and dodge as they swept across the trees and shrubs that lined the driveway.

Despite his calm words, if anyone had seen the expression on his face as the Suburban hit the pavement near the tiny St. Galen's Airport, it would have been obvious that he was anything but calm. By the time he eased into the silent town, the beast he had kept rigidly chained in front of the others had fought free. Drifting down the few narrow streets that constituted town, his dark face wore a look of savage concentration that would have caused many a brave warrior to step aside. Swiftly.

He stopped the vehicle in front of a small, ramshackle house and turned off the ignition. The house seemed to sit there sulking in the light from the streetlight a half a block away; the lawn, if it could be called that, overgrown and weedy, the garage door sagging half-open. Sloan considered the dwelling in front of him, trying without much success to tame the rage that clawed through him. This bastard, he thought, had hit out at Shelly. Had caused her pain and might have ruined her plans for the future of Granger Cattle. Personally, he didn't give a damn about Granger Cattle, but Shelly did, and that was the whole point. Shelly had her heart set on it and the son of a bitch who, no doubt, slept soundly inside this house had reached out and struck viciously at her. Jeb could spout the law all he wanted, but Sloan's mind was made up: Scott's attack couldn't and *wouldn't* be tolerated.

For a big man, Sloan could move like a shadow. Slipping

from the vehicle, he shut the door with barely a click, and, a second later, he was prowling on panther feet around the front of the garage. He stepped inside, the brief gleam from his flashlight revealing two mud-splattered four-wheel vehicles and Scott's truck parked inside the garage. Too much time had passed for the four-wheelers to tell him much, but he touched the hood of the vehicle nearest him, feeling for warmth anyway, not surprised that the engine was cold.

Stepping up to the door that led into the house from the garage, it took him only a minute to jimmy the lock. He smiled. Jeb had taught him that trick years ago.

Sloan slipped inside the darkened house, using another split-second gleam of his flashlight to give him the layout. The bedrooms lay down a short hall, and he eased open the door to the first one he came to, the sound of snoring reaching him as he stood there.

With a catlike tread he walked to the side of the king-size bed and flicked on the flashlight. The blinding light revealed Milo Scott asleep, his mouth half-open as he snored. Sloan was pleased. He would have been disappointed if his light had revealed someone other than Scott.

In his sleep, Scott frowned at the light and muttered something, turning on his side.

The urge to wrap his hand around Scott's neck was powerful, but Sloan retained enough of a sense of honor to find the thought of attacking a man in his sleep distasteful. He glanced around, his gaze lighting on the half bottle of wine Scott had left on the battered night table by his bed.

Smiling, Sloan picked it up and began pouring it over Scott's head. "Wake up, sunshine," he crooned.

The splash of cool wine brought Scott instantly awake, the blinding light from Sloan's flashlight making him blink as he struggled into a sitting position. "Wha—?"

Sloan flicked on the table lamp next to the bed. Laying down the flashlight, Sloan said, "Surprise."

"Jesus Christ! *You!* What the hell do you think you're doing?" Scott growled. He looked at the clock, then back at Sloan. "Do you know what time it is?"

"Yeah, time for you to pay the piper."

A crafty look entered Scott's eyes. "It's too damned early for riddles. You're crazy."

Sloan smiled, a terrifying smile, and reached over and grabbed Scott around the neck with one hand. "Crazy works for me. Actually," he said softly, "you're the crazy one—you should have known that turning Shelly's cattle loose was a crazy idea."

Scott looked smug, even with Sloan's big hand around his throat. "Now that's real curious," Scott said with a smirk. "Especially since me and my buddy, Ben, have been here together all night. Of course, we did go four-wheeling a couple of hours ago, but I don't remember seeing any cows." He smiled. "You can't prove anything." He glanced in the direction of the door. "Ain't that right, Ben?"

"You got it, bud," said Ben from behind Sloan.

Keeping his hand around Milo's neck, Sloan turned his head slightly and almost smiled at the sight of Ben Williams standing in the doorway, a double-barreled shotgun leveled at him. He had hoped to catch the two of them together.

"Move away from him, real slow," Williams ordered, his cold black eyes reminding Sloan of a rattlesnake. Williams was a tall, beefy guy with a straggly reddish brown beard crawling across his cheeks and chin. His gut strained over his black T-shirt, and Sloan figured Williams outweighed him by fifty pounds . . . and the other man held a shotgun. He'd come here for a fight, but he wasn't stupid, and only someone stupid took on a shotgun. But inwardly he smiled. Shotgun aside, things were working just about as he had planned.

"Sure," Sloan said easily, suiting word to action.

Just as he had known he would, the moment Sloan let go of Scott's throat and stepped away, Scott shot up from the bed and, putting muscle behind it, slammed a punch into Sloan's stomach. "Bastard!" Scott snarled. "You made a big mistake coming here. You've been wanting a lesson for a long time, and I'll be happy to give it to you." Over his shoulder, he said to Williams, "Keep him covered."

Scott's punch nearly knocked the air of out Sloan, and he gasped. Scott followed it with another one, laughing when Sloan almost doubled over, enjoying himself. Sloan let him get a few good licks in, judging his chances of taking both of them down. The shotgun worried him, but not much. Scott drew back his fist, ready to ram it into Sloan's face, when Sloan decided he'd been polite enough. He caught Scott's fist in one hand, the other hand dragging up a handful of the T-shirt Scott was wearing. In one smooth, powerful move, he threw Scott across the room, slamming him into Williams. Both men went down in a heap, the shotgun bouncing and clanging against the floor as it was torn from Williams's grasp.

With a flick of his foot, Sloan kicked the shotgun under the bed and, reaching down, half dragged, half threw the other two men out of the bedroom and down the hallway. The fight that followed was ugly, vicious, and brutal. It was two against one, but Sloan was more than a match for them. The battle spilled out of the hallway into the small living room, Sloan breaking Williams's nose and sending Scott flying with a crash into the table and lamp that sat at the end of the couch. It was not a pretty fight and there was as much destruction to the furniture as there was to the fighters. Sloan's lip was bleeding, his fists were scraped and cut, and he had to blink to keep the blood out of his left eye from a cut above his eyebrow.

Scott was smaller, but he was tough and wiry and a dirty fighter; Williams was heavier, a strong man, but he was slow. As he took a stunning blow to his right temple and the room swam, Sloan figured that if he didn't bring the fight to a quick end, they would eventually wear him down. He fought with a single-minded ferocity, heedless of the blows they struck, heedless of the damage they inflicted, his one thought being to take them down. And he did.

Concentrating first on Williams, in a series of lightning and violent punches, Sloan soon had the big man slumped and groaning against the far wall of the living room. A kick to the groin and an uppercut sent Scott spinning backward to land in a moaning pile on the floor.

Gasping for breath, wiping away the blood from his cut eyebrow, Sloan stood there, swaying just a bit from the damage he'd taken. His body was one long ache and, gingerly, he touched his ribs, wincing at the pain that lanced through him. Jesus. A broken rib, that's all I need.

He walked over to where Scott lay and nudged him with his toe. When Scott rolled over and looked up at him, Sloan said softly, "Stay away from Shelly Granger. She has any more trouble of *any* kind, and I'll come back to visit." Despite his busted lip Sloan smiled, a smile even more terrifying than his earlier one. "And if I have to come back . . . you won't like it . . . trust me."

Chapter Eighteen

⚬

Grimacing against the pain, Sloan turned around, stopping short at the sight of Jeb leaning against the jamb of the front door. For a second the two men confronted each other, then Jeb said dryly, "You forgot to tell him to cancel the lease with Shelly."

Sloan nodded. "Yeah, I did." He turned back to Scott and poked him with his toe. When Scott half sat up and looked blearily at him, Sloan said, "See Sawyer and tell him you want out of the lease with Shelly Granger. First thing Monday morning, you tell him you're eager to end it. No money."

Scott hesitated. Jeb strolled over to stand next to Sloan. "You have a problem with Sloan's request?" he asked politely.

Scott glanced from one face to the other, for the first time seeing the family resemblance. There was no yielding in either face, and, flopping back down on the floor, he muttered, "Sure. No problem. I'll call Sawyer first thing Monday morning."

"Appreciate it," Sloan said, and began limping toward the door.

Jeb regarded Scott for a moment longer. "I take it everything is OK here? No complaints, or anything like that?"

Scott flashed him an incredulous look. "Get out," he grated. "Just get the hell out of my house and take your trained ape with you."

Jeb grinned. "Glad to. Just wanted to make certain."

Jeb wasn't grinning when he caught up with Sloan, who was leaning against the front fender of the Suburban. "You OK?" he asked as he rested one arm on the top of the vehicle.

Sloan grimaced. "I'll live, but it'll be a few weeks before I want to do that again."

"Take it from me," Jeb said quietly, "*don't* do it again—ever."

Sloan squinted at him from his swollen eye. "You going to arrest me?"

"If you pull a damn fool stunt like that again, I will." He pointed a finger at him. "You're lucky, you know that. You took on two of them—not smart. And you broke all kinds of laws." When Sloan started to speak, Jeb held up a hand. "I don't want to hear it. I'm on thin enough ground as it is." Then he ruined it by grinning. "Nice work. I've been wanting to do that for a long time. I especially liked that uppercut you gave him after you threw him against the wall."

Sloan started to smile, then groaned as his split lip made itself felt. "How long were you watching?"

"Since you drove up." He jerked his head down the street. "I'm parked in Mrs. Nolan's driveway. Figured you'd drive right on past—which you did. Knowing you and how you feel about Shelly, I was pretty sure you'd come after him." He smiled faintly in the darkness. "Thought you might need some backup, but you handled it just fine, son."

Sloan shook his head, pain lancing through him. "Jesus! I'm too old for this sort of thing."

Jeb clapped him on the shoulder, and Sloan winced. "Remember that the next time you get all riled up." He sent him a considering glance. "You OK to drive home?"

"Yeah. I'm fine—or I will be once I've made it to bed—for a week."

Jeb laughed and sauntered off into the darkness.

Shelly woke Saturday morning tired, crabby, and depressed. The events of the previous evening were fresh in her mind and, as she dragged herself from the bed, she marveled at how swiftly a really great time had turned into a nightmare. One minute her only worry had been if she could resist Sloan's advances and then the next . . . She sighed. And the next, her dream for the future of Granger Cattle Company had been shattered.

The shower helped, but she still felt groggy and out of sorts. Looking at the clock and noticing that it wasn't much past 8:00 A.M. she wasn't surprised. She'd only had a couple of hours' sleep—if that.

She trudged downstairs, trying to work up some enthusiasm for the day. It was Saturday, not a normal workday, although on a ranch and with livestock there was no such thing as a weekend, but except for feeding and care of the stock, they did slack off some, and the hours stretched out endlessly before her. The loss of Beau weighed heavily on her and while she usually ran out to the cattle pens first thing every morning, this morning she was hard-pressed not to burst into tears every time she thought of the cattle. Poor Beau. As for Milo Scott . . . her face set, and her hands clenched into respectable fists. The next time she saw him, she'd probably forget she was raised a lady and kick his balls right up into his throat. She smiled at the picture. Yeah. She'd enjoy doing that.

Feeling a trifle better, she followed the scent of coffee and frying bacon to the kitchen. Maria was bustling around in front of the stove, and Acey was seated at the kitchen table.

"Morning," Shelly said as she helped herself to a mug of coffee and joined Acey at the table. She eyed him appreciatively. He looked almost rakish with his bandaged head. "How're you feeling?"

"Beyond my pride takin' a beating, I'm not doing too poorly. Head aches a little. Like I told Maria, when I explained what happened last night, the scratch looks worse than it feels."

After laying the last piece of bacon on a paper towel to drain, Maria turned around and glared at the pair of them. Hand on one hip, she demanded, "I suppose it never occurred to anyone to call me when all this was going on last night."

"Wasn't last night," Acey murmured. "This morning. Hell of a time to wake you from your beauty rest."

Maria snorted. "At my age I am beautiful enough." She fixed a gimlet stare on Shelly. "You should have called me."

Shelly grimaced. "Maria, it was one, two o'clock in the morning. There was nothing you could have done except lose sleep." She grinned. "And eat pie. I was never more thankful that you keep the freezer stocked with those apple pies of yours than last ni—er, this morning."

Maria looked slightly mollified. She turned back to her cooking for a minute and, after pouring pancake batter on the big black griddle on the stove, pointed a spatula at Shelly, and ordered, "The next time something like that happens, you call me—at any hour of the day or night."

Shelly nodded, her expression grim. "Let's hope nothing like that happens again."

"It won't," said Acey decisively. "We're putting locks on all the gates and, for the next little while, Nick and I are going to take turns patrolling the cows at night."

"Count me in," Shelly said. "If we take turns, no one has to lose much sleep."

Acey's dogs started up a ruckus, and they all heard the sound of a vehicle pulling in behind the house. A moment later, purple shadows under his eyes, Nick strolled into the kitchen. Spying the pancakes his mother was flipping on the griddle, he said, "Hot damn! Timed it just right for breakfast."

"Do you ever think of anything other than food?" Shelly teased.

Helping himself to a piece of bacon, he grinned. "Oh, yeah. Like Acey here, I think of women a lot. But unlike Acey, I get to *do* something about it."

Acey sputtered in his coffee. "I'll have you know that I *do* quite a bit about it, myself," he said grandly. "And better. You young studs think in terms of quantity—you're too dumb to know that it's quality that counts."

Maria and Shelly both groaned. "Please," Shelly begged, "not this morning. You're both studs, let's leave it at that."

"Damn right," Acey said.

Half an hour later, her stomach full of Maria's sourdough pancakes, Shelly drove the Bronco into town. She didn't know exactly what she was planning on doing, but double-checking that Beau's carcass had been removed from the side of the highway seemed a logical move. Sloan had said he would take care of it, and she didn't doubt that he had; she was grateful that was one decision she didn't have to make. She slowed when she reached the site of the accident, relieved that there was no sign of the dead bull. Don Bean must have been out early taking care of the grisly task. On her return, she stopped at his place, her face paling when she drove around back of his big metal shop and caught sight of Beau's remains lying stiffly on the back of a large flatbed truck.

Wearing a pair of grease-stained blue denim overalls, Don came walking out from his shop. After wiping hands the size of Virginia hams on a red rag, he stuffed the rag in his back pocket and pushed back the ubiquitous baseball cap on his head. Standing next to her vehicle, he said, "Morning. Sorry about your bull." He jerked his head in the direction of the flatbed. "I wasn't certain where you wanted the body dumped. Thought I'd call you in a little bit."

Shelly smiled with an effort, keeping her gaze averted from the truck. "Thank you for getting him off the road so quickly." She swallowed. "Uh, you're not going to drive him through town that way, are you?"

Don Bean was a big, beefy man, about six-foot-two, barrel-chested, and dripping wet, he weighed around 240 pounds. He was about Sloan's age and he'd been running his own business almost since the day he'd graduated from high school. If you wanted tractor work done, from road to ponds, you called Don Bean. Welding? Yep, he did that—when he had time. Timbering? When the rain quit, he'd be happy to do that, too. Construction? Well, he'd be willing to turn his hand to that—if the price was right. He was a well-known, well-liked good ole boy: His humor could be rough, his tongue brutal, and he didn't take crap off anybody. He was also known to be handy with those ham-sized fists, but his good heart and his good humor endeared him to just about everyone. Grinning at Shelly, he drawled, "Don't worry, the trip through town won't bother ole Beau none."

"I wasn't thinking of Beau," she said tartly. "I just don't think he's a pretty sight for any kids to see."

His bright blue eyes laughing at her, Don said, "Oh, in that case, I've got a couple of yellow tarps I can throw over him." He winked. "I planned to do that anyway. Don't want some do-gooder old lady having a heart attack or calling animal abuse."

"Thanks, Don, I appreciate it."

He waved her away. "No problem. Accidents happen. Don't give it another thought."

Shelly paid him and pulled away.

She wasn't in any hurry to go home, afraid that all she'd do would be to mope around the house and barns. Seeing M.J.'s apple red pickup parked at the side of the Blue Goose, she pulled in beside the other vehicle.

The aroma of frying ham and cinnamon rolls teased her nostrils as she pushed open the door and walked inside. Hank looked over his shoulder from where he was busy cooking up something on the grill and grinned at her. He tipped his hat. "Ah, good morning to you, darlin'. Couldn't stay away from my cooking, could you?"

Shelly smiled. "Well, I haven't actually tried your cooking yet—it was Megan's efforts I tried, remember?"

"So it was. So it was. But you're here now . . ."

Shelly shook her head. "But not to eat—just some coffee, maybe. I'm looking for M.J."

Several of the tables were full, mostly with couples or families; some she recognized, some she didn't; the ones she did called out a friendly greeting as she walked to where M.J. was sitting at a table for two tucked into a corner near the wood stove. As she joined M.J. she eyed the plate of sausage gravy and biscuits in front of M.J. and regretted her full stomach. Though tempted to try a half order, when Sally came to the table she settled for coffee.

Shelly and M.J. made conversation until after Sally had placed the heavy white mug in front of her and gone on to serve another table. Sally had barely turned away before M.J. pounced.

Brown eyes gleaming, food forgotten, M.J. leaned forward and said, "If you aren't the slyest thing. How *dare* you have a date with Sloan Ballinger and never breathe a word to me? Am I or am I not your best friend? Am I not the only person in the world who knows all your innermost secrets? Such as the fact that you have been known to eat peanut butter right from the jar—in bed?"

Shelly took a sip of her coffee. "How did you hear about it?"

"Bobba," M.J. said cheerfully, smiling at her. "And Chuck Brannigan. And Bill Tanner."

"Jeez, is there *any*body in the valley who doesn't know what happened?"

"Well it's not noon yet, so there's probably a few souls who haven't heard the valley drumbeat."

Shelly grimaced and shook her head. "I'd forgotten how quickly news spreads."

M.J. swallowed a bite of her biscuits and gravy, and, her face sober, she said, "Listen, all teasing about Sloan aside, I'm sorry about Beau. I know he meant everything to your plans. Were you able to find out how they got out?"

"Someone hit Acey on the head, opened the gates, and drove them down to the valley floor," Shelly said baldly.

"Oh, no. How horrible! Who would do such a thing—and why?"

"The favorite culprit at the moment is Milo Scott, but we don't have any proof."

"The lease!" M.J. exclaimed, her cheeks pink with anger. "That bastard! I'll bet he did it to get you to back off trying to break the lease."

"That's the best guess. I can't think of anyone else who would be that malicious. And it couldn't have been an accident—not with Acey getting his head bashed."

They discussed the subject for a few minutes, then, pushing aside her half-empty plate and reaching for her coffee, M.J. said, "OK, enough of that. Now give."

"It was just dinner," Shelly said, not pretending to misunderstand her. "We're trying to, um, be friends. Make a bridge between the Granger and Ballinger families."

M.J. hooted. "And I've got a bridge in Brooklyn I can sell you cheap."

Shelly flushed. "It *was* just dinner. And he was a perfect gentleman. We ate in Ukiah, seeing Reba and Bob Stanton, by the way, and arrived back in the valley in time to find Beau lying dead alongside the road."

"Gross. I guess that would pretty much put paid to any romance."

"Sure did." Honesty made Shelly admit, "I'm not so certain that it wasn't a good thing—not the cattle being turned loose, but having something to concentrate on other than each other." She frowned. "I don't want to rush into anything with Sloan."

"Rush? Are you forgetting that you've had seventeen years to think about him? That certainly doesn't sound like rushing to me." M.J. shook a finger at her. "And face it, kiddo, we're none of us getting any younger. If I had a hunk like Sloan Ballinger hanging around me, I'd be rushing *him*." Morosely, she added, "Good men are hard to find anywhere, and especially in the valley—I should know. Except for some 'prove myself sexy' romps right after the divorce, I've haven't been laid in months."

"Thought you were off men."

M.J. winked. "I like sex, and for sex you need men." She sighed, dropping the brazen attitude. "At least I do. Believe me, vibrators are not all they're cracked up to be." She fiddled with her coffee mug. "It's not as if I'm looking for another husband—there are the boys to consider, and between them, and running the store, it isn't like I have extra time on my hands. But sometimes, I don't know, I get lonesome for male companionship—and not just in the bedroom. Sometimes, the boys, the store, and my friends—even your scintillating presence—aren't enough for me. Marriage is one place that I don't want to go for a long, long time, if ever again, but I wouldn't mind having a no-strings-attached sexy affair with a decent guy."

Thoughtfully Shelly studied her friend. "What about Danny?" she asked curiously.

"*Danny!*" M.J. almost shrieked, her blue eyes bugging.

"Our Danny? Good God, I'd rather go to bed with my brother—if I had a brother." Scowling, she demanded, "Whatever gave you that idea? Danny Haskell is the last guy I'd go to bed with." She snorted. "Danny, I can't believe you said that."

"I can't either," Shelly admitted ruefully. "It was just . . . I don't know—you're single, he's single, and you can't deny that he's handsome."

"Yeah, but Danny . . . I dunno. It'd seem incestuous or something . . . I think." M.J. shook her curly blond head. "Nope. Not Danny." She flashed Shelly a lecherous grin. "But tell me about that cousin of yours. Didn't you say he was coming out to visit? Maybe I can make him feel welcome. *Real* welcome."

"Roman? I don't know how smart that would be. I adore him, but I can't say that he's dependable when it comes to women—he's always been the love 'em and leave 'em type." Shelly looked troubled. "No. I don't think you'd want to tangle with Roman. He's a great guy if he's your relative, but otherwise . . ." She shook her head. "No. You don't want an affair with Roman—Roman would break your heart."

"Probably, but the sex might be worth it."

M.J. was still half-trying to convince Shelly that Roman would be perfect to help chase away her sexual doldrums when they walked outside. Spotting Danny and Jeb standing by Danny's patrol car across the street, Shelly waved. Turning to M.J., she said, "I'll say good-bye now. I want to thank Jeb again for his help last night."

M.J. nodded. "You want to get together this weekend?" For someone usually so cheerful and bouncy, she looked downcast. "I miss my boys," she said softly. "The house seems so empty without them racing around and driving me half-crazy—even though I tell myself that I like the peace and quiet

when they're with their father." She grimaced. "Which is true
for about five minutes."

"Sure. Why don't you come to my place tonight? We can
make up a batch of caramel corn and watch *You've Got Mail*—
I bought the video last week. Bring a change of clothes and
stay the night."

"Thanks. I'd enjoy that." Impetuously, M.J. hugged Shelly.
"God, I'm glad you're home."

"You just want some homemade caramel corn, go ahead
admit it."

"OK, I admit it."

Laughing, Shelly waved her off and walked across the
street to join Jeb and Danny. Both men were leaning against
the patrol car, Danny in uniform, Jeb in jeans and a chambray
shirt, his features half-hidden by the broad brim of his black
Stetson.

"I really want to thank you for your help last night," Shelly
said to Jeb.

Jeb grinned, his teeth a brief flash of white underneath the
black brush of his mustache. "Well, I'll have to admit that
there are damn few people who could have gotten me out of
bed at that hour of the night. Of course, the apple pie went a
long ways toward making up for it." He faked a punch toward
her shoulder. "Don't worry about it, kid—families, even one as
convoluted and at odds as ours—tend to pull together in a cri-
sis." He sent her a considering glance. "You doing all right? I
know that Beau was more to you than just an animal in your
breeding program."

Shelly made a face. "I'm dealing with it. Nick and I need to
sit down and have a serious discussion about the direction
we're going to take now. It's hard, but I keep telling myself,
it's not the end of the world. Thanks for being there."

Jeb nodded absently, his attention fixed on something
across the street. A brief look at Danny's face showed the same

intensity, and Shelly turned around to see what they were staring at with such interest. All she saw was M.J. talking to Mac Ferguson, who owned the local, and only, gas station in town. Mac had moved to the valley twenty some years ago and was now about fifty. He wore glasses, sported a buzz cut, and was on the bony side. He was explaining something to M.J., waving his hands about wildly. Shelly couldn't see what there was about M.J. and Mac that held the attention of the other two men, and she shrugged.

"Guess I'll see you guys around," she said, and started to cross the street.

Jeb and Danny both jerked her back beside them. "Stay here a minute," Danny said, an anticipatory grin on his face. "You'll want to see this."

Mac finished his conversation with M.J. and started off down the street. M.J. walked the few steps to her truck. She swung open the door, let out a yelp and leaped back as dozens of bright yellow, green, blue, and red balloons exploded from the pickup. Balloons in every size, shape, and color floated around her, more spilling from the cab to the ground as she stood there gaping. With the door open Shelly could see now that the entire cab of M.J.'s truck was stuffed with balloons. M.J. staggered back another step, her foot coming down squarely on a blue balloon that burst with a bang. She jumped and squeaked.

Danny sniggered, and Jeb choked back a laugh.

Unaware that she had an audience, M.J. threw back her head, and yelled at the sky, "Damn you, Danny Haskell, wherever you are! I'll get you for this."

"Guess that's my cue," Danny said, his eyes bright with laughter. He hitched up his belt and swaggered across the street.

Standing behind M.J. as she stared at the contents of her truck, Danny asked, "Got a problem here, miss?"

M.J. spun around, noticing for the first time Jeb and Shelly laughing from across the street. Amused, she half laughed herself and made a face at them. "And I thought you were my friends," she hollered.

Looking up at Danny, M.J. said ruefully. "You got me. I owe you, and believe me you *will* pay. You've had your laugh—now what do you expect me to do with all these balloons?"

Danny looked innocent and scratched his head. "Gee, I dunno . . . make toys?"

Shelly was still smiling to herself when she pulled into the tiny post office parking lot a few minutes later. It would be interesting, she thought as she walked into the small cement building, to see what sort of prank M.J. came up with to pay Danny back. She checked her mail, not exactly thrilled to open the envelope from her bank and discover a cashier's check in her name for $48,000.00. It was the check to replace the one for the right-of way that Sloan had torn up. Now what did she do? She'd already failed with a straightforward attempt to right the wrong done by Josh for gouging Sloan on the right-of way buyout—and had it thrown back in her face for her efforts, thank-you-very-much. She wasn't about to try to give Sloan the money directly, having a pretty good notion that she'd get the same result. But she was determined to do *something* to right the situation. Mulling it over, she got in her vehicle and began to drive home. Passing the high school an idea occurred to her. Noticing a lone car parked in front of the administration building at the rear of the school, she took a chance and pulled in beside it.

The car probably belonged to a janitor or groundsperson, but she'd never know until she checked. Fate was kind to her: Sue Wiggins, assistant to the principal, answered her timid knock on the door.

They exchanged greetings, then Shelly said, "I didn't really expect anyone to be here."

Sue grimaced. "There's a rush report that Hickman wanted in the mail today, and I didn't get it finished yesterday."

Shelly hesitated. Sue was obviously busy . . . maybe this wasn't a good time to put forth the idea that had sprung into her mind the instant she had seen the high school. Then again, if she didn't do it now, she might talk herself out of it. Taking a deep breath, she said, "I hate to interrupt, but there's something I'd like to discuss with you—if you have a few minutes?"

"Sure." Her brown eyes curious, Sue invited her into the office. Sue Wiggins had been born in the valley, on the reservation, and like many of the Indians in the valley, carried in her veins almost as much white blood as she did Indian. She was about ten years older than Shelly, and while Shelly didn't know her exactly, she knew of her.

Her round face kind, Sue motioned for Shelly to follow her back to the small office where she had been working. Indicating a chair, Sue took another chair behind her desk, and said, "Um, I was real sorry to hear about your brother's death. He donated a lot of time and money to the school and could be relied upon to help the community and the schools in particular. It was such a tragedy."

Shelly expressed her gratitude for the condolences. They chatted a moment about Shelly's life in New Orleans and her return to the valley—how it had changed so little in seventeen years—and then Shelly guided the conversation back to her reason for dropping in.

"Uh, I was wondering," she began tentatively, "how one goes about setting up a scholarship?"

Sue beamed at her. "I see that you're going to follow in Josh's footsteps. Wonderful!"

"Oh! Did Josh set up a scholarship?"

"He certainly did! It must have been three or four years ago, he came out of the blue, just like you, put a $50,000.00 check on Principal Hickman's desk and said he wanted to set up a scholarship. We were floored—it was the biggest scholarship donation we've ever had. It was decided to put the money in stocks and bonds and that the interest each year would be put into one scholarship for one lucky student." She grinned. "It's called the Josh Granger Perpetual Scholarship Grant. Your brother was a generous man."

Shelly sat there, blinking at her. Her thoughts scrambled through her brain. Was it possible? The timing was right. The amount was right. And it sounded just like Josh. A slow tremulous smile spread across her face. And how like Josh to rob Peter to pay Paul and grab a little glory in the process. How like him to take the outrageous sum he'd charged Sloan for the right-of-way and put it into a scholarship. Her spirits lifted. Josh might have been a rascal, but at least he was a rascal with a kind heart.

So now what did she do? Even if Josh had used the money for a good cause, he had still taken gross advantage of the Ballinger family's desire to obliterate all signs of the Granger right-of-way. Any way you looked at it, Sloan was still out the $50,000.00—and he wasn't about to let her give it back to him. So that left . . .

Smiling hugely, Shelly plunked down the check she had received this morning. "I would like to open another scholarship account in the same amount—set it up exactly down the line like the one Josh set up—only its name will be the Sloan Ballinger Perpetual Scholarship Grant."

The thrilled expression on Sue's face faded the instant Shelly mentioned Sloan Ballinger's name. Uneasily, she said, "Well, I'll have to run the proposal by Mr. Hickman, but I'm sure that there will be no problem." The brown eyes troubled, she asked, "Er, this isn't going to get the school embroiled in some sort of feud between Grangers and Ballingers, is it? I mean, we appreciate your generous offer, and I would hate to turn the money away, but we can't afford to get caught in the crossfire between your family and Mr. Ballinger's."

Shelly shook her head. This was one area where she felt confident. Any feuding that might arise would be strictly between her and Sloan—he would never take this sort of argument public, nor would he involve any of his family. It was between them, and she rather suspected that once he got over his astonishment that he would see the humor in the situation. She hoped so.

Arriving home several minutes later, the check left with Sue Wiggins for the time being, she was smiling as she parked behind the house. Her spirits were lighter, and she was looking forward to M.J.'s arrival this evening. But the day stretched out in front of her, and she was at a loss how to fill the hours. She went up to her studio and spent the rest of the morning and early afternoon in fruitless pursuit of art. Ha! By the time she gave up, all she had to show for her industry were several dirty brushes and a canvas that depicted . . . something, but she sure as hell couldn't tell what it was.

Discouraged and feeling a little down once more, she trudged to the kitchen. Nick was seated at the kitchen table, taking a bite out of a sandwich that would have done Dagwood proud. The table was covered with condiments and several different kinds of cheeses and meats, and in the center sat a platter filled with lettuce, tomatoes, dill pickles, and sliced onions. Acey was seated across from Nick, and Maria was taking something from the refrigerator.

Maria looked up when Shelly entered, and smiled. "I didn't want to interrupt you when you were working, but I figured that hunger would bring you down soon enough."

Seating herself next to Nick and reaching for a plate and a

couple slices of bread, Shelly said, "Hunger or boredom, either one will send you in search of a way to end it."

"So which is it?" Nick asked after he swallowed. "Hunger or boredom?"

"Both, I guess," Shelly admitted, slathering mustard on her slices of whole wheat bread.

"With all the work there is to do around here, you're bored?" demanded Acey, his brows twitching.

"Come on, don't give me a hard time. You know what I mean." Turning the subject away from herself, Shelly asked, "So what have you two been up to while I have been slaving in the studio—creating nothing by the way."

The front doorbell chimed just then, and they all exchanged a glance.

"You expecting company?" Nick asked, with a cocked brow.

Shelly shook her head. "No—at least not this afternoon." Putting down her half-made sandwich as the doorbell chimed again, she stood up, and said, "I'd better go see who it is."

The doorbell was ringing insistently by the time she reached the front door. Irritated, she flung open the door and stood stock-still, staring openmouthed and wide-eyed at the tall, slim man impatiently pushing the doorbell.

At the sight of her, he ceased his actions, threw wide his arms, and, grinning from ear to ear, exclaimed, "*Ma chérie!* I find you at last."

With a joyful shriek, Shelly catapulted into his arms. "Roman!"

Chapter Nineteen

❧

Laughing, Roman Granger swung Shelly up into his arms. Heedless of the half dozen or so bags and suitcases that were scattered across the front deck, he whirled her around, and said, "You're a damn hard lady to find. When you said that St. Galen's was to hell and gone, I didn't really believe you." He gave a mock shudder. "I do now. Believe me, I do now. Thank God, there was some old fellow at the airport who was willing to drop me off on your doorstep—otherwise, I'd still be standing on the airstrip wondering where in the hell I had landed."

"It's a far cry from New Orleans, isn't it?" she said, smiling.

Putting her back on her feet, he said, "Far cry doesn't even begin to explain it. In case you haven't noticed, your beloved Oak Valley"—he spread his arms wide—"is in the middle of *nowhere*. And your airport . . . *mon Dieu*! As I live and breathe I do not think I shall ever feel as frightened as I did when the pilot pointed out the airstrip and said that he was going to land us on it." He shuddered. "I may never fly again."

"Come on, it wasn't that bad," Shelly teased. "At least the airstrip is paved."

Roman appeared struck by that statement. "And for that

I shall be forever grateful. I may even pay for a Mass or two to be said for the genius who conceived that brilliant idea."

There was only a slight resemblance between the two cousins. Since there were several generations between the original Jeb Granger who had set out for California after the Civil War and his younger brother, Forrest Granger, who had remained behind in New Orleans to rebuild on what was left of the family plantation, that fact wasn't surprising. The only physical trait they shared were the dazzling Granger green eyes. Roman's hair was black as the ace of spades, expertly cut and styled by a master hand, and while tall, he was slender, though his shoulders were broad and his body muscular enough to please even the most exacting critic. There was an elegance about Roman that bordered almost on the effete, and a few bullies had discovered to their pain that his long, whipcord-lean frame contained a great deal of strength and that he knew how to use it quite, quite effectively. Roman moved with a dancer's easy sinuous grace and if Sloan made Shelly think of a tiger, Roman called to mind the elegant, swift, and equally deadly cheetah.

"I know you said you were coming out for a visit, but I had no idea that you would show up so soon," Shelly remarked as she slid her arm around Roman's waist; he did the same to her, and together they walked to the front door.

Nick met them at the doorway and Shelly smothered a laugh as the two men regarded each other. Nick didn't appear to be terribly pleased with the way Roman's hand rested on Shelly's waist, and she could feel Roman's sudden tenseness at Nick's apparent ease in her house. Territorial males to the last, she could almost smell the testosterone in the air as they took the other's measure.

Concealing her amusement, she introduced them and they shook hands, mouthing appropriate greetings. Civilities out of the way, Nick struck first. "Come for a visit, have you?" he drawled. His gaze slid up and down Roman's casual sophistication, taking in the black silk turtleneck underneath the gray Bill Blass blazer, the knife-edged crease of his slacks, right on down to the gleaming black Bally loafers on his feet. "Think you'd have a better time in San Francisco."

Roman arched a slim arrogant brow. If he looked like a model out of the pages of *GQ*, Nick looked like he had just come in from the barn—which he had. In contrast to Roman's sartorial elegance, Nick's well-washed blue-striped cotton shirt was wrinkled, his blue jeans were faded and worn, his boots dusty. Roman frowned as he looked at Nick, the younger man's likeness to other Granger family members striking him almost instantly. Who the hell was this wolf cub that stared back at him with eyes he saw every morning in his own mirror?

"Perhaps," Roman replied to Nick with a cool look. "But since I came to see Shelly, San Francisco holds no interest for me." Roman smiled warmly at Shelly. "Unless, *ma belle*, you would like to take in the sights of that most romantic city?"

Nick stiffened, annoyed at Roman's easy manner with Shelly. "Shelly's got too many things to do around here to waste her time on sight-seeing," he said tightly. "Besides, she can see San Francisco whenever she wants."

Shelly laughed out loud and put herself between the two men. "OK, guys," she said, "it was fun for a minute or two to watch you strut your stuff, but enough is enough." She kissed Roman's cheek and then Nick's. "I'm not a bone to be fought over. Be nice. I adore both of you. Don't make me choose between you. Now shake hands and be friends, or . . ." and she frowned at both men, "I shall be very, very angry with the pair of you."

Nick grinned sheepishly, feeling foolish. Sticking out his hand again, he said, "Isn't she just the bossiest little thing when you get her riled? Pleased to meet you and welcome to Oak Valley—this time I mean it. Sorry for the bad beginning—shall we try again?"

Roman smiled ruefully, grasping Nick's proffered hand in a firm, friendly grasp. "Indeed, I shall be more than happy to start again. Acting the alpha male is so very fatiguing—which is probably why I do it so seldom." His voice warm, only the faintest hint of Creole in it, he said, "So you are Nick. Shelly regaled us frequently with tales of youthful crimes in which you figured largely—she, of course, or so she claims, was always innocent. She called you once, I think, an imp of Satan. In recent days, however, she speaks on the telephone of nothing but your helpfulness to her and the plans you two have concocted for the revival of the Granger Cattle Company. I'd be most interested to hear more of it." He grinned at Nick. "Don't let these clothes fool you—I have been known to get down and dirty with the best of them."

"Dirty is one thing I can guarantee you'll be if you hang around us for very long," Nick said with a smile. "Dust, heat, exhaustion, and aching muscles come along with the package, too."

In the kitchen more introductions were made, and Roman charmed Maria and had her looking flustered by exclaiming, "But you cannot be Nick's mother—you are far too young and pretty. It is a pleasure to meet you at last—Josh and Shelly have sung your praises to the skies—I feel as if I already know you." He grinned at her. "I have long heard tales of your scrumptious apple pies and wizardry in the kitchen."

Having watched this exchange with growing mistrust of Roman's charming manner, Acey was narrowed-eyed and pursed-lipped when he shook Roman's hand. Damned lounge lizard had no business waltzing in here and turning

Maria's head. Who the hell did he think he was hanging all over Shelly while flirting with Maria? Cousin, my ass!

Amusement gleamed in Roman's eyes, aware of Acey's instinctive reaction to a new man in an area he obviously considered his own. "Ah, so you are the venerable Acey," he exclaimed, "the wicked ogre of Shelly's childhood. She claims you would jerk her bloodied body up from the ground and put her right back on the wild, mean-tempered horse that had just bucked her off." Quietly he added, "I heard those tales many times, as well as the ones that show your patience, kindness, and affection for her. She said you taught her to ride and ride well and that having you around made up some for the loss of her father. She is very, very fond of you—and it appears with good reason. I am very happy to meet you."

"Ain't heard much about you," Acey said, trying hard not to like this smooth-tongued stranger. "Know you're a cousin and that you live in New Orleans, not much else." He sent Roman a squinty-eyed look. "She don't brag much on you."

Shelly choked back a laugh. "Come on, Acey, give the guy a chance. I've already warned Nick that I'm not going to take sides. If you want to act like a Neanderthal—go outside."

Acey held his ground for a moment, but seeing the affection in Shelly's eyes when she looked at her cousin, he drawled, "I knew that women's lib crap was a bad thing. Nowadays, women got no respect for masculine tradition. Guess we'll have to forgo beating each other to a pulp before we become friends."

"Sounds like a plan to me," Roman said with a chuckle.

The afternoon was busy. After lunch, during which he was peppered with questions in between managing a few of his own, Roman's numerous bags were dragged upstairs, and before too long he was regally installed in the guest suite across the wide hall from Shelly's room. Taking in the plush wine-and-gray patterned carpet, the breathtaking view of the mountains through the long windows, and the fine furnishings scattered through the suite, Roman sighed. "Yes, this is more like it." Grinning at Shelly as they stood in the pleasant sitting room that adjoined the bedroom, he said, "With all this comfort and elegance to look forward to, I'll be able to handle anything that Acey and Nick deal me."

"Other people might buy that languid, fastidious, city slicker attitude, but I know you," Shelly said with twinkling eyes. "I've no doubt that Acey and Nick will test you, but I'm quite certain that you'll pass with flying colors. Don't forget—*I* know you're not the prissy dilettante you like to pretend to be."

"Prissy! Now that's unfair," he said with a laugh. Putting his arm around her shoulder, they stood together staring out at the mountains in the distance. "Are you all right?" he asked softly.

Shelly nodded, emotion suddenly clogging her throat. She turned, resting her head on Roman's shoulder. "It's been hard, I won't pretend otherwise, but I think the worst is over." She looked up at him, her eyes troubled. "There's so much about Josh that I don't understand. There are things I've found out that make me wonder if I ever knew him at all."

Roman smiled down kindly at her. "*Ma belle*, your problem is that you saw him as some sort of godlike creature who could do no wrong." Roman grimaced. "And, while I disagreed with him, I can't blame him for letting you go on believing just that." Ruefully, he said, "We males tend to enjoy having females look up adoringly at us—even when we know we don't deserve it." His voice grew serious. "Josh was just human, Shelly, nothing more, nothing less."

She sighed. "You're right, but it's been a rough adjustment." She glanced at him. "Did you know about his gambling?"

"I knew he gambled, but I take it you mean more than just a weekend fling now and then."

"Yes, I do," she said softly. Over the years, she had come to rely on Roman almost as much as Josh. Three years her elder and decades older in experience, he had stepped easily into the role of older brother when Josh hadn't been around. It had been Roman who had helped her find her apartment in New Orleans and prowled antique stores with her for furnishings; Roman who had introduced her to the gallery owner where her work was displayed: Roman who had guided her steps during those first, painful, uneasy weeks in New Orleans. He'd always been there for her, and unlike her feelings about her brother, she had no illusions about Roman; he could be a devil, but he could also be trusted. And because she did trust him, she proceeded to tell him everything, Josh's gambling, the connection to Milo Scott, the raiding of the trust funds, Nick's parentage, the renewal, or semirenewal, of her love affair with Sloan, everything. She might have skirted around touchy issues like her relationship with Sloan, but essentially she left nothing out.

Roman blinked when she finished speaking, his expression astonished. He took a deep breath. "Man, and I thought New Orleans was Sin City. Sounds like little ole St. Galen's isn't doing so badly in the sin and corruption department. You and this Jeb character don't really believe that Josh was murdered by some drug lord, do you?"

Shelly made a face. "I don't know. I guess I want that to

have happened because it makes more sense to me than Josh committing suicide."

"Hmm, maybe, and I don't disagree that suicide is hard to swallow, but just look at how wrong you were about that money he took from Ballinger for that right-of-way. He deliberately scalped Sloan, but then he turned around and put the money to good use by setting up the scholarship." He grinned. "Now *that* sounds like the Josh we all knew and loved. He was a scoundrel with a heart of gold."

"But see, you knew that side of him," she said earnestly. "I didn't. And because I didn't, I guess that's why I'm having so much trouble believing that one day out of the blue he just decided to kill himself." Wryly, she admitted, "I really did think he walked on water."

"He didn't, trust me on that," Roman said. "Something else for you to think about—I'd be more than half-inclined to believe your Sloan's version of what happened on that night seventeen years ago." At her look of dismay, he added, "Josh loved you. But always remember that he wanted what *he* thought was best for you, and I can tell you that he sure as hell didn't want you marrying a Ballinger." When she would have protested, he held up a hand. "Listen to me. Being removed from the source of the feud, even though I'm as much a Granger as you are, I didn't pay a whole lot of attention to all the family tales about the dastardly Ballingers. But Josh did. He hated the Ballingers—dead ones as well as live ones—and what happened over a hundred years ago was as real and fresh in his mind as if it had happened a year ago. I know—every now and then I'd make the mistake of razzing him about the feud and would nearly get my head separated from my body for my efforts. I don't want to blacken his name or have you think ill of him, or even, God forbid, appear to be on the Ballinger side, but believe me,

Josh would have done *anything* to keep you from hooking up with a Ballinger."

"Did he tell you that?" she asked in a low voice.

"No. He didn't have to. All you had to know was how he felt about you and how he felt about the Ballingers to figure it out."

"You think the feud is stupid, don't you?"

Roman shrugged. "Not stupid, but you have to remember, my branch of the family was tucked safely away in Louisiana, and while word of the ugliness traveled back to us, none of us personally suffered at the hands of a Ballinger." He winked at her. "Now that isn't to say that we didn't take great offense at our kinfolk being mistreated by some damn Yankees or that if those same damn Yankees had come drifting down to N'Awlins we wouldn't have kicked their Yankee asses just because their name was Ballinger. We would have. Blood is blood." He grimaced. "Especially Rebel blood. We've been known to hold grudges for generations."

Shelly nodded. "I know. Sometimes I feel guilty for even considering letting Sloan back in my life. It's like I'll be letting down all those generations that came before me."

"That's true, but think of this; they're all dead, honey. Moldering in their graves. You're alive, and it's *your* life that you need to be thinking about—not some long-dead ancestor's."

The phone rang and, walking over to the gleaming walnut end table where the phone sat, she picked it up.

"It's only me," said M.J. "Listen, will you be terribly disappointed if I cancel out on tonight? My beloved ex just called and said that I can have the kids for the rest of the weekend if I meet him in Willits to pick them up. Guess he's got a hot overnight date."

"Oh, don't worry about it—we can do it some other

time," Shelly said. Glancing over at Roman, she decided
that cancellation of tonight's plans might just be the best
thing that could have happened. M.J. was too vulnerable
right now to be around someone like Roman. "You have a
nice time with the boys."

M.J. gave a wry chuckle. "Nice isn't exactly how I would
describe it, but I'll take an evening with my sons over anything else—no offense."

"None taken. Talk to you later."

Walking back to stand beside Roman, she explained,
"That was M.J. The two of us had planned to sort of have a
slumber party and watch a video, but something came up,
and she had to cancel." She nudged Roman in the ribs.
"Probably just as well—I don't want my handsome Creole
cousin putting the moves on her."

Roman arched a brow. "Are you warning me off?"

"Yep. M.J. is strictly off-limits—and I mean it. You can
seduce any other female in the valley, but leave M.J. alone."

"Ah, what a disappointment, since the entire purpose of
my whole trip was to finally meet and woo the infamous
M.J."

"Speaking of your trip," Shelly said smoothly, "why are
you here?"

Roman shrugged and glanced back at the view. "I don't
know. New Orleans suddenly bored me, and I wanted to get
away—and I was worried about you." He smiled over at her.
"Honest. This may have been home to you, but you've been
gone for a long time—I thought you could use some family
support. Sort of like better the devil you know . . ."

Her heart warmed. "I'm glad you're here. Acey, Nick,
and Maria, and M.J.—I have wonderful memories from my
youth of them and everybody has been wonderful, but
you're right, seventeen years is a long time. We've all grown
up, grown older, changed. They're not strangers, yet I'm

conscious, especially in view of what I've learned about Josh, that I don't really know any of them—not like I know you." She hugged him. "It's nice to have you here."

"I should damn well hope so," Roman teased. "I'll have you know that I gave up a weekend with a voluptuous Playmate of the Month to be with you."

"Did you really?"

"Yes." He grinned. "She terrified me—every other word out of her mouth had something to do with commitment." He shivered. "And you know how that word affects me."

"Poor baby," she sympathized, patting his arm. "I'd be more impressed if I didn't know that you're a master at escaping the clutches of women with commitment and marriage at the top of their agendas."

Roman laughed. "All teasing aside," he said, "I was worried about you. I cleared my schedule, turned the farm over to my assistant, and here I am."

The New Orleans branch of the Granger family had done very well for itself since the end of the Civil War. Money was not something that Roman or his other siblings had ever had to worry about. Through hook and by crook, and an expedient marriage to a Yankee heiress, Forrest Granger, Jeb Granger's youngest brother, had managed to amass a huge fortune, most of it in land, land that was now known as Granger Enterprises. These days they were a diverse corporation, but their roots were deep in the farming community and despite owning office buildings, several resorts, and oil fields, Roman was a farmer at heart. A staff headed by his father, Fritz Granger, known as Fritzie to family and friends, and Roman's two older brothers, Fritz Jr. and Noble, ran most of the businesses, while Roman oversaw the farming operations. Since he, too, had an excellent staff he was able to have as much free time as he wanted. Roman worked hard, but he was prone to playing harder.

The conversation slid to family, and several minutes passed as Roman brought Shelly up to date with the latest with relatives in Louisiana. They might have lingered longer, but Nick tapped on the door to the sitting room and stuck his head inside.

"Sloan's here," he said and grinned. "And man, oh, man you should see the bruises he's sporting. He *claims* he ran into a door, but I'd like to see Milo Scott. Bet he ran into a bigger door and looks worse."

Alarmed, Shelly flew down the stairs, skidding to a halt in the kitchen doorway when she caught sight of Sloan, who was seated at the kitchen table, helping himself to a slice of apple pie warm from the oven. He was absorbed in placing the piece of pie on his plate and didn't notice her immediately, which gave her ample time to take in his battered face.

He looked awful. A black eye, a gloriously purple bruise on the opposite cheek, a split lip and eyebrow, and various other nicks and scrapes were apparent.

Her voice calm despite her shock at the sight of his battered features, she strolled into the kitchen. Sloan glanced up at her and smiled, then winced when his split lip made itself felt.

"Nick said you ran into a door," she murmured, lifting up his chin and taking a closer inventory of his various wounds. "Must have been some door."

He grinned lopsidedly, and her heart turned right over in her breast. "Yeah," he said. "Big ole sucker. Knocked me flat. Just wasn't paying attention to where I was going."

Admiration in his gaze, Acey, who was seated across the table, said, "That's the thing about them damn doors, leap out at a fellow when least expected. Happened to me once or twice."

Nick and Roman followed her into the kitchen and introductions were made again. Both men were more subtle about their reaction to each other than Acey and Nick had been, but Roman was aware that he was being pretty thoroughly checked out. Either Shelly seemed to have surrounded herself with a bunch of very territorial and protective males, or Oak Valley bred them that way, he thought sourly. Nick and Acey's initial reaction hadn't bothered him; he'd been confident that any fight, physical or mental, would have seen him the winner, but Sloan . . . Sloan was a big bruiser, clever, too, from what he knew, and Roman decided that he'd really, *really* hate to tangle with him. Besides, Shelly was in love with the guy, and he'd learned long ago, never, *ever*, get between a pair of lovers.

Shaking hands with Sloan was like being caught in a bear trap and, delicately extracting his hand, with a pained smile, Roman said, "I surrender. You're bigger, tougher, and probably meaner than I am." He met Sloan's watchful gaze. "A couple things we should get out of the way right up front: I love my cousin in the most platonic way possible—believe me, I am not competition. I am not after her money or her land. I would never do anything to harm her, in fact I would do anything within my power to keep her from harm. So knowing that, could we please forgo the male bonding procedure? I've had a long trip, and I'm really not up to knocking heads."

"In that case," Sloan said with a wry chuckle, "I guess I can do as you ask. Besides, Acey's been filling me in and he says that you may look like you've never done a day of hard work in your life, but that I shouldn't let that fool me."

Nick and Acey both looked a little shamefaced. Pulling on his ear, Nick said, "We, uh, got off on the wrong foot with Roman."

"Yes, you did," Shelly said severely. "You both acted like a pair of glue-sniffing dorks." She glanced at Sloan. "And considering your argument with that door, I don't think you need to add any new bruises."

Sloan threw up his hands. "Truce. Truce. I won't lay a hand on him." He smiled at Roman. "Welcome to Oak Valley, and nice to meet you."

Roman replied in the same manner and shortly they were all seated around the kitchen table, devouring Maria's apple pie. Pushing aside his empty plate, Roman glanced at Maria. "That," he said in reverent tones, "was undoubtedly the best piece of apple pie I have ever eaten in my life. If you ever decide that you would like to move to Louisiana, you let me know. I'll set you up in your own business—of course," he added with a charming smile, "I shall probably want you to bake for me exclusively. Shelly has no idea what a treasure you are. And pretty, too."

Maria giggled softly.

Acey scowled, and muttered, "She's mostly retired these days. No reason she'd want to go traipsing off down South. 'Sides, she wouldn't want to go off and leave her children— or Shelly for that matter."

Shelly's eyes widened. Why, Acey sounded almost as if . . . She stared at the old cowboy. Could it be? Nick's gaze met hers, the stupefied expression in his eyes telling her that the same idea had just occurred to him. Well, well, Shelly thought as she looked from Acey's belligerent expression to Maria's oblivious one, would wonders never cease?

Aware that he had blundered somehow, Roman quickly changed the subject and a second later, they were all deep in a discussion of the ramifications of Beau's death.

"Sure is a damned shame," Acey mourned. "Beau was old, but I'd a bet we could have used him for at least one calf crop, maybe two or three—and by then, if we'd been lucky, we'd have a son or two of his to step into his shoes."

"So what are you going to do?" Sloan asked, pushing away his empty plate.

"Not much we can do," Shelly said. "We'll have to start looking for a herd sire prospect from somebody else's herd. It was bad enough," Shelly muttered, "that our cow herd had to be bought from someone else, even if the cows do go back to some good Granger bloodlines. But it was OK because we had Beau—a bull, bred and owned by Grangers. Now we'll be starting from scratch—not one animal will be Granger direct."

"Even my cows are a generation or two away from Granger bloodlines," Nick said heavily. "And the bulls I've leased over the years didn't carry any Granger blood up close." He made a face. "Too expensive for the likes of me to get my hands on a really great bull. To make a name for yourself in the cattle industry is so damn difficult these days. You can do it, but it sometimes takes years, and a lot of luck, before anyone notices that you have superior stock. Having Beau gave us a head start. He would have allowed us to begin reestablishing the Granger bloodlines up close—and the reputation of the Granger blood is famous and desired— it would have put us decades ahead." He stared moodily at the table. "Now we don't even have that edge."

There came the sound of vehicle tires crunching on the gravel, and a moment later the slamming of a door had all of them looking toward the back door. Jeb called out and strolled into sight a moment later.

Roman almost groaned out loud at the sight of Jeb. *Oh, Jesus*, he thought, staring at the massive shoulders and impressive height, *I'm a dead man*. To his relief, however, Jeb seemed delighted to meet him.

A huge, welcoming smile on his lips, Jeb stuck out his hand, and said, "Am I ever glad to finally meet you—although I almost feel as if I know you already—Shelly talks about you all the time. She says you're a great guy, and her word is good enough for me. Welcome to Oak Valley—if there's anything I can do to make your stay more enjoyable—you let me know."

Smiling, Roman said, "Are you sure you don't want to beat my brains out first?"

Jeb looked confused, then he glanced over at Acey, Nick, and Sloan, who all wore identical expressions of embarrassment. Light dawned, and Jeb laughed. "Oh, the guys give you a bit of the Me-Tarzan, You-stranger greeting?"

"But we're all the best of friends now," Sloan said ruefully. "And feeling duly chastened."

Jeb joined them at the table, eyeing the last piece of pie in the pan. "Anybody mind?"

No one did, Roman especially thinking that he'd rather fight a grizzly bear with cubs over the last piece of pie than Jeb Delaney. My God, the man was huge. And muscled. He brightened. And his friend.

Again the conversation drifted back to the previous night's tragedy and Shelly and Nick's plans for the Granger Cattle Company.

Shelly sighed. "Well, we're not giving up, that's one thing for sure." She smiled sadly at Nick. "Guess we'll just have to do it from the ground up like our, er, my grandfather did. Those Texas cows have a lot of Granger crosses in the background, and your stock goes back to Granger blood, too. We'll just have to start from there."

Jeb frowned. "Uh, I may be missing something here, but didn't Granger Cattle Company do their own semen collecting? I know your grandfather did, had that lab and all that fancy AI equipment brought in as soon as it became available, and I know that your dad did the same thing—your dad kept everything up-to-date. AI and doing their own collecting and storing was one of the things that made Granger Cattle Company so progressive—any new technology, they were Johnny-on-the-spot. Even Josh did—at least for a while." He looked at Shelly, who was staring at him open-mouthed. "I even think that he toyed with some embryo transplants, but gave up on it, deciding that AI was good enough for him."

Shelly and Nick's eyes were fixed on him like two pairs of green lasers. "Come on, quit looking at me that way," Jeb said. "You've both heard of artificial insemination." When they still both just stared, he growled, "Snap out of it. AI? Remember the boon of the cattle industry? There's got to be a semen tank around here somewhere. Besides, I seem to recall that several smaller breeders kept some straws in your tanks. Josh may have pretty much shut down the cattle operation, but even he wouldn't have dumped it. And as long as he kept the nitro levels up, you've probably got semen from some of the greatest bulls Granger's ever bred. Properly kept semen'll be viable for fifty years—at least that's the longest known right now, but I'll bet that you've probably got a lot of semen straws that belong to bulls your Dad bred."

Shelly swallowed. She looked at Nick. Nick looked at her. Hope blazing in her eyes, she stood up.

"The barn," she croaked. "The lab in the barn."

Like a tidal wave they swept out of the kitchen, Nick and Shelly in the lead, their pace increasing with every step they took, until they were running so fast that their feet hardly hit the ground. In through the wide double doors they flew, past her office, past the feed room, the tack room and wash rack next to it, to stop abruptly in front of the door to the lab.

Her hand was trembling so badly that she couldn't turn the knob. Nick's warm hand closed over hers, and their eyes locked. Together, they pushed open the door.

The lab hadn't been opened or used in a while, that was

apparent from the musty odor and the cobwebs, but it was clean, pristinely so, and looked as if it were ready to start up again at any moment—once several of the cobwebs were dispensed with. The steel restraining rack was almost in the middle of the room, counters and stainless-steel sinks to the right. A dust cover hid the microscope on the counter, but Shelly and Nick both recognized the shape. A portable ejaculator system in its case sat nearby, the lid open to reveal the bull probe and semen collector. A quick glance inside one of the cupboards showed packages of semen straws, J-Lube, gallons of blue Nolvasan solution, disposable plastic gloves.

Her heart pounding so hard she thought it would burst out of her chest, Shelly scanned the remainder of the room, her breath catching at the sight of two rotund objects not much more than two feet high sitting on a sturdy cabinet in the far corner of the room.

Standing in front of the innocent-looking objects, the others crowded around her, Shelly simply stared at the tanks, elated and absolutely terrified. Elated by what their contents might mean to her and Nick, terrified that there was nothing in them.

"Go ahead," Sloan said softly from behind her, his hand resting comfortingly on her shoulder, "open one."

"Carefully," Jeb warned.

Her breathing suspended, she carefully turned the lid and lifted. Wispy white smoke drifted from the tank and inside, ampule after ampule, each with dozens of semen-filled straws, rested snugly in the liquid nitrogen. The date on the inside of the tank revealed that its nitrogen level had last been checked and filled about four months ago.

"At least he kept the tank filled," Jeb commented. "Would a been a shame if he'd have let it go dry—you'd a lost everything." Since Shelly and Nick, who were standing side by side staring in awestruck silence at the contents, seemed incapable of moving, Jeb reached around them and took out the inventory that was taped to the inside of the lid.

He and Sloan glanced at it. Sloan whistled as he recognized the names of some of the outstanding Granger bulls of twenty to thirty years ago.

"The contents of that tank is worth its weight in gold," Sloan said as he tapped Shelly on the shoulder and handed her the list.

She and Nick read it together, dazzled at the prospect in front of them. With the semen from these bulls there was nothing to stop them.

Laughing and crying, Shelly threw her arms around Nick's neck. "Look out world, Granger Cattle Company is coming back."

"Well, ain't this just the dandiest thing that ever happened?" Acey demanded, a big grin on his face. He slid a sly glance at Maria. "Figure this calls for a celebration . . . and another of them deelicious pies of Maria's."

Chapter Twenty

After the discovery of the semen tank, no one had been in a hurry to leave and the afternoon had stretched into evening and Shelly and Maria had put together an impromptu dinner. Everyone had pitched in; Jeb and Sloan cleaning out the old brick barbecue pit off to the side of the house; Nick and Roman dragging over a redwood picnic table and benches; Acey helping Maria in the kitchen. At least that's what he claimed he was doing, but according to Maria he'd been sampling and snacking as much as he'd been helping. Another pie from the freezer was baked, and Maria made a crisp green salad and dips for chips while Shelly scrubbed potatoes for baking and made up a pitcher of iced tea; Acey had finally been sent to town for New York steaks. The meal had been great, and the conversation had been excited and full of laughter; the subject, of course, the semen tank and what it meant to Granger Cattle Company.

Everyone had stayed late, lingering over pie and coffee, but eventually one by one they'd wandered off until there were just Sloan and Shelly sitting side by side in the darkness, Roman seated across the table from them. After a few minutes, Roman yawned hugely and declared that he was exhausted. Rising to his feet, he bid Sloan and Shelly good night and disappeared inside the house.

"Tactful guy, that cousin of yours," Sloan murmured, as he placed his arm around Shelly and drew her next to him.

Shelly smiled. "He's known for it, believe me." Her smile faded, and she glanced at him, barely able to make out his features in the darkness. "I told him about us."

"Hmm, and what did our tactful guy have to say about that?" Sloan asked, nuzzling her ear, his mind on how much he wanted to make love with her, not on her cousin's opinion of their relationship.

Shelly hunched her shoulder, half-protecting her ear from his marauding mouth. "He said that I should maybe believe your take on things—that Josh would have done just about anything to keep me from marrying you—or any Ballinger."

Surprised, Sloan lifted his head and stared at her shadowy profile. "He did?" When Shelly nodded, he murmured, "Tactful and smart. You know I could grow to really like this guy."

Shelly pushed him away and stood up. "Will you stop it? I'm trying to have a serious discussion here."

Sloan rose to his feet, pushing aside the bench on which they had been sitting. Pulling Shelly into his arms, he said against her lips, "And I'm trying to seduce you . . . which one of us do you think will win out?"

Sighing, Shelly put her arms around his neck, and muttered, "That's not even a fair question." She kissed him gently, mindful of his split lip.

At the touch of her lips, Sloan groaned and Shelly jerked her mouth away. "Oh, Sloan, I'm sorry," she said, stricken. "Did I hurt you? I tried to be gentle."

"I'll tell you what hurts," Sloan said huskily, "and that's not having you in my arms and not making love to you." His mouth caught hers in a deep probing kiss, leaving no doubt in her mind about his intentions. He lifted his mouth, wincing just a bit. "I'll admit that hurts, too, but not as much as not kissing you." He smiled, wincing again from his split lip. "I think this is where I say be gentle with me."

The grass was cool and thick at her back as Sloan lowered her to the lawn beside the picnic table. For one flickering second Shelly hesitated, then Sloan's hand cupped her breast and his mouth found hers again and any remnant of reason vanished.

They made love to each other slowly, tenderly, Shelly mindful of his many cuts and bruises, Sloan gripped by passion, hardly even aware of his aches and pains. Fumbling fingers and hands dispensed with clothing and soon their discarded jeans and shirts made a soft nest on the already welcoming grass.

Time was suspended as they explored each other, Shelly's hands sliding softly over his hard body, the slight stiffening of his body here and there telling her more clearly than words when she touched a painful spot. Her mouth followed her hands and she pressed soothing kisses along his ribs, across his chest and shoulders before returning to his bruised face.

Half-sitting, half-lying beside him, she trailed her lips across his mouth, her tongue making dainty ventures into the intoxicating depths of his mouth, her fingers caressing the hard little buttons of his nipples. Sloan groaned, desire spearing through him at her arousing touch, one hand cupping a buttock, the other skimming up and down her back as she worked her magic.

"Did I hurt you?" she asked softly against his mouth.

Sloan shook his head. "No, but you're killing me, I can tell you that."

She chuckled and ran her lips up and down his throat, nipping softly as she did so. "Poor baby. Suffer."

Desire hummed between them, every touch, every caress, every kiss increasing the need for more and more and more . . . Their mouths locked together, their hands roamed with increasing urgency over each other as they teased and tormented the other almost to the point of madness.

With Sloan laid out on the ground like a feast before her, Shelly's mouth ravaged him, tasting the saltiness of his flesh, savoring the texture of his skin, the coarse hair on his chest, and the sleek muscles of his body. Sloan froze when her questing lips followed that line of hair that arrowed down to his groin, and he half growled, half groaned when her hot damp mouth closed around his erection. She drove him wild, the slick slide of her tongue on his sensitive flesh, the soft nibbles along his shaft, and when she took him fully into her mouth, he thought he'd die of pleasure. His hands clenched in her hair, his body arching in encouragement; he endured the dazzling torture of that sweet mouth as long as he could.

Unable to bear it a moment later, Sloan pushed her down on the ground, his mouth on her nipple, his hand between her legs, searching and exploring the hot dampness he found there. Shelly moaned, pushing up against his hand, silently inviting, demanding a deeper caress. He gave it to her, two fingers sinking into the satin heat, and her hips twisted upward to meet their thrust. Fire seared her belly, flames leaping into her veins as he plundered her depths, his fingers sinking deeper and deeper into her, taking her to the very edge of ecstasy. When his thumb found the swollen nub at the juncture of her thighs, and he brushed it once, twice, she screamed at the burst of pleasure that rocketed through her, cramming a fist in her mouth to block the sound. The world went incandescent, and she spun away, lost in the splendor of the moment.

It was Sloan's lips on her breast that brought her back to reality. Her fingers tugged at his hair, and his head lifted. Barely able to make out his features in the darkness, she kissed him, and said, "No one else. No one else has ever made me feel the way you do."

"Good," he muttered, "because it's the same for me. There's only you, only you."

His mouth came down hard on hers, but when he would have moved between her legs, she pushed him back, forcing him to lie flat on the ground. A siren's smile on her lips, she straddled him and took him inside her. Slowly, torturously she rode him, her flesh clinging and tightening around him. "My turn," she said softly.

"Oh, Jesus," he moaned, as she increased the tempo, the sweet slide of flesh against flesh, making him writhe in pleasure, "you really *are* going to kill me."

Breathless, ecstasy beginning its mind-blurring spiral again, Shelly said, "Then enjoy it, because I have no intention of stopping." And she didn't.

It could have been minutes or hours later that they both became aware of the world around them. They were lying naked on their clothes, Shelly's head resting on his shoulder, and they were gazing through the leaves of the oak tree up at the star-studded sky.

"Have you ever noticed," Shelly asked dreamily, "how many more stars there are here? How much brighter they are; how much blacker the sky is?"

"Hmm, yeah, you're right. It's the lack of outdoor light," he replied, one hand gently caressing her hip. "No light reflection to fade the stars." He shifted slightly so that he was staring down into her face. He kissed her. "Of course, I've always thought that it was the result of really good sex."

Shelly made a face and pushed him away. Sitting up, she began to put on her clothing. Standing to finish pulling on her jeans, her head bent, she asked quietly, "Is that all it was to you? Just good sex?"

Sloan had risen, too, and he sighed. He didn't say anything as he dragged on his clothes, and Shelly's heart sank. Had she been a fool . . . again?

"Come here," he said, and, catching Shelly by the arm, half walked, half dragged her over to the rear of the house. As she watched in bewilderment, he opened the back door and switched on the yellow bug light that hung above them.

His face washed in the yellow light, he stared down at her. "Look at me," he commanded softly, giving her a little shake. "I love you. I have always loved you. I will always love you. I want to marry you. I'm going to marry you. And no, it wasn't just good sex. It was *great* sex—the way it should be between people who love each other and plan to spend the rest of their lives together." As Shelly stared openmouthed at him, he shook her again. "Does that answer your question?"

Her brain went fuzzy. Feeling weak and dizzy, she could only stare at his beloved features. "But what about . . . I mean . . ." Her fingers suddenly gripped the front of his shirt. Desperately, she asked, "Are you sure? Do you really mean it?"

He smiled tenderly. "With all my heart." His finger lifted her chin, and he kissed her with great sweetness. "This isn't the time or the place that I would have chosen for this moment," he said softly, "but will you marry me? Please?"

Shelly's green eyes glowed, and there was a tremulous curve to her mouth. "Oh, wow!" she said, quite, *quite* unable to think of anything else to say.

Sloan quirked a brow, the one with the split in it. "Is that a wow yes, or a wow no?"

"Oh, wow, yes," she said breathlessly, not giving herself time to think. She flung herself at him and, wrapping her arms tightly around him, muttered, "Oh, yes, yes, *yes!*"

A killing weight he hadn't even been aware that he carried slid away from Sloan, and he crushed her to him. "This time," he vowed into her hair, "this time nothing is going to stop us. I want us to be married as soon as possible, and unless you want a big wedding with all the fanfare, I'd just as soon fly to Reno tomorrow and get married there."

Shelly stiffened. Pushing him away, she studied his face. He was serious. She hesitated, torn. She loved him. He loved her. They'd waited seventeen years for this moment. She didn't really want a big wedding—in fact Reno would do her just fine. But not . . . tomorrow. And there were, she reminded herself, still questions about the past, about just what had really happened that night she had found him in Nancy's arms. How could she marry him if she doubted him, if she thought him a liar and a cheat? If she couldn't trust him, what sort of marriage would they have? Oh, but she loved him! But how long would their love survive if she harbored suspicion and mistrust?

She swallowed painfully, some of her joyful exuberance draining away. She hesitated, wondering if she wasn't letting her heart rule her head. OK, so her heart was calling the shots, but one thing was very clear in her mind. She loved him. She'd never stopped loving him. And she wanted to marry him. It was a second chance for both of them, and she wasn't going to blow it because she was a coward. She'd find a way to put the past to rest . . . somehow. She wanted to marry him more than she had ever wanted anything else—this was a second chance for both of them and she was going to grab it with both hands and hang on for dear life. On the other hand tomorrow was just too soon to get married. "I'll marry you," she said slowly. "And I don't yearn for a big wedding: Reno will be fine." Her gaze met his. "But could we please wait a couple of weeks?"

Sloan's lips tightened. "A couple of weeks isn't going to change how I feel."

"And it isn't going to change my feelings either," she retorted, a little irritated. "It's just that right now, I've got a lot on my plate." She ran a hand through her tangled hair. "Roman just arrived; there's the settlement of the estate, the cattle operation—none of those things may seem important to you, but they are to me, and I'd like just a little time to get myself organized before taking such a huge step." It was on the tip of her tongue to mention Josh's relationship to Nick, but without just blurting it out, she couldn't think of a way to introduce the subject. She bit her lip. And yet, if they were to marry, he should know about it. Somehow she'd have to think of a diplomatic way to spring it on him. "My life is pretty complicated right now," she said softly, "all I'm asking for is a couple of weeks." She smiled. "After that I'm all yours."

Sloan growled and jerked her into his arms. "You're already all mine," he said against her mouth. "Don't forget it." His mouth came down hard on hers, all the love and longing he felt for her in that one kiss.

When Sloan finally lifted his head several minutes later, Shelly wasn't certain if her legs would hold her up. "Wow," she breathed. "You kiss me like that very often, and I'll never have a coherent thought in my brain."

"Good," he said, satisfaction in his voice. His fingertips caressed her cheek. "There is just one thing . . ." When she looked at him, he smiled ruefully, "You haven't said that you love me . . . do you?"

His expression was so vulnerable that Shelly melted inside. Her heart almost too full of love for her to breathe, she kissed him tenderly. "I love you. I always have. I always will."

Of course he kissed her again, a fierce joy in his heart. It was difficult to part, but eventually they did. Taking a deep breath, Sloan said, "Either we stop now or I'm afraid it's back to the grass for us."

Shelly laughed. "I'm not exactly averse to the idea, but the next time we make love, I think I'd like it to be in bed."

"Well, that's easily solved—if memory serves you have a perfectly adequate bed upstairs ... and I have a very nice bed. Which?"

Reluctantly, Shelly shook her head. "No. Not tonight." Shyly she said, "I know it's stupid and silly, but I don't want to spend the night with you until after we're married."

Sloan looked aghast. "You mean I have to wait until after we're married to make love to you again?"

Shelly giggled at his expression. "No, I just don't want to sleep with you until then."

"Honey, when I get you in a bed, we won't be sleeping, believe me."

Sloan had parked out front and hand in hand they walked through the darkened, silent house toward the gleam of light that came from the sconces on either side of the front door. It was difficult to part, and while they did get out the front door, as one they drifted to the covered swing seat on the deck and spent several moments kissing, caressing, and murmuring the soft, silly words that lovers always do. With Shelly's head resting on his shoulder, their hands entwined between them, they sat and talked and kissed and talked some more.

"I hadn't thought about it before now, but there *are* a lot of things that will have to be taken care of once we're married," Sloan said reflectively. He jerked his head in the direction of the house. "This house for one thing. What will you do with it?"

"I don't suppose you'd like to live here?" she asked, already knowing the answer.

"Josh's house? I don't think so." He smiled crookedly. "Some things are hard to change, and my feelings about your brother are one of them." When Shelly would have joined battle, he held up a hand, and said, "Whoa. He's your brother and you loved him—because of that, and only because of that, I'll try to keep a civil tongue in my mouth—but don't ask me to live in his house, OK? We don't have to live in my house either, although that would be my first choice. If you don't want to live there, I guess we could find a piece of property we both like and build something that suits the pair of us. But not here. Not in Josh's house."

The past, she realized, would probably always rise up between them, but surely their love was strong enough to overcome the bitterness that lay behind them?

Her hand tightened in his. "Do you really love me?" she asked softly.

"More than anything else in the world," he said huskily, kissing their locked fingers. "Never doubt it. I do love you." A thought occurred to him, and he slanted her a wry look. "Is this where you tell me to prove it by agreeing to live in Josh's house?"

"Would you?"

"If it was the only way I could have you, hell, yes." He grinned. "But I'll be honest—I'd probably find a way to burn the damn thing down before we were married for many months."

"To save you from becoming an arsonist, I won't insist we live here," she said with a laugh. "I guess we could start out living in your house and see how it goes from there."

"Good idea. In the meantime, you can be thinking about what to do with Josh's house." He hesitated. "Shelly, I know it's your property, and I don't want you to think that I meant that you had to sell it or anything like that, but we'll have to come to some sort of arrangement—although what it will be, I have no idea. We both have large holdings, and I don't see us merging our lands." He grinned. "My father would have a heart attack at the very notion of joining Granger land with Ballinger land." Gloomily, he added, "It's going to be hard enough for him to accept you as my wife. We may have settled our differences, but I don't know how the rest of the family is going to take our marriage."

Shelly stiffened. "Well, if that's a problem for you, you can just not marry me!"

Sloan shook his head, smiling at her. "Not on your life— we're getting married, and no one is going to stop that. The Granger/Ballinger feud is someone else's problem from now on—it's no longer *our* feud." He pulled her half-resisting form into his arms and kissed her. "Do you really think," he murmured, "that I'd let anyone come between us?" When she remained mute, he shook her slightly. "Shelly, I love you. And if loving you means telling my whole family to go to hell, I will. You're what's important to me, and an ancient feud started long before I was even born sure isn't going to determine my future. Got that?"

She relented, saying ruefully, "It's going to be a touchy subject for us now and then, isn't it?"

"Probably, but as long as we love each other, we'll muddle through it, won't we?"

She met his intent gaze, seeing the love blazing in the depths of the brilliant golden eyes. "Yes," she said confidently, "yes, we will."

A comfortable silence fell between them, and, hands entwined, they rocked in the swing, their thoughts busy. There would be difficulties ahead—both of them realized that— they were two strong personalities, and they had a history behind them, a history that was both family and personal, and it would always be lurking in the background waiting to spring up and cause complications. Shelly sighed, thinking of Josh's house. There was one complication already, but as she considered it, a solution, maybe a solution to several problems, presented itself.

"Uh, I was thinking," she began slowly, "about the house. Josh's house." She took a deep breath. "Nick could live in it." Growing more excited with the idea, she said, "It'd work out great. Josh only leased him the house and land where he's presently living; since I'm going to be living with you, he'd be right here where the cattle operation is centered— everything would be at his fingertips—the barns, the cattle, the office, the chutes, the lab, everything. It's more important that he be handy anyway—I'm the paperwork/telephone junky, and I can do that anywhere, even at your place, but he's the brawn and experience of our operation, and he really should be right here. What do you think?"

Sloan scratched his chin. "You know, I've been meaning to talk to you about Nick."

Warily she looked at him. "Oh? What about Nick?"

"It strikes me that you two are thicker than thieves— which is sort of surprising—after all, he was just a kid when you left. You come back, after being gone for years, and all of a sudden you're in a partnership together and he's treating your house like it's home. The pair of you get along very well for relative strangers . . ." He bent her a look. "Or is there something you'd like to mention about now . . . such as the fact that maybe Nick *isn't* such a stranger? That maybe Nick's uncanny resemblance to your brother isn't just a coincidence? That maybe Nick Rios is really a relative?"

Shelly gasped. "You *knew*?"

"Hell, honey, have you forgotten that we live in Oak Valley?" Sloan asked dryly. "The whole valley knows—or suspects—that Nick is Josh's son. It's been a topic of discussion amongst all the old tabbies in town for years. The first time I learned about it, I was about sixteen and overheard my mom and several of her friends happily feeling sorry for your mother that Josh had embarrassed her so."

"Oh, wow," Shelly breathed, her eyes huge. "Poor Nick. And Maria. No wonder she doesn't want to talk about it—I'll bet some of those old witches have gotten their claws into her in the past." She frowned. "Do you think Nick knows all the gossip about him?"

"Probably not. I can't think of a soul who is likely to walk up and ask him if it's true." One brow raised, he asked, "So is it true? Is Nick Josh's son?"

Shelly nodded. "I think so."

"Think?"

She made a face. "We have no way of proving it. Maria won't confirm it exactly, and even if she did say that Josh was Nick's father, it doesn't prove anything. My DNA would show we're related . . . but not that Josh is his father. Nick looks like a Granger—Roman spotted it immediately—but that doesn't prove anything either. Josh certainly made no effort to acknowledge Nick while he was alive—and his body was cremated, so we have no way of getting our hands on Josh's DNA to prove it one way or another."

"So what are you going to do about it?"

"I don't know. Nick and I talk about it all the time—at the moment, he's content, sort of, that I believe him and treat him like my nephew." Shelly's hands clenched into fists. "I've discussed it with the lawyer, but Sawyer, cautious bastard that he is, doesn't want to do anything—he says that Nick is just trying to get his hands on some of the estate." Her voice shook with anger. "It's just not fair—Josh should have made provisions for him. Nick should own half of the estate and he should be able to claim the Granger ancestors as his own. He's my nephew, yet we keep up this pretense in public that he's just the housekeeper's son. As it is, he's living in some kind of limbo, neither Rios nor Granger." She glanced at Sloan from underneath her lashes. "If I have my way, he'll be acknowledged and end up with half the estate . . . so remember that when you marry me, that you'll only get your greedy hands on half the Granger lands."

Sloan growled and pulled her up onto his lap. His mouth found hers and he kissed her hungrily, his tongue delving deep, his hand cupping her breast and squeezing gently. "As long," he said thickly, a second later, "as I am able to get my hands on *you*, that's all that matters to me."

Aroused and trembling, she brushed her mouth against his. "Feel free," she murmured throatily.

He did and he only let her go several minutes later when it occurred to him that if he attempted to make love to her in the swing he'd probably spend the next few weeks visiting the chiropractor. Setting her from him, he said reluctantly, "That's it. I have to go. If I don't, I'll do something that will spoil all my plans for our honeymoon."

"Oh, are we going to have a honeymoon?"

"I don't know about you, but I'm certainly going to have one." He leered at her. "I'm stocking my house with food and water, unhooking the phone, the fax, and the computer, and sending Pandora to stay with the vet." He kissed her nose. "And you, my sweet, will be locked naked in my bedroom for at least six weeks while I have my wicked way with you whenever I want."

"Sounds lovely. I can hardly wait."

"Which reminds me—I agreed to not getting married for a couple of weeks, but I hope you don't plan on practicing abstinence," Sloan said, nipping one of her fingertips. "I don't think we have to go so far as to announce our plans"— he made a wry face—"which would defeat the whole purpose of flying away for a private wedding, but on the other hand, I don't intend to be kept at arm's length either. I want to be with you." His voice grew husky. "And I intend to be with you—a lot. I'll draw the line at sleeping here, but you better get used to me being your shadow." He kissed her lips. "And I hope you'll come out to visit my place." He grinned. "Conjugal visits. We can practice being married."

Shelly blushed in the shadows, but she said airily, "Oh, I'm sure that I can live with those stipulations."

"Tomorrow afternoon?" he asked with a lascivious look.

Shelly laughed. "Maybe, depending on what happens in the morning." She grew serious. "I want to start checking some of the semen to see if it's viable. And if it is, as we're all pretty sure it is, Nick and I need to set up a whole new breeding program based on what's in those tanks."

"You and Nick are really determined about making Granger Cattle Company a success, aren't you?"

"We are. And we're lucky that our skills complement each other's—he has the cattle know-how that I lack, but I'm a demon with paperwork—his downfall. We make a pretty good team."

Sloan stood up, pulling her to her feet. His arms around her, he brushed his nose against hers. "But we'll make a better team, won't we?"

"Hmm, indeed we will."

They walked down the steps to Sloan's vehicle. Sloan opened the door, but he couldn't bring himself to end the evening. He'd never thought that he'd be given a second chance with Shelly, and he was, despite feeling a fool about it, just a bit superstitious. He'd been this happy once before; once before they'd declared their love for each other and once before they had promised to marry. . . .

His expression bleak, he glanced over at her. "You're certain about this? You're not going to suddenly change your mind on me, are you?" His gaze dropped. "Don't play with me, Shelly, not now, not this time. If you have any doubts, I want to hear about them now. What I don't want to have happen this time is for you to do another disappearing act on me. I don't think I could live through it again."

Tears shimmered in her eyes. "I won't pretend that I don't have some doubts—there's your side of what happened seventeen years ago and there's what I saw and heard." When he would have protested, she put a silencing hand against his mouth. "No, listen to me. It isn't going to do any good for you to protest your innocence—one of you, Josh or you, deceived me, and I have to decide, if I ever can, which one of you lied. I loved Josh, and I love you. But I love you so much that I want to marry you even if I have doubts. See? I have no pride left where you are concerned." A tear slid down her cheek. "It's hard, Sloan. I believed and trusted Josh all my life. And I *did* see you kissing her. And you did marry her within months of my leaving . . ."

His gaze hooded, Sloan nodded. "Yes, I married her—for all the wrong reasons. If you were hurt and miserable and felt betrayed, just remember I felt the same. No, not the same. Hell, for me it was ten times worse—I didn't know *why*. Jesus, the nights I lay awake wondering why, why did she do it?" His voice hardened. "You left me. You walked out without a word. I kept thinking it was a nightmare, that it couldn't be true." He laughed, an ugly sound in the night. "After all, you'd sworn that you loved me, you couldn't have left me. We were going to be married—you wouldn't have left me without one single, goddamn word. Well, I was wrong. You did. And once I got over being hurt, I got mad, and there was Nancy waiting with open arms. She didn't love me; she loved the Ballinger fortune. I knew it at the time, but yes, I married her—I married her to spite you; to thumb my nose at the world, to show everyone that your desertion didn't mean a damn thing to me. My motives might have been crass and stupid, but I suffered for it." His lips twisted. "And Nancy suffered for it, too. She found out too late that money wasn't everything, that being with the one you love is worth more than all the gold in the world." He looked away. "She loved Josh, and I think he loved her, so I guess in the end, you could say that we all suffered."

Her heart ached for him, for all of them. They had all made mistakes and paid dearly for them. Josh and Nancy were dead, while she and Sloan. . . . She and Sloan had a second chance.

She reached for him and with a muttered groan, he crushed her to his chest. "Don't disappear on me again," he said hoarsely. "Please."

Her face alight with love, she caressed his rough cheek. "I promise. I'll be here tomorrow and tomorrow and for all of our tomorrows. I love you. I always will." A tremulous smile curved her lips. "Nothing is going to stop us this time. Nothing."

Chapter Twenty-One

❦

$\mathcal{S}$helly spent a restless night, excited at the prospect of marriage to Sloan, a little apprehensive about the future, a small part of her worried that in the face of Sloan's powerful personality and her own yearnings she was letting her heart overrule her mind. She did have doubts—but not about her love or her determination to marry Sloan. For whatever reasons, they'd lost seventeen years. She wasn't about to lose the rest of her life.

Because of her restless night, it was late when she arose. By the time she came downstairs, it was to find Roman using a small drip percolator to brew some very black, very strong coffee. A pot that, Shelly guessed, contained warmed milk sat on a nearby burner. Acey was seated at the table, a mug of regular coffee in front of him, disbelief in his gaze as he watched Roman concoct genuine café-au-lait.

"You ain't actually gonna drink that crap?" Acey asked as Shelly walked into the kitchen. "I've seen crankcase oil lighter and thinner than that stuff."

Shelly laughed and dropped a kiss on Acey's white head—he'd dispensed with the bandage. "I hate to tell you this, but he drinks it every morning. It's a Louisiana thing. They all drink it that way—and in little bitty cups that most men would be ashamed to be seen holding."

Roman turned around from his task and grinned at her.

Picking up a dainty cup from the counter, he waved it in the air. "I packed mine, along with the percolator—when traveling west a man must take provisions."

Acey made a rude comment, and Shelly grabbed a mug of coffee from the white coffeemaker on the counter. "I may have lived there for a long time, but I never could get used to the coffee." Sitting down across from Acey, she took a sip from her mug and sighed. "Now that's how coffee should taste."

"So what's on the agenda for today?" Acey asked. "I told Roman that if you didn't have anything special planned I'd take him on a trail ride, kinda show him the place."

"No, that's fine." She glanced at Roman. "You won't feel as if I'm deserting you, will you? I really want to test some of that semen and see how viable it is." She looked around. "I'm surprised that Nick isn't here already."

"He's been here, ate you out of house and home, and is currently in the barn, I believe, drooling over the semen tank," Roman said, laughter in his voice. "You know, you people really need to get out more. A semen tank. You'd think that you'd found a gold mine."

"To us it *is* a gold mine," Shelly said, standing up. "Do you mind if I leave you with Acey for a few minutes while I go to the barn? I promise I won't be gone long."

Roman's handsome face took on an expression of horror. "Deserted! A man of my looks and talent deserted for a semen tank! My God, my vanity may never recover." He grinned at her. "Get outta here. Until you and Nick get over that tank, you're not going to be any fun anyway."

Shelly was gone before he finished speaking. She found Nick in the lab, just standing and staring at one of the tanks, his hands resting on it as if it held the secrets of the universe. He was so lost in the moment that when Shelly touched his shoulder he nearly leaped out of his skin.

"Holy shit!" he yelled, jumping backward. Seeing who it was, he exclaimed, "Dammit, Shelly, don't go sneaking up on me like that." Hand clutched to his chest, he stared at her. "You damn near gave me a heart attack."

"I'm sorry," Shelly said, trying hard not to laugh. "I thought you heard me come into the room."

Nick smiled ruefully. "Nah. I was so mesmerized by the tank that a B-52 could have flown in here and I wouldn't have heard it."

"So have you checked it out?" Shelly asked.

He shook his head. "I was waiting for you. Felt we should do it together."

Nervous and expectant, they opened the first tank and after scanning the inventory carefully lifted out an ampule and selected one thin straw for testing. It had been a difficult choice, but in the end it wasn't age or glory that made their choice, it was simply that there were a lot of straws from this particular bull.

The microscope was set up, and while they waited for the semen to thaw in the thawing unit on the counter, they made a more thorough examination of the lab.

Looking into one of the cupboards, Nick whistled. "Man, I don't know what Josh must have been thinking—he kept this part of the operation right up to date, but let the actual cattle breeding and selling go to pot. I can't figure it out."

"Me neither," Shelly answered, frowning as she discovered bottles of semen extender, tubes of K-Y jelly lubricant, and a couple of gallons of Nolvasan solution—the use-by dates indicating that they had been bought within the last few months. She glanced over at the microscope and thawing unit—they looked new, unused, and she suspected that they were. In fact, remembering the invoices she had pored over recently, she was pretty certain she had seen the paperwork on their purchase. So what had Josh been thinking?

Money had been running out by the time he had bought the up-to-date equipment and supplies, so why spend it on a cattle operation he'd abandoned? She sighed. It was another of those questions that they'd probably never know the answer to.

"Maybe," she said, thinking aloud, "he felt guilty about having let Granger Cattle Company fall by the wayside—maybe he was thinking of trying to start it up again."

"Could be—from the equipment and supplies in here that's what it looks like, but I dunno." Nick said, scratching his chin, "it just doesn't make a lot of sense." He shook his head. "We'll probably never know exactly what he planned—just put it down to one more mystery surrounding dear old dad."

Shelly glanced sharply at him, the bitterness in his voice almost palpable. "Do you hate him?" she asked quietly.

"No, but sometimes . . . sometimes, I wished to hell that Jim Hardcastle had kept his mouth shut." He looked away. "I'd have probably had questions later on," he grimaced, "since I seem to bear more than a passing resemblance to Josh. But it maybe wouldn't be the burning question that it is for me now." He shrugged. "A question we'll most likely never answer—unless, of course, Mom decides to come clean—which isn't damn likely. And even if she confirmed it, it wouldn't prove anything. So I'm stuck with the unanswerable question."

From the doorway, Roman asked, "But why? DNA testing would resolve the question for all of us."

Nick spun around, his gaze going from Shelly to Roman. "You *told* him?" he demanded, accusation in his voice.

Shelly shrugged, but it was Roman who answered. Strolling into the room and shutting the door behind him, he said, "Yes, she told me, but it wouldn't have made any difference—once I laid eyes on you I started wondering." He smiled. "You're right—you bear more than a passing resemblance to Josh."

"Yeah, well, it's going to have to remain one of life's little mysteries," Nick muttered, turning away and walking over to the counter. Staring hard at the thawing unit, he laughed bitterly. "You know it's funny—I can get a DNA report on a damn bull dead for thirty years, but as for proving Josh is my father . . ." He snorted. "That, my friend, is blowing in the wind."

"Perhaps," said Roman, walking up to stand beside him, "but you're neglecting the fact that we can do something to clarify the issue. I'm no expert, but I know that Shelly's DNA alone could prove that you are a Granger. Not Josh's son, but a Granger. My DNA wouldn't add a great deal to the mix since there are so many generations between, but if we used it, it would certainly be *added* proof that you are a Granger. Remember DNA is like playing the odds and using mine will only help tip the odds a little more in our favor. Not a lot, but definitely more." At the blaze of hope that sprang to Nick's eyes, Roman held up an admonishing finger. "You'll note that I didn't say that we can prove that you are Josh's son—only that we share a common ancestor . . . a Granger ancestor."

Nick swallowed, the desire, the hope he felt so naked that it hurt to look at his face. "You'd do that?"

"In a heartbeat." Roman grinned at him. "For my own protection, you understand—if we are relatives, you will only have kind thoughts of me, and I needn't fear some sort of painful Oak Valley initiation from you."

Nick couldn't speak. He couldn't make light of the subject, although he appreciated and recognized that Roman was trying to make it easier for him. He struggled for words, and for a terrifying moment, he thought he would break down and sob. To know the truth had been a dream for him for so long that suddenly having at least a partial solution presented was almost more than he could bear. He turned away. Swallowed thickly. "Thank you," he managed in a gruff voice.

Aware of the emotional impact Roman's offer had on Nick, giving him a moment to recover, Shelly said briskly, "Well, thank goodness that's one problem solved. We can make an appointment with the Willits Hospital and find out whom we need to see and how we go about collecting the DNA. And in the meantime . . ." She walked up to stand beside Nick. "In the meantime let's see if any of this semen is any good."

Taking the straw from the thawing unit, she snipped the end and carefully placed a few drops of semen on the glass slide. With fingers that only trembled slightly, she placed the slide under the microscope.

She took a deep breath and looked at Nick. "You want to look first?"

Nick hesitated. So much was riding on what those precious few drops of harmless-looking liquid contained. If it was bad news, he didn't know if he wanted to be the one to spring it. More to the point he didn't know if he could bear the disappointment. He grimaced and hedged. "Technically you own the semen," he said. "Maybe you should be the first one to look at it."

No more than Nick did Shelly want to look through the lens of the microscope and see . . . nothing. So many hopes and dreams were just a squint away, and yet she was reluctant to take that final step. Right now they still had hopes and dreams. The instant they looked into the microscope. . . . She swallowed, her fingers clenching and unclenching. Depending on what the microscope revealed, those hopes and dreams could be realized or shattered.

Roman glanced from one tense face to the other. Pushing

his way between them, he muttered, "Well, I for one can't stand the suspense." He bent forward and closing one eye stared down at the semen. A wide smile crossed his face. "Yes! Swimmers! I see swimmers."

Nick and Shelly gasped and shoved Roman aside, each trying to look down the microscope at the same time. Shelly won the battle and let out her own shriek of joy when her gaze saw the tiny twisting sperm. "It's true. Swimmers!"

Nick took his turn peering at the semen. "Man, look at those little suckers—each and every one potentially a calf. Hot damn! Are we lucky or what!"

Faces bright, laughing and gabbling plans for the future at the same time, Nick and Shelly did a jig around the lab. Roman watched amused. When he thought that they had celebrated long enough, he asked, "So what happens now? What's the next step in this odyssey?"

Shelly and Nick stopped their gyrations, but still grinning they walked over to stand beside Roman. Pushing back a strand of hair that had fallen forward in her wild dance with Nick, Shelly said, "I think a telephone call to the Angus Association in St. Joseph, Missouri, is the next thing. From what I've read, we'll have to run DNA tests on one straw of each of the bulls before we can start using the rest of it." She made a face. "I hate sacrificing even those few straws, but there isn't any choice. That's one thing Josh didn't do. And in the future, if we want to continue collecting and storing or selling our own semen, we'll have to meet the requirements of the Angus Association." Catching her breath, she took another look at the slide, a smile spreading across her face. "Aren't they beautiful?" she breathed.

"In a fashion," Roman murmured, a teasing glint in his eyes, "but as far as I'm concerned, when you've seen one sperm, you've seen them all."

Shelly hit him on the shoulder. "You would say that. These, I'll have you know, are *important* sperm."

"If you say so."

Together they cleaned up the lab and put all the equipment away. Shelly and Nick both suffered a pang at the disposal of the half-filled straw of semen. Each straw was so very precious—from the inventory, they knew that some of the bulls had less than a half dozen straws—and one of those would have to be sacrificed for DNA.

It was a cheerful trio that walked back to the house. Maria, home from Mass and looking very attractive in a crimson pantsuit trimmed in black braid, had joined Acey in the kitchen, and the two of them were sitting and drinking coffee. They both looked up when the other three entered, a question in their eyes.

"You'd better be smiling cause you've got good news," Acey said, "and not cause you've got gas."

"It ain't gas, old man," Nick said. "We only looked at one straw of Granger's Best Ideal—Beau's grandfather—and even though it's almost twenty-five years old, it looked damned good."

There was another round of dancing and whooping, and the next couple of hours were spent in joyful discussion of the future of Granger Cattle Company. By the time they finished lunch, there was a little drizzle falling and Roman's ride with Acey had been postponed. The group broke up, Acey heading to the barn, Maria to her house, and Nick back up to his place. The house seemed quiet and lonely after the morning's excitement, and Shelly suggested a drive into town.

Roman quirked a brow. "Does the town even open on Sunday?"

"Yes, it's open on Sunday. Just not a lot of places." She

grinned at him. "But then there aren't a lot of places in St. Galen's to start with."

Roman's first impression was not, well, impressive. The half-shabby buildings, some in desperate need of paint, some of them obviously empty for a long time, the uneven sidewalks, the overhead electrical wiring and poles reminded him of forgotten, decaying towns in the Deep South. He saw nothing that could explain the affectionate pride on Shelly's face as she pointed out the main features of the town.

His silence got through to her, and she glanced at him. "You don't like it, do you?" she asked in a small voice.

He tried a diplomatic approach. "It's, uh, different, not quite what I expected."

"You thought you'd find fancy brick sidewalks and filigree balconies and wrought-iron streetlights?" she asked with an edge. "Bistro joints with dainty little sidewalk tables?"

Roman grimaced. "No, not exactly. It's just that . . . that St. Galen's looks like hundreds of other sleepy little towns that progress has passed by."

"And *we* like it that way!" Shelly snapped. "We don't want a McDonald's on every corner, or, or Round Table Pizza or any of the other businesses that come with *progress*." She almost spit out the last word. Glaring at Roman, she said, "Let me tell you something—I know who owns every one of these buildings. I know their families, and my father knew their families. I know the history of the place. This isn't a town of nameless strangers. You may have your oh, so, la-de-dah hangouts in New Orleans, but I'll bet you don't know anything about who owns them—or their families."

Roman held up his hands in surrender. "I'm sorry. It's just that you talked so much about it that I expected . . ." He made a face. "I expected something different. I'm sorry."

Shelly kept her eyes fixed ahead. "It isn't the buildings, Roman, it isn't even the place—it's the people. They're the heart of Oak Valley. And sure, I wish sometimes that the overhead wires were gone and that a little more money was spent on paint." She sighed. "What I'd really like is a Chinese takeout or a really great pizza place." She cut her eyes at him. "One that delivers. But there isn't, and I can live with that because the area has so much more to offer. I can drive down to Willits or Ukiah and get those things that I just mentioned. But I can't get the, the slower pace of life, the pleasure of always seeing someone I know, of watching Jeb caution old man Shelton about driving that ancient wreck of his. It has no windshield and no one knows the last time it was licensed. Jeb won't turn him in—nor will any of the other deputies, because old man Shelton is a fixture around town—and he only comes into town from the hills once a week on Fridays for groceries." She grinned. "We all know when we see him coming to get out of the way."

Shelly came up behind a beat-up white truck that was stopped in the middle of the street. Two bales of hay and a pair of black-and-white cow dogs were tied in the bed of the pickup. She didn't recognize the driver, but she recognized Profane Deegan, standing beside the cab and carrying on a spirited conversation if his waving arms were anything to go by. When she would have pulled on by, Profane left off his conversation and waved her down.

His sun-wrinkled face sincere and his wiry salt-and-pepper beard spiking out in all directions, he leaned into Roman's side of the Bronco, and said, "I sure am goddamn sorry to hear about your bull, Shelly. You ever find the son of a bitch that let him out, I'll kick his ass back to Kansas for you. Goddamn shame."

"Thank you," Shelly said, a lump forming in her throat.

"Well, you know you can sure as hell count on me."

He looked expectantly at Roman and, reminded of her manners, Shelly introduced them.

"Damned pleased to meet you," Profane said, vigorously shaking Roman's hands. "Hope you'll stay a while." Pointing to the fellow half-hanging out of the pickup truck, Profane said, "This sorry-looking motherfucker here is Sam Higgins. He owns the Bar 7 out near the buttes. You remember his daddy, Shelly? Wild Horse Higgins?"

Shelly did, and a few minutes were spent in casual conversation, a couple of vehicles winding their way around the Bronco and truck.

Pulling away from the truck and Deegan, who was once more involved in his previous conversation, Shelly said, "*That's* one of the things that makes St. Galen's great."

"Profanity?" Roman teased.

Shelly laughed. "Yeah. When it comes from Profane." She laughed again, her earlier defensive mood gone. "And he *would* kick someone's ass back to Kansas if he found out that they'd turned Beau loose."

Still smiling, she parked nose first in front of the big log building that housed Heather-Mary-Marie's. Several cars, including a Suburban that looked like Sloan's, were parked in the same manner in an untidy row. As she and Roman exited the vehicle, she said, "Cleo only opens the store for a couple of hours on Sunday—mostly so the Lotto people can come in and check their numbers."

Entering the store, Shelly's heart leaped when the first person she spied was Sloan. Looking big and heartbreakingly handsome in well-worn black jeans and a plaid shirt, he was leaning on the counter, talking to Cleo. At the sight of Shelly, the expression on his face left no one in any doubt of his feelings.

Pulling Shelly into his arms, heedless of the interested

onlookers, he dropped a kiss on her smiling mouth. "Good afternoon. I missed you."

Flushing, a little embarrassed at the public display, Shelly stepped out of his arms. "Good afternoon to you, too. I, uh, missed you, too."

"Oh, go ahead and kiss him," Cleo said. "He'll pine and pout all day if you don't."

"Please do," said Roman, "and put the poor guy out of his misery." Brushing past the pair, he walked up to the counter and draped himself attractively on it. Grinning at Cleo, he murmured, "I'm Roman, by the way, her cousin from New Orleans—you must be the incomparable Cleo."

"My, my, aren't you just the handsomest morsel I've seen in many a year," Cleo breathed, patting her bright red hair. "And if I were thirty years younger, I'd be tempted to sling you over my shoulder and show you the storage rooms in back." She glanced back at Sloan and Shelly. "Go ahead. Kiss him."

Laughing, a little breathless, Shelly did. Aware of her embarrassment, Sloan let her get by with a chaste peck on the cheek, but he kept his arm firmly around her waist.

Cleo beamed at the pair of them. "Some things are just meant to be. And you two are one of them. I can't tell you how happy I am for you. When's the wedding?"

"Uh, we, uh haven't set a date," Shelly muttered, wishing for once that Cleo wasn't so brash. She was conscious of other people moving around in the store, some of them showing obvious interest in what was going on by the front counter.

Letting Shelly off the hook, Cleo just grinned, and said, "Well, when you decide you make certain you let me know." She glanced over at Roman, and asked, "How long are you staying? Short visit? Long visit?"

Charmed by Cleo and beginning to understand Shelly's

love of the place, Roman said. "Probably a long visit. We'll see."

The conversation became general, several people came in and out of the store—most to check their Lotto numbers and to banter with Cleo and be introduced to Roman. Shelly and Sloan grabbed a few minutes alone, standing in a quiet corner near the tiny changing rooms at the back of the store.

"I really did miss you," Sloan said softly, his gaze on Shelly's face. "Leaving you last night was one of the hardest things I've ever done."

"I know," she replied, her eyes shining with love as she looked up at him. "My arms felt empty, and my bed was lonely."

"We can fix that," he said, drawing her close, his voice deepening. "Come home with me now and let me show you how much I love you."

"I can't just dump Roman and leave him to drive home by himself." She kissed the corner of his hard mouth. "But I will come out this afternoon—late, say about four?"

Sloan sighed. "OK. 'Til four."

Saying good-bye to Cleo, Sloan, Shelly, and Roman exited the store together. Sloan stole another quick kiss, then walked over to where his vehicle was parked at the end of the row.

When Shelly would have slid behind the wheel of the Bronco, Roman said, "Why don't you let me drive? It's easier to remember streets and directions when you're the one driving—figure I might as well start getting familiar with the area."

Shelly shrugged, gave him the keys, and took the passenger seat. As Roman backed out of the lot, she asked, "How long are you going to stay?"

"Until you drive me away or I get bored." He slanted her a look. "Haven't been bored yet."

"You've only been here twenty-four hours. Be kinda hard to get bored."

"You know me—I get bored so easily."

They were on the point of passing the rear of Sloan's Suburban, still parked at the end of the row of cars, when Roman stepped on the brake. "And I'll be bored all afternoon watching you flit around trying to entertain me when you really want to be with him." He smiled gently. "Go. Get out of here. I know the way back to the house."

Her eyes strayed to Sloan's vehicle. "Are you sure?" she asked. "Isn't it sort of tacky abandoning you when you just arrived?"

"Be tackier hanging around the house when I know that you wish you were with Sloan getting your bones jumped."

Shelly flushed. "That obvious, huh?"

"No, but in case you haven't noticed I'm a man, and I have some inkling how Sloan feels in a situation like this. Go with him." When she hesitated, he added, "Listen, I'll be honest with you. I'm beat. It was a long flight, and it's been an eventful twenty-four hours. You go have fun with Sloan and let me go to the house and grab a couple of hours of sleep. Give me the directions to his place and I can pick you up this evening and save him a trip." He wiggled his eyebrows. "And what you two do during that time is your business." When she continued to resist, he said, "Why don't we see what Sloan has to say about it?"

Before Shelly could object, Roman had pulled in beside Sloan and, talking across Shelly, explained his idea. Of course Sloan came down on Roman's side, and before Shelly knew it, she was speeding down the road with Sloan, and Roman, with instructions on how to find Sloan's place, was heading back to the house.

Their relationship was too new, too fragile to take it for granted, and Shelly found herself oddly shy as the big vehicle ate up the distance to Sloan's home. She made polite conversation, unaware of the tender glances Sloan sent her way.

A snooty greeting from Pandora was just what she needed to snap out of it, and, sitting on the couch inside the cabin, she entered a stare-down with the little bundle of black-and-silver fur on the floor in front of her. Taking the glass of wine Sloan had poured for her, she said, "She doesn't like me."

"She's just jealous," Sloan said with a smile, taking a seat next to Shelly on the couch and pulling her against his shoulder. Nuzzling her hair and nipping at her ear, he murmured, "Now *this* is more like it. Remind me to do something really nice for Roman, will you?"

Making a noise like an outraged kitten, Pandora jumped up into Sloan's lap. She leaned confidingly into his chest and sent a very humanlike glare at Shelly.

"Pet her."

"I don't know. She looks like she'd like to bite me."

But at Sloan's urging she gently petted Pandora's head, surprised at how silky the fur felt and the fragility of the small skull. Pandora endured her touch, but after a moment, she got up, turned around several times, then lay down on Sloan's lap, her little butt firmly pointed in Shelly's direction, clearly giving her opinion of the intruder.

Shelly and Sloan laughed. Pandora gave them both an offended look, jumped off Sloan's lap, and trotted smartly to the kitchen. Her actions stated clearly, "Humans! Who needs them!"

Amusement dancing in her eyes. Shelly said, "Oh, dear. I hope I haven't come between the pair of you. She makes me feel like the other woman."

Sloan's eyes darkened, his mouth hovering above hers.

"There is no other woman in the world for me but you. Always remember that, will you?"

Shelly nodded, her throat tight, her heart almost bursting in her chest with love. Warmly, her fingers traced his hard face. "I love you," she said softly.

His mouth came down on hers and the world spun away. They never made it to the bedroom for that first urgent joining. Clothes, male and female, were scattered around the couch where they had tossed them in the wild drive to become one. They were frantic for each other, as if last night had never been, Sloan wasting little time on foreplay, Shelly already hot and slick when he parted her thighs and plunged deep inside of her. It was a desperate race to ecstasy and it took both of them hard and fast, Shelly's slim body arching up under his as the orgasm exploded through her, Sloan's hands tightening on her hips, his body pumping madly into hers as the same sweet release dragged him under.

Sanity came back slowly. Stretching beneath Sloan, Shelly kissed his mouth. "Wow," she said huskily, "you sure know how to show a girl a good time."

He bent his head and nipped her chin. "And if we ever make it to a bed, I'll show you an even better time."

Shelly giggled, but discovered he wasn't kidding. Picking her up, he carried her into his very masculine bedroom in the loft and tossed her on the bed, his long body following hers down. They made love again. This time slowly, gently, and with great tenderness, the words, "I love you. I love you. *I love you*," fervently repeated.

Eventually they left the bed for a shower, which turned into another passionate interlude. Dragging himself out of the shower, Sloan said, "If we don't stop this I'll be a dead man before the honeymoon." He shook his head. "Jesus, I haven't been this insatiable since I was a teenager." His eyes caressed her. "And only with you."

She smiled back at him, the smile of a woman who is, and *knows* she is, well loved. For a second Sloan looked tempted to crawl back into the shower, but then, shrugging into a pair of jeans, he left Shelly to finish her shower.

Leaving the loft and walking into the living room, he was met by a thoroughly disgusted Pandora, her expression saying clearly that she was not used to being usurped in this manner. And to prove it, she had chewed the toe out of one of Shelly's shoes. Sloan ruffled the fur along her back, and said, "Sorry, kid. You're just going to have get used to having another female around." He made his hand like a pistol, and, pointing at her, said, "Don't make me choose between you."

Leaving Pandora to pout in one corner of the couch, he gathered up Shelly's things and took them to her in the bedroom. Presenting the mauled shoe, he said, "Uh, I'll buy you a new pair."

"She's really taking this hard, isn't she?" she asked, concerned.

"Yeah, but she's normally a friendly little thing. She'll get over it . . . I hope." He glanced at her. "Will it be a problem for you?"

Shelly smiled. "Nope. I like dogs, and I think she's adorable. Besides, I can't really blame her—I love you, too."

He would have taken her into his arms and they'd probably have ended up back in bed, but the sound of a vehicle driving up broke the silence. Sloan glanced at the clock on his tall oak dresser. It was only 3:40.

Frowning, he said, "Didn't we tell Roman seven o'clock?" Shelly nodded.

Sloan grimaced. "I'll go see who it is. You go ahead and get dressed."

Still wearing only a pair of Levi's, his feet bare, Sloan

left the loft and walked across the living room, taking a peek out the window to see if he recognized the vehicle. He didn't.

There was a knock on the front door, and, frowning, he opened it.

Reba Stanton stood there, wearing a skintight pair of black leggings and a red-and-white patterned silk blouse tied in a knot beneath her voluptuous bosom. She tossed her blond hair back and smiled at his expression.

"Surprised to see me?" she purred.

Sloan nodded. "You could say that," he said. "What brings you out here?"

She smiled. "Can't I just come out and see an old friend?" Reaching out, she ran a teasing finger across his naked chest. "I thought we could discuss old times."

Sloan stepped back, away from her touch, and she followed him inside the house. Ill at ease, Sloan didn't quite know what to do. He was aware of Shelly in the loft, and the last thing he wanted was for Shelly to get the wrong idea. He'd already traveled *that* road once.

"Look," he said, "this isn't a good time." Bluntly he added, "And *we* were never such good friends. You and Nancy were good friends—not you and I."

Ignoring his lack of welcome, Reba prowled around the room, her eyes assessing to a dime the worth of the furnishings. "Hmm, you're right about that, darling . . . we were never friends." She smiled over her shoulder at him. "But as you said, Nancy and I were . . . and we shared many secrets. Like to hear some of them?"

"Not especially," he said impatiently. "I'm expecting company, and I'd like to finish getting ready."

Her face hardened. "Yes, I know. Little Shelly. At four o'clock."

"How the hell do you know about that?" he demanded.

She smiled a feline smile. "I was in the changing room at Heather-Mary-Marie's and overheard your conversation."

"If you know that, then why are you here now?"

"Well, you see, I thought I'd take a page out of Nancy's book and arrange a rather damning scene for dear Shelly to see." At Sloan's startled look, she smiled. "Oh, yes. Nancy explained everything. How Josh phoned her absolutely frantic that Shelly was going to marry you. It took them a while to figure out a plan to divide the pair of you, and it worked beautifully, didn't it? Shelly believed exactly what she saw." She sent him a droll look. "And you, poor sap, played right into it. What were you trying to do, protect Shelly? Is that why you said there was nothing between you? To put Nancy off the scent and keep her from sinking her claws into your darling?"

His voice thick, Sloan growled, "You guessed it."

"I always wondered. Anyway, it worked out perfectly, didn't it? Josh timed getting Shelly there down to the second, and when she saw you with Nancy..." She smiled. "Poof! No more engagement. Nancy and Josh were elated. Of course that was before Nancy decided she'd rather be married to Josh than you, but who knew?"

"What's the point of this?" Sloan demanded, his hands clenched into formidable fists. "You think that if you mislead Shelly again that I'll marry you?"

"Well, no," Reba admitted candidly. "I'm not after marriage. In fact I'm divorcing Bob. There's just one little hitch." She looked at him. "No money. That's where you come in. How much will you pay me to leave before Shelly gets here?" She put a finger to her lips and sucked on it. "I figure you'd be willing to pay a bundle—you're a very rich man."

Before Sloan's icy gaze, she undid the knot beneath her breasts and casually tossed off her blouse, leaving her upper body naked. Kicking off her shoes, she knelt on one of the cushions of the couch and posed seductively. She either didn't hear or ignored the soft growl that came from Pandora, who was still sulking on the opposite end of the couch behind her. "Well, what do you think?" she asked. "This should put an end to your little romance, don't you think?" Her lids dropped. "Unless, of course, you'd like to pay me oh, say a couple hundred thousand to leave before Shelly arrives."

Aware of Shelly in the loft, hoping she was hearing this damning conversation, Sloan murmured, "Suppose I agree. Once you leave here, you have no way of keeping me to my word. I could renege."

"Hmm that's true, but you won't for two reasons; one if you give me your word, you'll keep it, and two . . ." Her eyes full of malice, she said, "And number two—if you were not to keep your word, I'd find another way to turn Shelly against you. And I could do it. Look how easily this little tableau was arranged."

And Pandora bit her in the butt.

Chapter Twenty-Two

*I*n the loft, her blouse clutched to her breasts, Shelly listened in amazement to Reba's words. The full significance didn't fully penetrate—at least not immediately—she was too shocked at the woman's gall. And furious!

Scrambling into the rest of her clothes, the light of battle in her eyes, she was preparing to charge downstairs when Reba's shriek rent the air. Curious as well as furious, Shelly stalked out of the loft and into a scene of bedlam.

Reba, naked breasts bouncing like balloons on a windy day, had leaped to her feet and was twisting around, slapping at her rear end. Sloan, his face alight with unholy glee, was attempting to grab Reba, and as Shelly approached, above Reba's screams she heard a noise that she imagined would come from a stuffed toy—a very angry stuffed toy.

"Get it off me! *Get it off me!*" shrieked Reba, her face contorted with fury.

"Give me a second," Sloan said, choking back a laugh. "Pandora! Bad dog! Let go." He said the right words, but his heart wasn't in it and Pandora, hanging by her teeth to Reba's nicely rounded butt, only growled more fiercely.

Shelly's own amusement bubbled up, and, trying to keep her face straight, she grabbed Pandora and tapped her smartly on the nose. Startled, Pandora let go of her victim and for one split second looked like she'd latch onto

Shelly's hand. They eyed each other, then Pandora, deciding that Shelly was probably the lesser of two evils, turned to glare at Reba, still growling and ready to do battle.

Reba's face flamed as she met Shelly's amused eyes, and, snatching up her blouse, she put it on. Sending a lethal glance at Pandora and taking the offensive, Reba said, "I could sue you for what that vicious animal just did. And if there's any scarring, I *will* sue."

Thoroughly enjoying himself now, Sloan grinned. "Of course, that's your right. But if you *did*, then we'd have to explain how you were half-naked and threatening me with blackmail when the, er, incident occurred. Might make it easier for Bob to get a better divorce settlement, don't you think?"

Eyes hard as diamonds, Reba stared at Sloan. "It would be my word against yours."

"Ah, no, that's not true," Shelly broke in. "You're forgetting that I was in the loft . . . and heard every word. I found the part about how Josh and Nancy parted Sloan and me especially interesting. Oh, and I'm so sorry that you and Bob are getting a divorce, but I don't really think that Sloan should help support you in a lifestyle you'd like to become accustomed to." She smiled blindingly at Reba. "You see, poor Sloan is about to take on added responsibilities, and he'll need every penny he has." Shelly walked over to stand next to Sloan, who promptly put his arm around her waist and pulled her tightly to him. With Pandora cuddled against her chest, Shelly looked at Reba, and murmured, "Since you seem to take such a big interest in Sloan's, ah, affairs, you should be the first to know—we're getting married. Soon."

Aware that she had gambled and lost, only boredom showing on her face, Reba said, "Congratulations." Brushing past them, she added, "You'll understand if I don't wish you well."

The door slammed behind her, and Sloan and Shelly looked at each other and burst out laughing.

"My God," Sloan said, "I knew the woman was ballsy, but I didn't know that they were made of brass!"

"I feel like sending her a thank-you note," Shelly said, smiling at him. "Thanks to her, we now know exactly what happened that night seventeen years ago." She pressed a light kiss on top of Pandora's little head. "And this young lady deserves her very own piece of steak. Wasn't she brave?"

Sloan scratched Pandora's ears. "No. She was jealous as hell and was staking out her territory—but I agree about the steak." His eyes on Shelly's, he asked quietly, "How do you feel about learning about Josh's and Nancy's parts in our breakup?"

Shelly made a face and put Pandora down on the floor. "It's not the shock it could have been—Roman already warned me that Josh might have had a hand in the breakup." Her expression pensive, she leaned into Sloan. "I always looked at Josh like he walked on water, and since I've come home, I've learned that not only did he *not* walk on water, but that he wasn't always a nice man."

His arms around her, his cheek resting on the top of her head, Sloan murmured, "He was only human, honey. Just like us."

"Oh, but Sloan, the years we lost." She glanced up at him. "I'm sorry that I was such a fool and didn't give you a chance to explain."

He kissed her. "We can't do anything about the past— we've only got the future. Let's make it a great one, shall we?"

Misty eyed, she smiled up at him. "Oh, yes! And it will be great, just because we're together."

Naturally he kissed her again. And again. And again, which led to a slight detour into the loft. . . .

When Roman arrived just after seven he found Sloan and Shelly sitting on the front porch, Pandora between them. They looked contented and happy.

A smile on his handsome face, Roman said as he walked up the steps, "So, anything interesting happen before I got here?"

They both laughed and rose to their feet. Shelly set Pandora down and put an arm through one of Roman's. "You're not gonna believe what happened," she said, laughter dancing in her eyes. "Wait 'til you hear."

Dinner was a happy affair, and the three lingered outside at the back of the cabin long after dark, just talking, enjoying the silence of the night and each other's company. It wasn't until Roman and Shelly were on their way home that Roman was able to ask Shelly how she felt about Reba's revelations about Josh.

He was driving, and, shooting a look in her direction, he asked, "You OK about Josh's part?"

Shelly smiled sadly. "I think so. It hurts. And I guess I'm bitter. But like Sloan said, we've got the future." She looked across to Roman. "I feel such a fool for having worn blinders for so long where Josh was concerned." She bit her lip. "And I get angry when I realize that if he hadn't died, if I hadn't come home, that Sloan and I would have never gotten together again . . . and for that I can't forgive him."

"He's dead, Shelly. And you have to remember most of what he did was done for love of you. Never forget that he adored you. He wasn't trying to hurt you—in his mind, he was trying to make certain you didn't make a mistake. It could be argued he was trying to protect you."

"Yeah, right." She sighed. "I know. I know he loved me. And he tried to do his best, but sometimes . . . sometimes, you have to let people live their own lives—make their own mistakes."

"Everything cool between you and Sloan?"

She smiled. "Everything is A-OK."

"So, when's the wedding?"

"Couple of weeks." She flashed him a look. "And that's all I'm telling you."

⸻ ❧ ⸻

Shelly woke Monday morning with a smile on her face. She hummed as she showered and dressed and fairly danced down the stairs on her way to the kitchen. Acey was in his usual place at the kitchen table; Roman sat across from him; Maria was turning pancakes; and Nick was pouring himself a cup of coffee.

There was an unmistakable glow on her face, and Nick grinned. "What, you won the Lotto?"

Since her announcement to Reba of their plans, Shelly and Sloan had decided that there was no chance of keeping their impending marriage a secret. The when and the where they could keep to themselves, but not the news that they would marry.

"Better," she said, helping herself to coffee. "Sloan and I are getting married."

"And this is a surprise?" Nick asked, one brow cocked. "Anyone with half a brain could see how things were between you." He thought a moment. "Er, I know this is self-serving, but does your marriage change the plans for Granger Cattle Company?"

"No. The only change will be that you'll move here. Sloan doesn't want to live in this house, and I don't want it to sit empty." Ignoring Nick's sudden intake of breath and Maria's gasp, Shelly went on calmly, "It's a good plan.

You're the manager, and you get stuck with most of the physical work." She smiled at him. "My work is more PR, telephone, paper, and office stuff. This place is where the action is—the breeding barns, the lab, the office, everything. You should be here—not stuck up on the mountain, miles away. You're *needed* here. I'll be living at Sloan's place, and I can drive in to take care of the office—some of it I can do at home. I don't see a problem, do you?"

Nick cleared his throat. "Uh, not exactly." He leaned forward. "Shelly, are you sure?"

She smiled at him, affection in her gaze. "Yeah, I'm sure. This is where you belong—in more ways than one."

Nick's face worked with emotion. He stood up, swallowing hard. "I, er," he managed gruffly, "have to check some things in the barn." And rushed from the kitchen.

She met Maria's brown eyes. They were not friendly. "It is not kind of you to encourage him," Maria said grimly.

"And it is not kind for you to deny him the truth," Shelly said bluntly.

Maria's mouth tightened, and she put down the spatula. Turning on her heel, she stalked out the back door.

"Well, there's goes breakfast," Acey said, disgust evident. "Couldn't you have waited until she finished the pancakes?"

"I can cook pancakes," Shelly said, standing up and going over to the stove. She glanced back at Acey. "Anything else you want to say?"

He smiled that slow, almost shy, kinda sly smile of his. "Congratulations. I hope you and Sloan will be very happy. And I think it's about time that Nick came into his own. He's a good boy. I'm glad you're doing the right thing."

Shelly looked troubled. "Maria's not."

Acey stood up, putting his hat on his head. "Don't you worry none about Maria. She'll come around—she loves

Nick—most of her fussing is because she don't want to see him get hurt. And she knows she hasn't been fair about this whole thing—it's hard, sometimes, to get out of the corner you've backed yourself into. She'll do it. She loves you, and she loves her son. Don't fret."

After Acey ambled out, Shelly looked at Roman. "You have anything you'd like to add?"

Roman grinned. "No way. I want those pancakes you're trying to burn."

It proved to be a productive and busy morning. She and Nick packaged up the semen straws for shipment for DNA testing and took them into town to send overnight via UPS. They also sat down and worked out a breeding plan using the remaining straws in the semen tank—provided they were all viable, which was a real concern. The most pressing needs taken care of, after lunch and several phone calls, Shelly had the name of a physician in Santa Rosa who worked in the DNA field. He would take hers, Nick's and Roman's DNA samples and send them to a lab that specialized in that type of work.

Seated at the desk in Josh's old office, she stared off in the distance. Nick's words in the lab yesterday tumbled over and over in her brain. Hers and Roman's DNA would settle the question of whether or not Nick was a Granger, but it wouldn't prove that Josh had been his father—nothing would except Josh's DNA. Nick needed more than just the knowledge that he was a Granger. He needed to know that he was Josh's *son*. And while they would never be able to obtain a sample of Josh's DNA, she could, maybe, get a sample from someone more closely related to Nick than Roman. A lot more closely related. If they could get the sample . . . it would take them several steps closer to proving that Josh had fathered Nick. And if they could get Maria to tell the truth . . . Lots of ifs.

The phone rang, jerking her from her thoughts. It was Mike Sawyer in Ukiah.

"You are not going to believe this," the lawyer said. "But Milo Scott was just in here, looking like he had been dragged through a knothole backward, I might add, and he said that he didn't want the lease. He told me to draw up whatever papers were necessary to void the lease, and that that would be the end of it." Curiosity evident, he asked, "What did you do? Put the fear of God in him? After you beat him up?"

"Um, I don't know what you're talking about . . . but it's great news, isn't it?" Shelly said, thinking of Sloan's bruises.

She had barely put the phone down when the sound of a vehicle driving up to the back of the house had her wandering in that direction. Her pulse raced when she saw that it was Sloan.

Rushing up to greet him, she kissed him and batting her lashes, murmured, "My hero." At his look, she said, "I just got off the phone with the lawyer, and guess what? Scott is canceling the lease. You wouldn't know anything about that, now would you?"

Sloan's bruises hadn't faded much, and he looked like a slightly battered tomcat. "Nah. Haven't a clue." He bent his eye upon her. "But I do have a bone to pick with you . . ."

It was Shelly's turn to look surprised. "Me? I haven't done anything."

"Funny, but I got a telephone call this morning from Principal Hickman. He wanted to thank me for my generous donation." He gave Shelly a small shake. "The scholarship fund I so magnanimously funded? Ring any bells?"

Shelly grimaced. She peeped up at him. Toying with the top button of his brown plaid shirt, she muttered, "It's that damn right-of-way. You tore up the check, and I didn't see much use in giving you another one."

"So you funded a scholarship in my name with the money?" he asked incredulously.

She smiled. "Yes, I did. Wanna fight about it?"

He laughed, shaking his head. "Am I marrying a woman determined to get her way or what?"

"You aren't angry?"

He pulled her into his arms. "Right now, not much could make me angry. I'm just too happy that things are good between us. You want to waste your money on setting up a scholarship in my name—go ahead." He kissed her, his lips warm and compelling. "Forget about that damned right-of-way," he muttered when he finally lifted his mouth from hers. "I paid Josh for it and while he may have skinned me, I'd have paid him double just to have one more thorn between our two families removed."

Her arms around his neck, she kissed his chin. "Good thinking." She hesitated, then added, "Josh took the money you gave him for the right-of-way and set up a scholarship fund, too."

"Let me guess," Sloan said dryly. "It's in his name."

Shelly nodded. "Does that upset you?"

Sloan shook his head. "Like I told you—I've got you, and I'm feeling magnanimous. I won. And not meaning to be brutal—he's dead." He kissed her again, more urgently. "Let the past lie. From now on, our future is about us, not them."

Arms around each other's waists, they wandered out to the barn, where they found Nick, Acey, and Roman in the lab. Nick was still drooling over the semen tank, and Acey wasn't much better. Roman merely looked amused.

At their entrance, Nick left off his love affair with the semen tank, and, grinning at Sloan, said, "I understand that congratulations are in order."

"That they are," Sloan replied, shaking Nick's hand. "She gave me a chase, but I won."

Shelly snorted and rolled her eyes.

Acey walked up and stuck out his callused hand. "I surely am glad that you're marrying her. I've been telling her for weeks that she needed a good man." He winked. "It's nice when they take your advice."

Shelly shook her head. "That doesn't even deserve a comment."

Acey grinned. "Nope. 'Cause you know I'm right." He glanced at Sloan. "So when's the wedding. She's kinda close-mouthed about the date."

"Sometime in the next couple weeks," Sloan said easily. "We have to get things settled here, then we're flying to Reno to do the deed—just the two of us."

Acey looked askance. "That don't seem right. Think you should revise that plan and get married in the valley. Doesn't have to be a big affair, but there are a few of us that would like to be part of the celebration."

"And that," Sloan said dryly, glancing down at his bride-to-be, "is exactly why I wanted to get married before anyone even had a whiff of what was in the wind."

The truth of Sloan's statement became more apparent as the day passed. The phone began ringing almost constantly. First M.J. demanding to know if it was true that she was going to marry Sloan. Then Cleo called with the same question, and not five minutes later, Bobba. Turned out Reba had been into Heather-Mary-Marie's that afternoon and in front of a half dozen customers had coolly announced that she was just thrilled to pieces that Sloan and Shelly had overcome their differences and were planning on getting married. The news spread like wildfire—Jeb and Danny even drove out to the house to find out for themselves, both of them breaking into wide grins when they heard that this time the gossip was true: Sloan and Shelly were getting married. When Sloan returned to his cabin that evening he found his answering machine was full of calls from half the valley wanting to know if there was any truth to the rumor that he was actually going to marry Shelly Granger.

He returned Roxanne's call first. His sister was elated. "Oh, Sloan, I am so happy for you. I don't know what went wrong before, but anyone can see that the pair of you belong together." She hesitated. "Er, have you told Dad yet?"

Sloan made a face at the phone. "No."

"Um, how do you think he'll take it?"

"Probably badly, knowing how he feels about anyone named Granger, but that's his problem not mine. I'm marrying Shelly, and the fact that she's a Granger doesn't even come into it. Once we're married, she won't be a Granger, she'll be a Ballinger."

"You know," Roxanne said confidingly, "I hate to break it to you, but these days sometimes women keep their own name. Have you thought of that? Maybe she'll call herself Shelly Granger-Ballinger."

Sloan laughed. "Doesn't matter. All that matters is that I love her, and she loves me. And Pandora likes her . . . sort of."

Roxanne giggled. "And that, of course, puts the seal of approval on the whole deal. So when's the wedding?"

"I haven't a clue." He explained their original plan, but it was becoming pretty obvious that a quick, private wedding in Reno was fast disappearing. "All I know right now is that it'll be soon."

Shelly came swiftly to the same conclusion. The whole affair was spinning out of control and as the news spread, she realized that the sooner she and Sloan were married, the better off they would be. They put their heads together and came up with a plan that suited the pair of them. It wouldn't be the Reno wedding, but neither would it be a huge affair. They were determined to keep it as small and intimate as they could—without making enemies for life.

On Wednesday, Sloan, Shelly, Nick, and Roman drove down to Santa Rosa. The taking of the DNA samples was a simple procedure and by lunchtime they were comfortably seated in the Equus Restaurant at the north end of Santa Rosa. Ross, Sloan's younger brother, met them there.

What Ross thought of his brother's engagement to a Granger, he kept to himself, but then Ross tended to keep a lot of things to himself. He was nearly ten years younger than Sloan was and, except for his height, black hair, and tawny eyes, bore little resemblance to his older brother. He was lean, a rapier to Sloan's broadsword. He was more handsome than Sloan, his features finely chiseled, his hard mouth and jaw at variance with his extravagant lashes, but Shelly had eyes for no one but Sloan.

Seated in a quiet alcove, once introductions were made— he already knew Nick—and they had ordered, Ross leaned back in his seat, and, smiling at Shelly, said, "I hope you know what you're taking on marrying this big lug. He can be a tyrant. Believe me, I know. He was my boss at Ballinger Development and, upon occasion, he made my life hell. Are you sure you want to marry him?"

"Don't pay any attention to him," Sloan said, his fingers entwined with Shelly's. "He's just jealous I saw you first."

Ross grinned. Raising his glass of champagne, he glanced at Roman and Nick. "A toast? Shall we wish them many years of happiness? Or misery?"

Smiling, Roman murmured, "Oh, happiness, definitely happiness."

It was a happy, silly lunch, and well after 3:00 P.M. when the quartet headed back to Oak Valley, leaving Ross behind. Since Nick traveled on his stomach, they stopped in Willits and picked up a Papa Murphy's pizza to bake once they reached home.

The conversation at dinner that night was mostly about DNA and what it could prove and couldn't prove. Nick didn't offer much in the way of conversation, but Shelly watched his face, the way he listened intently to every word Sloan or Roman uttered. This meant so much to him. So very much. She was angry at Maria for not telling the truth; furious with Josh for leaving Nick dangling, and determined to do what she could to set it right—although, she admitted, it would never be totally right.

The idea she'd been turning over and over in her mind took full shape, and, pushing aside her empty plate, she said, "Nick gave me an idea the other day." When Nick looked at her, she went on, "You said something about being able to get DNA from a bull dead thirty years. . . ." She took a deep breath. "We don't have access to Josh's DNA, and while mine and Roman's DNA will prove a relationship between us, there is another source."

Nick's eyes were fixed painfully on her. "What do you mean? I know you've got other relatives scattered here and there, but their DNA wouldn't prove anything more than Roman's."

Shelly nodded and said very carefully, "If I had my father's body exhumed and had a sample taken—provided he hadn't been embalmed . . . while it still wouldn't prove that Josh was your father, if there was a match, it would be close enough to put to rest any lingering questions." Hastily, she added, "Not that I have any doubts."

Nick sucked in his breath, his face white. "You'd do that?"

She smiled gently at him, reaching across the table to squeeze his hand. "Yes, for you, I would."

With Jeb's help, they were able to discover that Shelly's

father had not been embalmed. As Jeb had explained, "I didn't really need to check—your dad had always been pretty vocal and downright vehement about the fact that he didn't want any damned undertaker fooling around with his body. I remember him saying time and again that if he had his way, he'd be buried in a wooden box the same day he died. He hated funerals and all the attendant fuss."

Because it was Shelly, the only surviving member of the family, requesting the exhumation, again with Jeb's help with the sheriff's office, permission to dig up the body was given. Within forty-eight hours, the sample had been taken and Shelly, with Sloan on one side of her and Nick on the other, watched as her father was reburied. She had thought she wouldn't feel anything—she had been a child when he had died, and she had few memories of him—but grief welled up inside of her as the coffin was lowered once more into the grave. Fighting back tears, she placed the bouquet of flowers she had brought with her on his tombstone. It seemed fitting and right.

Maria had been furious when she had learned what was planned. "This is wrong," she told Shelly. "It is not necessary."

"Does that mean that you're going to tell Nick that Josh is his father?" Shelly asked grimly.

Maria's lips trembled, and she bent her head and looked away. "I promised. I promised Josh that I would never say. He begged me to swear that I would never tell. You wish me to dishonor myself and break my word to your brother."

"But we're going to prove it anyway," Shelly said, her voice full of exasperation. "What difference does it make now? Josh is dead. It doesn't matter to him anymore. Is a promise you made to a dead man more important than your son's peace of mind?"

Tears in her eyes, Maria looked at Shelly. "You think this

is easy for me? You think I like seeing how much it pains Nick? You think I have enjoyed all these years seeing the yearning, the hope in his face? And each time he came to me for answers, I would not give them to him—you think I enjoyed hurting him?" Pleading, she said, "I would put the same argument to you—his father is dead, so what difference does it make? You have accepted him, you are making him part of your family. Isn't that enough?"

Her voice hard, Shelly said, "No. It isn't."

Chapter Twenty-Three

❧

$\mathcal{I}$n the end Shelly and Sloan's wedding was far larger than either would have wanted. It also didn't take place quite as swiftly as either one of them would have liked. But it turned out perfectly.

Interest in the valley had been high, and, giving in to pressure from Cleo, Acey, M.J., Roxanne, and Jeb to name just a few, they finally decided upon holding the wedding at the community center near the rodeo grounds. And half the valley was invited for the evening wedding. It wasn't a formal affair; the bride wore a new pair of Sassoon jeans and, as a sop to convention, a white silk blouse. The groom was in freshly pressed jeans and a black and white striped shirt, a red silk tie at his neck. Ross was best man and was the only one at the wedding in a suit. As he told Sloan later on that evening, "Dammit, you said informal; I thought you meant no tux."

As for the reception, it was held in the same place, and while a local band blared out country and western dance tunes, the guests ate good old-fashioned barbecued steak and beans outside in the pleasant June air. Everyone declared that it had been a great wedding and reception. The best.

Sloan and Shelly flew to New Orleans for their honeymoon. They were gone nearly three weeks, and though Sloan had to endure meeting many of the Grangers in New Orleans, he enjoyed prowling the streets of the French Quarter with his bride, seeing the place through her eyes and visiting her familiar haunts. Best of all, he was able to spend hours and hours in bed making love to Shelly. He was, as he told her the morning they flew back to San Francisco, a satisfied man, adding, with a wicked leer, for the moment.

Settling into marriage was easier than either one of them had envisioned. Quite simply they enjoyed each other—in bed and out. Once her things were moved into Sloan's cabin, she never gave Josh's house a second thought. In her mind it was already Nick's. She only suffered a pang as she packed up the items in the studio that Josh had had constructed with her in mind.

Sloan helped her and, seeing her face, stopped what he was doing and walked over and took her in his arms. "Don't, honey. Don't dwell on it."

She sent him a watery smile. "It's silly, isn't it? It's only a room, but knowing that Josh . . ." Her gaze blurred with tears. She took a deep breath. "I'll get over it." Flashing him a teasing glance, she said, "After all, you've promised to have another studio built for me next to the cabin. Bigger. More expensive." She kissed him. "Much more expensive."

Sloan laughed and patted her rear. "Gee, keep this up, and I'll begin to think that you married me for my money and not my body."

She dropped her hand and ran a light caress over his groin. His body responded immediately, the flesh hardening under her hand, and she grinned. "No contest, fella. I'll take your body any day."

His eyes darkened. "Prove it," he said huskily. And she did.

Nick's move into Josh's house the following week went smoothly. Since the house was furnished, Nick brought only his personal belongings with him. He told Shelly with a wry grin, "My furniture can only be classified early yard sale. Might as well leave it up there—we can use the place as a line cabin or something like that."

Shelly concurred. Watching him prowl around the spacious living room, she asked, "Are you going to be all right here? It's not a huge house, but it's a lot more space than one person needs."

He smiled. "I'll be fine. Just think of the wild parties I can throw." A lewd expression on his face, he added, "The women I can seduce."

"I hope," said Roman as he walked into the room, "that you'll give me forewarning so that I don't walk into anything that might shock me. I have such tender sensibilities, you know."

Roman had seemed disinclined to return to New Orleans, and he and Nick seemed to have worked out a living arrangement that suited them both. They shared the house, and Roman shared the chores both in the house and the barn. Shelly was pleased—she hadn't been quite certain how to handle the situation. It hadn't seemed fair to saddle Nick with Roman, yet she had been equally uncomfortable with the idea of telling Roman that he'd have to move out. And there was no question of Roman moving in with her and Sloan. Nope. Not a chance.

The two men went about their business while Shelly, oddly disinclined to leave, wandered around the house. Upstairs, she checked her former bedroom to be certain that she'd left nothing behind. She hadn't.

Nick had taken the suite next to Roman's—as he'd told Shelly, "I wouldn't feel right sleeping in Josh's room." Her lips twisted. It would probably be a long time before anyone slept in that room or that they stopped calling it "Josh's room."

Starting down the hallway, she hesitated when she came

abreast of Josh's room. Opening the door, she took a deep breath and walked inside. She'd gotten rid of his clothes weeks ago and had put away most of his personal things, but the room still felt as if Josh would come strolling in at any moment. His death was still unresolved in her mind. Suicide seemed so out of character, yet murder. . . . She shook her head. Neither seemed feasible.

She sat down on the bed and gazed around the room. She sighed, her fingers idly playing with the slim book of poetry that sat on his nightstand. She'd noted it earlier, but hadn't paid much attention to it other than to think that it was an odd choice for Josh. He'd never been much of a reader and had never cared for poetry. She sighed again. Another unknown facet of her brother?

Picking up the book, she fanned the pages. *Well, Josh, did you have a favorite poem? Something soothing you read before you fell asleep each night?*

She'd no sooner had that thought than the pages stopped flipping through her fingers and the book lay open—as if Josh had turned frequently to this particular page. And Josh had, she realized, seeing the thin slip of paper wedged between the pages like a bookmark. It was hidden inside the book, as if Josh hadn't wanted to mark the passage in an obvious manner.

Her gaze dropped to the page, the page that had apparently held appeal for her brother. It was a poem by Edwin Arlington Robinson, entitled "Richard Cory." Curious, she began to read.

RICHARD CORY

Whenever Richard Cory went down town,
We people on the pavement looked at him:
He was a gentleman from sole to crown,
Clean favored, and imperially slim.

And he was always quietly arrayed,

> And he was always human when he talked;
> But still he fluttered pulses when he said,
> "Good-morning," and he glittered when he walked.

Shelly smiled thinking that Richard Cory sounded a lot like Josh. Intrigued she read on.

> And he was rich—yes, richer than a king—
> And admirably schooled in every grace:
> In fine, we thought he was everything
> To make us wish that we were in his place.

Definitely, Josh, Shelly thought. But reading the last stanza, her heart began to beat in thick, painful strokes, and she was aware of a chill creeping into her bones.

> So on we worked, and waited for the light,
> And went without the meat, and cursed the bread:
> And Richard Cory, one calm summer night,
> Went home and put a bullet through his head.

Shelly couldn't breathe. The room spun around, and she was certain she was going to faint. She shook her head, fought for control. Only when she had command of herself did she look at the poem again, the last two lines leaping out at her.

> And Richard Cory, one calm summer night,
> Went home and put a bullet through his head.

The conclusion was inescapable. Like Richard Cory, Josh had taken his own life. She shuddered. Shut the book. Opened the book, reading as Josh must have done, again and again, the poem.

Like Richard Cory, Shelly thought numbly, Josh had hidden from the world the real man. Hidden whatever torments had led him to take his own life.

She sat there for a long time, the opened book clasped loosely in her hands, realizing that she'd only seen the face her brother had wanted her to see, and she wondered how many other faces Josh had hidden behind. Realized, too, that no matter how close, how dear, that no one ever really knows what goes on inside another person.

Closing the book, she set it down gently on the nightstand. She stood up, forcing her legs to hold her. Took a deep breath. Well, she wanted an answer, and she'd gotten it. The knowledge should have made her feel better, but it didn't, and she angrily pushed it away. *Damn you, Josh!*

Unable to bear another moment in his room, she rushed out, her fists clenched. She'd deal with it, and she sure as hell wasn't going to let it blight her happiness. It was over. Done with.

Despite her brave resolution, she suffered a pang as she drove away from Josh's house that afternoon. More than ever she realized that it was no longer Josh's house. It had been hers for a while, and now it would be Nick's. She wondered what her brother would have thought of his son living in the house. Would he have been happy? Angry? She grimaced. Like so many things connected with Josh, it was something she'd never know. During the drive home, she brooded over the brother she thought she had known, but when she reached the turnoff to the cabin, she firmly put Josh and his suicide aside. She'd have to talk to Sloan about it, but not today. Today the wound was still too raw, the knowledge too new and painful, and she wanted nothing to spoil the joy that she and Sloan shared. Josh was the past, and theirs was the future. It was that simple.

Thinking of Sloan, a soft smile lit her face, and warmth

flooded through her. Sloan loved her. She loved him. They loved each other. And *that*, she decided with a lifting heart, was the most important thing in the world.

Sloan had remained home that day—he'd a mare due to foal and hadn't wanted to be gone. When Shelly drove up, and he walked out of the cabin with a big grin, she knew his instincts had been right.

"What did she have?" she asked as she shut the Bronco door behind her.

He swept her up in his arms and swung her around. "The prettiest damn black-and-white filly you've ever laid eyes on." His warm gaze rested on her face. "And she's not for sale. Figure I'll save her for our daughter."

Shelly melted inside at the thought of bearing Sloan's child—boy or girl. They both knew that biologically time was fast running out for her, she'd be thirty-five years old in a few weeks and every year that went by decreased their chances of conceiving a child. Despite wanting a few years by themselves, they'd decided that if they wanted children, they had better not delay.

Her voice suddenly husky, she said, "Guess we ought to get busy then, don't you think."

His arms tightened around her. "Yes," he said gruffly, "I do."

June slid into July, August passed and suddenly it was September. Walking up from the barn one evening where they had gone to feed the horses, Pandora ambling at their heels, they were surprised to see Nick's truck pulling up at the cabin.

Nick spotted them and walked to meet them. He smiled at them and bent down and gave Pandora a swift pat. "She treating you any better?" he asked Shelly.

Shelly glanced down at the little ball of black-and-silver fluff. "Let's put it this way: She tolerates me. Sloan is her god, and I am simply useful for tidbits and petting when he is too busy to pay attention to her." She grinned and picked up Pandora. Nose-to-nose, she said. "Isn't that right, fur-ball?" Pandora stared at her, then gave her a tiny lick on the nose as if to say, "You'll do. Barely."

They all laughed, and, with Pandora in her arms, they continued the short distance to the cabin. A much larger cabin these days. True to his word, Sloan had had a studio with a breezeway connected to the original structure built, and the kitchen had been enlarged. As Nick looked around, Shelly said, "It was fine for a bachelor, but I needed more room to cook. Plus we're thinking of building on a family room."

Nick cocked a brow. "Am I to offer congratulations?"

Shelly shook her head. "Not yet. But we're hopeful."

Sloan grabbed a trio of cold Carta Blanca beers from the refrigerator and, after opening and handing one to Nick and another one to Shelly, asked, "So what brings you out here this time of evening?"

Nick's face changed, and Shelly realized instantly that his air of nonchalance had all been an act.

"What is it?" she asked anxiously.

Nick took a deep breath and pulled out a white envelope. "The DNA results arrived this afternoon."

"And?" she demanded. "Don't keep us in suspense."

Nick made a face. "I haven't opened the damned thing." He looked at her, and she saw the blind terror in his gaze. He swallowed. "What if it doesn't prove anything? What if I'm not Josh's son?"

"But what if you are?" she asked gently. "Open it."

He put his beer bottle down on the kitchen counter and, with shaking fingers, tore open the envelope. While Shelly and Sloan waited in an agony of impatience, Nick riffled through the papers. It seemed to take him forever to find what he was looking for, but they both knew the moment he found it. He blanched and gasped.

"What?" Shelly cried. Unable to stand the suspense a second longer, she grabbed his arm and began to read. She paled, her breath stopped, her eyes got big and round. She looked incredulously at Nick, who regarded her mutely, his expression dazed. "Oh, wow!" she muttered, her eyes locked on Nick's. "I never expected *this*! Who could have?"

"Well, goddammit, let me see," Sloan growled and, taking the papers from Nick's nerveless hand, studied the printed words. He glanced from one white face to the other. "Guess this sort of explains everything, doesn't it?"

His voice sounding thick and rusty, Nick nodded blindly. "Yeah. I guess it does."

The intensity, the enormity of the moment suddenly got to Shelly, and, tears welling in her eyes, she flung her arms around Nick. "It's not what we expected, but it's *wonderful!*" she said with something between a laugh and a sob. "Wonderful."

Nick looked at her, dawning wonder in his eyes. "Are you sure? You're not upset? Angry?"

"How could I be," she said softly, her face full of love, "when it gives me something I thought I had lost forever, something I never thought to have again . . . a brother."

Dear Reader:

Well? What did you think of *Return to Oak Valley*? I'm hoping that you enjoyed reading it as much as I enjoyed writing it.

Some of you are probably wondering why, after having written historical romances for over twenty years, I decided to try my hand at a contemporary. Let me tell you a big secret: I've been longing to write a contemporary since as early as 1980! You read the date right—*1980*. In fact when I signed my third contract for Avon Books (my first two-book contract by the way—*Gypsy Lady* and *Lady Vixen* had been contracted separately) I included a synopsis for a contemporary novel that I had hoped to write as my fourth book.

I envisioned it as an international thriller and the book moved all around the world from the United States to Iran, Morocco, and Mexico (I think—my memory is a little hazy on Mexico). Those were the days during the overthrow of the Shah of Iran, and I was going to use all the turmoil going on in the world at that time as the backdrop for the romance between the hero and heroine. Ah, the hero: Lance Devereaux. Seeing that name now I have to laugh. Have you ever seen a name that screamed fictional hero any louder? An interesting point: the heroine's name was to have been "Shelly." Which was something I'd completely forgotten until I sat down to write this letter. Guess when I get an idea in my head, at least *some* part of it sticks around in the old subconscious. That long-ago contemporary novel had a great title too: *While Passion Sleeps*.

Ah, now you're all going "but you published a book titled *While Passion Sleeps*." Yeah, you're right, I did—my third book. You'll just have to be curious about the original title for the third book, but in between the time I had submitted the book and the date of publication, there had been another book by a different author who had used a title extraordinarily similar, so my first title went out the window. It was crunch time, and we had to come up with a new title in a hurry (like *now*), so we stole the contemporary's title and Beth and Rafael's story came out as *While Passion Sleeps*.

By the time I had finished that third book and was ready to start the fourth, the Shah of Iran was old news and the plot of the contemporary was no longer current. I still wanted to write a contemporary, but since I was doing so well with historicals Avon was against the idea of a contemporary from me at that time. Maybe just as well, because for the fourth book I ended up writing is one of my personal favorites: *Deceive Not My Heart.* Guess things work out like they're supposed to—whether we like it or not.

The longing to write a contemporary novel never went away—which isn't to say that I didn't thoroughly adore writing my historical romances—I just wanted to try my hand at something different. Think of it this way—even if you eat filet mignon every night, after a while, say twenty years, a change of diet would be greatly, dare I say, *desperately* desired.

When Warner Books offered me the opportunity to write a contemporary I leaped at it (and for a fat lady it was quite a sight). Of course, we had artistic differences: I wanted to do a serial killer novel . . . in Oak Valley. In the end, since we all loved the general idea of a place like Oak Valley, we compromised and my beloved serial killer got the, er, ax.

Not having a nice, nasty killer lurking around in the background to add drama and excitement gave me some rocky moments with *Return to Oak Valley.* Not only was it a new direction for me, but I didn't have the safety net of a creepy villain to get me through—you have no idea how many times I thought *Oh, man, if only I had a killer.* . . . I never realized before how much I relied on my bad guys—or how much I enjoyed them. On the other hand, I never realized how wonderful it was to be able use the language and mores of everyday people.

OK, to answer the burning question: Is Oak Valley a real place? Well, it is and it isn't. The terrain is real. The atmosphere is real. But that's it, folks: Everything else is simply my imagination. Really.

Next burning question: Will I ever write another historical romance? Are you kidding? Give up filet mignon . . . forever? Never happen.

But until I finally get around to writing that next historical, I invite you to travel along with me, as we meet new characters and renew old acquaintances, and explore the gravel roads, the flatland, and the forested foothills that surround Oak Valley. Settle back, put up your feet, grab a lemonade, or whatever, and prepare to be, I hope, entertained.

Now let's see, where was I? Oh, that's right, working on *Coming Home* and serving up the romance of Roxanne and Jeb. . . .

Ta,

Shirlee Busbee

Standing on the small deck at the rear of her house and staring out at the hot, dry landscape below her, Roxanne Ballinger decided that she hated September in Oak Valley. And August and probably July, too. The valley was seared by the heat, the hay fields shorn of their crops lay fallow and burnt amber and yellow by the sun, except, as she reminded herself, in those places in the valley where the water table was high and the land stayed green all year. She made a face. Too bad her newly acquired house didn't overlook that area—it'd be nice to stare out at green fields this time of year. Then she shrugged. But if she overlooked those fields, she wouldn't have such a majestic view of Mount Sebastian in the distance and all the other smaller mountains and hills that tumbled down to the valley floor.

This was not, she admitted, the valley's most attractive time of the year . . . at least she didn't think so. And she wondered, not for the first time, what the hell she was doing here. And with a house of her own. She glanced back at the small A-frame building and amended her thought: a cabin of her own. She should be in New York. Tucked comfortably away in her elegant air-conditioned Park Avenue penthouse apartment. Looking forward to all the fabulous, sophisticated entertainment the city had to offer: anticipating the pulsating excitement she'd find on the crowded streets, ready to be seduced by the glamour and vitality of the city. Everything she could humanly want would be at her fingertips. And if she didn't want to venture out, a telephone call would bring all that the city had to offer right to her doorstep: clothes, food, jewelry, handsome men . . .

Thinking of the last handsome man who had shared her life, she grimaced. Todd Spurling was an executive editor at one of the major New York publishing houses, and their affair had lasted for a grand total of almost five weeks. They'd met this past June at one of the glittering pub parties being held for the launch of some celebrity biography, and it had been, she admitted, lust at first sight. As one of the top models in the business, her face had often adorned the covers of such magazines as *Cosmo*, *Vogue* and the like, and justly famous for the generous display of scantily clad limbs in the Victoria's Secret catalog, she was often seen at these sorts of parties. The life of a celebrity, she had discovered, was as much about seeing as being seen, and since she was considered one of the "beautiful people," she was invited everywhere. She had nearly refused to attend the party. She'd been unsettled and restless, having just returned from Oak Valley and her brother Sloan's wedding. The idea of being just another body in another scintillating crowd didn't exactly appeal to her—a feeling she had been experiencing more and more over the past couple of years. But in the end she had decided that a night of rubbing shoulders with the famous and want-to-be-famous might be more enjoyable than staring at the walls of her apartment and thinking black thoughts about Jeb Delaney. The jerk.

She had not gone to the party looking for romance. She snorted. Good God, no! In fact, she had been in a surly mood and rather off men in general. Jeb Delaney in particular. Cretin. Then she'd been introduced to Todd Spurling . . . Todd who was everything that Jeb Delaney was not: urbane, considerate, polite, and utterly smitten with her. Todd had also been tall, handsome, blond, broad-shouldered, and had the bluest eyes she'd ever seen. The moment their eyes had met . . . Her lip curled. The moment their eyes met, she started thinking with a different part of her anatomy than her brain. Apparently Todd had, too, because in less than two weeks after meeting, they'd been living together in her apartment. And three weeks after that, she'd tossed him out on his tight buns, his tight *married* buns, disgusted as much with herself as with him.

Roxanne shook her head, her glorious mane of hair glistening blue-black like a raven's wing in the hot sunlight. You'd think at my age, I'd know better, she thought wryly. You'd think that after nearly twenty years of living in the fast lane that I'd learn not to be so impulsive, that at the wise old age of thirty-eight, I'd not be so willing to fling caution to the winds and just leap into the nearest brawny pair of arms.

Finding out that Todd had been married, something he had conveniently forgotten to mention when they had been falling into bed together, had been a blow to her pride and her esteem. She had been horrified. For all of her wild reputation, and despite gossip and innuendo to the contrary, married men had been completely off her list. And while gossip and rumor had her sleeping with a new lover every week, the truth of the matter was that there hadn't been that many. She thought about it. Fewer than a handful. Maybe. She'd always been more cautious about sex than some of her contemporaries. She grimaced. Being raised in Oak Valley did that to a person. Even amongst the wealthy and powerful Ballinger clan. Values considered these days to be old-fashioned had been the rule, and though she had shaken the dust of the valley from her feet at nineteen, the mores of the valley had been a little harder to put behind her. Besides, with all the diseases out there, she'd never jumped into bed with just anyone. So why had she acted differently with Todd?

She bit her lip. She wasn't promiscuous. She'd never been promiscuous, not even in her rambunctious twenties when she'd been so greedy and eager to experience life and all it had to offer—so eager to gain polish and sophistication, determined to show the world that she wasn't just a beautiful bumpkin from some hokey place in the sticks. Sure, she'd made some mistakes. She wouldn't deny that. She'd been young, confident, OK, maybe arrogant, certainly convinced that the world was hers for taking. She'd been like a kid given free rein in a candy store, and, face it, New York was some kind of candy store for a young woman raised in a place without a stoplight, let alone neon lights, and nary a Burger King in sight. She could justify some of those early mistakes, but the affair with Todd Spurling bothered her. She'd simply taken one look into those mesmerizing blue eyes of his and . . . She snorted. And acted like a silly teenager in love for the first time. But it hadn't been love—she'd retained enough sense to realize that fact. It had been, she thought viciously, all Jeb Delaney's fault. The arrogant prick. Who the hell was he to look down that oh-so-handsome nose of his at her? Most people, especially men, fell over themselves trying to attract her attention, but not Jeb. Oh, no. He couldn't even be polite. And the contempt in his voice when he called her "Princess" . . . Her jaw tightened and her hands curled into fists at her sides. What right did he have to condemn her lifestyle? She'd like to bloody that handsome nose of his and slap that derisive smile off his mouth and into next week.

Roxanne took a deep breath. OK, enough of that. And if she was fair, she really couldn't blame Jeb for the fact that she had fallen into Todd's arms. Maybe a little. If she hadn't been so irritated, and face it, hurt by Jeb's manner and comments . . . if she hadn't gone back to New York grimly determined to show the world that she was *Roxanne,* darling of the media, the ideal sex goddess of half the panting male population, she wouldn't have given Todd Spurling a second look. Her lips twisted. She'd gone back to New York, defiant and dead set on showing Jeb Delaney that his words meant nothing to her. She sighed. And look where that attitude had gotten her. Right into Todd's bed. Ugh.

Her gaze fell to the valley floor. So here she was. Back in Oak Valley. A place she couldn't get away from fast enough nearly twenty years ago, but now . . . It was odd, she thought, how after all those years of happily being swept along by the glamour and excitement found in all those famous cities in the world she had visited and worked in, she found herself drawn more and more to the tranquillity and predictability of Oak Valley. Where once she had forced herself to return home for a short—very short—visit only every other year or so, the past couple of years, those visits had been increasing in both frequency and duration, the longing for the valley reaching out across the distances and tugging at hidden places in her heart. She had discovered amusements that had once held her enthralled were now boring and mundane. She smiled crookedly. Words she had once used to describe Oak Valley. Funny how life turned around on you. Now it was everywhere *else* that was boring and mundane and Oak Valley that held an irresistible appeal.

At first, she'd put this longing for the valley down as a whim, but instead of the need to be there decreasing, she'd found that it had grown. She was, she realized, tired of being *Roxanne*—the face and body that sold millions of magazines, and no doubt an equal number of pairs of scanty underwear—she wanted to be plain old "Roxy," the oldest Ballinger daughter. Sloan's sister. And Ross and Ilka and Sam's sister. She wanted to wear worn blue jeans and scuffed boots and wander into Heather-Mary-Marie's and be greeted by a half dozen people who had known her since she had been born and who were not the least impressed by her face, body, and reputation. She wanted a life that didn't involve being always "on," always photographed, always gossiped about. . . . She grinned. Well, that was going too far. The valley gossip was legendary, and she was quite certain that her purchase of a dead, reputed marijuana grower's property was currently the hot topic of conversation everywhere in the valley. Her grin widened. At least she'd taken some of the heat off of Sloan and Shelly and given the residents something new to speculate about.

The marriage of Sloan Ballinger to Shelly Granger in June had set the valley on its ear. Not only because of the swiftness with which the courtship had progressed but the very fact that a Ballinger was marrying a Granger. The Ballinger/Granger feud was the valley's favorite legend, and though most of the ugliness had happened decades ago, every time a Ballinger and Granger came face-to-face, the valley collectively held its breath and with bright, eager eyes watched to see if sparks would explode out of thin air. Mostly they did, but sometimes, as in the case of Sloan and Shelly . . . Roxanne smiled wistfully. In the case of Sloan and Shelly magic happened.

She gave herself a shake and turned back to the house. Cabin, she amended, and again wondered what the devil she'd been thinking of when she'd bought it. It wasn't as if the Ballingers didn't own thousands of acres in the valley and foothills and mountains surrounding the valley that she could have chosen to settle on. Nor was it as if she wasn't more than welcome to stay as long as she pleased in the family mansion and childhood home on the valley floor—her parents would be thrilled. And if she had wanted, her father, Mark, would have built her a place of her own on one of the many parcels of land owned by the family. She hadn't *needed* to buy 160 acres of mostly useless, mountainous terrain on the west side of the valley. It wasn't, even she would admit, a fabulous piece of land—altogether she probably had only about twenty acres that could be called flat. The rest was sheer, forested hillside with a small bench here and there. It wasn't even great timberland—too much underbrush, blackberry vines, buck brush, manzanita with oaks and madrones intermixed with the pine and fir. But it was hers, she thought with pride. Hers. Bought with her own money. Not family money. She didn't have to share it with a damn person. It was *hers*. And as for the cabin that came with the place . . .

Roxanne was positive that no other self-respecting Ballinger, except herself, would have considered the rough wood-framed building a prospective home. She laughed to herself. Call her crazy—her sister, Ilka, already had, and her parents, their expressions askance, had asked her at least a dozen times if she was sure that this was what she wanted? She had assured them that yes, she really did want the place. The land had its own beauty, but she loved the cabin. It had, she had pointed out to her stunned family, potential. It was small, but it had everything she wanted. Built at the very edge of one of those benches, the cabin was perched over two thousand feet above the valley floor. From the deck and from the east-facing floor-to-ceiling windows, she had stupendous views; the main level was one spacious room, except for a tiny bathroom tucked in one corner. The upper floor had a larger bathroom and two rooms. The decor left something to be desired, but she had no doubt that with a lot of elbow grease and a full checkbook, she'd have it looking just the way she wanted in no time at all.

At the moment, with the exception of a chaste twin bed, a battery-run lamp, an oak end table, a portable CD player, and a new side-by-side almond-colored refrigerator/freezer that had been set up to run on propane, the place was empty. The kitchen consisted of a stainless sink, propane stove, and a couple of metal cabinets shoved against the north wall of the cabin. Her nose wrinkled. Marijuana growers apparently didn't do much cooking.

Of course, she reminded herself, it hadn't been *proven* that the former owner, Dirk Aston, had really been a marijuana grower—that had merely been the conclusion of the valley residents. How else, they had asked, did someone unemployed and with no outside income earn enough money to live up there all by himself? And what about that new truck he drove? Where did the money to buy it come from? And why did he have those two greenhouses and black plastic piping running all over the place? Don't tell me he wasn't growing dope! When she argued that if his profession was so obvious that surely he would have been busted and the property confiscated, the sages had looked wise. Dirk was small-time, they'd said. Not big enough for CAMP and the DA's Office to go after, they'd said. Lots of guys like Dirk around, they'd said. Sheriff's Office knew who they were, but there were worse offenses than growing a little marijuana to keep them occupied. Sheriff's Office might harass guys like Dirk now and then, but no one took them seriously—bigger, more important fish to fry.

Roxanne didn't doubt that the valley had the correct reading of the situation, but it hadn't deterred her. In fact, if Jeb Delaney had kept his big mouth shut and hadn't warned her *not* to buy the property, she'd probably have gone looking for a different piece of land to buy. Probably. She grinned. But probably not. She *loved* this place. It was isolated, yet town was only about three miles down a dusty, twisting gravel road that took at least twenty minutes to traverse—in good weather. Her nearest neighbor was a couple of heavily forested miles away, and after the packed, surging humanity of New York, it was a great feeling to know that she could walk stark naked out her own back door and yodel at the moon, and no one would see or hear her. Not that she was going to do that. But she could. If she wanted.

Grinning to herself, Roxanne walked inside the cabin. Crossing to the new refrigerator, she took out a bottle of water and, after twisting off the cap, wandered out the back door of the cabin. It opened onto a small deck, too, this one covered, and she had a charming view of a small, meandering meadow before the ground rose, and forested hillside met her gaze. Like many places in the country, the rear of the cabin was both the entrance and the back door. It had always struck her as strange to drive up to the back of a house, until she took in the fact that the front had the views and no one in her right mind would sacrifice view for a front yard or driveway. The much-speculated-about greenhouses were situated to the south of the cabin, and, sipping her bottled water, she had just started to amble in that direction when the sound of an approaching vehicle caught her ear.

She wasn't expecting anyone, and, puzzled, she turned back to walk over to the wide gravel area where her own jaunty, rag-topped Jeep was parked. A second later, a red truck, a one-ton dually, roared up the last incline and stopped in a cloud of dust.

Recognizing the truck and the very tall, very big man who stepped out of it, her spine stiffened, and her fingers tightened around the bottle of water. Jeb Delaney. Absolutely the last person she wanted to see.

Like lord of all he surveyed, he strolled over to where she stood. Roxanne once surmised that the commanding air about him came from his job—a detective with the Mendocino County Sheriff's Office. There was a sense of leashed power about him, like a big, lethal tiger on a leather lead, but even she had concluded that it was nothing he did on purpose, it was just . . . Jeb.

Most people liked Jeb Delaney. Old ladies doted on him; young women swooned when he smiled at them; men admired him, and young boys wanted to grow up to be just like him. Just about everybody thought he was a great guy. Roxanne was not among them. He rubbed her the wrong way, and he always had. She couldn't be in his presence for more than five minutes before she was thinking of ways to knock his block off. She could never put her finger on just why he irritated her. She liked people—she couldn't have been the success she was if she hadn't. But Jeb Delaney . . . Jeb Delaney set her teeth on edge and made the hair on the back of her neck rise . . . and, a small voice nagged, excites you more than any man you've ever met in your life.

A big man, he stood six-foot-five and had the shoulders and chest to match. His arms were muscled beneath his plain blue chambray shirt, and the tight, faded blue jeans he was wearing fit his lean hips and powerful thighs like a second skin. Sunglasses, dusty black boots, and a wide-brimmed black Stetson completed his garb.

Watching him with all the enthusiasm she would have an invasion of rattlesnakes, Roxanne demanded, "What are you doing here?"

Jeb stopped about two feet from her and removed his sunglasses. His handsome face was expressionless as his gaze roamed over her, taking in the long, long tanned legs revealed by her pink-striped shorts and the firm breasts only half-hidden by the cut of her white halter top. There had been a few times in her career, not many, that she had posed nude, but she had never felt so very *naked* as she did at that very moment, with Jeb Delaney's knowing black eyes moving over her.

Her lips tightened. "I repeat: What are you doing here?"

"Just being neighborly?" he offered with a quirk of his brow.

She snorted. "Jeb, you live on the opposite side of the valley. Neighbors we're not."

He rubbed his jaw. "Yeah, I guess not." He looked around. "Seems an odd place for you to buy."

"And that's your business because . . . ?"

Jeb sighed and pushed back his black Stetson. "Are you always so prickly with everyone, or is it just me?"

She smiled sweetly. "Just you—I like everybody else."

He grinned, white teeth flashing beneath his heavy black mustache. It made him look like a brigand, a very, very attractive brigand, and Roxanne didn't like the way her heart leaped at the sight of that grin. The jerk.

Her foot tapped. "Are you going to tell me what you're doing here, or are we going to spend the morning exchanging insults?"

"Princess, I haven't insulted you . . . yet. You just keep tossing those smart remarks out of that pretty mouth of yours, and I might just have to do something about it." His gaze fastened on her mouth, and something dark and powerful leaped in the air between them. Then Jeb seemed to shake himself and take a breath. "Look," he said quietly, "I just wanted to see if the gossips were right about you buying this place—especially after I told you that it wasn't a good idea. Thought I'd take a drive up here and check it out. Since you're here, I guess this is one time that the valley gossip was right on the mark."

She was being rude. She knew it. She hated herself for doing it, but she just couldn't seem to stop. Looking down at her pink-painted toes in the flip-flops, she made the supreme effort, and muttered, "The gossips are right. I did buy it."

"Why? Like I said, this sure isn't the kind of place one would expect the exalted Roxanne of fame and fortune to buy. Now a mansion in San Francisco, where you could invite all your famous friends and hold wild bashes, yeah, I could see that. But here? A dead dope grower's digs in the middle of nowhere? Don't tell me you're thinking of turning your hand to growing a little marijuana on the side?" Coolly, he added, "Not your style, Princess."

She'd tried. She really had. OK, not much, but she'd made the effort, and what did she get for her efforts? Disparaging remarks and insults. "Is this an official inquiry?" she asked tightly. "Otherwise, my reasons are my own, and I don't have to share them with you. In fact, get off my property."

A muscle clenched in his jaw. "You know, someday, someone is going to teach you some manners."

Her lip curled. "You volunteering?"

His gaze swept over her. "Yeah," he said slowly. "Maybe."

He swung on his heels and climbed into the truck. The engine snarled to life, and, with more force than necessary, he spun the vehicle around and nosed it down the hill.

For several minutes after he'd left, Roxanne stood there staring at nothing. What the hell was the matter with her? With anyone else, she would have offered a smile, refreshments, and the hand of friendship. She bit her lip. So why not with Jeb? *Because I'm a bitch? Nah. Because he's a jerk.* Pleased with her conclusion, she headed for the greenhouses.

It was only ten o'clock in the morning, but already the heat was savage—by noon, every living thing, plant and animal alike, would be gasping for relief—relief that wouldn"t come until the sun set. Despite her brief apparel, Roxanne still felt the heat and after walking a couple of hundred feet to the greenhouses decided she'd put off investigating them until early tomorrow morning. Before it got hot. She grimaced. Yeah. Right.

She started back to the cabin when a rustling in the heavy brush to her right had her freezing in her steps. Visions of bears and cougars leaped to her mind—she knew the area abounded with them—and she cursed herself for not carrying some sort of weapon. Even a big stick would have been a comfort at the moment. Trying to remember everything she'd ever known about confronting a bear or a mountain lion, she faced the direction of the noise and edged backward toward the cabin.

The noise grew fearsome and just when she was certain she couldn't stand the suspense any longer, a horse and rider, followed by three dusty black-and-white cow dogs, burst into view.

Recognizing the wiry rider, a battered beige cowboy hat on his head, Roxanne's heartbeat slowed to normal, and a welcoming smile lit her face. "Acey Babbitt!" she exclaimed. "You nearly gave me a heart attack. I was certain that a bear had me in mind for breakfast."

Acey grinned, blue eyes bright in his sun-worn face. "And a tasty meal you would have made." Beneath an impressive pair of white handlebar mustaches, he smacked his lips. "Yes, ma'am, you do look good enough to eat—even to an old cowpoke like me."

She chuckled. "Why, Mr. Babbitt, are you putting the moves on little ole me?"

"Might . . . if I were twenty years younger and you were twenty years older," he said wriggling his bushy white eyebrows. "Of course, if you don't mind a fellow who creaks when he walks, I'd sure be still willing to give it a try."

Roxanne laughed again, not at all fooled by his abjectly hopeful expression. Acey Babbitt was seventy-five years old if he was a day and one of the dearest men Roxanne had ever known—and one of the biggest teases. His prowess with cattle and horses alike was legendary, and throughout his long career, at one time or another he had worked for just about every ranch in the valley, including the Ballingers. Just about every kid in the valley, including herself and her siblings, had learned to ride under Acey's gentle but steely guidance. And while he may have worked for others, his first loyalty had always been to the Grangers, and she knew that he was currently living on the Granger place, working for Shelly, Sloan's wife.

"OK, enough lecherous talk—you've convinced me that you're hell on wheels," she said with a smile. "What brings you out here?"

Acey made a face. "One of them fine expensive cows that Shelly brought out from Texas is due to calve and danged if she didn't find the only break in a fence for miles around. We discovered it last night about dark. Wasn't much we could do about it then, but Nick and I have been out since before daybreak trying to track her down."

Roxanne frowned. "Wouldn't she head for gentler ground?

Toward the valley? My place is so rough, I'm certain goats would turn up their noses at it, let alone a cow ready to calve."

"Don't want to hurt your feelings none, but you're right about that—this has to be some of the roughest ground I've ridden in many a day, and I didn't really have much hope of finding her. We figured right off that she'd head down to the valley, but we didn't find any tracks leading in that direction. For the last hour or two, we've been working up and down the ridge, hoping to see sign of her. No such luck so far."

"Well, I'll keep my eye open, but I don't think she'll come this way."

"If you do see her, just give the house a call." He paused. "You got a phone out here?"

"Cell phone. The magic of modern technology."

He glanced around. "I heard you'd bought the Aston place. Couldn't hardly believe it." His sharp blue eyes came back to her. "What are you going to do with it?"

"Not grow marijuana," she snapped, her green eyes glittering.

Acey held up a hand. "All right. All right. I just had to pry some." He bent his gaze on her. "You've been gone a long time, Roxy. Lived in New York and all them other fancy places. You were always too damned pretty for your own good, but you were also always a good kid. I figure you still are, but there are some folks who are a bit more suspicious. Lots of talk in the valley about what you're gonna do up here." He smiled at her. "Glad I'll be able to put their minds at rest."

"Are you serious?" she asked, astounded. "People really think I came home from New York to grow marijuana?"

Acey pulled on his ear. "No one with any sense . . . but you know, we got a few poor souls in the valley that got shortchanged in life—they have more chicken feathers in their heads than brains. Don't let it bother you none."

"Did you know Dirk Aston?"

"Not real well. And no, I don't know if he grew marijuana

up here or not. Wasn't none of my business. If you're real curious, you might talk to Jeb. I know he's a detective these days and isn't doing patrol, but he knows more about what goes on in these hills than just about anyone else." Acey wiggled his brows. "Except for maybe me. All kidding aside, you should talk to Jeb. He's a good man. A good deputy."

"Could we please talk about something else besides how wonderful Deputy Delaney is—I just ate."

Acey shrugged, but there was a little gleam in his eyes. "Sure. Anything else you want to know before I slope off?"

"I heard that Dirk Aston was murdered, shot, in Oakland. That he was involved in some sort of turf war? Is that true? Or just more gossip?"

"Maybe he was. And maybe he wasn't. Like Jeb says, Aston could have been just a victim of circumstances. Nothing to prove it either way. The way I hear it, drive-by shootings happen all the time—especially in that area of Oakland where he was found. Could have been that Dirk was in the wrong place at the wrong time. That's my take on it and the take of just about anyone with any brains. And as for the gossip about you growing marijuana up here . . ." He shook his head. "That's just plain foolishness. And anyone who knows you, knows it."

"Thanks, Acey. I needed to hear that." *Especially,* she thought to herself, *after Jeb's visit. El Jerko himself.*

He nodded, his eyes kind and shrewd beneath the wide brim of his hat. "Figured as much. Those fellows with chicken feathers for brains talk too much and half the time don't even know what they're talking about. Don't pay 'em any mind."

He glanced around. "So what *are* you going to do up here?"

She grinned. "Haven't a clue. Ain't it grand?"